ABOUT THE AUTHOR

Lexie Winston has been an astronaut, rock star, princess and time traveller. In her dreams. But none of the dreams have lived up to what becoming an author has been like. She gets to live in a world of pure imagination, and her heroines get to do the things she's always wished she could.

When not writing books, Lexie is a mother of two gorgeous teenagers and the wife to a patient and understanding man. They live in Western Australia and are lorded over by a black toy poodle. She loves camping, reading and if her iPad was stolen, her world would explode. (It has the kindle app on.)

Follow Lexie on

ALSO BY LEXIE WINSTON

The Collectors Division

(Reverse Harem Series)

Guardian

Guardian's Blood

Guardian Ascending

Arbor Vitae Coven

(Paranormal Romance Series)

Candy Conniptions

Dreamy Delights

Fangtastic Fireworks

Neighpalm Industries Collective

(Adult Bully Reverse Harem)

Abandoned Girl

Broken Girl

Seductive Sins Collection

Glorious Gluttony

Gangs, Guns, and Glory

GUARDIAN'S BLOOD

Collectors Division Book Two

LEXIE WINSTON

First published by Neighpalm Publishing in 2020

Copyright © Neighpalm Publishing 2020

The moral right of the author has been asserted.

Guardian's Blood : Collectors Division

Mobi format: 978-0-6487933-0-4

Print: 978-0-6487933-1-1

Cover design by Infinity Book Covers

Edited by Inked Imagination

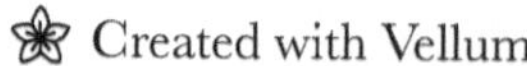 Created with Vellum

AUTHORS NOTE

The author's husband has asked for her to say that no marriages were harmed in the making of this novel. Also, much to the author's disappointment, nor do any of the situations reflect real-life experiences.
To all the readers who like to be surprised in their books and do not require trigger warnings or cliff-hanger warnings, please skip the next page and continue to chapter one. To all the special snowflakes who need a heads up, continue onto the next page.

This book is a Reverse Harem. The main female character will end up with more than one partner. There will be multiple sex scenes throughout the series that have more than two people participating. There will be MM, FF, MMF, MFM, and MMFMMMM. There may even be demon tails involved in the sex scenes. There is no dub-con or non-con in this book. Nor is there rape, sexual abuse, or emotional abuse. This book ends on a freaking massive cliff-hanger. Sorry not sorry, it's a series, and that's a great way to encourage you to read Book Two. I apologize for none of it. Now that I have given you this warning, if this is not your thing, read no further. But if this still interests you, read away, but please don't then turn around and give me negative reviews because you don't like any of the things I have mentioned. If

you don't like the story, that's cool, but complaining
about things I have warned you about isn't.
Saying that, I hope you all give the story a chance
and just skip past the things you don't like, because I
really think it's awesome.

Prologue

Jessamina

Darkness surrounds me. Muffled sounds echo in my ear as I float somewhere cold and vast. My consciousness is aware, but it's like it's separate from myself. I can't feel my body. No toes or fingers to wiggle; no eyes to open or mouth to call out for help. Only my thoughts in this deep, dark, empty space.

The last thing I remember is being bitten by that spider woman. The searing pain, then the dizziness. Mumbled words to a hazy figure whose arms were wrapped around me. A thought niggles at my brain, something that I'm supposed to remember, but it's just out of grasp.

Fuck! She was so quick, and my reflexes just weren't enough. The emotions in my brain bounce around like a ping pong ball—sadness, anger, frustration, and finally disappointment. *I* wasn't enough. I'm kicking myself, regretting my stupid pride and stubbornness. I should have had my damn blood activated. I should have taken everyone's advice and listened to the people who knew better. Who cares if my parents left me? Why did I let it stop me from being the best version of myself I could be? And the guilt, especially now that I know that they didn't just dump me. That I was hidden away to protect everyone involved.

Now I'm here, stuck in some stupid limbo, unsure whether I'm dead or alive. It feels similar to the void when stepping through the portal but with none of the intense pressure.

The muffled noises get louder, drawing my attention. The sounds are voices—voices that become clearer. A female voice, a musical tinkling that brings a sense of peace and contentment. Then there are two, maybe three, male voices as well, I think. It's hard to tell. The words are indistinguishable, and the tones start quietly but quickly develop into something else. Voices talking over each other, getting louder and argumentative. One voice is particularly aggressive, but still, I can't make out what's being said.

These voices fade and leave me in the empty void. Alone again with nothing but my thoughts and regrets. *Is this death? The afterlife?* I thought there would be more. Gods exist, so why wouldn't there be somewhere we went once life was over? Maybe I'm not dead, but where could I be? And where are the guys and Dru? What has become of them? What happened on Minzeon? Did they catch Loki?

Maybe he's responsible. So many thoughts tumble through my mind, haphazard and disorganized.

But no, the spider woman. She bit me; *she's* the one responsible. The poison, the pain! God, the pain!

At that thought, I become aware of an intense burning sensation, my nerve endings on fire. From feeling nothing to feeling everything, the sensation's overwhelming in intensity. With no body to move or mouth to scream with, I'm sucked into the abyss of agony, unable to escape. Time has no meaning, so I don't know how long I endure the pain, but eventually, it fades, and with it, memories also drift away like dust.

How did I get here? Where am I? What did I do to deserve this suffering? Pondering these thoughts, more muffled sounds reach me. Screams like those inside my mind. Are these an echo of my pain, or is someone else suffering as well? The screaming fades, and sobs replace them. Quiet cries of pleading. This time I can make out some of the words. *"Please,* and *why,* and *no, I can't, nooo.* That last cry, a soul-shattering sound, dissolves to nothing.

Again, I float, feeling pieces of me snapping off and drifting away. Memories and the other things that make me, me. *Why am I here? What happened? What did I do to deserve this torture?* I try to think, to create organized thoughts in a mind full of chaos. What had I been doing? I wasn't at the academy training to run the Gauntlet. I don't think I was with James and Livie. Straining, I push my mind, forcing it to remember, but the memories are just out of reach. Just as I think they're in my grasp, the pain returns. A firestorm of agony and despair because not only does it feel like my body is in pain, it feels like my soul is being eaten away. Piece by piece, the agony and destruction tear me apart. Like waves on the shore, a never-ending ebb and flow of misery. *How am I still aware? What is this torture?* My mind starts to shut down; no one can continue to endure agony such as this without losing something, and I fear that I'm losing it all.

A voice draws my attention. Musical and sweet, it calls my name, *Jessamina,* like an echo on a breeze. *Jessamina.* A little louder, and I stop floating. My eyes open, and I'm standing in a room. There's complete darkness except for one tiny pinprick of light. As it comes closer, it brightens until it's blinding, and I use my hand to shield my eyes. A hand touches me, pulling mine away. Standing before me is a woman, a painfully beautiful woman, and she smiles.

"Jessamina, I've been waiting for you." Her voice is like angels sighing, gentle and sweet but at the same time full of power.

"Why am I here? What's happening to me?" I ask, and sadness enters her eyes.

"This had to happen. To become what I need you to be, you must be forged in the fires of agony. We need both sides of you activated as well as the little bit extra I gave you. Forgive me for what you need to go through. It will be difficult, but in the end, you will be the savior we need."

"I'm not sure what you want from me or what you're talking about," I tell her, confused and disoriented.

"You won't remember this until it is needed," she tells me. The goddess is poised, but her hands are grasped together tightly, showing she's more anxious than she's trying to appear. I mean, it has to be Mylea, doesn't it? There's only one goddess, who else would it be? A nod of her head confirms my thoughts.

"What do you know about the original gods?" she asks, taking me by the arm so that we walk through the darkness together.

"Just what we've been taught. That there is one for each world, and they're the creators and protectors of each world's inhabitants."

"Mmm, yes, that's right," she confirms quietly, no remorse at the fact that not all of them followed that creed.

I stop abruptly at her words and look at her, my gaze hurling accusations moments before the words escape my mouth. "But it didn't work out that way, did it? Hammus was able to manipulate his people into war and destroy his world." I confront her with the truth, and shame crosses her face.

"Did you know that as the original goddess, I took the four gods as my consorts, and, for many, many years, things were wonderful? Our creations thrived, and the planets flourished until one day, there was a rift in the universe. A tear in the very fabric of space. We investigated, but nothing had come through, and the tear closed. But from then on, the balance of our universe was off, and Hammus started to behave strangely. First, he became jealous of mine and the other three's creations. Then he was convinced his people were conspiring against him. He secluded himself and proceeded to lay waste to his planet and people. Demons have very base instincts, and inciting them to turn on one another was an easy thing for him to do." Tears are flowing down her face now, her voice distraught at the weight of the memories.

"Why didn't you stop him?" I ask her.

"Because we couldn't. We were created to love each other, not to harm, so we can't raise a hand to each other without it returning to ourselves. Nor can we raise a hand to each other's creations either. Which I think is the only thing stopping him from coming after us and why he must use others to create chaos. But he has gone too far, and we need to find a way to stop him. That will be your task; *that* is your destiny."

My mouth drops open in shock. "You want me to take on a god?" I ask in disbelief.

"Not only take him on but destroy him," she replies, an edge of steel in her voice now. "And once he's destroyed, you will take his place." She puts her hand on my cheeks, a hardness in her eyes that's edged in the warmth one would expect from Mylea. "I have given you the tools you need to succeed. Did you know as Guardians you're taught to think logically and without emotion? Yet emotions influence our actions. Anger, jealousy, and greed all create negativity, but in opposition, kindness, love, and trust can be used positively. One cannot be without emotion; use this, Mina," she urges me.

"Unfortunately, once negative emotion grabs hold, it is hard to temper unless the person is open to positive emotions as well. Hammus was not, and you will find along the way that others you know and love have also succumbed. Trust in yourself and know that they can be influenced and their outcomes changed. Nothing is set in stone. You, and *only* you, will have the power to absorb his godhood once his physical being is destroyed. It will not be easy, and unfortunately, there will be losses along the way. Have faith that all will work out in the end." Tears are dripping down my face, and the fear in my heart is real. How am I supposed to do this?

She places a kiss on my forehead. "Now rest, Mina. Rest your body and your mind for what is to come next. And know that I am always with you."

With no other words, she disappears. And I am alone again, drifting. Once more, a wave of pain courses through my body, all thoughts of the goddess leaving me as I try to scream.

How long it continues, I have no clue, but after

a time, the pain flows away like a river to the sea. Now there is nothing left, nothing that tells me who I am. I know I must have existed, but there are no memories. Not even a name to call myself. *How did this happen? How did I come to be?* The pain has gone, and like a thunderstorm, it's washed away all that came before it. Confusion and sadness are all that remain now.

I float in a vast space, no sound, no senses at all. Just a wide-open, dark space. I am nothing. Absolutely nothing. Then, with agonizing clarity, noise surrounds me. Screams and shouts, begging, and pleading. Some I know are mine, but others aren't. Voices of men, women, and children all call out in despair, praying to a god that has forsaken them. A god that has pitted them against one another for the sake of sport. Who is this god? My thoughts echo theirs, turbulent and despairing, and I join in the chorus, crying for help. *Help me, please,* my mind begs. The pleading, desperate sounds of the hopeless are the final nail in the coffin. The last of my thoughts shatter and fracture, tumbling out into the vast abyss.

Chapter One

Zephaniah

Mina's skin looks pale and lifeless under the harsh, unforgiving lights of the hospital ward of the Collectors Division. Long-term patients are unusual; activated ABs usually heal quickly from any wounds, and illnesses are uncommon. The scent of antiseptic lingers in my nose, but under that is the putrid smell of rotting flesh. Mina's wound refuses to heal. Kept bandaged, it is a raw, gaping, hunk of meat that continues to look infected and inflamed. It regularly oozes thick, black, tar-like liquid. Frankly, the doctors are surprised that she continues to live.

Her small hand is cold and clammy, where it rests in mine, and her pulse flutters like the wings of a hummingbird under my thumb. The incessant beeping of the machines that monitor her heart and breathing rate are intrusive and annoying and wearing on my sanity. Blowing out a deep breath, I rest my head on the bed next to her. For the last week, we've all taken turns sitting with her. None of the doctors can tell us what's wrong. All we know is she was bitten by a black widow, and there's some mutated poison that they've never seen before flowing through her body. I just don't understand how this happened.

So many things went wrong during that operation. The warehouse ended up burning down, and the prisoners weren't apprehended. Not to mention what happened to Mina. She was assigned one of the least risky tasks and shouldn't have been in any danger. Secure the remaining Minzeons and get them to safety. What had happened to her, and where had all the spiders come from? So many questions unanswered. The Minzeons we questioned were terrified out of their brains, rambling crazily of a giant spider. A giant spider with a *woman's* head and torso, so it couldn't have been Anansi. But where did it go?

Looking at the dark circles under the eyes and pale, almost translucent skin of the woman I want to be ours, I whisper a quiet prayer to the goddess Mylea. *Please let her be ok.*

Soft voices draw my eyes to the next bed, and my sadness turns to anger and suspicion. *Constance! How is she alive?* We saw her fall off a cliff. Where the hell did she come from, and why was she in that warehouse of all places? I watch as Samuel hands her a bag of clothes to change into, his face suspiciously soft and eyes filled with a warmth that snake doesn't deserve. After being monitored here for the last week, she's finally being released today. She claims she can't remember anything, and the doctors are saying it's trauma-induced amnesia, but I call bullshit. Over two years and no memory of where she's been or what she's been doing? It seems a bit too convenient.

Samuel looks up and catches my eye, giving me a small nod. I thought he had lost his damn mind when he first brought Connie into the hospital along with Sander and Mina. He constantly got in the way of Constance's doctors and refused to leave her side. I thought he was going to go all gaga over her again, and once she was resting comfortably and the doctors had checked her over, we gave him a dressing down and told him to get his shit together. His face had fallen as he explained how he was shocked to see her, claiming his behavior had just been an automatic response to seeing Connie alive once more. At least he tried to make up for it by staying with Mina until Connie regained consciousness.

It's probably a good thing Mina didn't shoot her because now we can question her. I don't trust her, and neither do any of the others, so I ordered Sam to keep an eye on her. He was the logical choice, despite our concerns, and happy to comply. The others weren't interested at all, and they'd never be able to hide their true feelings. Connie had burned those bridges a long time ago, and Sander was downright hostile. The words that came out of his mouth when I had asked for volunteers shocked us all. He's still not particularly impressed with Samuel, but he's going to give him the benefit of the doubt. Sam needs to prove he's really over her and ready to be all in with Mina, or he's going to have to join another team. He was shocked when I told him that, but I'm not losing my chance at happiness—all of our chances for happiness.

Kissing him on the cheek, she takes the clothes and goes into the bathroom to get changed while Samuel makes his way over to us.

"Any change?" he asks hopefully. At the shake of my head, his shoulders drop in disappointment. He moves to Mina's side and grabs her other hand. Leaning down, he places a kiss on her forehead and whispers quietly, "Come on, Mina. We need you. Time to wake up." He runs his hand over her hair but moves away quickly when he hears Connie open the bathroom door and step out. Turning to look as she walks toward us, I study her. She's rail-thin and fragile-looking, and there's a slight tremor in one of her hands. Her long chestnut hair is stringy and needs a brush. She looks washed out and has a vacant look in her eyes. Nothing like the strong, vibrant woman who was once a part of our team. Now she looks like a junkie, jonesing for the next fix of her drug du jour.

Her eyes meet mine, and the vacant look disappears, replaced with something I *do* recognize from before, a calculating glint. Well, that's more like I expected; at least that hasn't changed.

She plasters a smile onto her face and saunters toward me with a walk that I guess is supposed to be sexy but just looks like she has a carrot up her ass. I think she's expecting me to stand up and greet her with open arms, but I shoot that down by staying where I am. She can't hug me if I'm sitting down. Shock crosses her face before she smooths it out. "Zeph, it's good to see you. You look well." She simpers, her eyes showing appreciation.

Not returning the smile, I grunt, "I wish I could say the same to you, but you look like shit." The smile leaves her face, and her eyes narrow and nostrils flare. There it is, that arrogant look that she always wore, the one that says she's better than all of us.

Hands on her hips, she raises an eyebrow. "Well, you haven't changed, have you? Still an asshole, I see."

I shake my head, unwilling to play any of her games. "I just call it like I see it. Care to explain where you've been or what's happened in the last two years, Connie?"

She stiffens in anger at my words but quickly hides it by adopting a pathetic look, tears filling her eyes on cue. "I wish I knew. Like I told Sam, I can remember going on the mission with you guys, but then everything is blank and hazy until I woke up here. The memories are disjointed and vague and don't make any sense. It's like they've been tampered with." Before I can reply, she turns to look at the woman on the bed. "Is *this* my replacement? Can't be worth much if she's lying here, not healing. Did Alpha have to scrape the bottom of the barrel to get a new team member?" Her voice drips with disdain.

Typical Connie. Deflect and insult. God, what was I thinking when I slept with this witch? Thank god it was only a couple of times. Looking at Samuel, I can see his hands clenched into fists, his body tight, before he takes a deep breath and answers. "This is Mina. You remember my foster sister, don't you, Connie?" She sidles up to him and wraps an arm around his waist. He stiffens slightly then slowly relaxes into her.

Her nose wrinkles up. "Hmm, yes. I thought she looked familiar. You poor baby, I'm so sorry your sister is hurt. I guess she didn't live up to all the potential the academy thought she had. What's wrong with her?" she asks, looking back up at Samuel.

Anguish crosses his face as he steps away from her, running his hand over Mina's cheek. "All new creatures that inhabit the realms are studied, and their features are noted and cataloged, as you know, but the poison in her body is nothing anyone has seen before." She nods her head as he continues. "All toxins have samples taken and antidotes created. Either we missed a creature, or this is something new and not of the realms."

"What about the demons?" she sneers. "Could they be responsible?"

Before Samuel can answer, a voice behind us does. "Unlikely to be demons. There aren't enough left for them to be causing problems. They just want to live their lives in peace."

Looking toward the sound, I see Brace and Janet, with James and Olivia behind them. Brace steps further in before he turns to me and continues with, "A meeting has been called, and you're all to attend." I start to shake my head, but he holds his hand up. "It's non-negotiable, Zeph. But we knew you wouldn't leave Mina on her own, so we brought someone to sit with her."

They all move to the side, and Maggie steps into the room. Her typical flawless appearance is disheveled and unkempt, and her face is tear-stained, but she's calm and collected. Her usual flair for the dramatics forgotten during such a grievous time. Her inner strength is shining brightly and a welcome relief. I feel comfortable leaving Mina, knowing Maggie is by her side.

"Maggie!" Connie exclaims, stepping away from Samuel and holding out her arms in another attempt at a hug.

She gets ignored as Maggie brushes past her, coming over to me and resting her hand on top of mine and Mina's clasped hands. "Go, Zephaniah, I'll take care of her," she says quietly. "Someone needs to find out who did this and how we can fix it." She helps me up and kisses me on the cheek before practically shoving me out the door. Turning, she shoots a dirty look at Samuel. "Go on, this is important. Stop getting distracted." Giving her back to him, she takes the seat I was in, grabbing hold of the hand I had been holding.

Connie pulls Samuel back to her side, fluttering her eyelashes at him. "Sammy was going to help me get to my father's place on Amilles since I'm not allowed to use the portal room without a Guardian present. They also told me they'd deactivated my world chip for safety reasons when I went missing, and they couldn't find my body."

"I sure am." He smiles down at her before looking back up at me. "Can you fill me in later?" Frowning, I nod. *Why's he acting like this? The meeting should be the perfect out for him to drop Connie for a few hours.* He's taking his act a little too far by ignoring a direct order from the top. That supersedes anything I've asked him to do, and he knows that. Or at least the rational Samuel would know that. I'm not sure who's in front of me right now.

"Ah, no, that's not going to happen. Connie, you're required to attend also," Janet tells her.

"They would like to question you regarding your, uh ... experiences."

"What… wait, why?" she stutters in surprise. "I can't remember anything. I've told them that." She looks up at Samuel again. "Please, I don't want to go through all that questioning again."

"Of course you don't have to," he reassures her, his hands rubbing up and down her forearms.

Frowning, Brace clears his throat, and Sam faces him in question. "Ah, yes, she does. If the Division has ordered her, there's no denying that order."

"But I'm not part of the Division anymore," she argues, her tone turning aggressive. Underneath it, I think I can almost detect a tinge of desperation, though I can't figure out why she'd be so reluctant to appear before the Archangels.

"It doesn't matter; you're a witness," Brace says firmly.

"A witness who doesn't remember," she hisses at him, a brief flash of crazy in her eyes before they clear again.

He shrugs. "They don't care. The Archangels want you there."

"There are ways to retrieve your memories, Constance." Maggie's voice is quiet but has a hint of steel behind it. "The Archangels have magic that we cannot even comprehend. Not only that, but the goddess has taken an interest in this case, so I'm sure she would step in if asked."

Connie's eyes widen. "Mylea has taken an interest? Why would she take an interest in one insignificant low-breed AB? Someone should just pull the plug on her machines and be done with it. She's probably in agony, and you guys are keeping her hanging in limbo." Gasps of shock and disgust leave the mouths of the people surrounding me, and James has to physically restrain and then carry Olivia out of the hospital ward, shouting back that they'll see us at the meeting.

Maggie is on her feet in a flash, finger waving in Connie's direction. "Now, you see here, you trumped-up piece of trash. Don't think for one second that you're fooling anyone with your amnesia story. Mina is special, and the Archangels know it, and so does the goddess. Not to mention, Peter has a sterling reputation with the Collectors Division and is well respected. He approached the council on her behalf, and they have granted him this investigation as a favor. In fact, they told him they would have conducted one anyway." Connie shrinks back into Samuel's side at the ferocity in Maggie's tone, and he comforts her while rolling his eyes at his mother.

Ignoring both of them, I move over to Maggie as she collapses into sobs again. Putting my arms around her, I hold her, patting her back as she struggles to compose herself once more. Her body is shaking with emotions, but I think it's mostly anger. Samuel just stands there awkwardly, his foster mother's distress not enough to shake him. He's going to have to be watched very closely.

"Dude, what the fuck? What is your problem?" I throw at his mind, but it either doesn't register, or he's ignoring me

Meanwhile, Brace approaches Connie. "We can do this one of two ways. You can either walk with us to the meeting under your own provocation, or we can cuff you and force you there. Your choice." She throws her arms in the air in agitation but nods her head, a snarl momentarily settling on her face before she seems to recognize how much attention she's under.

Her face clears of all frustration, and she wraps her arm through Samuel's. "Walk with me?" His gaze switches between hers and mine. He looks confused but eventually nods his head and escorts her out the door, Brace and Janet following close behind.

Maggie's hand on my chin draws my attention back to her. She drags my head down so that we are eye to eye, my forehead against hers. "I don't like that girl. Something is wrong with her, Zeph; she doesn't feel right. Something's not right with my Sam either. I know I'm a dramatic fool, but in the past, my tears haven't failed to gain his attention or sympathy. Not to mention he barely even blinked at my Mina in this bed here. Peter and I aren't stupid, you know, and we've been around for a long time. Peter may not be operational anymore, but we hear the gossip, the whispers that something big is happening." She gestures to Mina. "Fix it, Zeph. You and the others are the only ones I trust. I know you can do it."

Nodding my head, I kiss her before I leave. "I promise, Maggie.

Chapter Two

Lysander

Leaning against the wall outside the meeting room, my head throbs and my body aches. Symptoms of a bender that has gone on for too many days. My sister dragging me out of bed, shoving me in the shower this morning, and force feeding me breakfast is the only reason I'm now sober. I'm not sure if that's a blessing or not considering we're now sitting at this meeting. I haven't seen Zeph in days, his vigil at Mina's bedside overcompensating for how the rest of us have coped. Or not coped at all, I guess. Drusilla has cried for days and put no effort into hair and makeup, which, in itself, tells me all too much about my sister's growing feelings for our Mina. Only this morning is she showing signs of getting back to her normal, bossy self, but she still looks like she's been through the ringer. She felt an instant connection with Mina, much like I did, and she's really been knocked down by this. Not knowing what the future will bring is slowly tearing her up inside, and I can feel her pain, and my own, all too well. It's the twin thing. It's also partly why I've been drinking. Our emotions amplify each other's, and when I drink enough, that gets blurred and dulled. Right now, I desperately don't want to feel much of anything, let alone enough sadness and frustration for two people.

I had just watched as Mina's friends James and Olivia entered the meeting room. James had been carrying Olivia, and she had been ranting about something that I hadn't caught, but she was madder than hell, and he was trying in vain to get her to calm down.

Feeling a presence, I turn my head and watch Mav come down the hallway. He hasn't shaved in days, his hair looks like he's been running his hand through it constantly, and his clothes are wrinkled. Bloodshot eyes meet mine, and as he walks past me, he slaps me on the shoulder in greeting. *Goddess, he looks rougher than Dru.*

"You alright, man?" I ask, and he just grunts before entering the room. No words returning, only anxious feelings leaking through the connection. Who knows what's going on with Mav. He doesn't talk or show emotions; he keeps that shit bottled up inside. I don't remember when I saw him last, and I can't help but wonder where he's been all this time. Another part of me, the part that's a bit angry at myself for being so selfish, says, *Well, it's not like you've really been caring much about your team, is it?*

A nudge against my mental walls draws my

attention, and the familiar smell of sage and lemon reaches my nose as my pulse trips. *Trick.* I groan internally. I've been so horrible to him, and I'm not sure he's ever going to forgive me. My head comes up, and his icy blue eyes gleam with understanding, making my guilt lie heavy in my stomach.

"I'm so sorry," I apologize to him. *"I was such a dick."* I try to probe his emotions for how he's feeling, but he's locked down tight, and my heart sinks even more. He just stares at me, blank and emotionless. *How badly have I messed things up? We might lose Mina, and I can't stand the idea that I might be losing him too.*

A commotion in the hallway draws our attention, breaking the weighty eye contact between us. Connie and Samuel are making their way down the hall followed closely by Janet and Brace. She's got her arm wrapped through his and is leaning against him as she chatters loudly, no care at all for the somber moods surrounding her. He nods to us as he passes, but she just ignores us both. *Typical.* That suits me just fine. Sly nasty bitch, I don't want anything from her except to maybe get rid of her. Janet and Brace nod their hellos but don't stop to chat.

A hand on my arm drags my attention away from my angry thoughts. *"Never again."* His words are firm, and the hurt I initially feel through our connection makes my heart clench. *"You don't get to push me away when your emotions get the better of you.*

That's not how we work." Love starts to flow through the connection, showing that what he feels *for* me is much more powerful than how he feels about my recent idiocy. *"We deal with whatever the problem is, together. We're a partnership, and we share the burden. Always."*

I let out the breath I hadn't realized I was holding as relief flows through my body at his words and feelings. Thank god he didn't allow my destructive behavior to destroy our relationship. *"Yes, you're right, I really am sorry. It won't happen again,"* I swear to him. I grab hold of his arm, pulling him close and resting my forehead against his, our eyes locking. *"I love you."*

"And I love you too, you big idiot," he says back to me before speaking out loud.

"You will be punished for this, Lysander." Trick's eyes fill with heat as he promises me this, and my cock twitches in my pants. *That's* a good sign since it hasn't moved in days. He walks past me into the meeting room, brushing against my body as he goes. A smile crosses my face at the brief appearance of his dominant side, and a shiver runs down my spine at the thought of what punishment he may dish out. Not many others know that he likes that kind of role in our relationship. Everyone thinks that he's the quiet, submissive one, and they couldn't be more wrong. I love that he feels comfortable enough with me to show his dark side, and I love that I can do that for him. It's a rush.

Adjusting my cock, I follow him and find a seat at the table next to him. Looking around the room, I observe the various groups. Team Bravo and Echo are all here seated around the conference room table. Jagger's not sitting like the others but is standing apart, leaning against one wall, arms crossed, a scowl on his face.

Catching Dru's eye, I nod in his direction. *"We need to remind Zeph to do something about Jagger,"* I say to her through our mental connection.

"Yeah," she agrees, *"he looks like he's lost weight, and he's pale even for him."* Jagger's icy white hair and matching skin is such a contrast to his demon form, and now he looks almost translucent, like his blood has thinned.

"They must be starving him," she growls, anger filling the bond between us. My eyes scan the Team Bravo members at the table. None of them are particularly friendly now, nor have they ever been. Team pride and placement and the constant competition to be the best makes it difficult for the elite teams to be friendly with one another. But Brock's the only one I know who is an outright bigot, so the others must just be cowards who follow his lead.

Moving on, I can see the four members of Team Dragon who retrieved Connie standing in a huddle and keeping a close eye on her. Even though they weren't involved in the mission, they must be assigned to her now. Good, the bitch can't be trusted. I don't know where she's been for the last couple of years, but I'm almost a hundred percent sure she hasn't got amnesia like she claims.

"Sander, man, you're growling. Dial it down a bit." Trick's hand on my thigh draws my attention, and the growl cuts off before I draw more eyes to us than I'd like.

I'm pretty sure Team Dragon is suspicious too, or at least Mina's friends and former instructors are. It's good to have other eyes on Connie as well. Even though Samuel's supposed to be keeping an eye on her, I'm not sure I trust him either. Fucker has been awfully friendly to her since we found her, and while I haven't been the most attentive team member lately, at least I haven't been doting on the enemy.

Speaking of...my eyes find her across the room. She's standing further away from everyone else and is having quite the conversation with her father, Archangel Sabboath. He's a slimy dick, and I can't stand him; he has small man syndrome. Which I guess when he stands next to an Archangel like my dad, he is.

He's also the one who'd insisted Connie join our team. He was adamant that she be on Team Alpha, and Hugh was quite happy to comply with his wishes. We agreed at the time, but it had 100% bitten us in the ass.

I never liked her at the academy. She was horrible to Trick and me then, while she was always trying to weasel her way in with Zeph and Mav.

When they didn't work too well, she set her sights on Sam. He fell for her charms, and it wasn't long after they started spending time together that he started being horrible to Mina when she accompanied Peter to any of our classes.

Although they're whispering, the conversation looks to be quite heated. His arms are flying wildly, and the frown on her face deepens. She shakes her head, and he throws his arms up in what looks like frustration before storming to the table and taking a seat with everyone else. She follows closely behind and squeezes into a place next to Samuel. Putting her hand on his thigh and squeezing, she draws his attention, and he smiles at her.

"Dude, why are you looking at Samuel like that?" Zeph's voice sounds confused, and when I look at him, he's frowning at me.

"Yeah, man, you've got to stop," Trick adds in. Zeph must have projected his voice into everyone but Sam's head because they're all frowning at me. Drusilla, my ever lovely twin, smacks me in the back of the head.

"Ouch!" My exclamation is too loud for the room where everyone's whispering, and they all stop what they're doing and look at me.

Before I can answer Zeph, Raphael notices him and looks around to see that everyone is here. He and the other Archangels that took part in the mission are seated at the head of the conference table and have been having a quiet conversation while waiting for everyone to arrive. Hugh and Clementine are sitting next to them, each silently working on tablets in their hands, a distance between them that almost feels a bit tense.

"Finally, we can get started." His voice is exasperated, and he looks annoyed to the point that I wouldn't be surprised if he put his hands on his hips to show that he means business. "The mission to Minzeon was a bust. The Five were nowhere to be seen when we arrived or when the building was explored, and the people we rescued from the spiders are so traumatized their rambling doesn't make sense. They kept talking about a giant spider, but there was no sign of one except for the cocooned people we rescued off the roof. Matoz is still missing, and we have no leads to his whereabouts. Then to top it all off, the sprinkles on that shit heap of a mission, we have an agent in the hospital with something we've never seen before. Does anyone have any ideas on how we can catch the Five?" The table erupts into muttering voices as everyone tries to add their two cents.

I roll my eyes, my head is throbbing with all the noise. I'm really regretting my overindulgence now. Putting my head in my hands, I rub my temples. Trick's hand on my back rubs gently and soothes me greatly, and despite the pain, I'm glad that I'm sober enough to be aware of the feel of him touching me once again.

"I guess you won't overindulge that much again, will

you, brother?" Drusilla's voice is snarky inside my mind, and I throw her a mental middle finger. She snorts in return but tunes back into what everyone else is saying.

"Quiet!" Dad thunders, making me jump in my seat, and again Dru snorts. He's standing up, hands pressed against the table. "One at a time." The voices settle, but Sabboath gets to his feet.

"Where's Michael?" he sneers. "Surely, as the head of the Archangel council, he should be here. Is he too important to be involved in the day to day running of things now?"

That's actually an interesting question, and as one we all turn to look at the rest of the Archangels and wait for the answer. We shouldn't have bothered.

In return, Dad shoots him a look of utter disdain. "No, he's in a meeting with Mylea discussing options for finding Matoz. Not that it's any of your business, nor does he need to justify his actions to anyone. So sit your ass down," he growls. Sabboath does, his face covered in a scowl. Damn, Dad really told him. My old man seems like such a grump, but he's really a softie at heart. He just doesn't show it with anyone but my mom, Dru, and me. Though I've gotten the vibe that there's something he likes about Mina. I almost could've sworn that he was a *tiny* bit less grumpy the last time she'd been around him.

Zadkiel, Zeph's father, looks toward Connie.

"Maybe a long lost Alpha member can shed some light on the situation? How did you come to be in that warehouse on Minzeon? You were reported missing and assumed dead two years ago." Eyebrow raised, the curiosity is evident in his voice.

Everyone at the table is focused on Connie, and I can see panic cross her face briefly before she adopts a look of sadness. "I wish I could tell you, sir, but I have no memory of how I came to be there."

The skepticism on the faces of the Archangels is laughable. Chamuel growls, his next words coming out abruptly. "Maybe Raphael needs to have a look at you. There's no better healer than him. Or if that doesn't work, maybe we need to ask Mylea to. All the answers we need may be locked inside your brain. Your missing memories may be the key to all of this."

I nod my head in agreement with his words. *Yeah. that's right, let's poke around in that brain and discover all those secrets.*

Sabboath jumps to his feet, banging his hand against the table in protest. " My poor daughter has been through enough! Leave her be for now. If we can't find any leads, I will let you dig around in her brain, but until we've explored every option, she's off-limits."

I watch very closely as Connie breathes a sigh of what looks like relief. It quickly transforms back into her more typical smug confidence now that her father has protected her from those that aren't buying the bullshit she's trying to sell.

"Did Sabboath seem very quick to jump in and put a stop to that?" Mav's voice startles me. He hasn't said anything until now, and his voice is full of suspicion. No one responds, too fixed on seeing what happens, but I see some of my team members narrowing their eyes as they start to think about Mav's question.

"Very well then," Chamuel concedes, " but we will be re-visiting this in a week's time if there are no other options."

"We need to figure out what AoA's endgame is. What do they wish to achieve and why? Who's pulling the strings? Why did it escalate so quickly? First, we only heard rumblings, and then all of a sudden, they're breaking into the Menagerie and prison and causing chaos on Minzeon," Azrael muses, and Raphael agrees with a nod of his head.

"This is what's going to happen. Echo and Dragon, you're going back into normal rotation. Bravo, I want you to do some snooping. Ask around, poke your nose into places, see if you can dig up some info on what's going on. But be discreet, who knows what AoA will do if they discover you poking around. The five of you will be out of normal rotation for now."

Brock's been nodding while listening to their instructions but interrupts after the last direction. " Five of us? But there are six on Bravo."

Raphael nods. " Yes, but Alpha is down a member, so Jagger's going to join their team."

Relief at this command eases the tension in my team's bodies slightly. We still have a lot of problems, but Jagger is finally not one of them. Zeph looks pleased at this announcement, and I know he's also a bit relieved that the Archangels are stepping in to handle this without making us get into the middle of it. Jagger's face stays blank, but I see the tension easing from his body too.

"Welcome to the team, my brother. It's been a long time coming and we couldn't be happier." Zeph's voice is open and friendly as he broadcasts that to everyone. Jagger's Archdemon status allows him to tune into our team's mental connection,and he nods his head, relief evident through the link. A small smile graces his face, and he avoids looking at us for the moment, perhaps trying to save us from his former teammates' ire

"Thank you, I wasn't sure how much longer I could last if I'm being honest."

Hearing this announcement, Brock jumps up in protest. "What, no! Jagger's on our team. If you reassign him, we'll be down a member."

Again, Dad stands up, slamming his hands down on the table. "Who are you to tell us what we can and can't do? Sit your ass down and wait for him to finish." Brock's cheeks tinge red in embarrassment, but he sits down. I chucke to myself, but it must have gone across the team link today because again they all shoot me a look full of 'shut the fuck up.'

The victory of hearing that Jagger won't have to deal with this asshole anymore is just made that much sweeter by seeing Brock put in his place, and it gives me a special sense of satisfaction to know that my father is the one doing it. And I'm not the only one. Although they all want me to shut up, I can feel that they're all just as happy as I am. A smug smile crosses my lips at Dad's words, and Brock shoots me a look of hate when he sees it.

Raphael nods his thanks to Dad and continues. "As I was saying, Jagger will join Alpha, and you will get the first two picks in the next draft."

Sabboath looks furious at this announcement, and he barks at Raphael, "When did you become the director for the division? This isn't your decision to make." He turns to Hugh, an intimidating look on his face. Although he's small compared to the other Archangels, he's still a force to be reckoned with when facing down Hugh. "Surely, Connie will be re-joining team Alpha; it was her spot to start with."

"Well, yes, ahh... um, I mean..." Hugh stumbles out, the glare of the Archangel clearly getting to him as a drop of sweat forms on his brow. Turning to look at Raphael and Dad, his panic worsens. Nothing like being caught between a group of angry and frustrated Archangels.

God, I think, rolling my eyes, *could this guy get anymore pathetic?*

This time Dru actually kicks me under the table. *"Seriously, what the fuck is wrong with you? Has all that alcohol fried your fucking mental walls or soemthing? Turn it off! Your head is projecting everything, even the pain."* She rubs at her temples and I feel a little guilty as I rein it in. Looking at the others, they vary from annoyed, that's Sam-- shit, I hope he hasn't heard all of them--to amused, except Dru.

Dad shakes his head and smoothly intervenes, his voice firm. "We can hardly let a Guardian join a team when they don't have any memories of where they've been. It would be too dangerous, and Alpha wouldn't be able to rely on her."

"She will stay inactive until she can re-access her memories," Clementine chimes in, a tone of finality in her voice, and Connie's shoulders droop slightly. Trick, Zeph, and Dru look relieved, and although his face is blank, I know Mav will be feeling the same way.

"Thank god for Clementine. There was no way I was ever going to work with her again." I make sure to leave Sam out that time.

"Agreed," growls Mav.

"Agreed," Raphael echoes Mav. "Connie, you can return to your family home on Amilles for the time being. Let us know if any of your memories return. Okay, all of you are dismissed. Alpha, please stay behind."

Sabboath and Connie are the first to leave in a hurry after Connie places a lingering kiss on Samuel's cheek. Bravo, Echo, and Dragon drift out of the room, followed closely by Clementine and Hugh, who look to be having their own argument in hushed whispers. Now it's only Alpha, the Archangels, and Jagger left.

"Jagger, close the door and join Alpha at the table, please." Jagger does as Zadkiel asks and takes Connie's empty seat next to Samuel.

"We want to thank you for your time in Bravo. I think it's been going on long enough that we know they aren't the traitors. A bigoted bunch of assholes, but nothing is linking them with AoA," Azrael begins. "So you will be joining Alpha permanently. We know that's where you were supposed to be from the beginning, and we apologize for the wait and the appalling treatment."

Our newest teammate nods his head. "Thank you. They were leaving it longer and longer between letting me feed, and it was getting to the stage that I probably would've snapped before long. I would suggest not letting them have any more demons on their team. I have a feeling they get a sick satisfaction out of letting us suffer. Brock especially."

"We'll let Clementine know. She's reliable and won't let that happen," Dad grumbles. "Unlike Hugh. I think it's time we did something about that ineffectual waste of space. How did we let him get so far?" Dad's not mincing his words; I've heard him grumble about Hugh many times, and I guess he's taking advantage of this situation to start edging him out.

The Archangels exchange glances. "If I seem to remember rightly, that was Sabboath's doing. He put Hugh's name forward for the director position, and it was just around the time when the kids were born, and we were too distracted to do any digging," muses Chamuel. Surprised looks cover their faces at this revelation.

"Why do they all look so surprised?" I ask Zeph, and he shakes his head.

"I guess they'd forgotten. It can't have been easy, worrying about keeping us a secret and still making sure things ran smoothly with the angels and the CD. It really is a wonder things slipped by them unnoticed, but they shouldn't be so hard on themselves." Considering how dangerous that time must've been, he's easily sympathetic to the pressure our parents must have been under, as am I.

Shaking his head, Raphael continues. "We'll worry about him later. We wanted to speak to you all about Jessamina. She's not getting any better, and I've tried everything I know. We think activating her blood may be the key to getting her to respond to treatment." He looks at the six of us, a weight to his gaze that lets me know whatever he says next will be very important. "But as a member of your team, we are going to leave that decision to you."

"Especially because she was so adamant about not doing it," Dad adds in, his usual frown replaced by a look of sympathy.

I look at the other members of my team, seeing the strain of Mina's illness wearing on them. Bodies strung tight with dark circles under their eyes from lack of sleep and the constant worry. None of them look like they've shaved or brushed their hair in days. Drusilla has even bitten her nails down to the quick, and we certainly haven't been working as a cohesive unit. Most nights we try and get together for a meal, family-style, but that hasn't happened since the attack. I miss my family; I miss our down time together. Everyone seems to be avoiding one another, and I'm not sure if it's deliberate or a coincidence, but I've had enough. I'm also sick of Sam, or I guess the stranger who's taken his place. He's been downright mean and spending most of his time at the hospital with Connie, and with his wishy washy emotions, it's hard to predict what kind of reaction you're going to get when you do see him. Zeph has spent most of his time at the hospital by Mina's bedside, trying to keep Samuel in check, and I know he's exhausted.

My guilt flares. I've been such a self-indulgent dick. Instead of making sure my team was okay, I wallowed in self-pity at the thought of losing Mina, sniping at Trick every time he tried to comfort me until I finally drove him away. Not only have I betrayed my team by leaving them without the support I could've provided, but I made myself pretty much useless. What if something else had happened? What could I have done while I was disgustingly drunk?

Jagger is the only one who hasn't been around constantly, but he too looks worried, and I can't help but think the little interaction he did have with Mina had a significant effect. She's had an enormous impact on all of us in such a short time. She was always fun when she was younger, but we were all looking forward to getting to know her better and more intimately. I had hopes she would be what we've all been searching for, craving even. Someone to love heart and soul like our parents have with each other. Being such a close-knit team means that sometimes relationships with others cause problems. Someone doesn't get enough attention, so they try to come between us to quickly learn that's not how we are. We won't let another get in between us; we've done that before with Constance, and it's only recently we've been able to reconnect with a solid foundation. But with Mina, it's been completely different. She's also shown that she has no intentions of making us compete against one another for her affections. In the short time she had been with us, she already felt a part of the team.

I'd already known that I had feelings for her, especially after our one night together. I'd hoped that maybe it might have become more, but we got sent away for an assignment, and when I came back, I saw her in the same club with another guy. I was devastated even though I'd already thought it hadn't meant as much to her as it had to me. Now I know that was her inner demon driving her needs, but it still hurt like a bitch at the time. I'd even spoken to Trick about her joining us, and he was all for it.

Running a hand through his hair, Zeph looks toward the Archangels. "Do we even know who her parents are? How do we know if they left any blood for her? Or even if they're still alive? Was there any information in all the crap we unearthed at the orphanage?"

"Mina seemed a lot more open to finding out after she read that letter," Samuel chimes in. "But she didn't know where to start." This time the look the Archangels exchange is like they have a secret and are unsure if they should share it or not.

"He doesn't know yet," Azrael reassures the others. *Who doesn't know?*

Raphael nods. "Jagger, do you know the bar Eternal Damnation?" Jagger startles in response, a surprised look on his face. "There's a bartender there; her name is Siffa. Can you ask her to join us, please? You can teleport. No one will say anything." Jagger looks perplexed but quickly disappears.

"What's the demon owner of Eternal Damnation got to do with Mina?" Dru asks quietly. "I mean, she was lovely and kind to us, but I can't see how that will help."

"This is going to piss you all off, but let us finish the story before you all jump down our throats," Chamuel says calmly, leaning back in his chair.

"We know who Mina's parents are," Raphael tells us all. Disbelief covers the faces of my team members before noise erupts. Zeph shuts us down with one hand held up, and being good team members, we obey him.

"Seriously? You've known all this time?" The annoyance in my voice is unmistakable.

"Look, Mina being given up for adoption was not done lightly. In fact, it caused her parents to split up because they couldn't handle the grief of knowing their daughter was out there, but they had put her in such a dangerous situation that they couldn't be with her," Raphael explains.

"Damn near broke their hearts. Shells of people, they are. Instead of leaning on each other and taking comfort, they both threw themselves into their work. But you have got to realize it really was safer for her. Just like it was safer for you to grow up with foster parents. Luckily for us, we were able to have secret relationships with you, but it just wasn't possible for Mina's parents. If the world had found out, they would have been targeted."

"But why? What is it about her parents that would have made them targets?" Trick asks. He always keeps his head and can ask the right questions when the rest of us have exploded. *Goddess, I love him.*

"Yes, surely we need to know what's so secret that you hid it from us all?" Sam demands, standing up with his hands on the table.

"Oh, right, so now *you want to go to bat for Mina. Where was this before?* Zeph questions into his mind, not hiding his accusation from the rest of us. Sam has the sense to look ashamed, so I know he heard him, but he doesn't reply.

"Watch your mouth, boy; it wasn't any of your business," Chamuel growls at his son. "Sit your ass down." *I guess he's borrowing a page from Dad's book tonight.* He points at his chair, and Sam throws himself back into it at his father's words, huffing in annoyance.

Can you tell us now?" I ask, looking at the five of them, but before they can say anything, Jagger and the bartender from Eternal Damnation teleport into the room.

Siffa has her human form on today, no sign of anything demonic at all. She's wearing black skinny jeans and heels with a matching fitted top that makes the red of her hair and purple of her eyes stand out. She surveys the room, a blank look on her face until she gets to the Archangels, who have all stood up and are seemingly waiting for her to say something. A small smile crosses her lips when she sees them.

"Hello, boys! It's been a long time. What shit

storm has occurred that you're coming to me for help?' Her husky voice is pleasant, with a hint of steel behind it.

To my surprise, the five Archangels all move from where they're standing and greet this woman like she's a long-lost friend. Hugs and kisses all around, and they genuinely look happy to see each other. *Dad never mentioned being friends with any demons, and it looks like they're good friends at that.*

Zadkiel shows her to a seat at their end of the table, and she smiles and waves at the rest of us, shooting a wink at Dru, who shows the first bit of animation I've seen from her in days by smiling back. Meanwhile, Jagger returns to his seat as we look between the Archangels and Siffa for a clue as to what's going on.

"Imagine my surprise when one of my best friend's sons," she begins, gesturing to Jagger, "who I haven't seen in years, mind you, portals into my club and tells me that the Collectors Division wants to see me. He assures me I have done nothing wrong, so I can't imagine why I've been called for a meeting. But like a good little demon, I came right away." She smiles, the threat beneath it almost a palpable thing. "So, don't keep me waiting. Who's going to tell me what is going on?" she asks again, that steel filling her voice again by the end of the question.

A frown crosses my face. Jagger's father is Asmodeus, and he, along with two other

Archdemons, were the rulers in Habbalea before it was destroyed. As powerful as the three of them were, they were unable to prevent Hammus from infecting the other Archdemons with his hate and greed, and the destruction that occurred was catastrophic. All three went into hiding and haven't been seen in years. When Jagger appeared on our radar, it was the first time the Archangels had heard from one in years. His father had sent him to the academy, knowing he would get a first-rate education and training from the Archangel-run school. Raphael's awkward throat clearing brings my attention back to the room just in time.

"Well, Lucifer, I'm afraid it's about your daughter," Raphael announces.

Chapter Three

Zephaniah

Holy shit! Siffa, the owner of Eternal Damnation, is Lucifer, Archdemon and co-ruler of all demons. I stare at her in shock, unable to school my expression in time. She looks around the room, and when she realizes it's only the Archangels and Team Alpha, she shrugs her shoulders and releases her cloaking.

The power now emanating from her is enormous. The waves throbbing through the room raise the hairs on my arms and the back of my neck. That feeling that a prey animal must experience when faced with a predator after a meal. Her innate strength definitely rivals our parents', but they keep theirs on lock down for everyone's comfort. It's just not comfortable to be surrounded by so much power all the time. Had we been able to feel this, there would have been no doubt about her status.

And then the other thing that Raphael said slams into my brain. *Mina is Lucifer's daughter.* Mina isn't an AB; she's half-demon. The noise in the room is thunderous as the rest of Team Alpha explodes at this news. Unfazed, the Archangels pay no attention to us; their focus is on the deadly creature in front of them.

The look she shoots the others is cutting, and they all shut up. "When did we decide that this was a secret that was to be shared?" she asks our fathers, coolly.

"Mina needs your help, Siffa," Azrael tells her, putting a hand out for hers and squeezing it when she reluctantly accepts. "She was attacked during the last mission."

Lucifer sits up straight, worry in her face, and I'm struck by the depth of care. It's impossible to doubt that the letter Mina had found was genuine now that I've seen Siffa's expression at knowing her daughter is in danger. "I heard your last mission had gone balls up and that a Guardian was injured, but I didn't know it was Jessamina. What's wrong with her? She should be healing fine. Why wasn't her blood activated before she went on her first mission?" She looks between the Archangels and us, that worry quickly turning to anger so strong she practically vibrates with it. "Why is my daughter injured?"

"She refused to have it done. Mina figured if her parents didn't want her, why would she want anything from them," Samuel explains to the Archdemon, a look of disdain on his face.

"That's what she said the first time I saw her

again, but I couldn't believe it, didn't *want* to believe. We'd left her a note and trusted the nuns to pass on the information. We never expected that a good family wouldn't adopt her!" The devastation she feels becomes visible, her body shuddering violently as a sob escapes her mouth and a tear trickles down her cheek.

"We think the head nun had something to do with that," Sander adds in, his voice rough from his recent alcohol abuse. *Thank the goddess Dru got him sobered up for this meeting. I can't imagine handling this news with him drunk.* "But she's gone now, so we can't question her."

The sadness clears, and a look of glee fills Lucifer's eyes. "Mmm, yes, I know, shame that." Her smile brings a chill down my spine, and I can see Drusilla visibly shudder at the wave of anger that briefly consumes the room. My team exchange looks, but no one is willing to touch that, and the Archangels don't seem to care.

"I should have fought him harder on his decision." Her tone turns bitter as she narrows her eyes at the Archangels and adds, "And you assholes could have helped."

"Siffa, we tried, you know we did. He wouldn't be swayed." I'm about to ask who they're talking about, but Uriel gets in first.

"Enough, there is no point in dwelling on the past. We can't change it; we just have to look forward."

"What do you need from me?" Lucifer asks, sounding like she genuinely wants to help, and I think we're all going to have to trust that she does. I look at the rest of the table, and only Sander seems like he's going to say something, so I shake my head at him, and he shuts up.

"Mina's been poisoned with something we've never seen before. We're hoping that activating her demon side will burn the poison out of her and kick in her accelerated healing," Raphael explains.

Lucifer looks at Jagger before she answers, the worry in her voice evident. "We can do that, but I'm worried about her reactions. Demons go through a different kind of puberty than angels or even ABs, and when she gets my blood, she will too. I had Mina spelled so that she would avoid going through this."

"What happens?" Mav asks, breaking his silence. He likes to sit and take everything in before forming an opinion, so he hasn't said anything until now.

Jagger answers for her. "We go through a powerful hunger, completely insatiable. And it's not only for blood." He looks to Lucifer as if asking permission to continue, and she nods her head. "How often you feed your hungers depends on what they are. A demon that feeds on violence would be set up to fight as many demons as he could until the hunger faded. One that was ruled by their greed would be given everything they desired during that period of time. A demon not able to feed on what they need becomes a menace; their body starts to emit pheromones that influence the people around them to provide for the demon. It's a defense mechanism, a survival tool embedded into the demon's DNA."

"And what kind of demon are you?" Sam asks Lucifer. "Will Mina be the same?" The Archangels at the top of the table start to squirm, looking incredibly uncomfortable, while Lucifer just rolls her eyes at them. I have a funny feeling about this.

"Lust demon, commonly known as a succubus. Why else would I own a sex club? And yes, she will," she answers, seeming surprised at the question. "Are even the children of Archangels taught nothing about demonkind?" She aims a momentary grimace at the dads, and their discomfort only increases.

"So, does this mean…" Trick trails off.

"Mina is going to have to fuck until she satisfies all her appetites," Jagger confirms, a frown on his face.

"I will organize some demons to have on hand for her transition," Lucifer tells the group of uncomfortable-looking Archangels. "In fact, let's move her to my club. I'll clear it out until she's over the hunger. It will be the safest place for her."

"Now hang on a fucking second." My eyes fly to Drusilla, who has a surprising look of fury on her face. She and her twin can be a little hotheaded, but

I didn't think she'd actually mouth off to an Archdemon. Usually, she's the one with more common sense. "I have questions, damn it! Will she be in her right mind?"

"Probably not," Lucifer tells her.

"Is there no other option? Look, I don't think this is a decision we should be making. I barely know her, and she has no clue that you're her mother, and you guys are only just reconnecting." Drusilla gestures to us. "I think maybe we should invite Olivia and James in for this conversation," she pleads. "They're the ones who know her the best; they'll be able to tell us more."

Lucifer thoughtfully nods her head without hesitation. "Yes, you may be right; get them here." Dad leaves the room, and it falls into an uneasy silence as we wait for them to return. When they do, the situation is explained to them. The look of shock in their faces is amusing and must have been what we all looked like when we were told.

"That's the situation so far," Dad says. Olivia reaches over and grabs James' hand for support, and I can see him squeeze it. They're united in strength, good people for Mina to have at her back. I admire and envy their closeness, a pang hitting me when I think about how close we could be to never having the chance to develop that with Mina.

"I don't like the idea of Mina having sex with a whole heap of strangers," Dru explains to them both. "We thought maybe you could lend some insight."

James snorts, and a smirk crosses his face before Olivia elbows him in the side. He snorts again and gives it a rub before collecting himself. "Seriously, it explains so much," James says to Olivia. A look of confusion crosses everyone's face.

"What is it?" snaps Uriel, at the limit of his patience with being on the outside of whatever's happening here.

"Mina's like a dude. She had a never-ending revolving door of men and women, but she would hit it and quit it. No relationships, just lots of sex. Olivia and I thought it was because of her daddy issues."

Raphael stiffens at this comment, and a grimace crosses Uriel's face. The rest fidget, not meeting anyone's eye. Zadkiel clears his throat as he runs a hand through his hair, looking uncomfortable. Lucifer spares a look of amusement at them before a frown crosses her face. "Obviously, the spell I had put on her to stop her transition isn't working as well as I hoped. That would be the demon in her trying to get out. So how do you think she would feel about being activated and needing to have sex with a couple of strangers?"

"No different to any Saturday night." James shrugs, and this time Olivia hits him, hard.

"There aren't any other options? This will definitely happen once you activate her blood?"

Drusilla looks desperate for a solution; the distress in her voice is real.

"I'm sorry, there's not, but she's not going to care at the time," Lucifer assures her gently. "It's not ideal, but there is no way of stopping the hunger. Just ask Jagger." Dru turns to look at Jagger, and he shakes his head, confirming what Lucifer says.

"If it's any consolation, Mina really does like sex, and she really won't be concerned about having an overactive sex drive. It'll just be business as usual," Olivia says quietly.

"Most demons have a group of friends that help each other out, but they've known all their lives what they will go through," Jagger explains. He shifts restlessly on the spot, and his gaze bounces around the room before he meets my eye, and I can tell he wants to say more.

"What is it?" I ask him when he doesn't continue.

"I'm willing to help her out if you guys don't mind." This has everyone sitting up in their chairs, and even Sander shows some enthusiasm.

"Is this an option?' Trick asks Lucifer, and she thinks about it.

"Jagger? Yes, but he won't be enough, I don't think. If she's anything like I was, it went on for days."

"What about us?" Mav asks quietly. "Would we be able to help her out?"

"Do you think that's a good idea?" Lucifer eyes us up and down, a sympathetic look crossing her face. "You guys are just reconnecting; you don't think that seeing that will put a mark on your team before it's even really gotten started? She will fuck and feed from you all, and she won't be quite herself until she fills her needs. Are you willing to do that? To not know if she realizes it's you who she's doing these things with?"

As I glance around the table, the different looks on their faces are fascinating. Sander and Trick look like they're all in on the plan, and nothing will sway them. But they've always been all or nothing type people. Drusilla and Samuel look uncomfortable, the latter almost to the point of nausea, but I think Drusilla would get over her discomfort for Mina's sake. And Mav, his face is as blank as ever, but I know him, and I know behind that blank look his mind is a beautiful chaotic mess. With one revelation after another, the poor guy's head is probably spinning in this loss of control.

"Yes, I would do anything for her," Sander says, instantly looking better than he has in days. He and Trick exchange glances.

"I'm in too," Trick agrees.

Both Mav and Drusilla nod their heads, determination in their eyes. "Definitely, but I want to be on my own with Mina," Dru demands. "You can wait outside while it's my turn." The guys quickly agree to her terms. Smiling, I turn to look at

Samuel, but I can see the doubt in his eyes, and I understand it. Ideally, I don't want my first time with her to be when she's in a mindless frenzy, but I'm like the others, and I would do anything for her.

"I'm not sure," he says quietly. "I want Mina to remember our first time together."

Mav pats him on the shoulder. "I get that, man. I'm sure we'll be enough. You can keep an eye on Constance while we take care of Mina." I'm pleased to see him showing some sort of interest in a future with Mina even if he's not willing to help out with this. Maybe there's still hope for him.

Lucifer does too. "I think what you're all offering is very noble but consider it this way. Not only is she going to find out she's not an angel, but a demon, she's also going to have a demon form. How comfortable do you think she'll be going through this with all of you? None of you are currently in a sexual relationship with her, are you?" She looks around the table, and we all shake our heads. "Do you really think that's how she would like your first time to be?"

"No!" Olivia says firmly. "No, I don't think she would like it. Jagger would be fine; she doesn't have a history with him. But you guys... At one stage, you were the closest things to best friends she had. Mina would think you all deserve better than a mindless frenzy. No, I don't think it would be a good idea." She looks so upset that James wraps an arm around her, but he nods his agreement.

Lucifer looks at Olivia with affection, her eyes softening for the first time since she's joined us. "Thank you, Olivia. You're a good friend to Mina." Her gaze returns to us. "I appreciate the offer, but I think we will go with Jagger. Since he's willing, that opens the option to bring in only one other demon. If both are Archdemons, they'll be able to handle her between themselves with little to no risks. I wouldn't want this to affect you as a team." She reassures us, "The other concern I had with you all being involved is the blood drinking. Transition requires copious amounts of blood to be taken by the demon transitioning to speed up the form change. Demons produce extra blood because we all feed on it, and I wouldn't want any of you to be drained accidentally. Whether you could survive it or not, it's not a pleasant experience, and with everything that's currently going on, it would be dangerous to incapacitate another member of your team."

We all start to argue, but Jagger's voice is loudest. "Who are you thinking of, Siffa?"

"I was going to ask Malakai," she tells him, and he nods his head, looking both unsurprised and a tiny bit unsettled.

"I think he's a good option, and she could just drink from him. He probably wouldn't even be interested in sex," she reassures us.

That bit of information makes my head turn quickly toward her. "Why not?' I ask, the interest in my voice obvious.

"Is that Belphegor's son?' Chamuel asks curiously at the same time.

"Yes," Lucifer answers Chamuel and then turns to me. "Belphegor was the other Archdemon who, like Asmodeus and me, didn't succumb to Hammus's madness. We think it's because he's a sloth demon, and he really couldn't be bothered."

The Archangels around the table groan and grumble together. "So fucking lazy," Uriel spits out.

Lucifer laughs. "He wasn't any help when we were trying to stop the others from destroying Habbalea, physically, at least, but he is an excellent strategist."

I look at Jagger. "You know Malakai? How do you feel about this? You're the only one of us that can make this decision."

"He's standoffish and rude, and you'll probably want to punch him in the nose until you get to know him, but he's a good guy. He and I had been best friends for years before I came to the academy, and he got pissed at me. But he's only part sloth demon. His mother was a succubus too; sex will *definitely* be on the table," he reminds Lucifer. My relief at Jagger's words is staggering, and I'm surprised at how quickly I'm trusting him to make these decisions regarding Mina's wellbeing.

"What do you think?" I quickly ask Mav through our telepathic link.

"Man, I'm glad Jagger's here to give us some insight. I trust him, you know that," he replies gruffly.

"Fuck I never thought we'd have to making these decisions." Worry comes through, a feeling that I might try to hide from the others, but I know Mav can handle being the strong one for a moment.

"She's worth it though," he says firmly, and we both listen to what she has to say about this new demon.

Lucifer shrugs. "Even better. With the both of you offering her what she needs, she should come out the other side unscathed." She turns to us with a slight frown, concern clear in her eyes. "Please remember that Mina will have two forms, both demon and her normal one. She probably won't be able to hold her normal one consistently for the first couple of weeks, and you need to be comfortable with that, so it doesn't give her more things to worry about."

I hide a smile. Lucifer's mommy genes are kicking in swiftly, and you could almost feel like she's been looking out for Mina her entire life.

"She really cares about her, doesn't she?" Dru's question comes through, full of curiosity and an equal amount of warmth and admiration. It's definitely looking like Mina could have done *much* worse in the Mom department. . *"I can't imagine what she went through when they had to give her up."* Her sympathy flows through the connection.

"Yeah, it must have been heartbreaking. I can't imagine the tension it caused between her and her partner. Imagine losing your baby and your mate in one go." My sympathy toward the Archdemon grows at the knowledge that Jessamina's dad must have been her mate and that giving up their baby somehow destroyed that bond.

"Not a problem," Sander tells her, "demon forms are hot." *Can always rely on Sander to bring us back to the basics.*

She rolls her eyes. "Not all of them, but you're probably right, though there will most likely be horns, claws, fangs, and a tail, not to mention the wings."

But none of Alpha looks worried, and a feeling of pride flows through me. A lot of people turn their noses up at demons' alternate forms, but none of us have ever been bigots. We were raised to be tolerant and accepting of all, which unfortunately not enough angels are these days. And Sander is right; some demon forms are smoking hot. My cock twitches at the thought of how Mina may look. *Fuck, that's not appropriate! Especially with her mother here.*

"Is there something about Mina's demon blood that attracts us all to her?" I'm curious about our complete devotion to her.

Lucifer brow creases in thought. "Maybe the combination of my succubus blood, with her father's, has done something to her, but I'm not sure. It's something we can look into when we have her back with us."

"Who's her father?' Sam has more guts than the rest of us but is shot down immediately by Uriel.

"None of your damn business at this stage," he growls. "And if anyone's going to be told, I think it might be best if we talk to Mina first." *Okay, that's fair.*

"So, everyone, what's your decision? Shall we go ahead with this blood activation?' Raphael asks us, looking around the table. "All of you need to be okay." Everyone nods their agreement except Samuel.

"Is there no other way to heal her?" he asks Raphael.

"We could ask Mylea to intervene, but to be honest, she has enough worries on her hands with one of her consorts missing," he tells Samuel, a sympathetic look crossing his face.

"Yeah, and one of them is a raving lunatic," Lucifer mutters, pushing her red hair behind her shoulder.

Dad has been quiet the whole time, listening to the proceedings, but now he stands up. "This is really our only option, and you need to make a decision quickly before any of the damage goes too far. We don't know how permanent her injuries are, so get over yourself and make a decision," he commands Samuel, the annoyance in his voice unmistakable. A bit of his power slips his tight hold, and that, more than anything, betrays how serious the situation has gotten. Like me, he's usually good at holding things in when needed.

"Do it," I tell them, making the final decision. Samuel seems to be the only one not happy about it, and frankly, he's outvoted.

Lucifer stands up and nods in my direction. "I think you're making the right decision. If you can organize for her to be moved to Eternal Damnation, I'll return there and set up a room for the transition."

"We can use mine," Dru offers quietly from her side of the table, and Lucifer gives her a grateful smile but shakes her head.

"Thank you, honey. While your room is lovely, it's not very practical in that it's very …. white. And this could get very, well, messy." Dru's eyes widen at this response, and then a nervous giggle leaves her mouth.

"Also, let's keep this between the people in this room for now. You saw how Bravo treated Jagger. Unfortunately, they're not the only ones that hold a great disdain for our demon counterparts," Azrael instructs us. "Nobody needs to know what Mina is. Let's keep them thinking she's an AB for now." Everyone agrees with this.

"Alright, then shall we reconvene at Eternal Damnation within an hour?" Dad suggests and holds out his arm for Lucifer. She graciously accepts it, and the six of them make their way out of the room with James and Olivia, leaving behind our team.

"Are we really going to do this?" Samuel asks as soon as they're gone, aggravation evident in his voice, and I hold up a hand, stopping him in his tracks.

"Yes, we are. It's the difference between us having Mina or letting her fade away and never knowing if we will find a cure. And if a little bit of aggressive sex and blood is enough to sway you, then I question, are you really as committed to this, to *her*, as everyone else?"

Sander's face is dark with annoyance, like how could Sam even question our decision. A range of emotions cross Dru's face, but she settles on wary but determined. Mav stands up and paces back and forth; I know his thoughts are chaotic, but he stops and sits back down, nodding his head in agreement. Trick doesn't show much emotion except to shrug and nod. They all seem to be in agreement. As one, we all turn to look at Sam. All the attention on him makes him squirm, and he blushes slightly before his shoulders droop, and he nods in resignation.

Mav puts his hand on his shoulder. "It'll be ok, man. We'll be there for her until you and Mina are both ready. I don't think any less of you because it makes you a bit squeamish."

Samuel nods his thanks to Mav, but I hear Sander whisper "I do" to Trick.

Fuck. Dissension in the ranks, just what I need.

"Sander, he's entitled to his feelings, and we shouldn't make light of them. We need someone keeping an eye on Connie anyway, and I don't trust that job to anyone but one of us." Sander grumbles under his breath but doesn't say anything else. He's not one to let go of shit quickly, so I'll have to keep an eye on him and make sure this doesn't grow into something much worse between my two teammates.

"Samuel, you head to Amilles and keep an eye on Connie. I'll leave it up to you whether you do this at a distance or in person," I order him. "The rest of us will head to Eternal Damnation and take care of our girl." *Finally, we might get some answers to who or what did that to her.*

Chapter Four

Drusilla

Samuel doesn't join us when we leave the Collectors Division building. When we get to the ground floor, he moves to the next bank of elevators to take him down to the portal room, heading to Amilles to keep his eye on Constance. He just leaves without saying a word, not even good luck or keep me posted. Frowning, I stop and watch, a funny feeling building in the pit of my stomach. Something doesn't feel right about this. I turn to Zeph to tell him that, finding he's also watching Samuel walk away, a frown on his face.

"I don't like this. It doesn't feel right to be separating as a team at the moment. That Sam doesn't want to be a part of bringing Mina back to us," I tell him. "He's acting stranger than normal. I thought he would be the first person to jump at the chance to help her, yet he's the most reluctant." The others hear what I'm saying and stop just before the exit.

"So, we're finally addressing the elephant in the

room." Sander's sarcasm confuses me, and I raise an eyebrow in question, but the others don't look nearly so perplexed. He runs a hand through his hair in agitation. "Come on, you all know how I've felt about this. Let's just get it out in the open, let Dru and Jagger know what we've talked about over the years." Jagger looks just as confused as I do, and we trade glances between the other guys.

"One of you has to help us out. Jagger and I weren't around when you guys were training. What's Sander talking about?" I cross my arms and tap my foot, waiting for their explanation, my frustration clear. The four of them shuffle their feet and avoid meeting my eyes, clearly uncomfortable.

Mav awkwardly clears his throat but finally answers when no one else will. "Sam's always been a little funny when it comes to Mina. On the one hand, he wants to keep her all to himself, obsessive even, but on the other hand, he was jealous when she got more attention than him when we all trained together."

"What do you mean?" I ask, not seeing what this has to do with our current predicament.

"What he means is, Mina always got extra hurt when she was sparring with Sam. He was always very apologetic and had a convenient excuse, but it was like he was trying to prove he was better than her no matter the cost. A competition between him and her and who could get more attention from their parents," Trick adds in quietly, running a hand through his blond hair.

"Really?" I'm shocked at what Trick has just said; Mina's never shown any kind of animosity or wariness toward Sam since she joined the team, and she doesn't strike me as the kind of girl who lets herself get pushed around.

"Yeah, and he always made an extra effort to flaunt his relationship with Connie in her face when we went there for dinner. Kissing her and groping her in front of the whole family. It was embarrassing for Maggie and Peter, and Mina was mortified. Connie would just giggle and encourage him. It was like she fed off the tension. It got so bad that Mina stopped coming whenever she knew we were invited as well. Poor Maggie used to be sad she couldn't get her kids in the same room as each other, and Sam would always say it was a shame Mina was so selfish after they had taken her in when she had no one else. He could be such a dick," Sander tells me, aggravation in his voice. Jesus, I haven't seen him this worked up in a long time. It's not like him to say anything negative against one of the guys. "Mav and Zeph were always more private about what they had going on with Connie."

"Which wasn't much," Mav grunts, "mostly just convenience, I'm ashamed to admit." Zeph nods in agreement, fidgeting with embarrassment.

Sander continues, "When Trick and I told them

how horrible Constance was to you and both of us, they refused all her advances, but Sam didn't, *wouldn't*. Said he was finally glad to have something all to himself."

Zeph rubs his hand across his chin in contemplation. 'You know, I had forgotten about that because Connie disappeared not long after, but you're right. He got really mean and started babbling about being stuck with us and having no choice about doing things his way or making his own decisions. It was weird. Stormed off and was gone for twenty-four hours."

"Yeah, but he would disappear like that regularly. It started just as we first went to the Academy, and Mina moved in with Maggie and Peter. We thought he was going home to hang out there, but it turns out he wasn't. Remember, Maggie rang looking for him one day, and that's when we found out he wasn't with them," Trick muses.

"Right, I had forgotten that too. We didn't bother following up on it because we got sick of his temper tantrums and mood swings and stopped caring. It didn't happen much once we graduated." Zeph shrugs.

"That's weird. I always thought he worshiped Mina, borderline obsessively. I mean, I get it now that I've met her. She's gorgeous and sweet and kind, and he was always talking about her. I thought for sure he wanted her on the team, and Mina sure doesn't act like he had ever treated her badly."

Samuel has always been a little standoffish. He's polite and everything but never goes out of his way to show affection or hang out with me. Out of our makeshift family, he's the one who I like the least. Not that I would ever tell them that.

"Mina's always been about trying to see the best in a person. She even tried to be friends with Connie in the beginning, but that was *never* going to work. Connie saw her as competition. You never really know with Sam," Mav grumbles. "Moody asshole."

"Poor Mina, she's going to be so sad if she wakes up and Samuel's not there. I wonder if she knows how he feels," I question them.

Sander scoffs. "Doubtful, he was always nice to her afterward, going on about how he slipped, or she was clumsy, that sort of thing."

Trick shakes his head; there's a sense of sadness in his actions. "No, she's oblivious. She just wanted to be loved and accepted and thought she had finally found it with Maggie, Peter, and Sam."

Jagger claps a hand on Zeph's back. "Look, let's get through Mina's transition, and then maybe it's time to confront him about his attitude."

The demon's words make me think about how Mina would feel if she ever found out this information, and I make a promise to myself to never let her. The elevator finally arrives, and together we make our way to Eternal Damnation, our group deep in thought.

Siffa greets us when we arrive and hustles us through a closed, quiet nightclub and downstairs to the dungeon. The club is clean, but the stale smell of beer and sweat still lingers. She has a worried look on her face as we sit down on the couches arranged in one of the public areas.

"Transition is rough," Siffa confides in us all, "emotionally *and* physically. I wouldn't want that to be anyone's first time, let alone my daughter's. I'm just disappointed the spell to stop her transformation didn't work as well as it should have. A revolving door of strangers isn't great either. Just be aware, she will probably never be a 'one-man' woman," she warns.

"We have no problems with that; I think I speak for all of us when I say we would be happy to service her needs as long as she keeps it within our team,'" I reassure her, well aware that that's what everyone wants anyway.

Sander adds, "Hmm, may have to hit Samuel over the head with that one," disdain so clear that even Siffa gets a small frown. Just as he finishes saying this, a portal opens in the room, and a demon steps through.

I study this man with the eye of someone not interested in the opposite sex but still able to appreciate a handsome one. Relatively tall, with what looks like a long, lean build under his clothes, he's wearing casual jeans and a t-shirt. The boots on his feet are scuffed and covered in red dust. His eyes are bright purple, lined with eyeliner, and the pupil is thin and elongated like a reptile's eye. He has distinctive features that show some Asian heritage somewhere in his bloodline. Long, silky, black hair cascades over his shoulder streaked with purple highlights, and a cocky smirk graces his full lips.

"You called for me, Lucifer?" His voice has a lilting accent as he bows slightly to her.

"Thank you for coming so quickly, Malakai. Allow me to introduce you to Team Alpha, the top team in the Collectors Division. This is Zeph, Mav, Trick, Sander, and their communications tech, Drusilla."

Malakai eyes us all as we say a tentative hello, then his lip curls up. "Aren't there supposed to be six of you? What happened? Did you kill another member?" A stunned silence fills the air before Mav leaps at him with his hands out.

Before he can get close to him, Jagger jumps in between them. He stops Mav, putting both hands on his chest and pushing him back. Malakai watches on with a smirk not having moved to defend himself against Mav.

"I warned you he was an asshole," Jagger scolds. He turns and puts himself between them and hugs Malakai to himself while whispering in his ear. I watch as Malakai's tense body relaxes slightly against Jagger's frame, as if it was familiar and comforting to him. Malakai's eyes don't leave us, and the sneer on his lips doesn't move, but he nods when Jagger finishes and steps back.

"Actually, there are eight of us, now that Jagger has joined," Zeph growls at him.

Malakai's eyebrows raise, and he looks at Jagger in surprise. "Dude, you got out of Bravo, thank god." The relief in his voice is evident as he pulls him into another hug. Maybe he's not such an asshole after all. "Let's hope you get treated better by this team, but if you say there are eight to the team and only six here, that still means you're missing two. Not sure if you'll be safer."

"Fuck you," Sander spits at him, "you know nothing." The rest of the guys puff up their chests and snarl out their objections, and I see a small smile cross Malakai's face; he likes their reactions. *Is he feeding off of it?*

Rolling my eyes, I shout at them, "Shut up, all of you." The boys turn to me, more surprised at my volume rather than my words. "Can't you see he's enjoying winding you up?" They all turn to look at Malakai, who now has a shit-eating grin across his face. He holds his hand out.

"Can't promise I'm going to like you, but if you take care of my friend here, then that's all I care about."

The boys exchange looks, and reluctantly, they go about the male ritual of slapping hands. I roll my eyes, tapping my foot impatiently. Siffa just watches the whole exchange with amusement before clapping her hands together.

"That's enough of the male posturing bullshit. Shall we get on with what's important?" she drawls sarcastically, and my brother and his friends manage to show a little remorse. But only a little, the idiots.

Lucifer explains the situation to Malakai, and I watch him and his unchanging expression the whole time. I wouldn't want to play poker with this guy; he's entirely unreadable.

She finishes talking, and he turns to stare at Jagger. They stare at each other like they're having a conversation, and Jagger nods his head slightly. I wonder if Archdemons are able to communicate telepathically too. It seems likely since Jagger can hop into our team's connection with each other.

"Sure, I'll help out. It's no hardship fucking and feeding a pretty lady. She *is* pretty, isn't she?" he asks, and again Mav lunges at him. If nothing else, this just shows how badly Mav is taking all of this sudden change. Usually, he keeps his cool much better than he is right now. Jagger just throws his hands up in disgust and steps between them again. He shoves Mav away and rounds on Malakai.

"Stop being such a dick. This is important. *She's* important," he snaps at Malakai, and a sly gleam enters his eye as he holds his hand up again.

Siffa looks at him with anger. "That's my

daughter you're talking about." Malakai pales slightly.

"I'm sorry," he says to her, giving another bow that reaches lower than his initial greeting. Then to Jagger, "Ok, my friend, I'm sorry. If it means that much to you, I'll help and try to behave."

Just as Jagger lets out a sigh of relief and drops his hands, another portal opens in the underground room, and through it step Raphael and Uriel, followed by a floating hospital bed containing Mina. My heart sinks at seeing her like this, and tears fill my eyes. So pale and lifeless, I can only hope what we are about to do works, and she forgives us for making these decisions.

The bed floats past us as Siffa hurries away to show them to the room this will happen. Malakai shows the first sign of emotions as she drifts past, and a softer look crosses his face, compassion in his eyes along with a hint of appreciation. Everyone follows but him and me, and he catches me watching him.

"It's a little like that Earth story where the prince has to kiss the sleeping princess to wake her."

I snort. "Not sure a kiss is going to cut it this time, it's a much bigger job." A smirk crosses his face.

"And I've got just the right tool for the job." Ahh, there's that asshole. But I chuckle, and he slings an arm over my shoulder as we follow the others.

"So, Dru, was it?' he asks. "Tell me about the pretty sleeping princess."

"Well, I don't know her all that well yet, but she's funny, kind, and fearless, and I can't wait to get to know her. Not to mention, she has a banging body, a mouth made for loving, and kisses like a devil."

He smirks in my direction. "Now those are the details I like to hear. And she really let Jagger feed on her just after they met?' He sounds a little skeptical.

"Yep, that's the fearless, adventurous part."

"Sounds like this about to be a fun ride." He makes light of the situation, and I stop in my tracks and turn to him.

"Don't," I order, and he raises an eyebrow. "Just don't, I saw the emotions. I saw that there is more to you than just an asshole. Don't try and put on an act now. You can try and fool the others, but not me."

He runs a hand over his face, looking worn out all of a sudden. "Look, Jagger and I have been friends for a long time."

"And more," I coax, and he nods slightly before continuing.

"If he hadn't asked me to do this, I wouldn't. I've been hurt before, and I don't want to open myself up to being hurt again, but it's so hard to say no to him." *Hmm, they were* definitely *talking telepathically before.*

"So, I'll use sarcasm and assholism and whatever I need to keep the emotions and feelings at bay. Are you ok with that?" His confession is a balm on my soul. Relief that he may not be as bad as we first thought and can show kindness and compassion. Something I think Mina is going to need in huge amounts.

I pull him in for a hug and whisper in his ear, "It will be our secret."

He wraps his arms around me and hugs me. "Thank you," he whispers. "I needed that." Then his hand drops lower to caress my ass before giving it a squeeze, and I pull back in shock, torn between openly laughing and smacking his in return.

"What the fuck?" Sander growls from behind him, and Malakai winks at me before turning and sauntering off.

"Thanks, babe, I needed that," he shouts over his shoulder.

"She doesn't do dick, asshole," my brother snarls, causing me to snort with laughter as he follows after him.

Bloody Hell, it's going to be a long afternoon.

Chapter Five

Jagger

I scrub a hand over my face as I watch them place Mina onto a bed in the room Siffa has shown us to. Looking around, I decide it must be used for wet play as every surface is washable, including the mattress, and there are drains located in the floor. Not exactly the sexiest room in the place, but I guess it'll be suitable for what's to come.

It's hard to believe I'm going to help Mina transition her demon side. I never would have thought I would be so lucky. It's an honor to be asked to help because it's when a demon is at their most vulnerable, and for Mina it will be even worse. She probably won't understand what's happening until after it, and to be able to repay her kindness by helping her during this time of need is the best way I can think of to start my time on Team Alpha.

I just hope Malakai can keep his mouth shut and not antagonize the guys any further. He was pissed at me when I decided to go to the academy, but he chose to stay at home with his father. In any case, he's been pissed at me before, and we got through it.

"Jagger!" A voice startles me out of my thoughts, and I glance up to see Lucifer staring at me, an annoyed twist to her lips as she raises her brow and gives me a look that telegraphs her frustration. "You didn't hear anything I said, did you?"

Feeling a little sheepish, I shake my head, and she rolls her eyes. Before she can continue, the rest of Alpha and Malakai enter the room.

"Whoa, hold up, way too many people in this room now," she complains.

"We're just coming to say good luck," Dru tells her, nose wrinkling up as she looks around the room. "This is *awful*."

Again, Lucifer rolls her eyes, and I think it's safe to say she's getting impatient now. "Yes, it is, but we can hose down all the bodily fluids when they're done. Demons get a little, shall we say, enthusiastic during transition." Drusilla pales a little at the description but offers no further commentary.

Zeph's standing beside Mina on the bed, running his hand over her head. He leans down and whispers something in her ear before kissing her on the cheek.

"Hurry up," he growls to the others, "let's get this shit done."

He storms out, rushing past me, but I grab his arm, stopping him and pulling him close as I whisper in his ear. "I got this, brother. No harm will come to her on my watch," I promise him, and he nods his thanks, unwilling to look me in the eye and show just how upset and frustrated he is at all of this being out of his control. But I know my friend; I can see how much this bothers him. This is my chance to step up and do what's needed for the team, a way to show my gratitude to them and how much I appreciate their easy acceptance of me. Mav comes up and takes hold of his other side, nodding his head in thanks to me, and walks out with Zeph without looking back. He's another one that will bottle it all up.

Dru, Sander, and Trick all show little forms of affection before taking their leave until it's just Raphael, Lucifer, Malakai, and me left.

"Ok, so let me repeat what I said before when you weren't listening," she grumbles. I think the wait is taking a toll, but Malakai and Raphael just smirk at her.

"Transfusing my blood into her system should break the spell holding off her transition. From there, it's just a waiting game." She tugs at her hair in frustration and starts pacing. "I mean, for all we know this may not work, and she may not wake up at all. She may be lost to us — *me* for good."

Raphael steps in front of her and stops her pacing, grabbing her by the arms. "Look at me," he demands, and as she looks up, I can see tears streaming down her face. He pulls her into his embrace and starts rubbing her back. "Everything will be ok, Siffa. She will come through this, and you and her will build a relationship. Remember, Mylea said these things need to happen." My mind latches on to this bit of information. *Why would Mylea have anything to do with Mina? Why would she be involved in any of this?*

"What do you mean by that?" I demand of the Archangel, and the two of them break apart.

Raphael's face is like a thunderstorm, and from the stubborn set to his lips, I already know the answer we'll get. "Never you mind, we'll tell you when the time is right."

"Seems to me there are a lot of secrets that are being kept at the moment." My sarcasm is sharp, and Malakai's ever-present smirk changes to a wide grin, but he stays silent. In the wake of my stating the obvious, Lucifer visibly shakes off her distress and becomes all business again.

"As I was saying, we will give her the blood infusion and leave her in your hands. Both of you have been through it, so you know what to expect."

"Yup," Malakai confirms easily, his tone light. I think he's trying to make Lucifer more comfortable; I'm not sure it's working, but at least he's not being an ass at the moment. "Her body will go through the form change. I hope she's not too conscious for that; the pain was excruciating."

I shudder at the memories of my own transition. The extra appendages, whatever they may be, push their way through your body. It's like growing them but in time-lapse. The bony growths form, ripping through skin and muscle before becoming what is needed. They then form a covering in the case of tails or wings. Some demons are lucky they may only grow horns, unlike both Kai and me, who had a whole heap of things to grow.

"When she wakes, she will be ravenous, so it's probably better to feed her first, but I'll leave it to you guys to make the best decisions. I trust you both." Lucifer smiles slightly. "If things hadn't been taken out of my hands, the three of you might have been the three musketeers instead of the dynamic duo." She winks at our childhood nickname.

In that brief moment of reminiscing, Raphael inserts a needle into Mina's arm and hooks her up to a bag of blood. The liquid slowly flows down the tube and enters her body. "Alright, are we ready?" Raphael asks us, receiving a nod from both Lucifer and Kai.

"Ok, you know the deal. She needs to be able to hold her human form to leave the room. And not look at everyone as if they're a snack." Kai and I laugh, and it breaks the tension slightly, which I think is what she was aiming for.

Raphael slaps us on the back and wishes us luck as he leaves. Lucifer takes a little longer, giving us both a hug and shooting another glance at Mina over her shoulder on the way. Apprehension covers her face, but she pulls the steel door closed behind her. Not only is the room washable, it has a large safe-like door that can only be opened from the outside. This room is frequently used by transitioning demons now that our planet is inhospitable. There's a button on the wall to let people know when it's time to open the door, but we'll just teleport out.

The door shuts with an audible bang, and the mechanism locking is like a gunshot throughout the room, followed by intimidating silence. Seconds tick away as we both stand there watching the blood slowly enter Mina's bloodstream.

I search for something to say to Malakai, anything to get rid of the tension. It feels like forever since we've been alone. The last time we saw each other we parted badly and haven't really spoken since. He didn't understand that what I'd been asked to do was important. He didn't want me joining Bravo, knowing I would be treated badly. But finding traitors in the Collectors Division far outweighed my feelings of discomfort. Stubborn bastard he is, he won't start the ball rolling.

Giving up on waiting for him, I let my human form drop and embrace my demon one. My fangs and tail emerge, horns and wings becoming visible. My skin changes to its normal blue hue, and my hair lengthens and darkens to cobalt. It feels good, like stretching out your body after having an afternoon nap. Now that I'm a part of Team Alpha, I'll never have to hide this side of me again. I think that's one of the reasons Kai is so pissed at me. I left him to join the Division and ended up being in a bigoted team like Bravo, so he can't understand why I'd choose that life over staying with him. He likes to forget that Michael had explicitly asked me to do surveillance on their team from the inside.

"How many times are you going to make me say it, Kai?" I ask as I walk over to the couch on the side of the room. On the table in front of it are a range of drinks: bottles of water, soft drinks, and beer. Grabbing one, I flick the top off with one of my long claws and throw myself down, tucking my tail out of the way. Might as well make myself comfortable until Mina shows signs of waking.

Malakai shows no sign of having heard me. Still refusing to look at me, but as I watch him closely, I can see his body is curled tight from tension, and his breathing is faster than average. He's stewing in his anger and annoyance. Anyone would think I'd asked the favor of him, not Lucifer. It's not like I asked her to. Jesus, he could make a nun swear, he's such a dick. I'm going to have to goad a reaction out of him. We *need* to be on the same page to get Mina through this. Usually, it requires more than two to get a succubus through a transition, so hopefully Lucifer was right about our Archdemon blood making a difference. And, sex demon or not, pretty sure she wasn't keen on her daughter having a gangbang to ease the hunger.

"So, are you seeing anyone?" I ask casually,

leaning back on the couch and stretching out my arm along the length of the back.

"Fuck you, Jagger," he growls in return. I hide my smirk. *There* he is.

"Oh! What's wrong? Do I sense a bit of built-up tension? Mina's in for a treat then, isn't she?" Malakai explodes into action. Striding forward, he grabs the beer out of my hand, slamming it down on the table, and hauls me from my seat before fusing his mouth over mine.

It's like coming home. He tastes like sex and sin, and as our tongues wrestle for dominance in a clash of wills, he holds me tight against his body. My fangs nick his lip, and his blood is like nectar from the gods, spicy and exotic. His erection is thick and hard against my own as our kiss slows and becomes lazy and seductive. I run my hands through his silky hair, down his back, and cup his tight ass, squeezing it as he pulls back. He rests his forehead against mine and looks me in the eye, a swirling mix of hurt, and anger, and desire all setting me alight.

"Damn you to hell, Jagger. You're just going to leave me again. I see how you look at this girl, and I know how well you get along with Alpha. You're exactly where you want to be now." His breath is heavy against my mouth; then, he rips himself away, causing my heart to sink in my chest. *I thought we'd been making progress.*

"Is that what you wanted?" he yells. "You wanted to see if I still felt something for you? Well, fuck you. You know I always will, but neither of us bear a mark, so it isn't meant to be." *Ah, there's the heart of the matter.*

He snatches a beer off the table and storms away from me to the other side of the room where he leans against the wall, studying Mina as he takes a long drink of his beer.

My head hangs in shame at his words. Of course, having a mating mark or the lack of it, in our case, means something to him. Demons are the only creatures I know that receive a mark once they find their soulmate. It never mattered to me, but I know it matters to him.

His mother and Belphegor's relationship was always rocky due to their lack of the mark. Being a succubus, she couldn't commit herself to his father without the mark to stabilize her needs. If they had the mark, she wouldn't need anyone else to sustain the hunger. It's too much for one demon to endure on their own, and the donor could become drained of both life force and blood if they had to feed a ravenous succubus every day. Being someone's mate protects them from this, especially if they are not as powerful as the other. It also stops the need to search for more. Even though Kai's dad is more powerful than his mom, he couldn't keep her attention long enough, and she would often stray. His father had a hard time reconciling that reality, and it led to some bumpy moments in Kai's homelife that he's never been able to shake off.

We sit silently, and he finally calms down enough to change into his gorgeous demon form. Deep purple, almost-black velvety wings fold in behind him, his body a slightly lighter purple but no less vibrant. His hair stays the same; vain creature that he is, he loves his hair and keeps it in both forms. Black horns are curled up and away from his head. Thick at the base, then tapering as they get to the top. Kai's eyes are the other thing he leaves the same in his human form; he likes the shock factor when people notice the elongated, reptilian gaze. My eyes move down his clothing-clad body to his hands where his nails are longer and sharper and further down to his still bulging crotch. His tail, smooth like leather, long, slender, and cat like, whips back and forth in agitation.

I smirk, hiding it behind my bottle of beer; I adore revving this guy up. He loves to dish it out but gets annoyed when he has to take it. At least the aggravation will snap him out of his funk quicker.

"You know how I feel about you," I tell him. "I asked you to come with me."

He sneers. "Yes, but you know someone had to stay behind to help, and you were dead set on joining the Division, so I let you go."

"Well, we're both here now. Let's see where this takes us."

"Where it takes us?" he growls. "I know exactly where it will take us, right back to where we were.

You'll stay here, and I'll return home to help the cause. *Alone*."

I shake my head at him and his attitude. "I don't know, man. I have a feeling everything is about to change, and we're going to be swept along for the ride."

He looks at me in surprise before a frown graces his face again. "Oh, and why do you think that?"

"See that girl there?" I point to Mina with my bottle of beer then drain the rest and put it down on the table. Walking toward the bed where she's laid out, I study the blood going in; it's almost halfway through now. "I think she's the catalyst. I have a feeling she's going to be the one to bring about the change we need."

I turn to look at him, and his eyes are on Mina, an appreciative gleam in them even though she looks like a shadow of her former self. "You should see her when she's healthy. She has this glow about her, a fire in her spirit. She fed me, no hesitation, when Mav asked her to. Even though she had only recently discovered demons exist."

He snorts. "Are the Division still being racist assholes? No surprise there."

I frown at him. "You know that's all Hammus. He demanded that demons be removed from the curriculum, and the angels complied. They didn't want him turning his attention to this world. Anyway, she just offered up a vein to a relative stranger. That took guts, and I have no regrets about being here to help her with this."

He drains his beer empty and stalks back to the table to put it down before throwing himself onto the couch to wait. His gaze meets mine, and there's sadness and determination in it. "We'll do this, and then I'm done. I don't want you dragging me back again and again and having my heart shattered every time. I need to move on. I can't do this anymore, Jagger; it's time for me to start looking for my mate."

My heart skips a beat, and my stomach lurches with his announcement, but I keep my face from reacting. I can't get through to him, so I need to bide my time and be patient. I join him on the other end of the couch, and the room falls silent, with only the sounds of our breathing to break up the tension while we both sit and wait for the girl whom I hope will change everything, to wake.

As we watch, the blood flows steadily into Mina. A hitch in her breathing and a change to her pulse rate make me sit up. Sniffing the air, I notice that the smell of decay coming from her has lessened. Rushing over to her, I unwrap the bite wound and watch as the poison slowly oozes out of it. Bubbling and hissing, it evaporates into smoke. Lucifer's blood is doing what is needed, activating Mina's accelerated healing. Once the poison is ejected, the wound slowly knits itself back together.

The blood finishes its journey into Mina's vein,

and I pull out the needle, discarding it. As I watch, Mina's body starts to vibrate and change color; it has a pink hue to it that no human or AB could naturally produce. All of a sudden, her back arches, her muscles lock up, and a loud feral scream escapes her mouth.

"Fuck!" I pounce on her, holding her still as her body starts to convulse. "Get over here and help," I demand as Malakai freezes in shock, mouth gaping open in surprise. After the initial reaction, he hurries over, and together we try to restrain her, but her strength is phenomenal, and she's really thrashing around. Transition is painful, but I have *never* seen anything like this. My eyes meet his over her body as we try to stop her from hurting herself.

"Holy fuck! What have we done?" he whispers, and I just shake my head and pray to someone that she makes it through this.

Chapter Six

Jessamina

Pain like nothing I've ever felt before flows through my body like a river of fire, the flames burning hot and fast, scorching everything in their wake. This time, I'm aware of my body and the fact that I have limbs and can feel them moving. There's also a heavy pressure on my chest like someone has placed an anvil on top to hold me down.

The flames ebb slightly, but a continual heat pulses with intensity, and instead of pain, the sensation is distinctly sexual. My core throbs in need, and I can feel my heart rate increase as my breathing becomes labored.

I struggle to open my eyes, but my eyelids won't cooperate, so I lay motionless, unable to control the movement of my limbs. Sound reaches my ears, and for the first time, I'm aware of voices. One is familiar, but I can't place it, and the other I've never heard before. They're shouting at each other, cursing. I hear my name, but then my ears fixate on another sound, two actually. Thump, thump,

thump, and a whooshing, like liquid flowing. An intoxicating combination that causes my mouth to water.

Next, my nose picks up some scents. Something delicious, rich, and full-bodied. My hunger ignites, and there's a wrenching pain in my mouth as something explodes out of my top gums and pricks my bottom lips. *What the fuck!*

I move my tongue around in my mouth when the coppery flavor of my own blood hits my taste buds and recoil in shock when it hits a pointed fang that definitely wasn't there previously. Before my mind can compute any of this, a searing pain causes me to scream out loud again. It feels like someone is drilling steel bars into opposite sides of my head. My body convulses against the pain, and this time, something sharp punctures the flesh of my hands. The smell of blood reaches me immediately after the pain, and while I don't find it appetizing, the scent is much more...palatable than it ever had been before.

"Fuck, she's bleeding. Her claws punched straight through her palms," that familiar voice growls. "Can you stop it, please?"

"I can try, but this kitty just grew into a motherfucking feral cat, and those claws could take out an eye," the unfamiliar one complains before I feel a wet heat as something thick slides across my palm like a cat is licking my skin.

A rumbling sound starts to echo through the

room. "What the fuck is your problem?" the guy with the voice I might know snaps, and his friend replies with a snarl, his voice heady with lust when he groans.

"Fuck, man, she tastes amazing." A small chuckle is the only reply as the wet heat assaults my other hand as well. The chuckle makes my heart jump. My confusion is all encompassing. *What's happening? Where am I, and why can't I move? Who's in the room with me, and are they friend or foe?"* My mind tries to catalogue all the details that my training has told me are important, but instead of the foggy confusion of last time, I just find myself drawing an alarmingly lucid blank. My pulse pounds as anxiety builds inside me. That familiar voice means something, but I just can't put the pieces together

"Yeah, she does." With this chuckle, another wave of heat flows through my body, followed by an extreme hunger. *Oh my god, what is that?* My mouth is so dry, and my fangs throb, a new and altogether uncomfortable experience. *My fangs...that'll need some explaining.*

A vicious snarl from one and a growl from the other echoes through the room, and my eyes fly open. Looking around, I see what appears similar to a hospital room, but my eyes drag to the weight on my chest. Teal blue cats' eyes are staring at me with an intensity I can feel deep in my soul, and a feral longing pulses through my body. As my focus zooms out a little, I recognize the demon lying on my chest.

"Jagger?" My voice croaks a bit from not being used, my throat dry and parched after who knows how long spent unconscious.

His eyes widen in surprise, and I hear, "Holy Shit! She's coherent," whispered to the side of me, so I turn my head. Standing there is another demon, this one a total stranger. Purple skin with a long, lean body, his clothes fit like they were custom made for him. Reptilian eyes are surrounded by the thickest, darkest lashes I've ever seen, emphasized by the kohl he has lining them. A waterfall of pitch-black hair streaked with purple courses down his back, finishing the artistry that is this exotic, sexy man. My mouth waters, and all of a sudden, I want his cock in my throat more than I've wanted anything ever before. The growling in the room gets louder and more insistent.

"Quick, man, slash a vein and get some blood into her; otherwise, we're going to skip straight to dessert. Her pheromones are out of control," the purple-eyed beauty orders Jagger. Immediately, he runs a thick claw across his pec, which is right in front of my mouth, and blood wells in the wound.

"Drink, Mina, we'll explain everything," he coaxes. I can't even begin to compute what's going on. The blood in front of me has a heady, intoxicating scent, and I don't even think twice as I start to lap at the wound before latching my mouth to it and sucking hard.

"Fuck!" Jagger groans, releasing my arms as the rest of his body comes close to me. I can feel his cock thick against my thigh. It sends a delicious spike of heat flowing through my body, and my core clenches with need. I squirm, trying to get it to where I need it as frustration builds on top of the desire, the *hunger*, that's seeking to control every choice I make now.

Grabbing him tight, I pull him down and release the wound at his pec which is flowing too slowly for me. I sink my fangs into the thick vein in his neck and grind my pussy into his hard length, gulping up the life-giving blood that's flowing from this new spot. A shudder ripples through his body, and at the back of my mind, something tickles, telling me that I shouldn't be doing this, but I push it away to deal with at another time. The blood flowing down my throat is thick and potent and soothing. My body starts to feel like my own again, and the waves of pain ebb until they're just a dull ache. A clawed finger gently thrusts into my mouth, breaking the suction I have on Jagger's throat, and he rolls off of my body. The sexy, exotic demon is looking at me with heat in his eyes and perhaps a hint of concern, though I'm not sure if it's for me or for Jagger. "Let's give Jagger a break, hey? My turn, darling."

He climbs up on the bed as well and starts to lay

down next to me, but in a flurry of movement, I pounce. Pushing him back against the headboard, I straddle his lap and thrust my fangs into his neck before removing them and guzzling like a drunk on a bender. His shout of surprise and groan of delight as this happens brings a smile to my lips, and I continue to drink, his cock rubbing deliciously against my core as he thrusts in time to my sucking.

As my stomach starts to feel full, daggers of pain stab at the bottom of my spine. Letting go of the demon's neck, I howl in agony. Arching my back, I try to leap away from him, but he holds me tight. He's speaking to me, words that I can't make out through the pain. His hand rubs up and down my back as he croons, the soothing sounds penetrating my consciousness as I pant through the pain. I'm not sure how long I sit in his lap while the pain continues, but eventually, it too starts to fade as does his grip on me. By then, I'm too exhausted to go anywhere, and I slump forward against his chest. My breathing is labored, and I close my eyes, finding his chest so comfortable that I snuggle in, my own rumbling with delight.

"Is she *purring*?" Jagger's incredulous voice asks from the side of me where he's still lying on the bed.

I hear a snicker in my ear, and the smug voice replies, "Sure is." He pulls me tighter and nuzzles at my hair, whispering how well I'm doing.

"Do you think that was it?" Jagger's question

draws my attention, reminding me of everything I still don't know what about this situation. "Do you think she's done with transition?"

"I wouldn't have thought so. We haven't even gotten to the really good stuff yet," grumbles my body pillow.

My mind is still fuzzy, and while I recognize Jagger and that something is very different, I'm not sure where I am, how I got here, or even what's happening. I pull back slightly when something brushes against my arm. At first, I don't think anything of it, but a grunt from Jagger draws my attention. He has a somewhat strained look on his face as he watches something further down his body, and that look of pressure slowly morphs into one of desire. Turning my head, I watch as a black tail runs up and down Jagger's thick length that is pushing against his pants.

Hmm, that demon must be horny because I know Jagger's tail is blue, and it's not like he would be rubbing himself. Or maybe he would. Can you use a tail for jerking off? I'm about to start asking some questions when another wave of heat starts to roll through my body. *Fuck, now what?* My body goes tight as I brace myself for what's to come. This time the wave of heat isn't accompanied by pain. Instead, it's accompanied by a desire so strong I feel like my skin is too tight for my body. I start to squirm as my underwear floods, and my body pillow groans again.

"Do you smell that?" he asks, his cock hardening under me again.

I pull back and look him in the eye. "I'm really going to need your name before I fuck your brains out," I order, nearly panting through the heat.

"Malakai... Kai," he tells me, just before my mouth seals over his. In a clash of tongues and lips, I devour his lush mouth. In the rough crash of our mouths, I realize too late that he also has fangs after one nicks my lip, then he laps at the blood pooling from the small cut. I should feel shocked but having already experienced Jagger's bite, I'm actually looking forward to what Kai's can do.

"God, you taste amazing!" He pants before continuing to kiss me. Pulling away from his mouth, I move south, kissing and licking until I get to a nipple ring, which I circle with my tongue, laving it before I yank on the ring with my teeth. The deep guttural sound that leaves his mouth is intoxicating, as is Jagger's groan as he watches from the side. Knowing Jagger's watching us, entirely turned on, is intoxicating, and I revel in the feel of it as it creates another pulse deep inside my core. The throbbing is getting too much, and I know I'm about to do something desperate to relieve it.

Pulling away, I scramble out of the hospital gown I'm wearing until I'm sitting in his lap clad in only a pair of underwear. That too tight feeling is still riding my body hard, and my hands roam over my chest, trying to push it away. Looking away from

Kai, I suddenly realize something. "What the fuck! I'm fucking pink."

"I'd call it more of a magenta," the voice to the side consoles me. Turning my head, I can see Jagger watching me as if I'm a stick of dynamite about to explode, bracing for a reaction.

"But why?" I ask, confused. Before he can answer, a delicious scent hits my nose. Unlike Kai, who's spicy and exotic and tastes the same way, this one smells like cinnamon and sugar with a hint of pepper. Like a spicy hot chocolate, sweet with a bite. My face must show my intentions because his eyes widen right before I lunge at him. Not used to moving again or what's happening to my body, I underestimate my strength and speed, and we roll off the side of the bed, landing in a heap on the floor. Jagger groans underneath me, this one definitely a groan of pain. In my frenzy, I don't care, and I start tearing off his clothes with my claws.

"You ok, man?" Kai chuckles above as he looks over the edge of the bed, blood still trickling out of the twin holes in his neck and running down his throat, but I ignore him in my haste. Jagger shoots him a thumbs up as I wish I could get him out of his clothes faster. Suddenly, they disappear—Poof, *gone* like he was never wearing any in the first place.

"How?... what?... why?" I stutter, but I'm soon distracted as my eyes roam his blue body. Holy shit, this man has a physique that must have been sculpted by the goddess. Not an inch of fat to be seen as I watch his muscles ripple every time he moves.

"Thank you, goddess!"

Just as quickly as the prayer leaves my mouth, I hear Kai's voice above me. "Amen, sister." He's still watching us both from above with appreciation gleaming in his eyes. *Well, I can't say I'm opposed to that.*

"Looks like those powers might be kicking in," he muses, and Jagger nods his head in agreement, but I pay no attention. My eyes are drawn away from his sculpted body and zero in on the thick and juicy cock that bobs up and down like a snake trying to charm me.

"Oh yes, come to momma," leaves my mouth before I can stop it. Apparently, my inner voice is now my outer one. Leaning down, I move to drag my tongue along its length, but I stop and look at Jagger for permission. The shock in his eyes is comical, to say the least.

"Did she just ask for permission?" Now it's Kai's turn to be incredulous. "She's a lot more coherent at this stage than any I've ever been with."

Jagger nods his head, and I'm honestly not sure if he's permitting me or agreeing with Kai, but I've lost all sense of patience and run my tongue along the underside of his cock, coating it with my saliva before sucking it deep into my throat. The groan that bursts from his lips is pure music to my ears. His little thrusts drive my passion higher, as do the hands that are now on my breasts, pinching and twisting my nipples. I drag my mouth off him and circle the head of his cock with my tongue. Suddenly, another want hits me hard, and with a couple of licks to that thick vein, I plunge my fangs in, piercing it and letting his lifeblood run freely into my mouth and down my throat.

"Holy fuck!" he shouts, the desperate sound echoing through the room.

"Dude! How did she know to do that? She's amazing." Kai's voice is full of wonder as I feel him join us on the floor, his hands stroking up and down my bare back with a feather-like touch. Looking up, I see Jagger's head thrashing back and forth and his mouth open in pure ecstasy as he thrusts once, then twice, against my mouth before he's coming. Ropes of cum shoot out of his cock to fall back onto his stomach while his blood continues to flow into my mouth.

Running on pure instinct, I release his cock, running my tongue over the puncture marks before moving to lick his stomach clean. Pure energy shoots through me with every lick, his cum sweet and spicy just like his scent was. Leaning back, I lick my lips clean, and a growl starts to echo through the room. *Holy shit, is that me?*

"More!" the guttural demand falls from my lips.

"Here we go," Kai states with glee. He drags my body off Jagger's and throws me back onto the bed before stripping off his clothes and jumping on top and pinning me.

"More, *more*," I demand in frustration; my veins feel like they're boiling with desire, the sensation almost like a liquid heat that I can't seem to cool. Jagger climbs up to join us, and Kai rolls over so that I'm pinned on either side by the both of them. Kai's eyes are full of mischief and lust, and his voice is wicked with desire.

"Hang on tight, darling; we're going to give you more. We'll give you everything you need and then some." Then both their mouths descend onto my body.

Chapter Seven

Mavromichali

The central room of the dungeon has some comfortable couches that Lucifer offers us to wait on. Drusilla almost made me laugh with the way her nose screwed up in disgust, but Siffa assured us they're magically cleaned every morning. Raphael and Lucifer disappeared upstairs not long after the vault closed, with strict instructions to call them when they came out. Apparently, this could take days. We have permission to portal back and forth from home, but none of us want to leave.

While we wait, Sander has moved behind the bar, making us all drinks. "Might as well keep busy while we're waiting," he announces.

"Yeah, because that's what you really need: more drinks," Dru's voice is full of sarcasm, and she rolls his eyes at him before looking worried again. *Oh, goddess, please don't make me be stuck here with the twins sniping at each other for days.* "What do you think is happening in there?" she asks, and I can't help the snort that escapes my mouth.

The other three can't control their reactions and all laugh out loud with Trick adding in an incredulous, "Seriously?"

Poor Dru. She blushes a pretty pink before shaking her head. "No, I guess I mean, what do you think she'll look like?"

The rooms quiet for a while as we all think about it. "Lucifer's hot," Sander, the dog, states. "I'm sure Mina will be too."

"We don't know who her dad is, though," Zeph adds. "He could be one of those demons that don't have a second form. Or one who has oozing, pussy sores." Sander swallows nervously at his comment, but I know better than to react. Zeph's a fucker. I know he's messing with them, so I put them at ease. Poor bastards.

"Those kinds of demons are a lower life form," I tell them quietly. "Although they walk and talk, their intelligence is relatable to an Earth gorilla, with less reasoning."

They all look at me in shock.

"How do you know this?" Drusilla asks me.

"You shouldn't be surprised; you know what my proclivities are. I spend a lot of time here," I tell them, gesturing to the dungeon.

"But what's that got to do with it?' Trick has a confused look on his face. Realizing what I've led myself into, I mentally shake off the bit of hesitance left and decide that I need to just go for the truth.

"I talk to people; I make friends. It's not all fucking and pain. We have conversations." All three of them are frowning in confusion still, and I roll my eyes in frustration. "Most of the patronage here are demons." Finally, they clue into what I'm saying. Trick and Sander's frowns clear in comprehension, both of them breaking into wide grins, while Dru's eyebrows raise in surprise.

"So, you've had sex with a demon before?" Dru asks me carefully, and I nod my head in response.

"So has Zeph," I tell her.

Her head turns quickly in his direction, and he confirms what I said with a nod. Unlike Sander and Trick, who have sought relationships with both sexes in the past, neither Zeph nor I have. We both enjoy sharing a woman between us, and if it leads to more, then we don't shy away from it. He's also the only one I trust to give me the pain I need sometimes. Not often, but occasionally, I need to receive instead of give. When I feel my life is out of control, it helps me focus on what's important and what needs to be done. It helps me compartmentalize, and that's a skill that can be lifesaving when you're on an Elite team for the Collectors Division.

But right now, all I can think about is Mina and what she's going through on the other side. I *hate* not knowing.

"What you need to remember is that to feed, a demon, whether they're full or half, needs to drop their glamour and assume their demon form. You need to prepare yourselves mentally if you want to be what Mina needs," Zeph says firmly.

I grunt my agreement. "Especially because this will all be new for her. She hasn't transitioned like a normal demon or had demon friends around to support her. Her mental stability is going to be teetering on a very pointy precipice, and how you react to her will shove it one way or the other."

"So practice your poker faces and decide whether you're in or out," Zeph orders the three of them.

"I'm in. I'm *so* in," Sander exclaims, no hesitation. "There's nothing about that girl, even this unexpected bump, that could turn me away." He comes back around the bar with more beers in one hand and another girly drink in the other. Placing them on the table in front of us, he throws himself down next to Trick, wrapping his arm around him and pulling him close. He gives him a soft kiss on his lips before pulling away. "We've talked about this, and we both agree that we want Mina. Period!"

I raise my eyebrow at Trick questioningly, and so does Zeph.

"Don't look at me like that, assholes. You know he's the chatty one. I let him do the talking, but it doesn't mean I don't agree. We've always liked Mina, even when she was an annoying kid training with us, but we'd watched her grow and develop into a kickass woman and both decided if we ever got the opportunity, whether together or separately, we would make a move. That's why I was never jealous of Sander's night with her. Had I been at the club that night, it would have been both of us, but it could quite easily have been just me." Sander nods his head in agreement to Trick's words.

The four of us turn to Drusilla, who leans forward and grabs the pink froufrou crap Sander had made her before throwing away the straw and downing it in one gulp. She places it back down and takes a big breath before nodding. "I'm in. I want this. I haven't felt an attraction like this in a long time, and I want to see where it goes."

Zeph nods and smiles at her. "Don't stress too much, little D; I think you'll be pleasantly surprised. You remember how buzzed Mina was after letting Jagger feed? he was more than willing to offer to feed him again. It's how they keep their potential food source happy." Everyone falls silent at his words, contemplating the reality of the situation.

All this talking is starting to grate on my frayed nerves, and my foot starts to bounce up and down in annoyance. The tension in the room is so high I feel like peeling off my skin. I'm so agitated now that the conversation has dropped. We have no idea what's going on in that room, and the lack of control is driving me nuts. I jump up out of the chair and start pacing back and forth. The blood is rushing through my veins, and my heart rate increases with every step; between my pulse and my heart, there's a thump that's beginning to echo in my ears. My breath is erratic, and my chest heaves with each gulp of air I take. Not knowing is killing me.

"There's a gym in one of the rooms," Drusilla reminds me as she watches my heated path back and forth across the room. "Or what about the indoor pool? That should wear off some of that energy," she suggests kindly. I guess I must be making them all more anxious. My shoulder blades itch, and I release my wings. The whoosh of air as they expand blows Drusilla's hair back, and I stretch them out as wide as I can. Just as I'm about to return them to where they sit naturally, they're restrained and pulled back behind me, bending my body back and upward. The bite of pain in my wing joints shoots a sense of calmness through my brain, and I still, able to breathe normally for the first time in what feels like forever.

"Do you need something, Mavromichali?" Zephaniah's voice is low from behind me. My head drops in shame, and out of the corner of my eye, I can see Drusilla, Trick, and Sander exchange glances. They know I like BDSM, but I'm sure they thought I was always the top, so I guess it's a little weird to them that I let Zeph even take this much control so far.

"Are you okay with them knowing this? It might seem a little funny if we disappear for a while with no explanation." He sounds concerned, but he's right, and I don't

mind them knowing. It's not a secret; it just hasn't come up in conversation before.

"It's fine," I bite out, the turmoil still ruling my body. *"I need this more than I need to preserve a secret that's not really much of one."*

"See, our friend Mavromichali here doesn't just like to dish out a punishment; he also enjoys being on the other side. You might be familiar with the term 'switch'?" I struggle a little bit as I feel him relax his grip slightly, but he gives a sharp pull, and I instantly halt once more. The burn in my wing is ramping up again, and my cock hardens uncomfortably in my pants.

"For Mav, it's not all about the sexual gratification, though I usually allow him to find release in a willing hot mouth or a pretty pink pussy." Sander and Trick's eyes have glazed over with curiosity and lust, and although Dru wiggles with awkwardness, she's also fascinated and hooked on everything Zeph is saying.

He walks me forward to a room not far from the lounge area, my wings trapped in his hold, and I push the door open. He moves me to the center of the room and commands me, "Kneel!"

I do as he orders, head bent forward and my breathing already starting to ease. He releases my wings and moves over to the cupboard on the side of the room. We've been here enough times that each of us is familiar with the layout and toys that are made available for visitors.

"No, Mav here is all about control. He doesn't like it when things are out of his hands. His thoughts scatter, and he struggles to stay focused. That drives him into a state." Zeph moves back toward me with a long length of red hemp woven rope in his hands. "When I tie him up and give him something else to focus on, it helps to gather his scattered thoughts and find a center of balance. Then and only then is he allowed to give over to the release. It's all about the sensation, so it almost doesn't even matter what players are involved."

Movement to the side of me draws my eye. A black leather bondage couch is placed on the side of the room. Its curves are designed for the body to mold to it comfortably, allowing your partner to be put in various positions, and it has fastenings for creative ways of restraining. Dru perches on one end, and on the other end, Sander and Trick sit snuggled in close to each other.

"What Mav needs me to do is make it so he can't think of anything else, basically," Zeph continues as my clothing disappears, his magic tangible in the air.

A grunt of appreciation comes from the bondage couch, but Drusilla shuts that down quickly with a hissed, "Hush."

"Stand and put your wings away," Zeph commands me, and I do as he demands. Then with careful and precise movement, he proceeds to wrap my arms with intricate weaving until I am bound tightly with my arms behind my back. Pushing me down by my wrapped arms, he has me kneel again with my legs slightly spread so that my cock sticks up straight. He then binds my thighs and my shins, preventing any easy movement. My scattered thoughts are still spinning rapidly through my mind, but the binding has eased the panic, and a sense of calm starts to penetrate my soul.

Zeph's thick boots are heavy on the floor as he walks around me before moving back toward the cupboard.

"Mav, would you like them to leave?" he asks me, but I shake my head. No, these people are as close as family. If we go ahead with this relationship we'd all like to have with Mina, we can't be keeping secrets or be afraid of talking about things.

"No, it's not necessary," I reply quietly.

"Do you wish to stay?" I hear him walk over to them, something slapping against his palm. "Because if you choose to stay, you must know that everything I do to him is what he needs, what he craves. You must sit quietly and watch so as not to break my or his concentration."

My head is still bent in submission, but I hear one of them stand up, and I tense at the possible rejection. The person moves over to me, and I feel a small, gentle hand on my head. Drusilla's floral scent reaches my nose.

"Don't think that this is me judging you, but I don't like seeing you get hurt, whether it's what you need or not. I come to this club for other aspects and some light BDSM, and, well, I'm uncomfortable." Drusilla's voice is quiet in my ear, this moment just for my honorary sister and me. "These are my issues that have nothing to do with you and your tastes," she whispers in my ear before straightening up. "Also, I don't need to see you blow your load," Dru finishes, this time loud enough for the others to hear her parting words.

"Thank you, my sister, and I completely understand. I love you," I tell her, trying to reassure her down our link. The emotions flowing back are full of love

"And I you."

Trick and Sander snort, and the tension in my shoulders eases a little. I listen as she walks away and pulls the door closed behind her.

"Remember what I said," Zeph reminds Sander and Trick. "No noise." They must agree because I sense Zeph stepping up behind me once more.

"It's been a while, and the last few days have been nothing short of horrendous chaos. How bad is it today, Mav?" Zeph questions, and I pant out my response.

"It's bad."

"Alright then! You remember your word?" he asks me, and I nod.

"Cookies," I mumble, remembering I picked it because I always thought Mina smelled like cookies, and, well, back then, it was inappropriate of me to think of her that way.

"Ok then, let's get started." My body tightens in anticipation of the first strike; the wait is excruciating. Zeph likes to draw it out, making it worse before it can get better. There's a strategy to this though. The anticipation makes my mind focus on my immediate surroundings, searching for any slight indication that my satisfaction is about to begin.

With a whoosh through the air, the flogger strikes me in the middle of my back, the metal spikes on the end digging into my flesh. The agony is a sweet rush of fire across my skin, followed by a soothing warmth as blood trickles from the gouges, flowing down my back.

Zeph pauses and allows my abilities to heal the wounds before striking again. Over and over, he repeats the pattern until my breathing slows, and the chaos of my mind dims, getting calmer and more manageable with every stroke. It continues until my mind is quiet, and all I can focus on is the blood in my cock and the pulse of desire.

Zeph moves in front of me, and I can see that he's also naked, his cock standing at attention. He lifts my head with a finger under my chin and looks me in the eye.

"Would you like Sander and Trick's help with that, Mav?" Zeph's voice is a deep rumble as he looks at my throbbing cock.

My eyes widen in shock at his suggestion before turning to look at Trick and Sander. Now I know why he suggested it. They both have their cocks out and are stroking them as they watch, their eyes glazed over with lust. My cock twitches at the sight of them, and my mind jumps again in surprise. I'd never considered them as a sexual option in the past, but they don't seem too upset about the chance. Who knows what this will develop into, but I'm open to whatever comes, especially as Mina is going to bring us all together. It helps that AB culture has always been very open to fluid definitions of sexuality. Growing up in a world where pleasure is encouraged in all kinds of pairings makes many of us very willing to experiment.

Zeph must sense my indecision because the flogger comes down on my back one more time. "Yes or no? It's very simple."

"Yes," I grind out between clenched teeth, and instantly their clothes disappear. They both release their cocks from their hands and scramble to join us. Sander's in front of me, and Trick kneels in front of Zeph.

"You will not come until I tell you to," Zeph demands, and I watch as Trick takes his long thick member into his mouth and licks and sucks on it.

"Touch him, Sander. Light touches. Drive him mad," Zeph commands. Sander' licks my length lightly before sticking his tongue in the eye of my dick, and a long, loud groan escapes my mouth. The man has skills. Looking down, I see he has a hand on his cock, stroking it as he licks mine.

Watching Trick with his mouth on Zeph is such a turn on I struggle to hold in my release, grunting with the exertion, and I'm transfixed as Zeph takes Trick's head and starts thrusting deep before letting go, his moan echoing around the room while Trick's throat convulses as he swallows him all down. He steps back and pulls Trick to his feet, placing a searing kiss on his mouth and putting his hand on Trick's cock.

"Take him into the back of your throat, Sander," he demands as his hand moves up and down Trick's cock. Precum dribbling, Trick's panting gets faster; he's close now. My cock jumps, and liquid trickles from the tip as the wet heat of Sander's mouth wraps around it.

"Now, Mavromichali, come *now*." Zeph's voice is an ignition switch, and as Sander's throat tightens around me, I thrust as hard as my bindings let me, roaring out my release. My cum coats Sander's throat, a sense of rightness infusing itself through my body, and all is balanced within me again.

Chapter Eight

Jessamina

A snarl rips out of my mouth at his words, and before I can push them away, they both give me wicked grins and move. Kai's mouth finds a nipple, and he starts to lick and suck at it like it's his favorite thing in the world.

Jagger slides down my body, slowly placing kisses all over my sensitive skin. "Fuuuck," I groan out loud, and they both chuckle at my reaction. I have one hand in Malakai's luscious locks, and from his growling, I think he's enjoying the way I'm tugging on them. Jagger's mouth finally makes it to where I want it to be, and he wastes no time in making me feel good, using his tongue to flick at my clit expertly. Moving further down, he licks twice and then thrusts into the entrance of my pussy.

But unlike a normal tongue, his is now long and thick and feels similar to a cock, letting him hit all the right places. "Oh my fucking god," I shout out in surprise and enjoyment, and Kai chuckles.

"His tongue is talented, isn't it?" I pull his head

off my nipple, and although I can't say anything through my panting, he knows what I want. He opens his mouth and sticks his out. I watch as it grows, thickening and lengthening until he waggles it at me obscenely until it separates into two at the tip, now forked. I let go of his head and push it back toward my nipples. A benediction from my lips to the universe sneaks out, making Kai chuckle again against my breast.

With both of them doing their hardest to drive me insane, it's not long before I can feel my orgasm approach. The tingling reverberates through my body, and just as I'm about to explode, they both pull their mouths away.

"What the fuck! Don't stop," I shout at them, trying to shove both their heads back down. They do as I bid, but instead of finishing the job, they both plunge their fangs into my body. Kai into my nipple and Jagger just above my clit. A rush of bright white light fills my vision as my orgasm explodes through my body. My scream echoes around the room as they both drink deeply, and a never-ending wave of ecstasy continues to weave its way through my being. The tightness that had nearly driven me mad before is lessening bit by bit as we become more intimate with each other.

But as they both pull away, that heat of desire is *not* happy. It's not been appeased yet; my body's ready for another go-round. With a rumbling, irritated growl leaving my mouth, Jagger moves back up my body and joins Kai at my breast, where their mouths press against each other in a long deep kiss. The growling stops in an instant. *Damn, that's hot, watching them love on each other. I wonder if they'll fuck each other too?* "Can I watch you fuck?'" blurts out of my mouth before I can stop it. *Apparently, my inner voice is a stupid, horny bitch with no filter.*

They both climb further up and take turns kissing each other and then me, our mouths and tongues tangling indiscriminately. They taste like sugar and sex, and my fangs ache as I watch Malakai lick the blood that has trickled down Jagger's throat from when I drank from him. Another wave of energy flows through my body as their lust for each other fills the air. "Oh, I think we can do better than you just watching," he says as he moves away from Jagger's throat.

They both have their wings tucked tight against their bodies, but I reach out, one hand on each pair, and slowly caress, fascinated with the feel. Unlike angel wings, theirs are more of a velvety texture, smooth and soft. Both demons start to purr as my strokes get longer and harder. Pulling my hands away, I reach for one of each of their horns, needing to continue my inspection. Both of them must understand that I have to explore before they distract me with anything because they dip their heads enough that I can easily make contact. Wrapping a fist around one of each, I stroke over them lovingly, and both thrust their hips forward.

"Careful, love, they're as sensitive as a demon's dick," Kai jokes again. I let go, but before I can move my hand away, two tails appear, wrapping around each wrist and holding them in place. I study them. One is blue like Jagger's body, and the other's purple, so it must be Kai's, but I could have sworn it was black before.

Shaking off my surprise, I put my hands back onto the horns, and the tails release me. Huffing in amusement, I stroke up and down a few more times, waiting for them to be appeased. "They have a mind of their own," Jagger tells me, "and they like to get their own way. Nobody knows why."

While I'm pinned on either side, my naked body is still exposed, their tails gently caress my body. Similar in feel to the wings, they're soft but don't have a velvety texture; the tails are more like leather. They softly knead over my breasts before moving down to my pussy, where one stops at my clit, and the other moves further south, pausing at my entrance.

"What are they doing?" I ask the two demons, who just smirk in amusement, and Jagger shrugs his shoulders.

"Told you, they're independent. I mean, I'm definitely not opposed, but this isn't up to me."

Before I can do anything, I shout out in surprise as one of them pushes deep into my channel, and the other one starts to vibrate against my clit. "Oh, oh, ohhhh," my voice sounds out again. The tails are relentless, and before I know it, another orgasm explodes through my body. Gripping tight to the horns in my hands, I ride the wave igniting all my nerve endings, a sheen of sweat covering my entire body.

As the feelings fade, I bring my attention back to Jagger and Kai, who are exchanging kisses while their tails violate me in the most delicious ways. They gently maul each other's mouths, fangs flashing, sending a shot of desire straight back to my core. *Goddess, I'm still a horny bitch.* "Fuuuck," I complain, my voice on the side of whiny. "I need more."

They stop kissing, and Jagger brings his mouth to mine. "We know, baby. How do you feel about being the meat in our sandwich?" he asks, wanting permission. Well, that's very thoughtful of him, but right this very instant, all I want is cock, and two is always better than one.

"Abso-freaking-lutely," I reply, and he pulls me away from Malakai and puts me on all fours. "How about your mouth shows his cock some loving like it did mine," he suggests as Kai reclines against the headboard, his hand stroking his thick cock while he licks his lips in anticipation.

I crawl forward until it's in line with my mouth then circle my tongue around the rim of the head, licking and laving before running my tongue along the length. I think about what he had shown me before and wish that my tongue would do the same, honestly not expecting anything to happen. As I think this, a burning sensation occurs along its length, and before my very eyes, it lengthens and splits in two. I scream in panic and haul myself backward, slapping my hand over my mouth.

Kai follows me forward, removing my hand. A tear trickles down my face, and he wipes it away, the touch gentle enough to soothe away my immediate panic. "It's okay, sweetheart. It's normal. Have some fun with it, and we'll tell you everything after the hunger isn't riding you so hard.

Again another thought tickles the back of my brain, but it disappears as I grasp for it. Shaking my head, I ask, "What the hell is happening to me? Something's not right." I've never had so little control over my own body before, and even though I have no complaints about the pleasure Kai and Jagger are giving me, there's still something completely overwhelming about it all. Jagger snuggles into me from behind and whispers sweet encouraging words in my ear, and with the desire still wreaking havoc on my body, I shudder from his touch. The evidence of my desire trickles down my leg. "I've always enjoyed sex, but this is ridiculous," I complain.

"It's all natural, baby. Trust Kai and me, and we'll look after you," he tells me. Even though I barely know anything about Jagger, I know the one thing that matters most: Alpha trusts him. No matter what craziness is going on, I know that he wouldn't be anywhere alone with me if my team hadn't given their approval and trusted him to take care of me.

Nodding my head, I know deep in my soul that I can trust them. I push Kai back into the position he was in, and I wonder if I can wrap my tongue around either side of his cock. Pushing my concerns to the side, I attempt to give it a go, and Kai's shout of pleasure as my tongue does as I bid distracts me from my worries.

"Bloody hell, Jagger, hurry up and get in her and distract her, or I'm going to blow before anyone is ready." His demands are low and harsh, and the way his clawed hands flex on the mattress, I know he's telling the truth.

Jagger's rough palms rub up and down my back, his claws lightly scratching my skin. He grips my hips tight, and with one thrust, he buries his cock deep into my cunt. Grunting my pleasure, my mouth too full of Kai's cock to do much else, he groans in response. Jagger grabs hold of my hair, and between the two of them, they set a deliciously furious pace that has my toes tingling and my pussy tightening around Jagger's hard length. It doesn't take long before that blaze ignites again, and with a final thrust, they both grunt, and we all detonate together.

I swallow down Kai's cum with enthusiasm as Jagger continues to thrust through our orgasms, his cum filling my channel. It's scalding hot, but it doesn't burn; it just sends me blazing higher.

Licking Kai clean, I pull my mouth off his cock and lean my head down, enjoying the aftershocks of my orgasm while Jagger still gives little thrusts. Kai's calloused, hot, hands touch me, running up and down on my head, but wait, that's not my hair he's touching. *What is that?* Taking my hand, I feel for what he's doing.

"Fuck me! I have horns," I shout out in surprise. They don't feel quite as big as either Jagger or Kai's. They're probably a hand and a half long, still long enough to get a good grip on. Rubbing my hands up and down, the rough texture almost tickles my fingertips, and I realize the horns have ribbed lines running around them all the way to the top in a spiral.

Kai's smiling at me as he continues to rub up and down the ridged protrusions, and it feels like he's rubbing his fingers over my clit. "Gorgeous horns, they are too, love." He leans forward and licks one, and my pussy clenches in surprise again.

"Holy shit." My words come out in a moan.

Jagger pulls out, and he climbs up next to Kai so that I'm looking at both of them, my eyes starting to droop. For the first time since I woke, I'm feeling full, and my energy levels plummet. I push my way between their bodies, and they wrap themselves around me.

"I have so many questions, but I am *so* tired.

Can we rest first?" My voice is rough as my eyes start to close on their own.

They both place gentle kisses on my lips. "Rest, baby, that was only the beginning,"Jagger says in my ear.

Kai follows with, "We've got you," and that's the last thing I remember

— • ◆ • —

The first thing I notice when I wake up is that I'm horny again. *Fuck!* The second thing I realize is that my stomach is rumbling with extreme hunger, and there's a burning feeling in my throat and gums. Before I decide what to do about both of those, Jagger and Kai's voices register, so I pretend to be still asleep. *Maybe I can get some information first.*

"I can't believe how coherent she is. Usually, it's a mindless frenzy, but she was aware from the start." Jagger's rumbly voice is low in his attempt not to wake me. I thinking my hearing may have gotten more sensitive because I can hear everything he says.

"Dude, she looked at you for permission." Kai's lilting accent is strong in his amazement, and I can't help but fall into the sound, finding it relaxing. "I've never heard of that before. And she's transitioning so much faster than anyone else. What she's done usually takes days."

"Yeah, I'm sure that's got to do with her parent-age, though," Jagger replies.

"I wonder what else is going to happen," muses Kai. One of them moves on the bed, and that's when a delicious scent hits my nose, and all else is forgotten. My fangs explode in my mouth, and I pounce on the nearest body.

Before I can attach myself to one of them like a leech, I get restrained by two muscled purple arms. "Whoa, hold up there, baby demon." I flinch at Kai's words, but he distracts me by sucking one of my ears into his mouth. "Let's do this the right way." He holds me against his body with one arm and parts my legs for Jagger with the other.

"Get her ready for us, will you, honey?" My core clenches at his endearment for Jagger, and Jagger's head ducks down between my thighs and starts showing my pussy some loving. He licks and sucks and bites until I'm thrashing in Kai's arms, then his tongue moves further south until he's circling my other hole. His talented tongue pokes around down there before he runs a finger through the mess he's made of my pussy, lubing it up and pushing it through the tight ring. I grunt my surprise, but a loud moan follows that as he slowly works his finger in and out.

Kai pinches and caresses my nipples, his mouth placing wet kisses up and down my neck as he whispers dirty words in my ear. Jagger's tail gets in on the action by rubbing my clit while Jagger increases the number of fingers until he has three stretching me in preparation for his cock. Goosebumps erupt across my skin in anticipation of what's to come.

Jagger removes his fingers and pulls me away from Kai. As he reclines back on the bed, he helps me lower myself down onto Kai's cock, stretching me fully, and the burn feels so good as I bounce up and down until he's deep inside me. I grind myself up and down a couple of times, and Kai's fingers convulse against my hips with the movement, his eyes wide and breath quickening.

Jagger's hands on my back gently push me forward, and I brush my lips against Kai's, but before I can deepen the kiss, Jagger's cock pushes against my back entrance as he slowly works himself in with little groans of pleasure. My mouth widens in shock at the feeling once he is fully seated, and we all pause to adjust.

"Now, darling, this is what's going to happen. When you orgasm, you're going to bite me, Jagger will bite you, and I'll bite Jagger," Kai whispers as he pushes my hair back to the side, giving Jagger access to my neck. Meanwhile, Jagger wraps an arm around my chest, giving Kai access to his body.

"Hopefully, this will help push you toward the end of transition." I'm feeling too many sensations to acknowledge what Jagger has just said but nod my agreement anyway. Both my pussy and ass are full of hot hard cock and it's an overload for my nerves, my brain short circuiting from all the stimulation.

With a nod, they both start with alternate thrusts, one in and one out, and then swap, and nothing I've ever done before can compare. The rush of sensation to my nerve endings is mind-blowing, and I try to hold it at bay to extend the feeling, but I fail and can't hold it off any longer. Rushing through my body like an out of control freight train, my orgasm explodes, and I bite down on Kai, triggering the guys' reactions. Sensations are pushed to the next level, and I lose all sense of being. The blood in my throat, the suction on my neck, and the flow of desire drive me over the edge. Again and again, like a tidal wave of sensation, pleasure crashes over and through me.

I'm not sure how much time has passed before I finally start to become aware again, but the ecstasy fades and is replaced with a searing pain in the middle of my back, just below my neck. Both Jagger and Kai shout as well, not in pleasure but in pain too.

"What the fuck was that?" Kai pants as Jagger pulls himself from my body. Kai's eyes widen in surprise, and I turn to look. Sitting on Jagger's pec just above his heart is a mark. The black mark is in the shape of a heart with an infinity symbol slicing through the middle. Circling it are two different kinds of patterns. Leaning forward, they confirm I have a matching mark, but it's larger and in the middle of my back.

"Mate marks." Kai's face is taken over by awe as Jagger's eyes widen in surprise and mine in confusion. "We're mates." Kai's whispered voice is full of smug satisfaction as another excruciating pain starts to invade my body.

"What now?" I scream as the tearing sears my back. I try to arch away from it, but I can't escape, and Kai's cock is still buried deep in my cunt, making the movement all the more awkward. He grabs me by the shoulders and shakes me.

"Breathe, Mina!' he demands, and as I take a big gulping breath, wings erupt from my back, and my mind can't take anymore. Everything goes black.

Chapter Nine

Jessamina

When I wake, Jagger hands me a bottle of water, and after taking a couple of gulps, I find myself standing in front of a large mirror. What was opaque black glass turns reflective when Jagger flicks a switch.

"Oh my god! I'm demon Barbie," I complain, absolutely stunned at what I'm seeing. Kai spits his water all over the floor in laughter at my comment, but I don't pay any attention as I study my form.

I still have the same figure with plump, perky breasts, slim and toned waist and legs, with rounded hips, but the rest is so very different. My eyes are red, with what looks like flecks of flame in them. My skin is magenta, but my claws, hair, tail, and horns are black. Yep, that was *my* tail I noticed before. And if that's not enough to blow my mind, I have wings. Huge-ass, candy pink wings with gold striations through them. And if the colors weren't bad enough, they don't look like either angel wings, with their neat feathers, or demons with their velvety texture. No, I have feather boa wings. Fluffy pink feathers that wouldn't look out of place on a Vegas showgirl.

"Fuck my life." My wings rustle behind me in agitation, and my tail flicks back and forth. "I'm a demon, and there is absolutely nothing even remotely intimidating about me." I pout my disappointment as the two other demons step up beside me. They've both put on pants, while I'm still stark naked, but their strong, muscular bodies look like lethal fighting machines. I look like an advertisement for Pornhub's fantasy collection.

A rush of air escapes my lungs as I sigh. Turning around, I look for the hospital gown I was wearing, but Kai clicks his fingers, and suddenly, I'm in a large pair of sweatpants, and a man's tank top with slits for my wings. Picking up the soft cotton, I take a deep breath, and Kai's intoxicating scent fills my nostrils. Oh, he's given me *his* clothes to wear. A warm gooey feeling fills my heart, and the space on my back, where my mating mark is, throbs with heat.

Making myself comfortable on the nearby couch, I pull my legs under me and nail the guys with a serious look. "Ok, who's telling me what the freaking fuck is going on? I'm a demon!" I'm stunned, seriously stunned. Not that long ago, I didn't even realize they existed, and now I am one. "I have so many questions."

"What's the last thing you remember?" Jagger

asks as he and Kai join me on the couch, squishing me between their big bodies, their warmth sending reassurance and calming my racing heart.

I think back to the last thing, feeling a faint sense of unease as I try to touch the memory. "I was on Minzeon for a mission. The Five were causing havoc, and I was helping evacuate the workers. It's fairly fuzzy after that, but I vaguely remember something about spiders."

Over the top of my head, Kai and Jagger exchange glances. "You were injured and in a coma, and there was nothing anyone could do. You were dying." Kai's voice is solemn as he gives me this information. He grabs my hand and squeezes it in comfort. Jagger's hand comes onto my thigh, stroking me, and I'm not sure he even realizes he's doing it, but the small gesture brings me such joy. I've had a lot of one night stands, but casual touching and the intimacy that comes along with it is something that I'm a little starved for.

"And because you hadn't had your blood acti-vated, there were no extra healing abilities to help you out." Jagger's voice is gentle, but I still hear the slight reprimand in his voice.

I flinch at his words, but he's right, and I'm now kicking myself for my arrogance. After finding that letter from my parents, I had been planning on asking for the activation, but I was still selfishly biding my time. I was stupid, thinking I could battle magical creatures as a human. Well,

I guess it turns out I was never human in the first place.

"The only way the Archangels thought you would survive was to activate your blood. Team Alpha, after some advice from Olivia and James, voted to go ahead with it. It turns out that Team Alpha's parents have always known who yours are and were able to get your mother to comply."

Jagger's words have me gasping in surprise. "Really?" I ask incredulously. I wonder what the odds are that team Alpha didn't know? I mean if they're parents did maybe they did too and they've been pretending all this time. "Urial stood there on selection day and pretended not to know anything about me. What an asshole.'

"Yeah, apparently you're somewhat taboo, and they were worried for your safety, so she gave you away for your protection but loved you no less. Your mother was devastated when she heard what you had been through. Your parents had thought you'd be adopted instantly; they never thought you'd be mistreated." Kai's voice is still gentle, and his hand rubs up and down my thigh like he's having trouble keeping it to himself. I can't help but wonder about the mysterious demon. *What has his life been like? How does he know exactly how to break this news to me?* Jagger, too, is playing with my hair, stroking it reassuringly. These two beautiful men are very attentive towards me. Feelings of contentment and happiness keep assaulting my mind, but I almost feel a weird sense of detachment from them. It's not that I'm *not* those things too, but they almost feel like an echo of something. *What is that? I don't think they're mine.*

"What's with all this, though?" I gesture to my new and enhanced body, my tail wiggling underneath me where I'd trapped it when I sat down. I move slightly, and it gets free and starts rubbing on Malakai. He chokes down a cough of laughter, but his eyes are amused.

"You, my beautiful, are the daughter of an Archdemon like Jagger and me. Your mother is Lucifer, demon co-ruler."

I think my brain misfires as I take in that information. "Lucifer? What's she like? Do you know her?"

Jagger's hand stops stroking my hair. "Yes, we know her well. Our parents," he gestures between the three of us, "are best friends and lead the remaining resistance against Hammus." Whoa, all this information is giving me a slight throbbing behind one eye.

"You know her, too," Kai adds as we watch his purple tail entwine with mine and writhe around like snakes. The feeling goes straight to my core, and a pulse of desire flows through my body—his breathing hitches as I grab hold of his tail and unwind it from mine, needing to focus.

"I want more information before we start anything else," I scold the tails. "What do you mean, I *know* her? The only other demon I've met apart from you guys is Siffa at Etern....." My voice trails off as I put two and two together, and they both nod their heads.

"Oh." My voice is quiet as I think things through. "She said she was a succubus demon and fed on blood and sex. Is that why I just allowed you guys to fuck me until my brains were just about leaking out of my ears?" Kai starts to nibble on said ears, and the tent in his sweats pulses with my words.

"Yup." He keeps biting, and my nipples pebble, so I grab him by his silky black hair and yank his head backward.

"Down, boy, I need answers." I turn to Jagger, who has an amused smile on his plump blue lips, and my mouth waters at the thought of sinking my teeth into them. *Oh my god, this is ridiculous.* I roll my eyes in my head as I try and get my thoughts straightened out. His smile widens as if he knows my thoughts.

"I don't mind if you bite my lips; I like your fangs," he tells me, and I look up in surprise.

"I didn't say that out loud," I stutter in surprise. I'm sure I didn't.

"No, that's the other thing we need to talk about," Jagger reassures me, wrapping a large hand around mine and squeezing it tight. "Those marks that appeared when we all had sex and exchanged blood are mating marks. Only demons and their mates have them. Hammus did care about us once upon a time before he got bitter and twisted, and he made it so that demons were able to find their ideal matches."

"But you both got the same mark as me. You're *both* my mates?" I say, reaching up my other hand to run a finger across the black mark on his pec.

"Yes," he replies, watching me before pulling my finger to his mouth and placing a small kiss on the tip, avoiding the claw. "Demons are not often limited to one mate. Which is a blessing now that there are so few demons left. Most women have at least two or three, and not many demons are heterosexual either. Sex is a way of survival, a food source, for a lot of them, and they'll take it how they can get it."

"Mates can speak to each other telepathically," Kai tells me before sitting upright in surprise as if something had just occurred to him. "That must have been why you and I always could," he says to Jagger in shock, "but we needed Mina to activate the actual marks." A wide smile spreads across his face as I digest the information.

"Where does that leave me with Team Alpha? I had finally committed to giving a relationship with them a go." My heart thunders in my chest at what the answer may be. Imagine being so close and having it all ripped away, I'm pretty sure we're all going to be heartbroken, or at least I know I am. I try and lock those feelings down tight and not show any expression. The last thing I want to do is hurt these two wonderful men, but Alpha and I have history. Jagger knows that.

A rumbling sound comes from Kai and Jagger's chests. *Well, that's not good. Oh my god, I've fucked everything up. Already.* "Can demons even have other races as mates?" I ask them, and Jagger starts to shake his head, but Kai cuts him off.

"Actually, they can. In the colony, we've seen this happening more and more often. My father hypothesized that it's natural selection working its best to help rebuild the population, but I think others have had a hand in making this possible." Jagger's eyes widen in surprise at Kai's words. "In fact, I heard him and Asmodeus arguing about it just before I came here, and if Azeyr has been meddling and made angels possible demon mates, he may be the next god that goes missing. But Dad argued that there weren't enough people who knew about this revelation for it to be something to worry about."

"Okay then, that's something we need to tell the others when we get out of here," Jagger tells him, and Kai's shrugged response is a little belligerent.

"I'm sure Lucifer will tell them if she wants them to know." My mind is reeling with all this information, and I'm not sure what to focus on, so I ask something else that's bothering me.

"If demons have multiple mates, how do they know when they've found them all?" The guys look to each other in surprise before their eyes drop to their marks.

"The marks turn golden," Jagger replies before running a hand through his cobalt hair.

"Sorry, in my excitement at getting a mark, it slipped my mind that it's not sealed yet."

"Yep," agrees Kai, "looks like you've got more out there, baby. You're going to have to keep kissing frogs to find your prince or princess." He sounds slightly disappointed, but then a smile crosses his face, and he looks more cheerful. "At least you'll always remember your first and best," he says cheekily.

His words are reassuring but I still have some worries. "Look i can tell you two have history, you obviously feel something for each other and now I've messed all that up and linked you to me. Are you sure thats not going to be a problem?"

They both laugh uproariously at my words and I feel a little disgruntled crossing my arms in embarrassment.

"Oh no don't be like that." Jagger pleads, "we didn't mean to upset you."

"No we didn't." Kai adds in. "Yes Jagger and I have been partners for a while, but it's been rocky for various reasons, but trust us that having you unite us is like a dream come true." He pulls my arms away from my body and places a quick kiss on my lips

The tension in my body releases as I laugh out

loud at his antics. Then I ask something I've been thinking about since I asked about Team Alpha. "Is everyone okay? My team, I mean. Was the mission a success even though I obviously failed my task?" Looking down at the hands in my lap, I feel one of them ruffle my hair before I look back up.

"Everyone's fine, worried about you," Jagger answers, but Kai grunts, and I raise an eyebrow in question.

"They seem a bit touchy to me," he says, shrugging his shoulders, one of his hands still in my hair. Jagger growls at him in response, but the sound has a playful edge to it that tells me it's just another part of the chemistry these two have together.

"That's because you were an asshole." He reaches around me and smacks him in the back of the head. Kai winces dramatically but then smirks again.

"So, what now?" I ask them both now that my worries have been relieved.

"Now we need you to feed again. You're probably going to need to stay in here for a little longer until small things don't set off your hunger. You're also going to have to prove to us that you can change back and hold your human form."

"I'm fine," I insist, "not hungry at all." I ignore the slight twinge in my belly, but then Kai, the cheeky bastard, grabs hold of my horns and rubs his fists up and down. *Jesus, is that what it feels like getting a handjob?* My eyes roll back into my head, and before I know it, my fangs are in Jagger's neck, and I'm slurping down his blood like it's my last drink ever. Kai's chuckles echo through the room when my mouth leaves Jagger's neck, and, using my claws, I rip his sweatpants apart before impaling myself on his cock.

The sharp bite of pain as his thick dick penetrates me brings a semblance of coherence to my mind, and I hang my head in shame. *Okay, maybe not fine.*

Jagger gives me a sympathetic look and hisses at Kai, "Shut up, you dickhead." He starts to move me up and down on his cock, slow and steady and oh so good. I put my mouth back onto his neck and continue to suckle his delicious blood as he builds me to a mind-blowing orgasm.

Once I'm coherent again, I wrap my arms around Jagger and snuggle into his chest. His scent of sweet cinnamon envelops me and fills me joy.

"The most important thing we now need you to do is assume your other form," Kai tells me a little grumpily. He should learn to keep his mouth shut if he wants to be in on the loving. "Demons have two forms, but with your dual nature, we don't know what will happen with you."

"I'm not a full demon?" I ask, surprised. "Who's my daddy?"

Jagger chuckles at my question, his chest rumbling under my cheek. "We don't know who he could be. They wouldn't tell us, so that's probably something you need to talk to your mom about."

Wow, my mom. Never thought I would hear those words said to me. "So, how do we do this?"

"Well, for demons, we sort of will a glamour on top, and everything just disappears until you look human again. Angels can retract their wings into their bodies. The magic of it is all a bit confusing, but the main thing is it's all about how badly you want it."

When Jagger finishes what he's saying, I feel two hands against my wings. I turn my head to see Kai stroking them until he gets to the base where they attach to my back. The strokes feel so good; my nipples are erect, and my pussy clenches around Jagger's still hard cock deep inside me. He growls with the movement, and I'm so tempted to turn this into one more round.

Kai pushes at a spot dead center between my wings, and with a whoosh, they disappear. "Holy shit. Where did they go?" I shout in surprise, and he shrugs his shoulders.

"Not sure, into your back, I guess. It's just something I learned from a pretty little angel that I....." He trails off when he sees the looks that both Jagger and I are giving him.

"Nevermind," he mutters, rubbing his hand across his face in embarrassment.

"Well, that's one thing down."

"We also need to assess what abilities you have

and get a handle on those before you leave, so you don't accidentally set things on fire or something. Don't forget, many people are still scared and bigoted toward demons due to Hammus's actions. We don't want you to suffer through the hate if you can avoid it, so tight glamour control is essential," Kai finishes.

"Yeah, you saw what happened when I wasn't feeding regularly; I struggled to hold my glamour, and with the vibrant skin colors we've all got going on, people tend to notice pretty quickly when our glamours fail," Jagger reminds me, and a smile comes to my face when I think about the confusion and curiosity that I felt when I first saw him.

"Okay, so a list of things to do." I have some goals now. I can work with that.

"But before we do, I want some loving too." Kai nuzzles against my back and whispers in my ear, "How would you like to watch me fuck Jagger while you suck on his cock?"

My body flashes hot with want, and I nod my head, my answer coming out in a groan. "Fuck yes."

Chapter Ten

Malakai

I watch my mate as she practices her new powers with our other mate, and a deep feeling of rightness infuses my heart. It's hard to believe that I was lucky enough to be given these two for the rest of my long life. Someone is looking after me, and it's not that evil one that calls himself our god. Jagger has been a significant part of my life for years even though I felt hurt by his decision to attend the academy not long after we had started our relationship. My feelings for him were deep even then and continued to grow whenever we saw each other although my anger at him taking a position with Bravo and subjecting himself to the bad treatment caused a rift in our relationship. If I'm honest, I was just as mad at myself for making a difficult job more difficult as I was with him. This new connection, knowing that we're mates, has soothed my wounded heart.

I watch as Mina picks Jagger up and flings him across the room with her telekinesis. He hits the wall hard and slides down it into a heap, and her proud look turns to one of horror as she rushes over to check on him. My heart warms even more at her concern. Not only is she sexy but she's caring and compassionate too just like Drusilla said. Jagger wouldn't have been hurt too badly, but her hands run over him to check for injuries as he milks it for what it's worth, and I can't hold back my smile. Mina helps Jagger up when she realizes he's faking injury, grumbling about him being mean. Yes, I am thrilled about being attached to these two.

The only thing I worry about is who else will be in our circle and how we'll find them. I'm not an easy person to get along with, and I can't abide morons. *I hope that I like whoever else ends up as her mate.* I know I can be an asshole, but trust has been very hard to come by on Habbalea. There's also this fierce protectiveness that has hit me, so may the goddess help whoever is added if they hurt either one of them.

Shaking off the worry, laughter bubbles out of me when Mina makes Jagger's clothes disappear and then dresses him in an outfit that must be from her own closet. He looks ridiculous, teetering in high heels and a black body con dress, though his muscles do look fabulous. I wipe a little drool from my mouth; that man has always had such power over me. Her laughter is light and joyful, echoing around the room. Her infectious pleasure seems to shine out of her, filling my heart. Jagger hasn't seemed so light and free in a long time. Even though he's grumbling about looking ridiculous, I can feel through our link that he loves it and is so very happy. That's all I've ever wanted for him: happiness.

We've been here over twenty-four hours now, and many rounds of fucking and feeding have taken place. My cock stands at attention from the thoughts of all those rounds. They were wild, and Mina was *insatiable*. Until she finds more mates, I'm afraid and embarrassed to admit that we may not be able to keep up with her. She's so much hungrier than either of us have seen before, and although my cock thinks it can keep up, I'm damn near exhausted.

Flopping onto a seat, I blow out a deep breath, and my body screams in protest; all of my muscles ache. Over the last few hours, my body was contorted into positions that it's never experienced before, and I'm no blushing virgin. Our new mate is just that...creative. That, combined with all the magic we've used to demonstrate things to her, has me almost running on empty.

Jagger and I talked while she was sleeping after another round of sex, and we're going to ask Alpha to help out with the schedule if one of us can't be around. She's attracted to them already, and they're all interested in starting something with her. I just hope that our mating marks don't put them off. They may not like the fact that she's mated, that they may never be a permanent part of her life, but we can only ask. She needs to feed, and if she doesn't, her body will force the issue. I would rather they be aware and consent than be caught up in the pheromones. Mina would be devastated if this happened, and they hadn't consented.

My attention returns to the present when Mina shouts at Jagger, "What the fuck?", and I look toward them both. Jagger is now back in regular jeans and t-shirt, but Mina is wearing a white unicorn plushie costume with a rainbow mane. I double over with laughter at the look on her face when she yanks the big head off. She is *not* amused.

She throws the head of the costume at Jagger, growling at him, and he catches it before lifting an eyebrow at her.

"Oh, so you can give it but not take it." We watch as she struggles to hold her form through her anger. She has done a great job of maintaining what she looks like, but one thing she can't change is the two red streaks that are now a permanent feature in her hair. Not sure why it's red when her demon form's hair is black, but I'm not going to complain. I'm realizing that our mate looks abso- lutely delicious now matter what she is or *isn't* wearing.

Her eyes glow red, but nothing else changes, and with some deep breaths, she manages to get them to turn back to her normal lavender color. For her to have such control after only a short period is staggering. Usually a demon will struggle to assume a different form. It's unnatural to them so it takes a lot of hard work to get it fluid and to hold it, but Mina seems to be natural in either form.

She's mastered a lot of the abilities a demon possesses like telepathy, telekinesis, and manifestation, to name a few. She's definitely as powerful as her mom, but her ability to master them is unprecedented; Jagger and I struggled for months when we went through transition. Poor Jagger had to be careful during sparring at the academy. Uriel actually took most of his combat classes so that he could clean up any escape of magic.

It really makes me wonder who her father is. For her to be so powerful so quickly, he must be someone with a lot of power. Before my mind can speculate any further, her stamping foot draws my attention. Just to stir the pot a little more, I walk over to her and wrap my arms around her. "Oh, babe, didn't know you were into this kind of thing. I'm down if you are." I snap my fingers, and a butt plug with a rainbow ponytail appears in my hand.

She looks at it and bites her lip. "No to the outfit, but you can hang on to that for later," she tells me with a wink before changing her outfit again.This time she's wearing her own sweats and tank top. It looks like she's going for comfort over style or function at the moment.

"So, how about we blow this joint?" Jagger asks

her, running his hands through his short white hair, now that we have both assumed our other forms.

A worried look crosses her face, and she turns to look at the steel-reinforced door, a frown wrinkling her forehead. "How are we getting out? You said it's locked from the outside."

"Come on, demon baby, we thought you would show us your wicked portal skills." I rub my hands up and down on her arms, keeping my voice light, so she doesn't feel any pressure. Her body's taut with tension under my hands.

"What if they're disgusted by me now?" Her voice is tiny, and insecurity practically radiates off her.

Jagger strides over to us and wraps his arms around her too so that she's now a Mina sandwich. My cock twitches in anticipation because it has no sense of timing, stupid thing. I reach down to adjust it, and both Mina and Jagger look at me, amused. Shrugging my shoulders, I ignore them.

"Mina, they're your friends and teammates, and they're also my friends and teammates. They've never had an issue with me, and I'm a demon," he reminds her gently. Poor lamb, there's so much change going on, and it can't be easy to assimilate it all. She nods her head and places a quick kiss on his lips then turns and puts one on mine. I try to slip in some tongue and hope we can delay this departure a little longer for another round of sex, but she shoots me down with a frown and pulls away.

"As much as I'd like to stay here in our bubble," she assures me, "that's just avoiding everything I have to face out there. And one thing I'm not is a coward."

"Ok, sweetheart, we need to get you to open a portal. It's important that you have this ability in case you ever need to escape capture. I'm going to get Kai to do it, and I want you to put your hand on him and look for the magic," Jagger explains to her.

"Look for the magic? What the hell does he mean?" Her voice is so cute and confused that it has us laughing out loud. Not to mention the fact that I don't think she intended to broadcast that into our minds. With our reaction, she realizes her mind connection is wide open and promptly crosses her arms in defiance as a blush heats her cheeks with a red flush.

"I'm sorry you think it's funny, but you're going to have to explain it to me because what you said makes zero sense." Caught up in the moment, her chastisement reeks of insecurity, and even though we didn't mean to, it seems like we embarrassed our mate. That's definitely not something we want to do, especially since there'll be a great many things more that she'll have no idea about. Jagger's laughing cuts off, and he steps up to me rubbing the tops of her arms with his hands.

"Oh, baby, we're not laughing at you not knowing; how would you? You just have the cutest little confused voice." Her annoyed look slips at his sweet words, and he places a kiss on her forehead as he steps back.

"Ok, so, magic has different frequencies, waves so to speak, and although most people can't see it, Archdemon and Archangels can if they look closely enough. Different kinds of magic have different signatures, and a portal spell looks like ocean waves. It's about focusing on where you want to go to activate the portal magic and then directing those waves where you want it to appear. Remember, very specific thoughts because if you just, say, think of Blue Lake, you might appear *above any* blue lake."

Nodding her understanding, she steps up and places a hand on my back, and I can feel her listening to my thoughts. *Mina's bedroom,* I think, holding out my hand. I concentrate on the size and release the wave of magic. She's squinting to see the hazy shimmer of the wavy lines, her frown of concentration smoothing out as she finds them. She watches them expand outward from my hand until they form a shining portal a couple meters ahead of us. It's wide enough for us to step through, and she waits for me to take the lead.

"See the size? That's another thing you need to consider as well. The bigger the portal, the more energy it requires. This size is nothing, but if you're opening one for an army, then you'll need to focus more energy," Jagger explains, and my body involuntarily reacts. Jagger's teaching voice flat-out does it for me, and a wave of desire flows through me, but I think my dick is broken because it doesn't move. Mina has worn it the fuck out. *Well, there's a first time for everything, I guess.*

Mina's eyes widen as she looks at him in a new light. His knowledge and experience shine through in the confidence that accompanies every word. It's as sexy as fuck, and she sees it too. Her stomach rumbles, and the perfume of her desire surrounds us; she's hungry again.

"Mina, are you hungry again?" Jagger asks, surprise in his voice, and I wince at the tone. Not waiting for her reaction, I cover my crotch with my hands.

"Mina, my dick needs a rest, baby; let's do this first, and we can see about getting you another meal," I joke, trying to ease the tension, but I have to admit I'm actually serious. Her eyes drop to the ground in embarrassment, and she hunch her shoulders in self-consciousness.

"Oh, baby, no, it's okay." Jagger wraps his arms around her and hugs her tight. "This is just all new for the three of us. You're like nothing we've seen before, and we're going to have to adjust our thinking. Don't be upset."

"No, Mina, I promise, just give him a couple of minutes, and my dick will be at your service." She rolls her eyes at my words, and I grab her hand and pull her through the portal, Jagger following closely behind. Looking around the room, she starts to smile.

Jagger's face must mirror mine because he looks as surprised as I am at her room. A single bed covered in soft toys, poster-covered walls, and the very faint smell of Mina, like she hasn't been in it for a long time.

"Huh, not quite what I was picturing, to be honest," I tell her, sitting down on the bed and pulling a stuffed unicorn into my lap. It's cute and has a goth look to it, all black hair and black eyeliner with a skull painted on its rump.

"I see what you mean about being specific now," she says to Jagger, trying to contain her laughter, and he growls at me.

"You're an idiot; this is her bedroom at Maggie and Peter's house. I *just* warned her about being specific." He smacks the back of my head again, and a noise downstairs has us all looking at the door in horror.

"Ok, Mina, nothing like learning under pressure. Take us back to the lounge downstairs at Eternal Damnation," Jagger instructs quickly. We can hear footsteps on the stairs, and a growing sense of desperation blooms inside me. *This is not the way I want to meet her adoptive parents.* I watch as she concentrates, tuning into her thoughts, and she's pictured the room perfectly. She holds the size in her mind and wills the magic into existence, holding her hand out in front of her.

The portal whooshes into existence just as a woman's voice calls out, full of hope. "Mina?" As the footsteps get louder, Mina goes through the portal, and I stop Jagger before he can follow.

"Just to give you a heads up, if any of those fuckers make her feel bad or even look at her sideways, I'm going to destroy them," I growl at him.

He shakes my hand off his arm and growls right back, "I won't stop you" before he steps through. The door handle rattles and starts to turn as I leap through, and she lets the portal dissipate just in the nick of time.

When I catch up, I find Mina surrounded by Team Alpha. Jagger has been pushed to the side, and they're peppering her with questions and affection. Drusilla has tears streaming down her face as she holds Mina tight and babbles about how she thought she would never see her again. The other four guys look like they're only just holding their shit together.

"I'm going to find Siffa and Raphael," Jagger tells me inside my head. *"Keep an eye on her; those eyes keep flashing red. Their scents might drive her to feed."*

I nod my head at him, and he turns and heads toward the elevator, giving Mina a few extra moments before she meets her mother for the first time since learning what she truly is.

"How are you feeling? Did the wound heal?" Zeph asks as he extracts her from Drusilla's arms and pulls her tight against him. I think the outward show of affection surprises Mina, but a small smile crosses her face as she reassures him.

"I'm good; actually, I feel incredible. Thank you. The wound healed up before I even regained consciousness."

"Do you remember how it happened?" he asks quickly, the team leader in him kicking in. I keep a close eye on her to ensure that his question isn't upsetting her. She seems steady enough right now, so I hold back the asshole in me that's just too tempted to come out.

"No," she says, shaking her head slowly. "It's all kind of fuzzy, and if I concentrate too hard, it hurts."

"That's ok, sweetheart." His words are soft and reassuring like he really is putting her feelings before his job as Alpha leader. "We'll work it out eventually." He releases her, letting her be for now.

Sander and Trick move in when Zeph lets go and sandwich her between them. They both whisper things in her ear, and a pretty blush covers both her cheeks that causes a rumbling growl to escape my chest before I can stop it, and the three of them turn to look at me. Trick and Sander are scowling, but Mina just laughs and blows a kiss in my direction, shocking them both into silence. Mav uses the opportunity to take hold of her arm and steer her toward the sofa. He helps her to sit before taking a seat next to her, pulling her in close to his side, a very protective position. Clever bastard picked the only two-seater in the room, so I wander over and perch my ass on the arm next to her.

"You okay?" I ask her through the mate bond. She doesn't reply but sends me love and reassurance that speaks loudly enough for now.

"We have some questions, but we'll just wait until Jagger returns with the others so that you don't have to repeat it all later," Zeph tells her, and Mina nods her head, the nervous anticipation in the room now huge.

Mina's nerves are glaringly obvious, and her foot bounces in anticipation. I knew Drusilla was a clever girl when she called me out earlier, but what she says next confirms it. "How about this, instead? We'll head back to our place and give you a chance to talk to Lucifer without us all here? We've got plenty of time to hear everything, and now that I know you're okay, I can be patient for a little longer." Sander, Trick, and Mav look reluctant, but Zeph agrees with Drusilla and gets them all moving.

The look of relief on Mina's face is heartbreaking. I just want to wrap her up and protect her from all this, but I know I have to be strong. They all give her kisses on the cheek and start to teleport out one by one until only Zeph remains, and he looks at me with a raised eyebrow.

"I'm staying," I insist, my voice all rumbly. My mate instinct is riding me hard, and I need a few more moments to get a handle on this. "We need to speak to Siffa about a few things that happened." He goes to say something, but I hold my hand up, stopping him. "We'll fill you all in later," I reassure him, and with that, he too leaves.

I slide into Mav's vacated spot, and Mina snuggles in, leaning her head against my chest. We sit and wait in comfortable silence for Jagger to return. Twenty minutes later, I hear the elevator to the basement open, and Raphael and Jagger step out. Mina's body tenses, but she stays where she is. I watch as the elevators start to close again, but Raphael rolls his eyes and shoves a hand in between the doors to stop them from closing.

"Good lord, woman, you're one of the fiercest warriors I know. How about you grow a backbone and get out here and meet your kid?" She must say something back to him, but I don't catch it, and I don't hide my smirk at his reply.

"Well, you won't know if she doesn't like you until you try." His voice is filled with exasperation, and I get a feeling he's been nursing her insecurities since we've been gone.

Maybe he's Mina's father, but that would mean Trick's her brother. I shudder at the thought. Nope, they would've put a stop to that straight away if he was. Demons are pretty free-loving, but incest is still a taboo.

I watch the doors reopen once more, and Lucifer steps out, her body braced like she's going to war. "I think your mom's nervous," I whisper in Mina's ear. Mina takes a deep breath, stands up, and walks toward Lucifer while Jagger, Raphael, and I brace for what's to happen, but Mina just wraps her arms around her mom and pulls her close, hugging her tight.

"I'm so excited you're my mom, and I can't wait to get to know you." Her voice is choked with sentiment with this statement.

Tears are streaming down Lucifer's face as she too embraces Mina. They're both shaking with emotion, but the tension in the room breaks. I'm so proud of Mina; she let go of all her insecurities and is embracing this change like a champion. I can only hope everyone else does the same. They pull themselves together and move over to the couch and sit down, and Jagger, Raphael, and I join them, Jagger and I taking another couch and Raphael in a chair on his own.

"We've so much to talk about," Lucifer starts, but Raphael interrupts.

"Siffa, we talked about this." She throws him a hostile look, while Mina's face is curious.

"We need to have a rundown of what you remember. The Collectors Division needs to hear your version of events," he tells her gently, and she nods her head.

"It's fuzzy and vague, like a memory just out of reach. But I'll let you know as soon as I remember." He looks frustrated, "Are you sure you can't remember anything? Do you remember seeing the workers you found?" he pushes, but Lucifer's low growl has him holding up his hands and backing off.

"Alright, we can put that off for a day or two then," he relents.

"First thing we need to talk about your transition. I expect the boys filled you in on most of it." Lucifer is all business all of a sudden, having wiped her face and gotten control of her composure. She seems to have braced herself for the coming conversation; she's all tense where she sits next to Mina on the couch. Her hands are clasped tightly in her lap like she wants to reach for Mina but isn't sure she would be welcomed.

"Can we do this at home, please? I want Team Alpha to hear everything too," Mina pleads, grabbing hold of Lucifer's tightly clasped hands, which loosen a little at the contact.

A frown crosses Siffa's face. "Actually, I think it would be a good idea to stay here for a few more days, just until you're settled. You need to learn to feed off of others, and here's the perfect place to do it."

Jagger starts to growl loudly at the suggestion, and it actually makes me feel a bit better that he's having some control issues as well. He's always been the more settled of the two of us, so him being rattled makes me feel like I'm doing better than I think. I place my hand on his thigh and rub up and down in comfort. Lucifer lifts an eyebrow at him, but it's Mina who breaks the tension.

"Ah, yeah, so the thing is..." Mina looks like she's at a loss for words, so instead of using them, she just turns and lifts her shirt, showing Lucifer the mark in the middle of her back. Lucifer's widen in surprise and then soften.

"You have a mate," she whispers in awe, and then it occurs to her who, and she looks at us, eyeing where my hand still rests on Jagger's leg. "Both of you?" We both nod, pulling down the neck of our t-shirts and showing her. A huge smile crosses her lips. "In your face, Asmodeus!" she shouts with glee, and Mina looks shocked at the outburst.

"Ah, care to share with the room?" Raphael asks her, amused, and she looks a little sheepish.

"I swore to him that they were meant to be. Before we gave Mina up, the two little boys would barely leave her side. They were always hanging over her crib, and when she would cry, they would be just as upset."

"So, that's where you guys were hiding when we couldn't find you," Raphael muses, looking thoughtful. She nods, a cloud crossing her face before she changes the subject quickly.

"Hmm, wonder what that's about," I say to Kai in his head, and he nods slightly.

"I saw it too. We can dig later," he reassures me.

"Okay, but the mark is black, so that means it's not sealed. You have more mates out there, and you need to sample the goods to find them."

Again, Jagger and I start growling, and she waves a hand at us. "Hush, you know it's our way; you'll get over these issues for your mate." A frown crosses her face, and her voice is no-nonsense as she basically tells us to get over ourselves, putting us in our place. That's easy for her to say, but the reality is very different, it's instinctual, nothing I could help anyway.

"You're right, Mom," Mina says, and Lucifer melts at the use of the M-word, an excellent distraction technique from our beautiful mate. I'm impressed and half in love with her ruthlessness already. "But with everything that's going on, I was going to ask Alpha for help feeding me for now."

"I'm in," a voice says behind us, and we turn to find Team Alpha standing behind us. Raphael must have used his telepathy to call Trick back. Standing in front of the group is Sander, the one who'd made the offer to help Mina feed.

"Tell us more," Zeph demands, joining Sander at the front of the group."In fact, tell us about it all.

Chapter Eleven

Jessamina

Everyone makes themselves comfortable and waits for someone to start talking. Thank goodness, Jagger takes the lead, glossing over the more intimate details and simply sharing that my transition had been very fast after I'd regained consciousness.

Kai chimes in with how coherent I'd been and how amazed he was that I'd been aware of what was happening. A look of relief flows over my mom's face at this news, which makes me smile. *I can't believe this gorgeous woman is my mom.* We've got a long way to go, but so far everything has gone smoothly. Before I even left the room, I'd decided to let go of all grudges and preconceived notions. To embrace who I am and the people who did what they had to, to make sure I was safe. That what they did came from a place of love. Occasional thoughts of doubt will probably be a common occurrence, but I plan on nipping them in the bud before they can take hold. Having mature conversations with

Lucifer about all that went on will go a long way to stopping those thoughts.

Thoughts about moms make Maggie pop into my head. She almost caught us in my room. *Wouldn't that have been a shock for her?* Then I shudder in realization that I'll have to explain all of this to her. *Oh goddess. That is not going to go well.*

Tuning back into the conversation, Jagger is talking about how quickly I picked up the Archdemon magic. Nobody talks about my alternate form, just that I can hold it well, and I'm willing to avoid that little nugget of truth for now. Looking around the room, I feel blessed to be surrounded by those who love me, but I suddenly realize something. Sitting up straight, I draw everyone's attention.

"Where's Samuel?'" An awkward silence greets me, and everyone does what they can to avoid my eyes.

Dru huffs out a sigh of annoyance. "He's assigned to Connie," she says, voice snippy.

"Connie?" I ask, looking at Zeph. "I thought she was dead?" Before he can answer, Sander snorts, drawing my attention to him. He's wearing a ripped pair of jeans and a tight t-shirt, and I can see his nipple rings through the fabric. My mouth starts to water, but his comment distracts me.

"So did we, but ding dong the witch apparently isn't dead."

The sarcasm is strong with that one. I look to

Zeph for confirmation and see him running his hand through his hair in agitation, a deep frown on his face as he avoids my eyes. Finally, he gets it together and looks at me.

"No, it turns out we were mistaken. She has no explanation for her whereabouts, as she claims to have amnesia."

"That's who we found you with in the warehouse. Are you sure you don't remember what happened?" Mav's voice is gentle as he prods, but my mind is blank.

"No, I really don't," I apologize, shaking my head. "But why is Samuel with her?"

"We're not sure if we trust her or not; amnesia seems too convenient an excuse." Raphael explains, "She seems attached to Sam, so we asked him to keep an eye on her, and he was happy to help out."

"Oh." My disappointment is intense, and my eyes travel around the room, watching as the rest of my team exchange glances. There's a story there, but I'll ask about it later.

"Let's get back to Mina's transition," Kai redirects the conversation, and my heart rate increases because I know they're about to talk about the mate marks and me needing to feed twice a day.

I'm just about sick at the thought of how they'll react. I know in the back of my mind that Sander and Trick have fed Jagger before. But now they'll be feeding *me*, and I'm not sure I can separate the fucking and the feeding just yet. Or if they would want me too or if they are okay with it all.

Lucifer words are gentle as she begins. "I know that the academy has had to erase most of their curriculum on demons, but did you guys know that demons have predetermined mates? There's someone or a few someones out there for all of us. Up until recently, non-demon mates were few and far between; only a few of us were known to have one that wasn't a demon. Over the last few hundred years, that has begun to change, be it natural selection or divine interference, we're not sure." She pauses and waits for Team Alpha to digest this information. They look at each other then between Lucifer and me and Kai and Jagger, their confusion at why she is telling them this evident. My foot starts to bounce up and down in anticipation as Kai rubs his hand up and down my thigh, the move soothing me slightly.

"It's okay, baby demon. We've got you," he whispers in my ear.

"Well, it turns out Mina, Jagger, and Kai are mates."

Team Alpha explodes into shouts of confusion and anger, and I shrink in on myself a little. Lucifer sees my reaction and bursts into her demon form, a snarl on her lips. Her wings are spread, and her tail is twitching in agitation.

"Silence!" Her voice booms through the room. Wow, my mom is a badass because she instantly silences everyone. "You will let me finish," she demands before settling herself and re-assuming her other form.

"What I was trying to say is that the mating mark isn't sealed." She gestures to Jagger, and he pulls at the neck of his shirt again to show my team what it looks like. "See that it's still black. That means she has more mates; once it turns to gold, the group is whole. Until the mating is complete, the three of them are going to be horny as can be while they look for the remaining members. It's a weird chemical thing, kind of like a heat, and those with mate potential will be attracted to them the most. Mostly Mina, being the catalyst to their mating, but Jagger and Kai may experience the same thing too, to a lesser degree or maybe not at all. It's all about attracting the potential mates and making the strongest bonds for protection."

My eyes widen at her words. *Huh, the guys never mentioned that aspect of it. So I'm basically going to be a walking, talking ball of sex pheramones until my mating group is finalized...* Turning to look at them, Jagger has a sheepish blush and is avoiding eye contact with the team, while Kai is smirking that stupid grin of his again.

"Sorry, Mina, we didn't want to stress you out even more," Jagger apologizes in my head.

"What was going to happen when I started being approached by random people and propositioned?" I snap back, my annoyance clear.

"We would have run them off, don't you worry." Kai's voice is arrogant, that ass. Shaking my head, I listen as Lucifer continues.

"The problem is we don't really want to advertise Mina's status as a demon just yet. There are other issues which, no, before you ask, you are not privileged to know them yet. Especially before I get to talk to the people involved, mainly Mina and her father."

This comment has me sitting up and taking notice, and Lucifer realizes. "I promise, honey, we'll talk about this soon," she reassures me with a gentle look on her face. Deciding to continue with my trust, I let her go on.

Jagger takes over where Lucifer finished off. "Because of the situation, Mina, Kai, and I were hoping you would help with feeding her. We should be ok," he says, gesturing between Kai and himself, "as we transitioned ages ago, but as a newly-transitioned demon and the nucleus of this mating, she's going to be hungry."

"Very, *very*, hungry," Kai adds in, heat in his voice.

"So if I get what you're asking, you want us to feed Mina, both hungers, while you bring her out to try and find your other mates." Zeph's voice is unimpressed, and from everyone else's faces, I'd say they agree with him.

"No, with everything that's going on, it's not a good idea for her to search for her mates. So yes, we're asking you to help your teammate out," Jagger replies firmly. "Actually, you'll be helping two teammates out because you'll be helping me too."

"Look, it's not like we, or any of us, planned this," Kai interjects, starting to get defensive. "We have no control over these things. You guys were Mina's first worry when this all happened. Jagger and I were beyond thrilled, but she was worried, too worried to enjoy it for what it was, a revelation. Don't think that wasn't a kick in the nuts for us." I stiffen up at his words and try to pull away from him. *Fuck, I really screwed that up. I hadn't realized they'd been upset at my reaction.*

Kai doesn't let me get far, putting a hand on either side of my face and placing a gentle kiss on my lips. "It's ok, baby, we know you weren't trying to hurt us. You didn't even know, but we'd been hoping to find our mates for years."

I look to Jagger, and his eyes are full of love. "He's right, sweetheart, don't think about it again."

"I'm just trying to explain it's not easy for any of us and that your team was in your thoughts," Kai tells me, pulling me back against his side. Looking around the room at my team, they all appear a bit lost in thought.

"You know what, why don't you go home with them tonight, Mina, and we'll talk in the morning," Mom says to me. I think she understands how over-whelming this all is, and to be honest, all the swirling emotions are making my hunger rise. "You can all talk about it in the comfort of your home." Looking around, everyone seems to agree.

"Can Kai come too, please?" I ask politely, and they reluctantly agree with my request. We're kind of a package deal now, and I know it may be hard for them to accept, but the thought of not being with him at the moment makes me feel ill. He squeezes my hand in thanks.

I'm not sure what's going to happen now since everything seems to be up in the air, but one thing I know for sure is I need my mates. I know they'd talked about Jagger moving in, but hopefully they'll consider finding room for Kai as well. He can always have my room, and I'll flit between his and Jagger's. With him and Jagger also having some kind of relationship, it just feels like we'll be incomplete if he doesn't stay with us. *God, what's going to happen when he has to return home?* My stomach rolls with all the unanswered questions.

Kai stands up and pulls me with him. "I need to return to my home to get a few things, so I might be gone a little while, but I'll return," he assures me before giving me a searing kiss filled with promise then teleporting away.

"I need to go and pack up my room at Bravo's apartment," Jagger tells everyone. "God, I hope they're out on assignment." He winces at the thought of seeing them.

Raphael answers this question. "Actually, they're

not home. They've gone undercover in the city to get more info on AoA. It should be clear."

Jagger's sigh of relief is immense, and a pang hits me at the thought of all the unfairness that he suffered at the hands of his old team. *Thank the goddess he's with us now.* "Can I leave you guys to look after my girl? Her eyes are glowing; she's starting to get hungry."

Team Alpha all turn to look me in the eyes, and I laugh at the intense concentration. That seems to break the tension, and everyone relaxes.

"Of course, we'll look after her. She's still part of our team even if we're not destined to be with her." Drusilla's words are fierce, but the look in her eyes is sad, and I understand how she feels. I had hoped to explore my relationship with this gorgeous woman more, and I'll just have to enjoy what I can for now, knowing that someday we might end.

The feeling of immense relief that flows through my body at her words is vast. I throw myself at her, wrapping her in my arms and pressing my lips to hers. She doesn't react at first, and I think I may have scared her, but it's not long before she responds, her tongue darting out to lick at the seam of my lips in return.

I try to take the kiss further, but Jagger pulls me away. "Whoa there, beautiful, maybe wait until you get home and explain a few things to them all." I must look confused because he adds, "You need to tell them about your other form or show them."

With his reminder, my desire instantly cools. After nodding my head to show him I'm ok, he kisses me and disappears.

"I'll talk to you tomorrow." My mom gives me a big hug. "You can do this," she whispers in my ear. "I love you, and I'm so proud to have you as my daughter." Tears trickle down my face, and she wipes them away. "You're so brave." She places a kiss on my cheek, and she and Raphael, who waves goodbye, leave via the elevator.

"Are you alright to teleport on your own?" Zeph asks me gently. "Or would you like one of us to help this time?"

I give him a grateful smile. "That would be great, actually. I'm kind of tired, and I wouldn't want to end up on Habbalea or somewhere like that by accident." One by one, the others depart, leaving me with Zeph. He goes to wrap his arms around me, but I stop him. Looking down at me, his eyes are filled with questions. Glancing down at the ground, a little embarrassed by my request, I ask, "Can you wrap your wings around me like the last time we did this?"

A finger under my chin has me lifting my head. Zeph's eyes are full of heat at the reminder of the last time we did this, and an answering sensation overtakes me as well.

"Absolutely," he says, and his beautiful wings appear, stretching high above him. They shudder, fluffing themselves up before wrapping around me and cocooning us together. My fangs drop down in my mouth and pierce my bottom lip, but Zeph's only reaction is a slow blink despite my mortification. I run my tongue over the wound, and it heals instantly, my nipples pebbling at the feel of his cock hardening against me.

"Ready, sweetheart?" he asks, his rough voice sending a shot of desire to my core. I nod my head, unable to look away, and we arrive back at the apartment in the blink of an eye.

I'm reluctant to leave the safety of Zeph's arms to face the others, but his bellow of annoyance has me jumping away and turning to see what the problem is. To my absolute shock and amusement, I find the other four playing a rousing game of rock, paper, scissors.

"What the bloody hell do you think you're doing?" Zeph's frustration at his team is evident.

Drusilla waves a hand at him. "Hush unless you want in on this! I'm winning."

"What on Earth are you playing for?" he asks incredulously.

"Rights to feed Mina first," replies Trick, and my heart soars. Zeph's jaw drops open before he quickly rushes over to join in, his wings disappearing, and it's my turn to be amused. Crossing my arms, I watch as Dru beats the boys, one by one. I can see they're not amused.

"Yes!" She fist bumps the air before they all turn to see me watching them. The five of them look like sheepish kids caught with the hand in the cookies jar.

"If you're ok with it, I'd love to help you feed first." Drusilla has the grace not to gloat, and I decide to let it go. At least they're not horrified at the thought. Unfortunately, that reminds me I need to tell them about the thing.

"That would be great. Thanks, Dru, but you all better have a seat first. There's one more thing you need to know about feeding me." They all find a place on the comfy couches, but I stay standing. Pacing back and forth, I think about how I can tell them this. Should I show them and get it out the way? Rip it off like a band-aid?

My pacing must be too much for Sander because he jumps up and grabs me by the waist and sits back down with me on his lap. "Just tell us, love," he demands.

"When I feed, I need to be in my demon form." It all comes out at once, a torrent of words, and I wait for the explosion.

"Is that all?" Sander asks, and I nod, confused.

"Mina, Zeph and I have been with demons before," Mav assures me quietly, "and Trick and Sander have fed Jagger. None of us are strangers to it."

I look to Drusilla, and she shrugs. "I've never been with a demon before, but I've seen demon forms, and that doesn't bother me."

The relief I feel is huge, and I relax into Sander, my body previously held tight for a confrontation.

"But let's not tell Samuel about this arrange-ment at the moment. In fact, the less he knows, the better. We don't know if he'll let anything slip to Constance, and we're pretty sure we can't trust her," Zeph instructs us all. My heart aches at not being able to trust him, but I understand the importance of not letting anyone else know at this stage. Just as he finishes what he was saying, the door to the apartment flings open, and Sam strides in.

Chapter Twelve

Samuel
Twenty-Four Hours Earlier

I hurry away from the team without a backward glance. My concern for Mina has seemed to fade over the week, and it's not like she hasn't got enough people worrying about her. I'm not entirely sure why I was so enamored with her in the first place.

Connie was always my number one girl, and now she's back, and I have a chance at something good without having to share her with my brothers.

All week, the memories of them fawning over Mina, Maggie and Peter telling me all about how good Mina was doing at the academy have plagued me. The bitter, jealous feelings I had back then have returned tenfold. They're so bad I can't wait to get out of the building.

The elevator to the portal room opens, and I step in, its doors closing before I can turn around. No last glance at my team to make me feel worse.

I'm sure they're all shaking their heads at me, but they don't know what it was like.

They were only children, and their parents doted on them. Sander and Dru weren't, but they might as well have been one person when we were children. To have Mina come in and live with my foster parents, taking up all of their attention, was harsh. Is it any wonder I wanted Connie to myself? Sharing blows.

I get down to the portal room, and they set the coordinates that I give them to take me directly to Connie's house. Those were the instructions Sabboath sent to my wrist guard. He wants a rundown of what was discussed when everyone got kicked out. Stepping through, I shield my eyes. Everything on Amilles is so much brighter than anywhere else. The air is cleaner, and the cities and countryside are always pristine and clean. It's like the angels don't like anything marring the perfection. Not sure how Sabboath got away with his house though. Turning I look at the monstrosity. It's made with a substance like Earth's mother of pearl; it shimmers and shines, peachy-pink in the light. It's way too big for only two people to live in, but Sabboath likes his symbols of status. Shaking my head, I hurry up the front path of the garish mansion.

Before I can knock, the door is flung open, and Connie throws herself into my arms. She goes to kiss me on the lips, but I stop her before she can.

Huh, not sure why I did that. She looks a put-out, so I hug her a little tighter until she relaxes in my arms, all forgiven.

Pulling away, she grabs me by the hand and pulls me inside. "Come on. Daddy is waiting for us." I let her drag me around while I study her. She's been put through the wringer wherever she's been. When we were at the academy, she was fit and healthy, with muscles from all the training we did. But now, she's lost so much weight and is gaunt and pale. Mina looked similar on the bed in the hospital, too. Thinking about Mina brings pain to my heart, and I rub that spot on my chest, not knowing what my body is trying to tell me.

Connie sees me rubbing at the pain, and a slight grimace crosses her face. Before I can think about it too much or ask her any questions, she drags me into an office. I've seen nothing of the house on the way through it, my mind preoccupied. That's not like me. We're taught to be hyper-vigilant about our surroundings. *How is it that I keep getting distracted?*

Sabboath is sitting behind a huge desk that emphasizes his smaller frame. He's never been like the other Archangels; unlike the dads who are all big, brawny, muscular guys, something that happens during an Archangel's transition, he's on the thin side with stringy black hair. He's shorter and, dare I say it, sickly-looking. Now that I look closer, he has a touch of green to his skin tone that's eerily similar to Connie's, but she's been missing for two years.

What's his excuse? I'm not sure how he achieved Archangel status, and he won't tell anyone either, so it remains a mystery.

His voice has always been a bit whiny, and it's with that tone that he now demands, "Report!" like he's a general in the army. My skin prickles with annoyance, but I ignore it.

Connie pulls me down on a leather couch that he has in the room and pats me on the leg. "It's okay, Sammy, tell Daddy everything that happened in that meeting." A wave of disdain flows through my body at her touch, my mood darkens, and I snatch my arm away from her. I try to tell them that Mina is Lucifer's daughter, but the words can't come out. Instead, my throat closes up, and I start to bark like a dog.

Their faces are confused at my reaction, but the more I try, the more I bark. A few moments later, Sabboath's face turns thunderous.

"Someone has put a geas on you," he yells, throwing a paperweight across the room in his anger. It embeds itself into the wall a little to the right of my head. Once I stop trying to tell them what happened, the barking stops.

Sabboath is out of his chair, furiously pacing up and down while muttering things to himself. Connie's hand is tight on my thigh as she looks on in worry. "Please, Sam, try and tell him something." Her voice's laced with fear, and she starts to shake slightly. Wanting to help her feel more at ease, I stop and think about what I could tell them.

"Mina isn't an A..." My throat closes up again, but the barking doesn't happen.

Connie bounces up and down on the chair. "Huh, ok, how about I guess?" I nod at her.

"Ok, Mina is not a, hmm, what starts with A," she muses, thinking hard.

Fuck! I think as I roll my eyes. *The girl isn't too sharp, but she used to give great blow jobs. Whoa, where did that nasty thought come from?* Shaking my head, I focus on Connie.

Putting my arms out to the side, I flap them like wings and then point at her and myself, but she still looks confused. *Goddamn game of charades could take forever.* Sabboath stops his pacing and looks at what I'm doing, some of the tension bleeding from his body as he stills. "She's not an AB?" he guesses correctly. I nod my head and point at him.

"Well, what is she?" Connie asks, confused. I put my hands up to my head and mime horns. "She's a demon?" she gasps in shock, her nose wrinkled up. "Ew, you were living with a filthy demon all this time?" She sounds disgusted, and I'm honestly a bit surprised. I didn't realize her hate for demons was so strong.

Meanwhile, Sabboath looks thoughtful. "Hmm, that's interesting but not relevant to our cause. They didn't discuss anything else?"

Shaking my head, I'm able to reply, "No, it was

all about Mina. You heard all the other plans." He looks disappointed and dismisses us with a wave of his hand. We step out of the office, and he slams the door behind us, a loud click telling me he's locked it.

I try to leave without Connie hanging all over me, but she grabs hold of my hand again.

"Shall we go to my bedroom, Sam?" she asks, and I think she's trying to be seductive, but she just looks unwell.

"When was the last time you ate some real food?" I ask her, concerned.

She tries to wave me off. "I'm not hungry; I don't need food." But I won't take no for an answer. I'm too concerned about her.

"How about you and I go out and have some dinner at a nice restaurant? You can get dressed up, and we'll make an occasion of it. A celebration that you're alive and back in my life."

She looks thrilled with the idea, a little tear appearing in the corner of her eye. "Oh, Sammy, that would be great! Just you and me, like the good old days." She smacks a kiss on my cheek and runs away to get changed as I huff out a laugh. *Except the good old days weren't just you and me, were they, you whore?*

Fuck! I scrub a hand through my hair, pulling at the short ends in frustration. *What the fuck is happening to me?* I'm all over the place. I want to let Connie kiss me, but I feel guilty about it because of Mina. Part of me has deep feelings for Mina, but they always seem to be overshadowed by negativity. Especially this week.

When she first joined the team, I was ecstatic and so pleased to have her with us, but since her failure on mission, my feelings have changed. Seeing Connie made me realize how much I missed her, and how Mina had weasled her way into our team. Poor Connie must think I replaced her, and I don't owe that family and team-stealing bitch anything. My brain throbs with indecisiveness. I feel like I may be going insane with all of these dark, nasty thoughts plaguing my brain. Just like that, though, the thoughts disappear, and I shake off all the bad feelings until the guilt kicks in again. I really should be with the team, waiting for Mina's recovery.

Needing a drink, I'm about to go in search of one when Sabboath's voice on the other side of the door draws my attention. Putting my ear to it, I try to hear what is said.

"No, that's all I know. One of their teams is going to be doing some snooping around the city. At this stage, it's directed at Reath only, but you can be sure when things lead to Amilles, he'll send a team to investigate here, too."

I try to wait for more, but a maid comes around the corner, and I have to leap away from the door so that she doesn't see me listening. Hurrying away, I try to find a sofa to sit on while I wait for Connie.

Finding a room with a bar, I pour myself a big

glass of Cherub, an angel spirit similar to Earth's bourbon but a hell of a lot stronger. It has the smooth taste of whiskey on the way down and an aftertaste of licorice. They named it after an Earth angel myth as a pun because cherubs are cute, and there is nothing cute about this drink.

Slamming it down, I leave the glass on the wooden surface and throw myself on the couch to wait for Connie.

I don't have to wait long before she's back, wearing a skimpy dress more suited to a stripper than a casual dinner celebration, but who am I to protest if she wants to show me the tops of those tits? Looking at them, I can't help but compare them to Mina's. These are tiny little sacks of nothing compared to Mina's cracking rack. *God, again with the nasty thoughts.* I dig my nails into the palm of my hands, but the nastiness continues. *But it's alright, we'll feed her up, and hopefully, she'll gain back a bit of the curves I enjoyed bending over our couch when no one was at home.*

I adjust my cock, which has tightened in my pants, and Connie sees my reaction and simpers at me. An abrupt pain in my heart sends a shooting pain downward, and my cock is instantly limp again. *What the hell?* I'm starting to feel sick with all the conflicting thoughts and feelings, and I grab hold of the couch next to me to steady myself. Connie doesn't give me any chance to think about it before we're out the door and in a hovercar on the way to the best restaurant in the capital of Amilles.

The restaurant is full of angels, and their noses turn up as I walk in, but when they see Connie follow me, those sneers turn to fake smiles. The AB daughter of an Archangel is someone that they could impress. I imagine they would shit their pants if they knew I'm an Archangel, too. One day I won't have to hide it, and I'll show all these assholes whose butt they can kiss.

We're shown to a table and seated before the first kiss-ass approaches us. Daubjdiel is one of the angels that lectures at the academy on angel traditions. Why we need that kind of class, I don't know, but it's included in the curriculum. She's a pompous, stuck up woman who I think is trying to get into Sabboath's pants, as she was always very kind to Connie at the academy but a downright dragon to everyone else.

"Connie, darling. We had heard you'd been found and returned to us safely," she fawns, giving Connie air kisses on each cheek. "Your poor father must be so pleased." She's giving Connie a look I can't quite decipher, so I ignore it for now.

Connie replies gracefully. "Oh yes, bless his heart, I'm not sure how he survived without me, but I'm sure it has to do with you and some other wonderful people in our angel community," she gushes, really laying it on thick.

"And rumor has it you're suffering from amnesia," Daubjdiel continues, and Connie's eyes narrow slightly. "We're all praying that your memory is recovered soon." She pats her on the hand reassuringly, and Connie thanks her again before she leaves us to our menus. Dinner continues without us getting a chance to talk much, as angel after angel approaches the table.

When we finish our coffee and desserts, Connie orders a hover car to take us to a club on the other side of town. We settle in for the ride, but I put some distance between us so that we're not touching but she doesn't seem to notice. While we were at dinner, I seemed to come out of my angry fog, and I'm testing a theory about Connie's touch. She continues gabbing about people we saw at the restaurant, not noticing that I've strategically taken a seat where she can't easily touch me.

"And did you see what she was wearing? I wouldn't be caught dead…" Her whiny tirade continues, but all I hear is blah blah.

I wonder how Mina is? If adding Lucifer's blood into her body, allowing her to transition, has helped counteract the venom… I can't believe she's a demon. Not once had that occurred to me. Does it matter to me if she's a demon? I think about that last question for a moment, and to be honest, I don't care one bit. Meanwhile, just Connie's presence is seeming more and more abhorrent to me with each passing moment.

"Are you even listening to me?" Connie's hand on my arm and her annoyed tone have me focusing back on her. She's finally moved over, almost sitting in my lap now. Shaking off my thoughts about Mina, I smile and quickly apologize. "Sorry, sweetheart, I was thinking about something else. I guess I'm a little tired, and I think I'll skip the club and head home to bed."

A gleam enters her eyes at my words, and instead of dropping her off at the club and going home without her, she quickly asks the cab driver to take us both home.

"I like the way you think," she purrs as her eyes fill with lust. "We haven't had any alone time together in ages."

At these words, my bipolar body has two *very* visceral reactions. My cock hardens in desire for all the things I could do to her before that sharp stabbing pain hits me again and causes my stomach to roll with nausea. Hiding my grimace, I look out the window, so she doesn't see my reaction. To stop her wandering hand from reaching my crotch, I hold it in mine. I agree, spending the trip home thinking about the things I'm going to do to her.

Immediately after entering the garish mansion once more, she tries to drag me up to her bedroom. Thankfully, someone is looking after me tonight though, and Sabboath tells her he needs to speak to her in private. Taking advantage of their distraction, I follow a maid who shows me to my room. All the emotional ups and downs of today have me exhausted, and I collapse into bed once I remove all my clothes.

———•◦•———

I spend the following day with Connie, and we meet some old friends from the academy for lunch. It's funny, I remember training with all these people, but none of them are in teams anymore. When I question one of them, he tells me it wasn't for him, and the gig he has now is much more interesting. I start to ask him about it, my internal sense pinging, but Connie puts her arm through mine and drags me to the bar to buy her another drink, and it slips my mind.

It's not until that evening, when I'm sitting with Sabboath and Connie, having a drink and discussing what we'd done that day, that I get a message from Zeph saying Mina is awake. He follows that announcement up by asking if I want to come home and see her. I ignore it, but it keeps beeping at me until Sabboath finally snaps, "What's the problem, Samuel?" He glares at my arm with annoyance as if I should have no other concerns or contact when I'm having my time monopolized by him and his daughter.

"Oh, Mina's awake," I tell him, not thinking anything of it.

Both he and Connie jump to their feet in surprise. "She is? God, I thought she was done for."

Connie's voice is panicky in a way that I don't entirely understand. Part of me is totally mystified by why this would matter to her so much, while another part of me whispers that I should be alert, that there's something here to pay attention to.

"Well, you better get there and see what she has to say about what happened to her then," Sabboath insists and starts to guide me towards the door. I'm surprised by their sudden enthusiasm, but I guess I better do the right thing. I've been ignoring messages from both Maggie and Peter too, and goddess knows my adoptive parents won't be happy about that. Hopefully, I can kill two birds with one stone on this trip and then come back and live in luxury in the guise of keeping an eye on Connie. She gives me one lingering hug goodbye, whispering something I don't quite catch as I head out the door.

All of a sudden, rage flows through my body. *How dare Zeph make me feel guilty about seeing Mina! They're the ones who suggested I stay here in the first place.* Determined to give him a piece of my mind, I press the button to activate the portal at my coordinates, and when it opens with a whoosh, I step through and make my way to our apartment.

Chapter Thirteen

Jessamina

"You're awake." His tone is flat as he walks into the apartment and closes the door behind him, diming my hunger for a moment because a fresh wave of hurt overwhelms me.

Not wanting to move, I stay in Sander's lap. I'm comfortable and feeling so many different emotions at the moment that if he wants to show me any affection, he needs to come to me. Watching him closely, he takes off his jacket, hanging it on the peg before moving further into the room. He's changed drastically in the week since I've seen him. He looks like he's lost weight, there are bags under his eyes, and his hair looks unwashed. His skin even looks like it has a tinge of green to it. I wonder if he's not well but shake my head at that thought. ABs don't get sick. Something is obviously bothering him.

"Hi, Sam. It's nice to see you," I reply, trying as hard as I can to keep my voice neutral. A small smile crosses his lips before he's frowning again.

"What did you want me for, Zeph?" The look of

shock on Zeph's face at Sam's comment is so comical that I almost laugh. I don't think he was expecting Sam to question why he called him, thinking that Sam would want to be here to see me. That makes my heart sink. *What the hell have I done to Sam to make him act this way again?* Goddamnit, I thought this shit had stopped. My hands clench in anger, and a soft growling escapes my mouth. Sander shushes me and wraps his arms tighter to comfort me.

"Nothing really, just wanted you to know that Mina's back, and there have been some developments."

"And you couldn't just message them to me?" Sam sneers as he grabs a beer from the fridge before joining us, but even then he stands a little bit apart. Now over his surprise, Zeph has an annoyed look on his face. There's a storm brewing between Sam and the rest of the team, and I hope he's prepared for what he's bringing out in the others.

"Now he's done it," Sander whispers in my ear, and I shiver as my body informs me it is *way* past time I eat.

Before Zeph can start in on Samuel, I stand up. "If it's alright with you all, I'm heading to bed. Today has been huge, and I'm exhausted." The guys all give me sympathetic looks and wish me good night, but Dru throws me a wink and tells me she'll be there shortly. I think she needs to hear what Samuel has to say, whereas I just don't care anymore. That little flame I had in my heart for him is slowly withering away.

I make my way to my room. Opening the door, I look around. I don't know why I thought it might have changed, but I'm pleasantly surprised it hasn't. A strong sense of relief has me collapsing onto my bed, all sorts of thoughts and worries plaguing me at the moment. It's nice to see something stayed the same even though I haven't.

My magic wand is on my bedside table. Grabbing it, I hug it to my body. "Hello, my old friend," I whisper, and with a shock, it pulses with magic, a bright yellow and blue light, before turning dull again. I carefully place it back where it was, looking between me and it. My hands tingle with power, and a wave of electric current sparks over it before winking out. *Whoa, it's never done that before.*

Lying on my bed, I decide I need to make an effort to get up. I'd really like to have a shower and clean up before Dru comes to feed me. We're sort of skipping a few steps in this relationship process, and I want her to see that I want to make an effort for her. Dropping my glamour, I assume my demon form. I leave my wings inside, having discovered how not fun they are when they get wet. *Not even sure those floofy things are going to let me fly.* I brush aside the grumpiness that comes with that thought, not wanting to let that take over my time with Dru. That's a job for tomorrow; maybe I can get someone to throw me off the top of the Collectors

Division building. *I get the feeling Sam might be willing...*

Stripping off my clothes until I'm in my underwear, I'm just about to run the shower when the door to my bedroom flies open, and Samuel steps in. His look of shock at my appearance would be comical if I didn't see the small glimmer of disgust in his eyes or the way his body tensed up when he caught sight of me. Right, well, he's the last person who's going to see my full demon form apart from Jagger and Kai. I miss them already, and they haven't even been gone long.

God, I can almost literally see the emotions flitting across his face one by one, disgust, but that fades, and then there's happiness and then sadness. Bipolar Sam at his best, I brace myself for his words. He runs his hands through his short hair in frustration and clenches his fist, opening and closing it before he finally says something.

"You really are a demon," he states, using that same flat tone. Shaking his head as if to clear it, he tries to bring a smile to his face, but I can tell it's forced. Seeing it, I just get mad. Picking a pillow off my bed, I throw it at him, but he bats it away. Holding a hand out, I use my powers to pick a shoe off the floor and fling it at him, then a hairbrush from my bedside table then a book sitting on the desk. One after the other, they fly at him in anger, but he just holds his hand up and stops them, making them drop to the floor. A growl escapes my mouth, and I stamp my foot in frustration. Anguish crosses his face at my reaction to him, and I can see he's trying to think of something else to say even though he's already said enough. *What happened to the Sam I used to know? The one who would support me and take the time to be like family to me?*

"Hey, dickhead, you wouldn't have to look at it if you didn't barge in unannounced," I snarl, turning my back to him. I'm pretty sure if it could, my tail would be giving him the finger right at this moment. My stomach rolls with nausea, and my head throbs in pain. The hurt I'm feeling rolls through my body, and I physically feel like I'm going to be sick. Closing my eyes, I pray for him to leave, needing him gone so that I can preserve what little bit of confidence I have left.

Someone must get the message because I hear the door close quietly behind him, and that's the straw that breaks the camel's back. I open the shower and turn on the water then sit on the floor and let the tears flow. Great big wracking sobs escape my body; this is all *way* too much for one day.

Underneath the patter of the water, I hear the door to my bedroom open and close again, and I quickly assume my human form. I feel more vulnerable in my demon form than I do being naked in front of anyone, and Sam's reaction did nothing to build up my confidence in my demon appearance.

Drusilla's voice shouts out from my room,

"Mina, honey. I brought you some food that was just delivered; I'm sure you haven't eaten normally for a while and could do with a hot meal too."

I hiccup snort through my sobs at the thought; all my meals are hot one way or another. Poking her head around the door, she sees me at the bottom of the shower. "Mina, what's wrong?" Her concern causes more tears to flow and possibly some wailing because, before I know it, Dru is stripped down to her underwear and joining me in the shower. She wraps her hands around my arms and hauls me to my feet before drawing me into her soft embrace. I shudder with the effort to hold my form; it feels like it wants to rip out of my skin, and, gritting my teeth, I hold it in place.

"What's wrong, sweetie?" she coos gently. "Tell me all about it?" And through my sobs, I manage to tell her about Sam barging in and his look of disgust.

"Oh, honey, Sam's a lot of things, but he doesn't hate you. He doesn't even hate demons; he's been friends with Jagger for years. Something's going on with him, and we think it has to do with Connie being back around. We'll figure it all out. You've been through so much in the last twenty-four hours, not to mention almost dying before that. I think what you need is some food and some sleep. Everything will seem better in the morning." Drusilla turns the taps off and opens the shower screen, grabbing us both towels. She strips off her underwear quickly, and we dry off, putting on two robes she conjures out of thin air. They're soft and fluffy, and I feel comfortable and warm, and all my frayed, frazzled, emotions start to settle. Drusilla's calmness brings comfort to my soul.

I follow her out to the bedroom; her dark hair is plastered against the back of her robe. Using my new powers, I click my fingers, and the water is drawn out. I flick it back toward the bathroom, and the ribbon of water flows away and down the drain. Instantly, her hair is dry. She turns and winks at me. "Thanks, that's a neat trick. You've got great control of your powers already." As she turns, her robe gapes a little, and my eyes are drawn to the rounded globes of her breasts. That triggers the memory of what she looked like naked. Creamy pale skin and nipples like ripe raspberries, her body rounded but toned and her mound with a small landing strip of dark hair.

I can't believe we showered together, and I didn't think to look at her almost naked body. The image in my brain triggers something deep within my soul, and my hunger comes racing back with a vengeance. The need to ravish her before plunging my fangs deep into her vein rides me hard, and I swallow with anticipation. But first, there's a tray with two bowls of stir fry on it, and she went to the trouble of looking after my other needs, so the least I can do is eat it for her. Climbing up on the bed, I pat the covers, gesturing to her to sit with me. Smiling, she joins me and hands me one of the steaming bowls, and we quietly chat about mundane things while we eat our food. Avoiding any of the issues that have been plaguing me for what seems like forever but in reality is such a short time.

"You know Maggie will be here first thing in the morning, don't you?" Drusilla asks, and a look of horror must cross my face because she's instantly alert. "What? What's wrong?"

My fork clatters to the bowl from where it has slipped out of my hand. "Lucifer's coming, too."

Comprehension crosses Dru's face, and she tries so hard; I can see the struggle broadcast across her face, but she just can't hold it in. Peals of laughter escape her luscious lips, and tears stream down her face. "Oh my god, you are so screwed." I quickly grab at her bowl as she starts to roll around on my bed.

A knock at my door distracts me from her hysterics. Maybe it's Sam coming back. Biting my lip, I contemplate ignoring it, not sure I want any more surprises, but the knock sounds again a bit more insistent. Bracing myself, I flick my hand to unlock it, and it swings open to reveal Sander and Trick. Breathing out a sigh, I realize I'm disappointed it's not Samuel, but Dru's laughter keeps me smiling.

"Everything okay in here?" Trick's voice is gentle, and Sander has a worried look on his face that just turns to confusion at seeing his sister.

They come in, Sander shoving Dru back up, and Trick takes both bowls from my hand before he climbs up behind me and wraps his arms around me.

Dru finally gathers a breath and tells them why she's laughing. Sander's laughter joins hers, but Trick whispers in my ear, distracting me. "Are you okay? Sam stormed out like a hellhound was on his heels." This information sobers me up, and I turn to look at him. His dirty blonde hair is tousled like he's been running his hand through it, or maybe Sander has, and his arctic blue eyes hold worry for me. My heart warms that these guys are so understanding during such a difficult time for all of us. I'm not the Mina they thought they would have on their team, but they're taking on all my extras like they don't even matter.

Placing a gentle kiss on his lips, I assure him I am, or I will be. His eyes widen behind his black-framed glasses before they heat, and he leans in for another kiss, but a hand appears in front of his mouth.

"I don't think so. I won fair and square. Out, both of you." Drusilla's recovered, and her voice is firm and final. I hide a smile at her dominance; it's cute that she's telling them off. Trick pushes her hand out the way and gives me a quick kiss then grabs the bowls and leaves. Leaning over his sister, Sander does the same. "Sleep well, beautiful," he tells me and follows Trick out.

The door closes behind them, and I get off the bed, grab a couple of bottles of water out of my mini-fridge, and hand one to Dru. She cracks the top and takes a sip while I do the same. By the time I've finished and put the lid on, she's looking at me impatiently. "Well, come on then."

"What?" I ask her, confused.

She waves her hand up and down. "Let's see it." *Oh, fuck, my demon form.* She must see my body tighten up because she promptly shakes her head, a kind but stern look on her face that tells me I am not getting out of this. "None of that. Ignore the shit that came out of Sam's mouth for now. Tell me about what Jagger and Kai thought."

I think about the words Jagger and Kai used, and a soft smile comes over my face. "There, see, they had some good things to say, didn't they?" she asks, and I nod my head, dropping my eyes to my lap. But she grabs me by the chin and lifts it again. "Mina what's on the outside doesn't matter." She puts her hand to my heart. "Because I know on the inside you are kind, funny, sweet, and brave, and I find those things very attractive. Lots of people do." She lets go of my chin and waves her hands. "Well, hit me with it."

Taking a deep breath, I drop my robe, and Dru's eyes heat with desire at my naked body. *Let's hope they stay that way.* Releasing the breath I'm holding, I let go of my glamour and release my wings.

Too scared to look at her reaction, I keep my eyes to the floor.

Drusilla's breathing increases, and with a lusty sigh, I hear her say, "Fuck me!"

Looking up, my confidence soars at the look on her face. She gestures for me to spin around, and turning, I show her the whole look. Her inhale of surprise at my tail reminds me of the things Jagger and Kai did to me, and a rush of adrenaline fills my body at the thought of the things *I* can do to *her*.

When I finally face her again, she gets off the bed and walks toward me. "I've never been with a demon before, and I'm so lucky my first is going to be as gorgeous as you are. Can I touch you?" she asks, the awe on her face making my cheeks heat, though I'm sure she can't tell because I'm pink anyway.

Nodding my head, I grumble to her, "I look like a demon Barbie doll." She just purses her lips while running her hands over the feathers of my wings. A bolt of lust tingles my core, and I start to purr as she circles my body, her hands continuing to touch my tail and horns with seductive, gentle caresses that quickly have my nipples pebbled and the proof of my desire on my thighs.

"I used to pretend I was going to marry Barbie over in the fictional character realm when I was smaller. She's gorgeous, if a bit stiff." A giggle escapes my mouth.

Drusilla moves back around in front of me.

"You're beautiful, Mina." She strokes my black hair. "When I imagined what you would look like, this was not it. I thought you'd be red like your mom and the streaks in your hair."

She runs her hands through my long black hair, brushing her thumbs against my horns, causing me to moan at the same time. Her eyes light up. "Are they sensitive?" she asks softly and wraps a small hand around each of them. She has to stand on her tiptoes to reach them, and she pushes against my body as she does, my face just about in her cleavage. Her floral scent hits my nose, and I groan with want.

"Drusilla, what you're doing is basically the equivalent of giving a guy a handjob. So you need to decide if you want to continue this because I'm about to lose it," I grind out, my teeth clenched, fangs throbbing with want.

She pulls her hands away quickly, and my heart drops, but before I can let her off the hook, she quickly undoes the tie and drops her robe. Her curvy petite body is naked and completely on display for me like a fucking meal fit for a queen.

Without any delay, I pick her up and carry her back to the bed, looking her in the eye the whole time, but there is no fear or reluctance to see.

"Sweetheart, I'm going to eat you all up," I growl and proceed to do so.

Chapter Fourteen

Jessamina

Dru's eyes are wide with anticipation as I crawl my way up her body, placing soft kisses across her stomach and over her plump breasts. My tongue finds her nipple, and her cry of delight as I nibble and suck on it, scraping it with my fangs, is music to my ears. Moving to the other side, I give that one the same treatment before I crawl further up, kissing and nipping my way until I get to her mouth.

Pulling back, I ask her once more, "Are you sure about this?" I look down, knowing what I need to say but needing that moment to gather the courage to do so. "I'll probably bite you and drink your blood," I tell her, watching for any hesitation. "I still can't separate the two acts yet. Are you alright with that?" Her eyes are glazed with lust, and her soft mound rubs against my thigh, her pussy already weeping with want.

"Yes, please. I've always wanted to know what

being bitten felt like," she rasps out, her breath coming in pants, completely turned on.

Without waiting any longer, my mouth meets hers, and we kiss with slow, languid movements that quickly turn frantic until she's writhing and moaning beneath me. Moving my lips from hers and looking down, I can see my tail's gotten in on the action. Caressing up and down her body with soft gentle movements until it's penetrated her pussy. Dru's wet damp heat envelops it, her pussy walls fluttering while it thrusts in and out. My heart skips a beat, worrying about her reaction, but when I bring my head back up and meet her eyes, she doesn't seem the least bit concerned.

"Oh my god," she calls out, her hands gripping the sheets, but I'm not ready for her to come yet, so I quickly move the tail away. It twitches in protest, almost trying to find its way back to her, but I manage to control it this time. *Such a greedy thing.*

"I guess I didn't warn you about that." I start to apologize, but she slaps a hand over my mouth.

"Don't say another word; your tail has become my new best friend. Did you know it changes shape when it's inside?" My eyes widen with amazement, and she kisses me like I'm her last breath of air and then pushes my head down toward her pussy.

A wicked smile crosses my mouth at her bold-ness, and I slowly make my way down, kissing, caressing, licking, and sucking every inch of her skin in an erotic tease. She's panting and moaning as she thrashes underneath me, her passion a smorgasbord for me to feed on. Her emotions are sweet and fulfilling, and I gorge on them, a syrupy buffet that I can't get enough of.

Jagger and Kai warned me that because she couldn't actually come inside me like a male does, I would have to feed from feelings as well as what I could swallow. That conversation was fun, and the boys' reactions from it were doubly fun. I could feel they were turned on by the thought of me and Drusilla together, and one day I might ask her if she wouldn't mind if they watch. Just for fun.

I finally make it to her soft naked mound, where I swipe my tongue across her clit a few times, circling it until her breathing hitches before pulling away. She groans a little in frustration. Moving further down until I get to her swollen, pink lips, I lick a path straight through, reveling in the flavor that is Drusilla, sweet with an earthy taste. I wrap my mouth around them and suck, her moans increasing immediately. Pulling away, I will my tongue to expand and extend like Jagger's did. Once it does, I use it to fuck her sweet cunt until she's begging for more. Just as I feel her pussy start to flutter around my tongue, I withdraw it, generating a shriek of disappointment that causes me to smile, but I quickly replace my tongue with my tail and wrap my lips around her clit. Tail fucking combined with my mouth sucking, Dru's orgasm hits her like an explosion. Just as it does, I bite down into her mound above her clit, and the explosion turns atomic.

Her screams are silent and back arched as I drink my fill of her sweet blood while my tail fucks her through it all, her tight wet heat pulsing and gripping hard. Slowing, I wait for her to come down until she's limp and sated below me. Running my tongue across her mound, I lick the two holes closed and climb up her sweat-covered body until I'm lying next to her.

I wait for her to recover, not wanting to kiss her because I have the taste of her blood in my mouth, but she doesn't seem to care. She rolls over and wraps her arms and legs around me, and we kiss lazily, tongues rolling against each other. Her emotions batter me with their ferocity, and I drink them down. The high of the orgasm followed by feelings of love and acceptance throb through my body filling me up, both emotionally and physically. My mind and soul are overflowing with the kind of feelings I've always craved.

She pulls away and rests her forehead against mine. "Holy shit. That was amazing, thank you." She starts to move down my body, teasing, "My turn now," but I notice something on her shoulder blade.

Grabbing her, I stop her from moving. "Oh my god!" She must hear the shock in my voice because she tries to see what I'm looking at, her face taking on a surprised curiosity that's quite adorable when her nose crinkles in question.

"What's that on my shoulder? I can't see it properly." She's craning her neck but can't make it out.

"Mate marks," I whisper, "my mate marks. But they're different from Jagger and Kai's; yours has another section. I can't believe you didn't feel the pain." My heart is racing with excitement but also nervous about how she's going to react.

"YESSS!" she shouts, jumping up and down on the bed in celebration. "I'm mated to the sexiest Archdemon on the planet, and I probably didn't feel the pain because my orgasm just about made my head explode."

Dru starts to do a happy dance, and I watch as her naked ass wiggles in front of my face, a bemused smile crossing my lips. She drops to her knees in front of me and kisses the heck out of me. "I get to have the best sex of my life forever, and I have a gorgeous, kind, sweet, and funny girl to share my life with. I could not be happier!" she declares, a smile taking over her face that tells me, even more than anything else, that the excitement and happiness she's showing is genuine.

"You don't care if you have to share me?"

"Fuck, no! I'll be honest; if you did that to me every night, I might not want to leave the bed ever. Either that or you might kill me."

I laugh and hug her tight against me, whispering "Thank you," in her ear.

She jumps up, running into the bathroom to have a look, and I watch her turning until she can see them. A smug smile crosses her face before she runs back to look at mine, and I can feel the soft touch of her tracing her hand over it. "Yours has grown, but it's different than mine."

"Yes, it seems like you're all getting different marks, while mine is a combination of all of them."

She untangles herself and winks at me before getting up and grabbing a bag off the side I hadn't seen yet. From it, she pulls some toys and throws them on the bed before climbing back up. She wiggles her eyebrows. "I might not have a tail, but I have a few tricks of my own up my sleeve." She spends half the night showing me exactly what.

⸻ • ◆ • ⸻

The next morning, I wake, warm and snuggled with my body wrapped around Drusilla. Placing kisses against the back of her neck, she mumbles in her sleep as I climb out of bed and leave her to rest a little longer.

I know that Maggie and Lucifer will be invading our home at any moment, and I need some sustenance to have a hope of surviving what's to come. Blood, some sex, and a fucking cup of coffee. Not wanting to feed from Drusilla again, just in case I drank too much last night, I go in search of Jagger. He'd messaged me last night that he had arrived and was all moved into the spare room that was previously an office. He hadn't wanted to interrupt my night with Dru, so he hadn't done it telepathically. How sweet is my blue demon?

I quickly run down the hallway in my naked demon form, praying nobody opens their door before I get to Jagger's room and crack the door open slightly. It's pitch back, but I can hear the soft sound of his breathing. Sneaking my way to where I think his bed is, I pull back the covers and climb in next to him. I run my hands down his spine, finding nothing but deliciously bare blue skin, before sliding them around to the front of his body. Running my hands over his firm pecs, I reach for a nipple, giving it a loving tweak.

He grunts in response. "You better be here for breakfast, my pretty pink princess, because I'm starving," he growls. His tail wraps around my waist and hauls me up as he rolls over, and when it lets me down, I'm seated firmly on my sexy, blue demon's lap.

A little lamp turns on next to the bed, and I lick my lips when I see the want in Jagger's eyes. Without any warning, he lifts me up and drops me down on his hard dick. It takes a couple of thrusts, but finally, he's seated deep, and I'm purring with pleasure.

Slowly, I start to ride his cock. My hips swivel every couple of thrusts, but he mustn't be able to wait because he grabs me by the thighs and starts to help. His thrusts are increasing the sensations until we're both moaning and groaning with pleasure. He pulls himself into a sitting position, looking me in my eyes as he brings me to a toe tingling climax. As I scream his name, he bites down on my neck, sending the orgasm to greater heights. My pussy is clenching his cock hard, and after only one or two more thrusts, he comes too. I thrust my fangs into his chest, just above his mate mark, and we both drink down each other's rich blood in large mouthfuls while riding out the pleasure before pulling away and sealing the holes.

I slump in his arms, and he rubs his big hands up and down my back. "Now that's what I call a wakeup call." His grumbly words are smug but rightfully so.

"I missed you," I tell him as we sit there enjoying the moment."Have you heard from Kai?" He rumbles in pleasure and places kisses up and down my neck.

"Yes, baby, he's fine. He linked with me last night and said he might be a day or two." I pout when I realize Kai hadn't spoken to me and almost yelp from the admonishing nip my lip gets in response. "Don't sulk. He didn't want to disturb you when I told him you were with Drusilla," he reassures me. Half-tempted to keep the lip out to see if I'll get another nip and possibly some other fun afterward, I tuck it away, not wanting to be too dramatic this early in the day. "Did you have a good night? Did our team take care of you?"

I reply with a murmured "Mmhmm," reliving my wonderful evening with Drusilla. Feeling lethargic, I let my eyes start to close until I remember what's happening this morning.

"Holy shit!" I shout, climbing off of Jagger's lap and looking around for clothes before remembering I came down here naked.

He has an amused look on his face as he lies back down, one hand propped under his head as he watches me flap around. "What's wrong with you?"

I stop dead. "Both my moms are going to be here this morning. *Together*. At the same time. Together."

He just laughs at my despair and gets up, going over to a chest of drawers and pulling out a pair of sweatpants to slip on. Demon and angels' clothes must be spelled to fit around appendages because their wings and tails never seem to be trapped by anything.

"Come on, maybe it won't be so bad. It could be worse; all the other mothers could be here too."

I feel the blood drain from my face at the thought of meeting all of the team's mothers. I mean, Jophial was lovely, but what are the chances she's still going to be so sweet when she finds out I'm a demon and have two demon mates? Mothers are protective, aren't they? I mean, Maggie is, and I'm not even hers biologically.

Not wanting to think about it, I scramble around in his drawer for a t-shirt and pair of boxer briefs, which I pull over my body and then change my form. They hang on me, but I don't care. My insecurities kicking in again, and I like the feeling of being hidden.

"Honey, why are you doing that? Aren't you sick of holding it?" Jagger's voice is curious, and while holding the human glamour does take a little getting used to, it's no different for me than being in demon form. But that's not the main reason. I don't know if Sam is still here, not to mention the others haven't seen me yet.

Instead of answering him, I just rip open the door and head down the corridor to the main living area of the apartment. The noise on the other side is a little chaotic as I finally arrive. It looks like everyone but Drusilla is up, and they're having a loud conversation for first thing in the morning. I can see Sam there, and he seems to be happy, joking and laughing with his team as usual.

I'm reluctant to join them, but Jagger, following behind me, has no such worries and drags me with him to the kitchen bench. Calls of good morning sound out as we approach. "Morning, everyone," he calls to the others before grabbing two plates and filling them with the breakfast things that are laid out. There are eggs, bacon, sausage and hash browns, and a massive stack of pancakes with all the fixings. He passes me the first one, then sits down next to me and starts digging in. I look around, bemused, but the guys have continued their conversation, so I take his lead and quietly eat my breakfast. A cup of coffee is placed next to me, and I look up, shocked to see Sam is the one to pass it to me.

"Mina, if we could talk privately in a minute, I need to say a few things," he says with an apologetic tone in his voice. I nod stiffly, not sure I'm quite ready to hear his words. He shattered my heart last night with his reaction.

Jagger gives me a little nudge of support, and I answer Sam, realizing I've just been looking at him with who knows what expression on my face."Yeah, ok, but Maggie and my mom will be here soon, so maybe after that?" He looks shocked when I say Mom, but he quickly schools his features and agrees to my terms.

I'm concentrating on eating my breakfast when a set of lips against the back of my neck has me arching into them, and Drusilla's husky voice whispers in my ear, "Hello, mate." She's quiet, so the guys don't hear it, but Jagger certainly does. He stiffens up and glances at the two of us.

"Drusilla got the mate mark last night when I drank from her," I tell him telepathically, *"but we're keeping it on the down-low for now. She doesn't want to upset the rest of the team."* We had discussed it last night, and I agreed with her for now, still a bit caught up in trying to process my own feelings. I'm so glad to

have Drusilla and my demons, but I'm not sure if I can handle juggling everyone else's emotions if they're less than pleased to know that Dru has my mate marks. .

Jagger narrows his eyes at the both of us but nods his head in agreement. *"Yeah, I felt it, and my mark grew as well. I just wasn't sure which person it had been. Smart thinking to keep quiet for now. We don't need to have anyone else upset,"* he replies, eyeing Samuel, and Drusilla's eyes widen when she hears him too. She places a kiss on his cheek, looking relieved at his easy acceptance, and goes and grabs a cup of coffee.

"Did you sleep alright last night?" Trick asks us both, and Sander sniggers, ridiculous man child that he is. "You're practically glowing."

Again, Sander snorts, and I narrow my eyes at him, wondering if he put Trick up to that. Before I can answer, Dru takes care of her brother for me. "Oh, yes. Mina fucked me so well I thought my brains were going to leak out of my ears." The room is shocked into silence, and we watch as Sander turns a little green before everyone bursts into laughter simultaneously.

Mav high fives Drusilla, and Zeph shoots me an amused look to which I just shrug. Jagger just can't help himself. "Once you've gone demon, you'll never go back," he says smugly like it was him that put that smile on her face. Without missing a beat, I pinch him.

"What are you so happy about? *I'm* the one she's bragging about."

"Yeah, but I bet Kai and I helped you with a few of those moves." He winks at me, and a blush crosses my cheeks.

"Well then, Jagger, thank you too, for all of my orgasms last night." Drusilla bows in his direction before laughing again. She pats Sander on the cheek. "That's one point to me." She pats him a little harder a second time before taking her coffee cup and heading back to her room. Finished with my breakfast, I put my plate in the dishwasher and do the same. I need to get appropriately dressed before the moms get her.

Sander's spluttering is still loud enough to hear as the hallway door closes behind me, and a smile crosses my lips. *Maybe this day won't be so bad after all.*

Chapter Fifteen

Jessamina

I am so fucking wrong; it's ridiculous. Today is heinous. If I could warn my past self, I would have run around with arms in the air, screaming "Abort! Abort!" and tell past me to hide under my blankets and not to come out until they'd left.

They, being the two rigid women sitting on opposite ends of the couch while I sit uncomfortably between them.

Maggie was the first to arrive. Thank god! I was able to explain the situation, and bless her heart, the fact that I'm a demon didn't even faze her. Unfortunately, when she found out who my mother is and what kind of demon I am, well, you could say her head just about imploded.

Maggie's pretty open to most things, but owning a sex dungeon to feed is her hard limit, and, well, Lucifer may as well be the literal antichrist.

She tried to convince me that I could find a nice AB husband and settle down and have a couple of AB children, so I then had to tell her about demon mating marks. She hasn't spoken a word to me since I told her I'm mated to Jagger and Kai and possibly have more out there.

Lucifer arrived not long after this, and apart from Maggie's frosty greeting, they haven't spoken a word to each other, and I haven't been able to ask my mother any questions that I need to. I can't say I blame her for the silence after Maggie started their relationship by calling out, "Hey Trollop!"

Thank goodness my mother is more rational; otherwise, Maggie's head might have literally exploded on the spot if Lucifer had felt offended. Silly dramatic woman. Jealousy is a funny thing. I mean, polyamory's not an uncommon thing in our society, and I know Maggie has no problems with it. I think the fact that I now have another mother figure in my life plus two mates to lean on is making her feel like I won't need her anymore, and that's really not the case. But there's no point in trying to tell her that right now. I'll give her a couple of days to calm down, then maybe I'll get Peter to help me talk to her when she's feeling a little more reasonable.

The rest of the team made themselves scarce, but I'm about to try out my telepathic link with my newest mate. *"Drusilla, so help me god if you ever want sex with me again, you better find Sam and tell him to get his ass out here. If he ever wants back into my good graces, he can do it by getting Maggie out of here. I need to talk to Lucifer."*

A light giggle comes through the link. *"Okay gorgeous, I'll find him and twist his arm. Hang in there."*

The silence is excruciating. I know both of these women love me, and I love them, but the new rule is they're not to be in the same room at the same time ever again.

While I wait for my rescue, I study them. Both women stopped aging in their thirties and are gorgeous, but Maggie has adopted a more mature look to her dress and mannerisms, whereas Lucifer exudes sensuality even dressed in jeans, a fitted top, and heeled boots.

Finally, Samuel opens the door from the bedroom area and, with a smile on his face, greets our foster mother. Pulling her to her feet and wrapping his well-defined arms around her, he squeezes her tight. "Hi, Maggie, I've missed you." She has a shocked look on her face, but it's the perfect distraction because she melts and starts fussing over him.

Thank goodness she's the only foster mom that's still around. All the other foster parents didn't have anything to do with the academy, unlike Peter, so they stepped away once the team joined, and the birth parents took over in secret. I think they were actually made to forget; they'll go on to have their own children and be none the wiser.

"We haven't caught up in a while. How about I take you out for lunch?" he suggests to her, and she fluffs her hair and smiles at him.

"Oh, Samuel, that would be lovely. Just the two

of us?" she asks, hopefully, looking around the room for someone, Connie maybe, and when he nods, she beams.

Picking up her purse, she places a kiss on the cheek. "We'll talk soon," she tells me before bustling out the door with Sam. Just as I'm about to breathe a sigh of relief, she calls back over her shoulder, "Goodbye, hussy."

As the door slams, Lucifer and I look at each other before we both collapse laughing. "I'm so sorry," I apologize through my chuckles, and she waves me off, wiping a tear from her eye.

"Don't be, she's a hoot, but don't tell her I said that."

Finally, we settle, and I make us both a coffee. Once we're sitting comfortably, I tell her about Drusilla getting the mate marks, and she's thrilled that I've found another one. God, I can't believe how right this feels. Having Mom here, and her being happy for me and accepting of everything. My soul and heart are overflowing with joy. There are still some growing pains, doubts about why they gave me up, because I still don't know the whole story. But I'm willing to wait like she'd asked. I've not known for over twenty years, and a few more days or even weeks isn't long in the scheme of things. This makes me think of another question that has been burning a hole in my mind, and I can't hold it back any longer.

"Is my father your mate? Are you cheating on

him with the dungeon?" She looks shocked at my question before her eyes soften.

"Yes, your father is my mate, and he is the only one. No, I'm not cheating on him. I don't have sex with any of the patrons; I just absorb all the lusty feelings and emotions they put out. Kind of like you and Dru last night. Am I right?" Nodding, I think about it; I had fed on the emotions more with Drusilla, compared to sex with the boys.

"There's so much I want to tell you, but I'm not sure who can be trusted, and as a new demon, your mental walls are not going to be as stable as say Kai and Jagger who have had years to perfect them," she says, grabbing my hand and squeezing it. Before I can reply, the hallway door opens, and the rest of the team pours out.

"Hugh has called a meeting; he wants details and won't take my word for it that you don't remember. Everyone is required to attend." Zeph's voice is annoyed, but I can tell it's directed at Hugh and not me. "You're going to have to finish this later." He looks apologetically between Mom and me.

She nods, standing up and running her hands over her jeans. "That's okay. There are things I need to attend to as well. Remember, the geas I placed on you will prevent you from revealing I'm Jessamina's parent, but it might also stop you from saying anything it thinks is related to that topic. Best to generally steer clear unless you want it to try and shut you up. All is not right at the CD, and I'm pretty sure AoA has managed to turn a few of the staff working there."

"What do you know about the AoA?" Zeph asks her suspiciously, and I look at him, shocked.

Mom walks over and puts her hands on both his cheeks. "Never you mind. Raphael knows what I know, and he will let Team Alpha know if he thinks it's relevant. We all have our secrets to keep," she tells him before placing a kiss on his cheek. With a wave and a shouted "I'll see you soon, my beautiful daughter," she teleports out.

A dazed expression is still across Zeph's face as I snort my amusement. My mom packs one hell of a punch. "Come on, lover boy," I tease as I nudge him, "haven't we got somewhere to be?"

He shakes himself and heads for the door. "Yes. Mina, you need to suit up. We're back in circulation."

This information has my adrenaline rising in panic. Looking at the others, I notice they're all dressed in the black uniform. Mav and Zeph are both pulling on their boots while trick shrugs into his jacket that he pulled off the hook. Sander has flopped down in Lucifer's vacant seat and has a dagger in his hand, casually cleaning his finger-nails while Drusilla looks on in horror. "Don't do that on the couch!" she shrieks at him. He rolls his eyes, and the dagger disappears into thin air, and there's a little smirk to his lips that makes it all too obvious that he's baiting her. *That disappearing trick again.* .

Before I can ask how he did it, my eyes are drawn to Jagger and the way my mate fills out his CD uniform as though he was born to wear it. Trickling through my attraction to him, nervousness twists inside me at being in front of the council now that I've transitioned.. He must feel my uncertainty through our bond because he crosses over to me and hugs me tight. "You can do this," he reassures me. "Do you need some blood before we go?"

"No, I'm good for now." And it's true. After filling up on Dru last night and Jagger this morning, I'm feeling good. Sander huffs his disappointment, and the others laugh while I quickly run to my room to get changed and grab my wrist guard and magic wand.

———•·•·•———

Connie

"Quickly, Connie, I've been called back to the Collectors Division, and you can attend too. We're going to question this new girl that you bit." The disdain in my father's voice is as cutting as it has been every time he's yelled at me since I returned to the house. I roll my eyes at his words. He's always harping at me, but what can he do? It's not like he hasn't already done his worst to me. Ruined my life by using me as a guinea pig for his experiments. Promised me things he just wasn't able to deliver. He used to terrify me, but now he just makes me mad. Everyone else gets the new and improved formula, while I get stuck with what I am.

Yes, I almost got caught, and yes, I fucked up, but I wasn't expecting her to survive. *No one ever has before,* I think, rolling my eyes again.

"Is that a good idea, Daddy? What if she points the finger at me?" The look he gives me would cut a lesser AB to the quick, but I've become immune. My father is a pompous, jealous ass, who has gotten us in a situation we can't get out of and is dragging me down with him. I believe in our cause, but I was never supposed to get caught on Minzeon. It's his fault he didn't delay them longer. Now I'm trapped and being watched, and before long, they're going to want to probe my brain, and I won't be able to hide anything. Thank goodness this whole Mina thing has them distracted. Now we need an exit strategy from the CD but Dad keeps hanging in there, too hungry for any chance to have a victory over the Archangels that he's so envious of.

"My source says she doesn't remember, so we should be fine, but I have a plan to get them out of the way," he tells me as we leave the mansion.

"And Sammy, Dad? When are we going to bring him over to our side? You know that's what you promised me if I did all of this for you." I know

I'm whining, but it's the only thing that seems to work these days; he's so preoccupied. I'm excited about him making good on his promises. Finally something for me other than being his whipping girl. Sammy will be all mine, and there is nothing else the rest of that asshole team will be able to do to get him back. The transition is permanent, as I know intimately.

"Yes, yes. When Alpha gets called off on an assignment later this evening, I'll request that Sam remains behind to look after you. After all, they have enough members now that the demon has joined their group and the girl has recovered. We'll inject him with the formula tonight, especially now that I've perfected it. What would you like him to transform into, my sweet?"

"Oh, a dragon would be nice, Daddy." Not like my ugly spider. "Why couldn't you have made me a dragon?" I pout at the memories.

"Because insects were the only thing we had gotten right back when we started with you, and even that wasn't a perfect shift." That's right, fucked me right up. I shudder at the thought of what I went through. The pain was excruciating. Even now when I transform, it's slow and uncomfortable, not like the newer members of our cause. The lucky ones that benefitted from my suffering. The thought has me seething with loathing for my father, but I suck it up and smile prettily for him.

"That's good to know, Daddy, because I don't

think my voice is affecting him anymore, or at least it seems to be waning quicker than it used to," I complain.

"That's because the siren part of your formula was diluted, and constant contact is needed for it to be effective," he explains to me again like I'm an idiot, and I just want to stab him in the back. What little true affection existed between the two of us died long ago. Ours is now a relationship of necessity, though my father is egotistical enough to not realize that, still seeing me as his obedient daughter.

I will suck it up until I get what I want, which is Sam. I need him like I need to breathe, and I can feel him pulling away every time he leaves. It's that fucking bitch Mina.

She has some kind of hold over my Sammy; maybe she's got some kind of siren in her.

But that can't be right, I think, shaking my head. That's only something Daddy has been able to do. Stealing magic from the fictional creatures in the realms and putting them into ABs is a breakthrough no one else has ever achieved. I smack my head in frustration at the voices bouncing around, and they quiet down again. I'm sure no one has ever been clever enough to think about it before my daddy. The side effects are far overshadowed by the benefits, and there's no one around with the kind of mind that's needed to figure out how to manage the process. No one besides him, that is.

He stops just before the portal. "How would you

like to be reinfected with a newer potion?" he asks me, rubbing his hand across his chin. "You could be a dragon like your friend Sam?"

His suggestions strikes me mute, and I look at him with horror. Fuck, the thought of all that pain and the chance that my results would once again be compromised has my stomach reeling with nausea. Who knows if the original form would mix with the update? I could turn into something even uglier, more twisted than what I've already become. .

He's looking at me like he's expecting me to be ecstatic, and I guess part of me is. I always wanted to be something more than just a spider. Swallowing down my nerves, I muster up some semblance of enthusiasm since I don't want him getting suspicious of me. There's no escaping this anymore. I've made my bed; I need to lie in it. "If it makes me like Sam, then, of course, I'll give it a go," I tell him. Daddy seems happy as I follow him through the portal, crossing my fingers that bitch doesn't remember anything between now and then.

——■•••■——

Jessamina

The meeting room's packed when we arrive and find a place to sit or stand. I'm a little distracted because I still haven't heard from Kai, and I can't reach him telepathically.

"Jagger, I can't reach Kai. Do you think he's okay?"

"He's fine, sweetheart. I spoke to him not long ago," he reassures me, which isn't altogether that reassuring since it makes another troubling thought come to mind.

"How come you can speak to him but I can't? Am I broken?" Surprise at my question comes down the link.

"No, baby, I'm sure you're fine. Maybe it's the distance. Sometimes I can't get through to him either," he tells me, but there's a carefulness in his words that betrays he's thinking about this more deeply now. *"Don't worry about him."*

Easy for him to say, he hasn't got an ache in the heart like a piece is missing. Then again, he might. I watch him rub his chest in the same spot I do, and my mind gives me a little reminder of how the two of them had looked at each other, kissed each other. The two of them have a new spot for me in their lives, but they also have spots for each other that were reserved decades ago.

Before I can ask him about it, I'm approached by the other Archangels that were on the mission with us, aka 'the dads.' "Mina, so good to see you up and about." Zadkiel pulls me in for a hug, and my eyebrows shoot up. Wow, ok, we're hugging now. Over Zadkiel's shoulder, Uriel crosses his arms, a scowl on his face. But he must see my confusion because a smile crosses his lips briefly, and he shoots me a wink before adopting the grumpy look again.

"Yes," he grunts his agreement.

"You look so much better than when we last saw you," Azrael muses as I pull back from Zadkiel.

"All shiny and healthy, looks like you've transitioned well." Chamuel's comments have them all clearing their throats uncomfortably, and that has a smile crossing my lips as snort of laughter escapes. Sheepish looks cross their faces, and, as one, they all turn to head back to the table.

Raphael offers me his arm and escorts me to a chair while whispering in my ear, "Follow my lead, and I'll try and keep everything on the right track. Your mom has made sure we can't talk about some things anyway."

I can't hide my surprise as my head turns to look at him in shock, eyebrows raised in question. The others might have acclimated to the idea of their parents being friends with an Archdemon already, but it still strikes me as a bit weird that Mom is so close with the dads. He ruefully rubs his hair and laughs. "She has a few tricks up her sleeve that I didn't see coming, though it's not a bad thing," he adds, looking around the room. Everyone is looking at me expectantly, and I sit in the seat he shows me to.

"Only waiting on a couple now," he announces to the room, and I look around. Sam is still missing. I guess he needed to give his apologies to Maggie and then find a place to discreetly change clothes and teleport here, all without getting caught.

Just as I'm thinking this, two more rush into the room. A tall weedy-looking Archangel if the murky green wings he's displaying are any indication and my least favorite person in the world. Connie.

I hadn't seen her since before she went missing, and time has not been kind to her, not even recognizing her until I looked closely. She looks like a drug addict, and I can see a slight tremor in her hand. *Nerves,* I wonder, *or something else?*

"Where's Michael?" the Archangel I don't know asks. "Still too busy to be coming to meetings?"

"Yes, he is," Uriel answers without elaboration, and the newcomer's face settles into a scowl to rival Uriel's, seemingly uncaring that he's coming off as a major dick .

"Who's that?" I whisper to Drusilla, who's sitting next to me for moral support. She leans in.

"That's Connie's father, Sabboath."

Connie walks over to Mav and leans against him, proceeding to fall when he moves away from her. "Where's Sam?" she asks, looking around the room in concern. "He was gone all night." There's a pout to her lips and a possessive twist in her tone that nearly makes me growl. For a moment, I feel a bite on the edge of my fingertips, and I have to slam down with my self-control, hoping that no one noticed the tips of my claws starting to emerge.

"He stayed the night at our place, had breakfast

with us this morning, and was taking Maggie out for lunch. I'm sure he'll be here soon," he replies gruffly. Her eyes meet mine, and a hint of worry crosses them before a smug smile takes over her face, and she saunters over to where I am. She looks at my hand in Drusilla's and instantly dismisses me as a threat.

"Hello, Mina, it's been a while. So glad you were able to recover from your injuries. Strange that you got hit so hard. I guess you must just have inferior blood, almost like a demon." I hold in my shock at her words, but Dru's hand twitches in mine. With barely a moment's pause, I plaster an insincere smile on my face.

"Connie, I'd like to say you look well, but you look like shit. Have you been trying out some newfangled recreational drug? Maybe that's why you're having trouble remembering things."

A furious look crosses her face. "I hear I'm not the only one, bitch."

At those words, Sabboath drags her away to the other side of the table, drawing everyone's attention until Sam hurries in, apologizing for his tardiness. She tries to catch his eye, but he joins Team Alpha instead.

"How does Connie know about me being a demon?" I ask Dru, knowing I can't ask the others aloud right now, but needing to do something with the confusion and shock that hit me. .

"I'm not sure she does. She might be just saying it

because she's a bigoted bitch," Dru says even though I can feel her worry making our bond and her response feel tight.

"It can't have been Sam, right? He wouldn't do that, and he has the geas on him too?" I ask her. She doesn't respond, but her worry increases through the bond, and my heart sinks. Why is she so worried about Sam? Looking over at him I catch him staring at me, lips downturned and eyes full of confusion and anguish. When Raphael clears his throat and starts to talk, he breaks eye contact and shakes his head as if to clear it. Now Dru must feel *my* worries increase because she squeezes my hand tight in support as we listen to what the Archangel has to say.

Chapter Sixteen

Samuel

I rush into the room, and the meeting gets started. Standing with Team Alpha, my head feels the clearest it's been in days. My mind is not a confusing ball of messed up dark thoughts, and it feels like a weight has been lifted off my chest. As I listen to the Archangels run over Mina's memories with her, my mind starts to wonder.

What's wrong with me? I keep having Jekyll and Hyde moments, and they've gotten progressively worse since I've been with Connie. It was like that before, too, when we were at the academy. I would find myself deliberately hurting Mina during sparring without not knowing why. There would be a surge of extreme anger, and I would lash out, but the minute I hurt her, her pain would break through the haze, leaving behind immense guilt. God, I couldn't apologize enough. It made it worse that she trusted me so much she bought every word of it.

Sabboath and Connie catch my eye across the room, and she winks in my direction. A shudder threatens to escape, but I hold it in, somehow knowing that it'll be more dangerous for me to reveal the chaos of my mind to her than anyone else. Looking around the room, everyone is paying attention to Raphael questioning Mina. Well, everyone except for Uriel; he's watching me. He looks between Connie and me, his eyes narrowing, and I nudge Sander in the side.

"Can you ask your dad if I could have a word, please?" I ask him telepathically. He nods his head, and after a minute, Uriel nods in acceptance. Feeling a bit relieved, I tune back into what's happening around me.

"I think I need to have a look inside your brain to see if we can trigger anything," Raphael is saying to Mina.

Before she can reply, Sabboath jumps in. "I think we should give her a few days grace like you've given my Connie. See if anything comes back on its own," he suggests, and I swear you could have pushed Trick's dad over with a feather.

"I'm not sure that's the best course," Raphael argues. "Anything she knows could be vital to our fight against AoA. It would be best if we could access it now."

"But it also could do more harm than good," Sabboath responds. "After all, she almost didn't recover. Actually, now that I'm thinking about it...how *did* she recover?" He looks between Mina and Raphael, pushing for the information he already knows and hoping to stall Raphael by pushing for answers they don't want to give. The real question is why he wants to give Mina the few days away from the Archangels' prioring intervention.

"Ah, ok then, but we do need answers. AoA has been ahead of us on everything, and we need to get in front, play offense as opposed to defense," Raphael backtracks smoothly, avoiding the question

"Yeah, because our defense is letting us down, and we're losing the metaphorical Superbowl," Uriel chimes in, the two of them looking pleased with their Earth references.

Clementine stands up, rolling her eyes at them. "If we're done with the analogies, can we move on, please?" The Archangels nod graciously and let her take the floor. Sabboath looks animated for the first time today, and Connie is practically dancing in her seat. They both look like Earth children waiting for Santa on Christmas Eve. They must have a plan, something that they've organized and haven't told me about. Otherwise why would Sabboath be advocating for Mina? That's not like him at all, so he must want her in circulation. My heart sinks at the thought of her walking into trouble. I really need to speak to Uriel *now*.

"We've received a distress beacon from Habbalea again." Team Alpha slumps in defeat, and Sander actually groans out loud. She holds up her hands. "I know what happened last time, but we can't just ignore it in case it's a demon stuck on the planet. You know its atmosphere and weather aren't conducive to living. It's an easy mission to ease back into after your break. Get in, have a look around, and get out if there's no one to be found."

Team Alpha nod their heads and prepare to leave the room, but Sabboath chimes in. "I would like Samuel to stay and keep my daughter safe, please. This seems like a convenient distraction, and, well, I wouldn't want her to disappear again. My heart broke when she disappeared last time, and I'm not sure I would recover if it happened again" I roll my eyes, finding it ridiculous that he's really laying it on so thick. Connie's behavior in the past has shown a different kind of relationship to what he's portraying.

Then I think for a moment and my body freezes, heart skipping a beat when I realize what he just asked. I *really* don't want to do that. I look to Clementine, who is conferring with Uriel, hoping she's got some reason for why my team desperately needs my company. "That's fine," she replies to him, "but Uriel needs to speak to him first."

Sabboath's eyes narrow, but he smiles wanly and agrees. "Connie and I will meet you at home then." They both depart, leaving the rest of the room looking undeniably relieved to have the poisonous father/daughter duo out of their midst.

Team Alpha surrounds me, and I grab Mina by the hands and pull her to the side. "I don't know what's been happening to me, and I don't know what will happen in the future, but I'm sorry for my behavior. Tell me you'll see me when you get back, so we can actually have that talk?"

She looks down at my hands wrapped around her then back into my eyes. The confusion I know she's feeling shines bright in them, and I don't blame her, guessing my own mirror that same feeling. My heart sinks, thinking I've truly made an ass of myself this time. "Ok, Samuel, but you really hurt me. I feel like you dont care because you weren't even there when I woke up. What happened between the attack and now, that changed your attitude? It feels like it was when Connie was around last time. Is she your focus once again?" I'm done putting up with it. I'm dealing with a lot right now, and something tells me that life isn't going to get any less complicated. I need to know that anyone who I trust is worthy of that, that they won't make me doubt myself or what I can bring to this team. If you can't do that, then we'll have to reevaluate what the relationship between us can ever be.".''

Now that Connie's not here, I pull her close and whisper in her ear, "I know I screwed up the whole demon form thing, but I was surprised. Your demon form is beautiful, just like your soul." I can feel the tension in her body lessen as her body relaxes against mine. Her scent fills my nose, and a bolt of lust hits my groin. I almost groan at the feeling but manage to keep it in, enjoying this brief moment where I can just hold the girl that I know I've wanted in my arms for so long. *Why is it so easy to admit that to myself now? Where's this me keep disappearing to?* She pulls away from me, but I hold onto her hand. "I'll do better, Mina. My emotions are all over the place, but I promise I'll do better. You're right, and I need to treat you the way that you truly deserve," I swear to her. She still looks unsure, but she smiles and nods her head. I wish the rest of them good luck, and when Sander still looks at me with anger in his eyes, I know Mina's not the only one I have to fix things with. Watching them walk out the door, I pray that they stay safe and I get a chance to make things right. Clementine and Hugh follow them out a moment later, and I'm left with just the Archangels as I hear the door close behind me.

Dad approaches me first. "What's going on, Sam? You don't look well."

Collapsing into the seat, I put my head in my hands. "I think I'm going crazy; there's something wrong with me." Despair coats my words as I speak, my dad's presence allowing me to let those feelings touch me without putting up a wall to protect myself. "A nasty voice in my head is telling me to do things like hurt Mina. It used to happen before, and I never put the two together." My eyes meet theirs as I look up. "I think Connie's doing something to me."

The five Archangels exchange glances, and

Raphael sighs deeply. "We've long suspected that Sabboath and his daughter Connie are associated with AoA and possibly the person in charge," Zadkiel tells me, his fingers steepled in front of him.

"But finding outright proof has been difficult, and we cannot accuse him without it," Azrael chimes in.

"We can check you over and put some protection in place, but how would you feel about being a double agent? We need someone on the inside, but up until now we haven't been able to," Dad tells me. "With Connie gone, Sabboath was very careful with his movements and words."

"Tell it like it really is. Everyone we send looking ends up fucking dead," Uriel spits out. "We're not telling anyone as yet, but we lost Bravo."

"How can you lose a team?" I ask, confused. He waves a hand, and five photos appear on the holo-screen above the desk. Five bodies strung up. Two have been hanged, while the other three are staked to crosses, and it looks like they've been eviscerated as well. My mouth drops open in horror. *Oh, lost as in dead, fuck me!*

"This was a favored method of some of Hammus's pet Archdemons during their war. But they're all dead now; this is AoA, or whoever the puppet master is, sending a warning not to stick our noses in."

Uriel conjures up a bottle of what looks like whiskey and slams it down. He conjures up more, one glass landing in front of each of us. Everybody raises a glass in silent respect for Bravo and slams them down. The whiskey burns its way down but brings a sense of calm.

"This is going to be dangerous, Sam, but you've the skills to get yourself out if you need to, and they don't know that. So even if they take away your wrist guard, you're safe," Dad tells me, worry coating his voice.

I don't even have to think about it. "Yes, I'll do it. I need to know what they've been doing to me. I've been horrible to everyone, but especially Mina, and I need to do something to make it up to them. There has to be a way that I can feel like myself again, feel *good* about myself again"

Raphael fidgets a bit, which isn't like him, and the others won't meet my eyes. "You can't tell them," Dad blurts out. My heart drops at his words as I realize I might as well kiss any relationship with Mina goodbye.

"They need authentic reactions, so they won't set off any suspicion," Azrael tells me. "I know my son; he wouldn't let you do it on your own." He's right. Mav would want in on the plan.

"We promise we'll smooth it all over once we get what we need," Zadkiel assures me. "Zeph will understand that it was ordered. They'll forgive you."

I'm not sure if I truly believe that statement, but I nod my head and agree. Before I can say anything else, a bright light fills the room, and when it clears and my eyes recover, standing before me is a woman so beautiful she brings tears to my eyes. Rubbing at them, the brilliance dies down a little until I can see her normally.

The dads all get down on one knee and bow, Dad nudging me until I join them. Holy shit, this must be Mylea. What could the goddess want?

"Samuel Mason, you're to be rewarded for your honesty in admitting you were struggling and your bravery for agreeing to what will be a challenging task for you." Her voice is musical and transcendent, bringing a sense of peace and tranquility which has been missing in my life just recently. She places a hand on my head. "I will clear out the darkness and put a protection on you," she tells me as her hand starts to heat. "This does not mean you'll not have to do some things you may not want to. But it will protect you from the more harmful ramifications, and it will also protect you from any questioning that you won't want to answer," she says mysteriously as her hand cools and leaves my head. I slump on my knees, and Dad grabs hold of me to keep me upright.

"Know this, Samuel, though it may be a struggle, I'm always with you." And with that, the goddess disappears.

The six of us get back to our feet, though my head is a bit foggy, so I sit back down in a chair. "Okay, then. It looks like you have better protection than we thought you would. Divine intervention bodes well." Raphael has a pleased look on his face, and some of the anxiety has cleared from Dad's.

"Why did she do that?" I ask, still a little fuzzy. "I thought the gods and goddess weren't allowed to interfere."

"They're not supposed to," Zadkiel muses, "but when you look at it, Hammus has been doing it from the start. Did you know that the people of Reath originally had magic? Potions and small abilities like telekinesis and telepathy. That's the magic that slowly escaped and infected Earth, and then there was none left here. The balance was thrown out, and that's when he started his crusade. His demons would never have had a war if he hadn't influenced them."

The dads all look thoughtful as I look around the table at them. They also look tired, which is not like them at all.

"This is probably Mylea's way of evening the playing field. They can't interfere directly, but she and the other three have made small plays here and there over the years. They've been playing the long game, and they're waiting to see how it pans out. Matoz missing is a bump in the road that was never expected," Azrael explains wearily.

"No, but that's our job to worry about," Uriel says, standing up. "We're about to join Michael; he has a lead. So, let's get this finished," he grumbles, and a blazing sword appears in his hand. "I need to stab something." He swings it, and it sings as it swooshes through the air. Uriel makes me smile; at least the grumpy bastard never changes. He's nothing like the twins.

"Report when you can," Raphael orders. "If I'm unavailable, report to Jophial. She's always around here somewhere and can pass me the information. Don't trust anyone else," he warns me.

"Thank you, Sam." Dad hugs me tightly, and I can feel how proud he is through the way his arms crush me to him. "You're making a big sacrifice, and we recognize that." With those words, the Archangels leave, and I wearily make my way back to Sabboath's house, wondering what's in store for me, hoping I survive it, and praying that the team forgives me for my deception.

—— • ◆ • ——

Sabboath approaches me as soon as I enter their mansion. "Samuel, could you join Connie and me in my office?" Surprised to see him waiting for me, I follow him into the room. Connie's bouncing up and down on the sofa, her excitement palpable, and a sense of caution immediately overtakes me. Sabboath takes a seat behind his desk and steeples his hands together, looking at me cautiously.

"Now, Sam, I've gotten the feeling in the past that you aren't happy with your position on Team Alpha and within the Collectors Division." I think about his words, and I guess when I'm with Connie, that's how I feel, though I'm sure that's more her influence than real.Not sure whether I can give a convincing affirmative, I keep my mouth shut, hoping he'll make the effort to fill the silence.

He continues without an answer from me. "We too feel like that and have done something about it. Connie thinks you have the potential to be an asset to our cause, and I'm leaning toward believing her. You're a powerful young man who has shown his loyalty to Connie by the way you take care of her so well, both now and in the past, even if it does cause a rift sometimes between you and your teammates." He gives me a knowing look, but I'm surprised he's scrutinized my team and me so closely. Then his actual other words register. *Huh, they're not beating around the bush. This is the information I need. Can it really be this easy?* I think, my suspicion rising even further.

"We would like you to join the cause, but I'm afraid it requires further proof of loyalty." Connie puts her hands on me, and this time the tingle of the darkness that appeared every other touch is absent. Whatever Mylea did is protecting me. I blow out a big sigh of relief; luckily, they must assume it's nerves.

"What kind of proof?" I ask. The concern in my voice isn't for show; I'm genuinely worried about what I'm about to be asked to do.

"We have created a formula that gives our members the ability to shift forms." His words shock me, and the drop of my jaw is a real reaction. Shifting is something that's only in Earth's fictional stories. No one has had that capability before. *How did they manage that?*

"Shapeshifting?' My tone is incredulous, yet Sabboath is smiling smugly, every ounce of his pride showing he means what he's saying.

"Exactly! It gives our members the edge over the Collectors Division and normal ABs. We would need you to take this formula to prove your loyalty to us." *Fuck, ok.* Well, I need to trust Mylea and hope like hell that she's protected me like she promised. Just as I'm thinking this, the spot on my head where she touched me heats up, and my nerves disappear. I guess I don't have a choice now that they've spilled their guts. Probably end up dead if I say no. Thinking of my team and those last moments of Mina in my arms, I take a deep breath.

"I'm in," I declare, and a satisfied look crosses his face; like the ridiculous cliché he is, he rubs his hands together and sneers.

"Excellent." I feel a prick in the back of my neck, and I turn to see Connie placing a syringe on a coffee table. Her lips are twisted into an evil grin, one I've never seen on her face before, and excitement practically oozes off her.

A searing pain starts to flow through my body, and I hunch over in agony, clutching my stomach. She begins to stroke my head, cooing to me. "Oh, Sammy, it hurts so much, but when it's finished, you will be better. Stronger and more powerful." Her voice has a touch of crazy in it that I can't deny any longer. *Is that to be my fate too?*

"What animal did you end up giving him, Daddy? Did you give him a dragon?" Her voice is grating, but *holy shit*, did she just say dragon?

"Why give him a dragon when I can make him so much more?" Sabboath's smarmy voice is the last thing I hear before I escape the agonizing pain that is now contracting my body.

Chapter Seventeen

Jessamina

After kissing Dru goodbye, I follow the others as we make our way down to the portal room. Sander's constant grumbling is getting on my nerves after my surprise interaction with Samuel.

"God, Sander, won't you shut up? What's the fucking problem?" I finally snap at him as we enter the second elevator for our trip down. The surprise on their faces makes me snort, and I realize I was out of line. They've also seen sassy Mina before, but I don't think they've seen nervous and cranky Mina much in our years together. I fiddle with my magic wand in my hair and avoid looking at them as I apologize. "Sorry, Sam has me all confused with the hot and cold shit, ignore my grumpiness. But seriously, what is wrong with you?"

"Habbalea's atmosphere is slightly toxic after the war, and normal ABs have to wear breathing gear, and because they don't know we're not normal, we're going to have to wear it too," Trick explains to me, looking at Sander sympathetically.

He's wrapped his arm around him, but it doesn't seem like Sander is taking much comfort from his partner's effort.

Mav slaps him on the back. "Sander here is slightly claustrophobic and doesn't like to wear the gear." His voice is amused, and I frown at him, not sure what's so amusing about the whole scenario.

Feeling sorry, I step up to Sander and wrap my arms around him, hugging him, and Trick in the process. He returns the embrace and snuggles into my neck, tickling me, his familiar clove scent surrounding me and bringing comfort. "There's no need to tease him about it," I scold Mav. "How about I give you an incentive? If you wear the BA and don't complain the whole time, you and Trick can be my dinner!" I suggest to him, knowing that it'll kick him out of his funk quickly.

He pulls back to see if I'm serious, and when he sees me smiling at him and nodding my head, he fist bumps the air. "Fucking deal." He holds his hand up for a high five from Trick, who indulges him with a smile on his lips and a look full of heat shot at me.

Mav's smug look disappears, and Jagger and Zeph laugh, the latter slapping his hand on Mav's back. "Bad luck, brother."

The elevator doors open, and we all step out, the atmosphere lighter than it had been moments ago. Zeph leads us to the left into an equipment room to pick up the BA headgear. The room is empty of any personal but is filled with the smell of metal and rubber from the stored equipment. I can see backpacks hanging on hooks, and there are shelves lined with various tools, weapons, and PPE gear that may be needed while on assignment. Swords, nets, and chains litter the surfaces so that any AB who stops here will be more than prepared for their mission. One wall of shelves is filled with rations. Water pods and other liquids as well as field ration kits for sustenance for long assignments. Another shelf is dedicated to protective clothing, including one bundle that is labeled acid proof and another with the caption, fireproof.

"What the hell is this for?" I ask, holding up a wetsuit that looks to have built in flippers but only comes to up to the waist. Zeph is busy handing Mav and Jagger the headgear while he signs some requisition forms, but Trick and Sander both look at what I'm holding and laugh when they see what it is.

Trick comes over and takes it from me. "I keep forgetting how new you are to all this." He pulls open the zip and puts it down on the ground for me to step into. I play along and put my feet into it, and he pulls it up the length of my body until it sits at my waist.

"These are for use in the mermaid kingdom, or Poseidon's realm, or anywhere really that involves time underwater. This is a male suit, but for this demonstration it really doesn't matter." He zips it up in the back. Meanwhile, Sander's face has taken on a cheeky grin that is undeniably attractive. *I'm looking forward to paying out on our deal later.*

"I dont know...I think Mina should have taken her other outfit off for this demo." He wiggles his eyebrows, and Trick rolls his eyes, knowing better than to feed into Sander's teasing. He reaches into the front of the waistband and presses a button. The material instantly molds to my form, and a tearing sensation in my neck takes me completely off guard. Crying out in pain, I slap a hand to the spot where the ache is and gasp in shock. Running my fingers up and down the side of my neck, I feel three slits have developed in the skin and are now moving in and out with every breath I take.

"A mermaid spell?" I ask, incredulous. They both grin at my surprise. Normal ABs can't breathe underwater, so this must be the solution they came up with.

"Can you do normal bodily functions in this?" I ask, my mind having instantly dirty thoughts. I always wanted to know how mermaids have sex. Sander's eyes twinkle, and I bet he's also had the same thoughts. He leans in and whispers in my ear.

"How about when we get some time off, you and I test that out?"

My nipples pebble with the thought, and I shiver with excitement, hoping my eyes aren't flashing red. "You're on," I tell him, and Trick just rolls his eyes at the both of us.

"Hey, stop messing around!" Zeph sounds exasperated, and I'm half-expecting him to put his hands on his hips and start tapping his toes. "We've got to go."

"Sorry," I apologize, feeling guilty, but Trick and Sander just ignore him as they help me out of the suit. Once the button is pressed again, the gills disappear and my legs unlock, and they can peel the suit down. Putting everything away, we take our headgear from the others, and then we head to the end of the long, cavernous room for another world jump.

Clementine is already down there, clipboard in hand. "Alright, a quick in and out. We've programmed in the coordinates where the distress signal came from. It's one of the destroyed cities, so it may take a while to search. Let us know if we need to expect refugees and activate the chip when you're ready to return home," she orders before wishing us luck and stepping back as the portal opens.

Placing our headgear on, Drusilla's voice echoes in my ear as she does a mic check. Once she's satisfied we're all online, she gives us the go-ahead. "Guys, we need to make this quick. There's another solar flare predicted in a couple of hours, so if you don't want to be stuck again, you better haul ass."

The four of them groan, and Jagger and I watch as they all grab already packed survival bags off the wall to the left of us. "You two grab one as well. If we do get trapped, there are some caves we can hide out in, or sometimes the cities have an intact building," Zeph says.

"Last time, we were trapped for three days," Trick warns us as we watch Mav run back to the equipment room.

Jagger and I grab a pack, and I open it and look inside. A week's worth of water pods are inside as well as military-style food rations, a space blanket, and a medical kit. I'm just throwing mine over my shoulder when Mav returns and hands out guns to us all along with an extra BA canister he'd grabbed from the supply room. I store these inside as well, and we step through the portal. This time the journey is short, and I experience nothing like what I had in the past. Instead, my portal experience seems blessedly normal. It's with a sigh of relief that I get my first look at Habbalea.

Lightning flashes through the hazy atmosphere as my gaze scans our surroundings, finding a ruined medieval city built into a cliff face not too far from where we've landed. Between us and it is a waste-land of rocky outcrops and dead trees, the atmosphere so charged I can feel the ends of my ponytail reacting to the static.

A rush of dry air blows a dust cloud around, and it quickly turns into a funnel that races away from us in the opposite direction. I follow its path, watching it cross a desert plain, building and pulling more and more debris into its funnel, a destructive force with nothing to stop its path.

A noise draws my attention back to the others. They've started walking toward the ruins, and one of them kicks a rock that rolls a distance before coming to rest again. "This castle was Lucifer's stronghold during the war," Jagger tells me through the BA as we follow them, his voice carrying an eerie quality to it. "And one of the last things to fall before the resistance defeated Hammus's followers."

"What was his goal for all this?" I look around at the destruction before us, shaking my head. It must have once been a beautiful city but now is a pile of rubble and ruin. The castle towers and some of the buildings are the only thing still recognizable. The castle, carved out of the stone cliff, was a little hard to destroy, I guess.

"Nobody knows," Zeph says, looking around and keeping an eye out for someone who may have sent a distress signal, but there's no sign of life. The atmosphere is creepy, and a feeling of being watched pricks me in the middle of my back. Uneasily, I turn on the spot. but there's nothing to see.

"Dad says nobody knows for sure, but the Archdemons he was able to influence lost their minds completely and had to be cut down. Your mom, my dad, and Belphegor are the only ones that were able to resist the pull, but they were the three oldest. They think some escaped the chaos but haven't been seen again, and the concern is whether he would be able to grab hold of their minds and infect them too. Better they stay hidden wherever they are."

"Guys," Drusilla's voice comes through our coms with a hint of fear, "something is coming up behind you, and it's moving quickly."

Turning, we watch as a massive plume of dust moves in our direction. We quickly toss our survival packs behind some rubble in the hope that they will make it through and wait to see what's coming. The guys fan out forming a v formation with Zeph in front, Sander and Trick on one side, and Jagger and Mav on the other, leaving me in the middle, protected. Rolling my eyes, I stay where I am for now. I appreciate the thought, but I'm hoping I won't need it. As we wait, adrenaline rushes into my system along with another kind of hunger. This time, it's not blood or sex that I want. This time, I'm ready for action.

"Looks like a sandstorm," Mav responds, and she quickly replies.

"Ah, no, not unless sandstorms have a heat signature."

"Fuck!" Zeph releases his wings and pulls a blazing sword from thin air. Ripping off his BA, he throws it to the side. "No time for pretend now," he announces, and we all follow suit, donning weapons and removing the BA. I activate my magic wand, and it separates into two daggers that start blazing with a light that shoots a rush of power up my arms. *Whoa!*

"Nice weapons, Mina." Sander whistles, and I watch as Jagger assumes his demon form. I stay in my normal one, and he gives me a weird look.

"They haven't seen it yet," I tell him telepathically, and he frowns, choosing to reply out loud.

"No time to be shy, Mina, demon up." The others give me nods, and I roll my eyes, hoping they're the kind of men I thought they were.

"Okay, but don't freak out," I warn them. "Oh, and the wings are staying in until I learn to use the useless things." They all give me funny looks at that but agree. Letting go of my human form, I embrace my demon. A shudder of relief flows through my body, and my tail stretches out behind me, the sensation akin to one of those perfect back stretches that feels so satisfying.

"Holy shit!" Sander, of course, can't keep his mouth shut, but it's whispered with reverence instead of the horror I'd been anticipating. Sucking up my nerves, I look up and see their eyes are full of admiration and an unexpected heat. Before anyone can say anything, a humongous roar rips across the plane; the ground is vibrating with whatever is coming.

"Fuck, what could it be? Nothing that big lived here to start with, and even if it had, the atmosphere would make it unable to survive." Trick's voice is full of concern, but behind him, his wings shiver with anticipation. Similar to his father's, his wings are an ombre fade of green, but there's no white. They start light at the top and darken until they're a very dark green at the bottom.

"Not sure, but it has to be magic," Zeph replies. "Nothing else makes sense." The cloud is almost at us, and still, we can't see what's coming.

"I thought magic couldn't be used in other realms," I shout out over the incoming noise.

"It can't be, but that doesn't mean that they can't drop a magical creature here," Mav tosses back. His wings are a solid black that fades out to gray with a shiny reflective silver along each feather, giving a holographic look to them. He launches himself into the air, big wings rippling with the effort, and hovers above the ground in anticipation for the coming fight.

"What the fuck." Jagger's horrified voice draws my attention away from all the beautiful, 'normal' angel wings and back to the creature before us. Out of the dust appears a creature I'd only ever read about at the Academy. One that usually keeps to itself inside the mythical creatures realm, one that looks decidedly pissed off. The giant Japanese lizard roars out its anger, and this time everything shakes around us.

"Well, at least he should be easy to dispose of." Sander's cocky words make my confidence soar, but Zeph soon destroys that.

"Don't be so enthusiastic; we don't know what they've done to it. Jagger, you and Mina deal with it down here, and we'll deal with it in the sky," he orders, and we all nod our response. Jagger and I start to run toward it, and a feeling of purpose flows through my body.

Yes. This is what I've been missing. I've been floundering with all the new stuff and getting back to basics, to what I had always planned to do with my life, feels right. A calmness and clarity I had been missing flows through me, and that hunger for action intensifies.

While he's distracted by the angels in the air, I launch myself at the big lizard's legs in the hope of severing some tendons, but before I can get too close, his giant tail swings around and smacks my body, sending me flying sideways. The air explodes out of me in a groan as I hit the ground hard. Shaking my head, I assess the damage, but what I see when I look down stuns me. Shimmery pink and golden scales cover my whole body, and as I feel around, up my face too. I stick my dagger into one, and it bounces off of it, no painful sensation. Crap, this is awesome. They're similar to the scales on the dragon I met what feels like a lifetime ago.

Jagger's shout of pain quickly brings my attention back to the fight, and I jump up and rush back in. Dodging the tail this time, I lunge at the lizard and quickly use my two daggers as climbing picks to pull my way up his body. He has stab marks all over him from the others' swords, and its bellows of fury are starting to sound like bellows of pain. We need to end this poor creature's suffering. It's not his fault.

My scales protect my body from his rough hide, and I make it to his head unscathed. Sitting on his neck like a rodeo rider, I can hear the angels in the sky screaming at me, but I have this sorted. My body feels like it's running on autopilot, knowing exactly what it needs to do. Fusing the daggers back into a sword, I raise it high above my head and plunge it down through the middle of his neck.

A last pitiful roar sounds out, and the creature instantly disappears back to the realm it came from, but now I'm left plummeting through the air. *Crap! Didn't quite think that out.* Before I hit the ground, a pair of warm, strong arms wrap around me, stopping my descent. Looking up, the fury in Sander's eyes is astounding. I'm not sure I've ever seen him look at me like that before, and guilt slightly dims the triumph I felt a moment ago.

His white and gold wings beat furiously to keep the both of us in flight. "Damn it, Mina! What were you thinking?" he demands as he brings us back to the ground.

Unsure how to diffuse the situation, I kiss him on the cheek. "My hero," I tease him, and his eyes soften. "Can't say I was, really. I sort of went into autopilot."

"Dru's screaming in my head, demanding to

know what's going on. I think I'll skip telling her about the part where you almost fell to your death even though you have wings," he tells me sarcastically and puts me down on my own feet. He wanders away to have a telepathic conversation with his sister. My telepathy still seems to be wonky, as I'm not able to hear her. The same as I still can't hear Kai, so it must be a distance thing like Jagger said. I must need to stretch my telepathy muscles.

"What's this?" Awe fills Jagger's voice as he runs a hand over my scales, a shiver of desire following the trail of his hand. That's weird; I can feel *that* but not a blade. *Maybe it's the succubus part of me?*

"Nice, right? When I took that first hit, these appeared. It seems like they're blade and big lizard proof. Not sure I want to test them out on a bullet, though." I try and keep the words light.

The boys release their weapons to wherever they came from, I must ask about that sometime, and get rid of their wings, while Jagger stays in his demon form. I'm about to will mine away, but looking down at my body, I realize that when my scales covered me, my clothes disappeared. So I either walk around naked or leave myself covered by my armor. Looking around at all the sand, I decide to stay in demon armor but try something new. The ones on my head disappear as I think about them and will them away, and I leave the ones covering the rest of my body. *Cool!*

Mav grabs our packs and hands them back to

us, so I rustle around for a water pod, my throat itching with thirst. When I down a couple, I realize that water is not going to cut it, and my fangs almost burst through my gums when I acknowledge the real source of my thirst. "Ah, guys. I'm going to need a drink," I tell them awkwardly.

Sander replies, distracted, "Haven't you got any water pods in your..." He breaks off, and his eyes widen when he comprehends what I mean. "Oh. A *drink*."

"Yeah, I guess fighting a big lizard gives a girl a thirst." I'm looking at the ground a little embarrassed. *First the demon form, now this. Can't a girl catch a break?*

"Well, it's a good thing I'm here, then isn't it?" The familiar voice has my head shooting up, and like a slow-motion movie scene, Kai comes strolling out of the ruins of the castle not far from us.

"Dude, you've been here this whole time," Jagger growls, "and you didn't help?" Though the growl says otherwise, I can feel that he's happy and relieved to see Kai. Despite his reassurance about my faulty telepathy, he must have really been worried about what our mate had gotten up to.

Kai holds his hands up in defense. "Whoa, big guy, I only arrived to watch our princess deal the fatal blow."

"Where did you come from?" Zeph's voice is heavy with suspicion as Kai gets to me and pulls me in for a searing kiss. My heart skips a beat, but the pain I was feeling at his absence eases. He then pulls Jagger in for a kiss, too, before replying.

"Follow me. It's time you met the resistance." He walks back into the ruins, leaving us to follow behind like puppies. Zeph and Mavromichali growl their annoyance, but we follow along as requested, curiosity only growing with each step.

Chapter Eighteen

Jessamina

Kai leads us out of the weather and deep into the ruined castle, and it's suddenly eerily quiet like all the sound has been cut off. We enter a cavernous throne room carved into the rock behind the castle, with destroyed decorations and furnishings littering the polished floor. On the wall at the far end is a giant tapestry featuring a beautiful woman surrounded by four out-of-this-world handsome men.

"Who is that?" I ask, my voice echoing around the space. I'm pretty sure I know, and for some reason, the woman looks familiar, but I'm not sure why.

"That's the goddess Mylea," Zeph replies.

"And her four consorts, including that bastard Hammus," Jagger growls, pointing him out. He's sitting slightly apart from them with a calculating look in his piercing blue eyes. His coal-black hair seems to absorb all the light surrounding it, and his pale complexion shines out of the piece of work.

He has a menacing feeling about him like his eyes would follow you around the room no matter where you went.

Kai heads directly to the tapestry and pulls it away from the wall. How cliché, a secret passageway. I roll my eyes, and he blows me a kiss. "Come on now, be adventurous. Oh, and you may want to tell Dru what's happening because she won't be able to reach you after this. Just tell her to tell the CD that it's a solar flare." With that, he disappears behind it, leaving us to follow.

"That guy's a real asshole," Sander growls before putting on that face that shows he's having a telepathic conversation with Drusilla. When he's done, he pulls the tapestry aside and gestures for me to go first.

The tunnel is narrow enough that we can only walk in single file. It has a damp unused smell about it, and I hear, rather than see, creatures scuttling about in the shadows. The tunnel opens out into a larger room, but as I wait for the others behind me, I look around. There are no exits, and the walls are straight up and down, not even a way to climb them; they're unnaturally smooth. Looking up, there's a hazy light, but it's not an open space. It seems more like a reflective window or something.

The others are muttering as Jagger, who was bringing up the rear, finally enters the room. Kai is just leaning casually against one of the walls, his smug ass look on and a claw flicked out, cleaning his nails. Rolling my eyes, I'm about to tell him off when suddenly the floor rumbles and starts to move downward. We're all thrown slightly off balance with the sudden movement but quickly right ourselves. Kai, of course, is steady as a rock.

"Hammus really did a poor job of looking after his creations," Kai starts conversationally, not concerned in the least that the floor's moving, so we all relax too. "And when he had all but crushed this world's spirit, three Archdemons decided that the demon way of life needed to be preserved and started planning a resistance."

The elevator thing rumbles as it continues its descent. The temperature drops the further we go down, but I seem to be unaffected by it. Score one for demon genetics. "Pockets of surviving families were found and spirited away to a secret location right under the nose of those hell-bent on destroying them. And those that continued to create chaos were taken care of by the Archangel council. Finally, it was declared that demons were all but extinct. Of course, there were some located on Reath, but Hammus was not willing to go against Mylea to hunt those down. Since Habbalea now had no remaining life on it, or so he thought, Hammus looked toward new interests beyond his own planet."

The elevator finally comes to a shuddering halt, and two large metal doors open. "I just don't understand why the other gods didn't stop him," I muse, unable to reconcile how someone could destroy his own creations.

"Because their hands were tied. When they came into existence, they were unable to lift a hand against one another, probably due to their mate bond. It's the way it's always been," my mother explains, stepping into the elevator and wrapping her arms around me. Shock at seeing her must show on my face, and she laughs.

"Come on, this is another one of those things that I couldn't explain earlier. Let's get you guys cleaned up, some food, and we'll talk."

Lucifer and Kai lead us through a subterranean city flourishing with life. Demons are scattered throughout, families with playing children, couples laughing and kissing, and thriving business full of patrons. There are cafes and shops, and I even see a little day-care with children playing on swings and throwing balls. Most adults are in their demon form, no fear of being persecuted.

The guys' faces are filled with amazement, Jagger included. "*This* is what you've been doing?" he asks Kai incredulously, the look in eyes and the stiffness of his body showing how hurt he is. "This is why you wouldn't leave with me?"

Kai nods his head, and I look at Jagger in shock. "You didn't know about this?"

He shakes his head. "No, when I went to the academy, my parents had a place on Reath, and I lived there. Lucifer and Belphegor did too. That's where I thought Kai was the whole time, sulking about me leaving."

Kai scoffs and rolls his eyes. "Thanks a lot."

"Why wasn't I told about this?" Jagger asks, hurt in his voice as he looks between Kai and Mom.

"Your dream, from day one practically, was to join the academy," Mom says gently, "and your dad didn't want to force your hand. After a few years, he still thought you would join us eventually, so why not let you spread your wings." Some of his hurt disappears, and he nods thoughtfully.

"I guess that's fair," he says to her but turns to Kai, pointing his finger, "But your guilt trip at me going to academy when you were keeping a secret wasn't fair. You're an ass." Kai has the grace to look ashamed but doesn't respond.

"And now?" Zeph buts in. "What's the point of us all knowing now?" We arrive at a building that's a replica to the castle upstairs with two giant wooden doors that are opened by two armor-clad demons who salute as Mom walks by.

"Look, I'll tell you, but why don't you freshen up? Most of you are covered in blood and don't smell so great." The guys sniff the air and realize that mutant lizard blood stinks, their faces twisting in grimaces that almost make me laugh out loud. She leads us through the castle, which has people buzzing everywhere.

"How long ago was this war?" I ask Jagger curiously since none of this information is taught anymore, and there are so many people around.

"About a thousand years ago, give or take." That stops me dead, and Mav runs into the back of me with a grunt.

"What's wrong?" he asks, steadying himself on me.

"My mom's over a thousand years old," I tell him, still in shock, and he laughs.

"Yeah, all the parents are. Archangels and Archdemons are relatively immortal; not much can kill them. Plain angels and demons are also pretty long-lived even if they don't make the transition to arch status. Demon and angel societies were pretty interwoven before the war. Hammus destroyed everything."

Shaking my head, I allow him to pull me along, so we don't get left behind. "Does this mean I'll live that long? That we all will?" My voice is a little sad at the thought of outliving my friends and Maggie and Peter.

He must know what I'm thinking because a gentle smile takes over, and comfort washes over me through our connection. "Yes, but you'll still have them around for a good while. You know AB aging slows to a snail's pace compared to normal Reathians." Don't think about it now."

Lucifer's stopped in front of some white double doors, a patient look on her face like she has nothing better to do than show her daughter and a bunch of angels around this demonic underground sanctuary. "I'm assuming you'll want to stay together, so this room has been prepared for you guys. I'll give you a couple of hours to rest, and then we'll talk." She places a kiss on my cheek and leaves, an aide I hadn't noticed before trailing after her. Kai opens the door with a flourish and saunters into a beautifully appointed suite, the rest of us trailing after him.

"Bedroom, bedroom, bathing room," he says, pointing to one door after the other before throwing himself on the sumptuous seating area that's in the center of the room. He throws his booted feet up on a coffee table and reclines back. "You reek. Please clean yourselves," he demands. "There's a bathroom through that door there." He points to one. "And the bedrooms also have some attached as well." Then he closes his eyes and proceeds to have a nap. Jagger, Mav, and Zeph disappear toward the bedrooms leaving Sander and Trick with me.

"What an assh..." I slap my hand over Sander's mouth, cutting off his words, and shove him in the direction of the bathroom door.

"Shut up, I'm hungry," I tell him, and I hear Kai's chuckle echo behind us. "I've got first dibs on the bathroom," I shout behind me, before anyone else can move. "Are you coming, Trick?" Sander's eyes are wide with shock, and amusement flows through my body, but the hunger quickly eats that up.

It's like all the distractions are making hunger worse, and it's eating up all the feelings around me. These needs have to be dealt with. A rumbling starts to come from my chest, and Sander's eyes widen even more before narrowing with desire, and he turns and leads the way. Trick is close on my heels, so my inner horn bag starts to purr, the rumbling a soft vibration that's almost comforting.

As we reach the bathroom, I get a good look around while Trick closes the door. Muted grays and blues are predominant, and a large steaming pool of water with a slight sulfur smell fills most of the room, steam lazily drifting off it. It must have a thermal supply source. On one side, there are a couple of showerheads on the wall, with drains underneath for rinsing off before getting in the pool. I point the boys in that direction.

While they do that, I continue to explore. There's a long bench with three sinks recessed into it and a large mirror on one side. I take my magic wand out of my hair and place it on there. Then next to that is a large shelving area, some filled with fluffy white towels, while others must be for discarded clothing.

A pair of hands rests on my hips from behind, bringing my mind back to my present needs. Trick nuzzles his face into my neck, his voice husky in the damp atmosphere. He must have put his glasses somewhere. That thought makes me stop suddenly, and I turn to face him. "If you're an Archangel, why do you wear glasses?" Sander chokes on a laugh as he approaches my other side, and Trick blushes like a virgin in a whorehouse.

"Look, I'm just not comfortable with being fawned over by women, so glasses make me look nerdy and put them off," he tells me, trailing off quietly when I look at Sander incredulously.

"Is he serious?" Sander nods, delighted with my response. I start shaking my head, unable to understand this lapse of logic. "But... but....."

"I know, *right*. I tried to tell him, and he wouldn't believe me, so I had to start a rumor to get them to leave him alone." Sander's smirk covers his whole face when Trick looks at him.

"What rumor? What do you mean?"

I take his face in both hands. "Trick, honey, the glasses don't work. You've got this sexy bookworm nerd thing going on that makes me want to jump you. Am I right?" I ask Sander, who's nodding enthusiastically.

"Sure are, and that's why I had to tell all the ABs at the academy that he only liked dick. *My* dick to be specific, and that I'd maim anyone who touched him even if they were female."

Now my curiosity has risen. "Is that true, though, are you only interested in Sander that way?" I ask, my hope shattering at the thought that maybe Trick's only here because of him.

He must see my hesitation because he sweeps me into his arms and lays a wet passionate kiss on me while rubbing his very hard, very naked cock against my armored scales. Holy shit, I forgot they were naked; I pull away quickly so that he doesn't rub himself raw.

"No, Mina, believe me, I've been having inappropriate thoughts about you longer than I probably should have. Sander and I've been talking about having you between us for longer than we should have. When I heard he had gotten to be your first, I was green with envy. I wish I'd been there that night too. "

"Between us, under us, on top of us..." Sander's voice is light as he steps down into the bath, dragging Trick with him, their eyes on me the whole time.

"Now I want to see that body. We saw your demon form in clothes, and we've seen that space-age dragon scale armor thing you're rocking, but I want to see all the pink bits now," Sander commands, waving his arms around until Trick grabs his arms and pulls them behind his back, restraining them, before he bites Sander's ear hard.

"What have I told you about demanding things?" Trick's dominant side has arrived, and Sander squirms with excitement and bows his head in submission. God, that's sexy, and I find myself squirming almost as much as Sander. Their top halves are out of the water, and Sander's sexy tattoos are glistening in the steamy air, his nipple rings calling to my mouth in a way that makes my fangs drop down. "What do you say?" he demands.

"Please, sir, I want to see Mina's body," he begs, and Trick eyes me with the same dominant look.

"Well, Mina, you heard him, show him what he wants," he commands, and I will the armor away until my naked magenta skin is on display, also dropping the glamour on my tail and horns.

"Turn," he demands and lifts Sander's head by his hair. "Watch her!" My inner core is on fire from his dominant streak. He's usually the quiet one, and I love seeing this side of him.

I turn, letting them see all that there is, but keep my eyes down in case the sight of the tail and horns disgust them. They haven't said anything once I've done a full rotation, and I start to rethink this all. Is it another reaction like Sam's?

"Look at me." Trick's voice is full of authority that I can't and don't want to resist. Looking up, I can see he's still got hold of his arms, but he's making a little thrusting movement with his hips, and Sander is gasping with enjoyment. "Do you like what you see, Sander?" he asks, nibbling on his neck while still restraining his arms behind his back.

"Yes," Sander groans in delight.

"Yes, what?" Trick demands and bites into his shoulder hard enough that I know Sander will be marked. *Oh, I'd love to leave a matching mark on the other side.*

"Yes, sir." Sander moans a little at the bite, his eyes glazed.

Trick looks up at me, calculation in his. "Mina, go shower then come and sit on the edge of the pool."

I quickly run over to the rinsing bay and turn the water on. It's freezing and sends goosebumps rushing over my skin, but I wash off the blood and sweat from the fight and then return to the edge of the pool and sit like Trick told me to. My nipples are rock hard at his demands and the lingering chill of the water.

When I sit, he walks Sander over toward the side of the pool, closer to me. I'm pretty sure he has Sander impaled on his cock, and I shiver with anticipation. I can't see, but that makes it even more delicious. Before we can get any further, Kai throws the door open. "Sorry to interrupt, but we've got trouble up top again. They must be searching for you, and we can't send a team in case anyone is watching."

Instantly, Sander and Trick switch to work mode and separate, both heading to the steps, drying off, and putting their dirty uniforms back on. No concern that Kai can see that they're rocking hard ons and his eyes are scanning their bodies appreciatively. They must be used to it. Me, well, I look at Kai in horror. "I haven't fed; I need it." Sander and Trick exchange worried glances.

"Go, I've got this. We'll catch up," Kai tells

them, then strides over to me and lifts me into his arms.

"Sorry, baby, blood is going to have to hold you over." He tilts his head, and I'm so worked up I won't complain. Instead, I sink my fangs in, groaning before an orgasm screams through me like an out of control wildfire. Just taking his blood was enough to trigger one. He grunts, and his hips thrust a couple of times before he holds himself tight against my body, riding out what my fangs have triggered. After drinking my fill, I lick his neck and step back.

"Thanks, I feel heaps better," I tell him, and he winks, instantly changing into clean clothes.

Kissing me, he says, "Put on your sexy armor; we need to catch up." Thinking about it, I'm enveloped in my scales, but this time my tail and horns are left on display. I grab my magic wand, and with Kai's arms wrapped around me, he teleports us topside.

Chapter Nineteen

Jessamina

When we get topside, I start to run outside the ruined castle, but Kai grabs my hand to stop me. "I can't come," he tells me a worried look on his face. "Someone must be spying on you for this to be happening, and I can't be seen with you. It was bad enough I showed myself before, but I didn't think anyone would be watching." Of course, he's worried; he has a city full of people to protect.

"And I need to go and talk about an evacuation plan with Lucifer in case whoever is here discovers us and then I'll be back up on standby in case you need me."

A small frown crosses my face in worry. "Okay, be careful, I'm sorry this has all happened." For an asshole, he really cares about his people, so I smack a kiss on his lips and hurry out to join my team as Kai disappears to go and make contingency plans.

When I reach the outside, I skid to a halt. The lightning storm that was flashing when we first arrived seems to have broken, and rain is pelting down, making visibility difficult. Looking through the downpour, my eyes are greeted by something out of a horror movie. The dry, dusty area is now a muddy mess, crawling with giant insects. Spiders, ants, scorpions, and even flying ones like wasps. All super large, almost the size of a small pony, and some even more extensive.

"Holy crap! Where did all of these come from?" I shout over the thundering sound of rain and the hissing and clicking of insects. The guys hack at the creatures, blood and guts flying, but they disappear soon after. The angel-runed weapons the guys carry are doing what they're supposed to, unlike with the lizard.

Mav and Zeph are in the air taking on the flying creatures, and I'm going to leave them to it. I still don't know if my floofy things will even let me fly, and I'm certainly not attempting it in the pouring rain.

I opt to join Trick, Jagger, and Sander, who seem to be working quite well as a team, on the ground. The rain is cold on my face, but my scales seem to be impervious to temperature change, so I launch myself at the insects.

I start hacking away, and every time I hit something, it disappears in a flurry of blood. Cutting a path through to the guys, I join them in their fighting circle. One by one, we take out the creatures in front of us. Using the magic wand as a sword, I slash and stab my way through the animals, our backs to one another while keeping an eye on our peripherals. My blood is pumping and my breath heaving before too long, but the wave of monsters doesn't seem to have an end.

Suddenly, Jagger slips in a puddle of mud, putting down his hands to stop himself from going further, and he doesn't notice the giant scorpion that has snuck up from behind. Its stinger dripping with poison hovering just above him.

"Watch out," I scream and jump into the air, but a bee flies toward me at the same time as I try to protect him. My heart drops as I turn my body away, and the stinger flies closer to Jagger's exposed neck. As my sword stabs into the bee and the stinger is about to reach Jagger, I feel my tail morph. Instead of the shape it's taken each time, it now has a razor-sharp edge. Without conscious thought, it flicks up and slices the stinger from the scorpion's tail, sending it flying into the incoming insects. The scorpion screams in pain, but I now have time to thrust my sword into its body once the bee disappears.

"Fuck, thanks." Jagger heaves as he notices the scorpion, but I don't have time to reply before we're back at it, my tail now joining the team.

"This is ridiculous," Zeph screams from above us. "Someone must have an open portal, so as they regenerate, they're channeling back through."

"I'm going to look," I shout back. "Kai's

worried that they saw him here and now have an idea that this place is significant. We can't let whoever's here report back."

"They may have already," Mav points out, his voice barely heard.

"Doesn't matter! They need to be stopped; we can't go on indefinitely. Find the portal and take care of the person." Zeph lands, his wings knocking a wave of insects over before they disappear into his back. "Mav, get down here and go with Mina; we can fight them off just as well down here."

Mav lands not far away and retracts his wings as I cut another path through to him. "I saw the direction they were coming from. Come on, this way," he shouts and starts to run, me following quickly on his heels.

We dodge the incoming creatures that seem to be slowing slightly, stabbing and hacking where we need to, but they seem to have a destination in mind and mostly ignore us the further we move away from the center of the destroyed city. Mav runs down an alleyway and leaps up some crumbly buildings until we're at a higher vantage point. A portal is open below us, insects flowing out of it at a rate that should honestly be alarming. I scan the area for the person responsible.

"There!" Mav points at the corner of another crumbly building, and I look, expecting to see an Archangel because they're the only ones who can open portals, but to my shock and dismay, the person is wearing a CD uniform and has a wrist guard aimed at the hole to keep the portal open. So that tells me it's not an Archangel. I feel a sense of relief; not that I suspected any of the dads, but there are a few others.

"Shit! Can you see who it is?" I ask Mav, disappointment flowing through me at the confirmation of traitors in the CD, possibly someone I know. It was easy to pretend when it wasn't right in front of you.

He shakes his head. "No, the BA gear makes it difficult. Come on, we'll get closer. The rain should hide us well."

We head back the way we came. Dodging and ducking around the fallen buildings, we get closer to the portal user. Hiding behind the corner of what looks like it used to be an apartment, we peek around.

"Holy shit, is that..." my voice breaks off as Mav confirms my question.

"Yep, it is."

The person who now looks to be shaking with strain is none other than Hugh Elmstone, director of the Collectors Division. Mav growls, "We always guessed he was responsible for a lot of the shit going on. At least now we can prove it. Slimy bastard."

We duck back around the corner. "Right, we need to capture him; we can't let him get away," he tells me. "Which means we need to destroy the wrist guard to close that portal and prevent him from opening another one. We also can't let him send any messages."

I flick the sword into a whip and nod. "I can do that if you can distract him."

He shakes his head. "No! I don't want him to see us; otherwise, he may go straight through the open portal. He's got nothing to lose now. "

I look around to find something to distract him with. *If only invisibility was a skill we possessed.* Not finding anything, I look back at Mav, and he has the weirdest expression on his face. "Mina, where the fuck did you go?" He puts his hands out and feels around like he's gone blind all of a sudden.

What the hell is he doing? There's no time to fuck around. I would expect something like this from Sander but not Mav. "I'm right in front of you," I hiss, grabbing hold of his hand, and shock takes over his face before he slowly smiles.

"You're invisible," he tells me, his voice filled with awe. "Like a chameleon, you've blended with the wall. Move away so I can see if you stay invisible." With a frown on my face, I walk away from the wall and around behind him. At first, I think he's fucking with me because I can still see myself, but as I move, his eyes remain where I had been.

"Did you move?" he asks, and I lean over and whisper naughtily in his ear.

"How do you feel about invisible blow jobs?"

His whole body stiffens at my words, and a growly sound comes out of his voice. "Later, remember that later." He turns around and squints slightly. "I didn't see you move at all, but if I look very carefully, I can see a slight haze where you are. The rain seems to miss you, but everything is so wet he won't even notice that. This is going to work perfectly." He rubs his hands together in glee, and I roll my eyes even though he can't see it.

"What I want you to do is use the whip to destroy his wrist guard and then wrap around his body to secure him. Can you telepath Kai and ask him to teleport here? He can take him back for questioning," he instructs me.

"Yes, ok," I agree but ask, "why not take him yourself?"

"Well, one, I don't think he needs to know that I'm an Archangel yet, and two, I'm sure that they have wards on the city to stop random people from teleporting directly in, just like the CD does."

"Oh, yeah, I hadn't thought about that." I feel a little embarrassed, so I'm glad he can't see me.

"Ok, you ready?"

"Hang on, let me tell Kai," I reply. "*Kai, can you teleport to me in a few minutes? We've caught the person responsible and thought Lucifer might want to question him too.*"

"*Sure can, demon baby, be careful.*" His thoughts are affectionate as they return, bringing warmth as though he's wrapped his arms around me.

"*I will. I have a neat new trick, can't wait to show*

you," I tease him, and a curious feeling comes down our connection, but he doesn't say anything else.

With that, I tell Mav I'm ready. "Be careful," he cautions me.

Whip in hand, I creep around the corner of the building we were hiding behind. Hugh isn't too far away, but his back is to me, so I need to angle myself sideways as to get around in front of him, and on the side, he has his guard. I move slowly, careful not to disturb the ground around me. He's angled off to the front of the portal so that the insects don't try and attack him, so I need to get between him and the insects. Hopefully, the invisibility works on them as well as it worked on Mav.

Sneaking closer, I can hear him muttering to himself. Something about being rewarded and finally being recognized for his help and blah, blah, blah. What's the point of a villainous monologue when no one's around to hear it?

I get careless, kicking a rock that rolls perilously close to his feet, and freeze, but he doesn't even notice it over his ranting. I finally get to a point where I can reach his wrist with my whip. Flicking it back, I lash out. With a crack, the wrist guard shatters, no match for the runed weapon. Hugh shrieks with fury as the portal instantly cuts off, blocking off the exiting insects. I heave a sigh of relief. *That's one thing taken care of.*

He spins around, looking for the culprit, but sees nothing and starts to panic. Before he can take more than a couple of steps, I have the whip wrapped around him, trapping his arms against his body. He tries to struggle, but the only thing he manages to do is tip over.

He splashes down, the muddy ground softening his fall and splashing into his mouth, and he sputters and coughs, trying to spit it out. Profanities spew out of his mouth as he tries to see what has caught him. Meanwhile, Mav comes around the corner and stops in front of him, looking down in disgust. I go back behind the wall, turn visible, and follow him out. Not sure Hugh's going to be going anywhere for a while but no point in giving him info that he may pass on to others.

"Team Alpha," Hugh hisses, then does a double take when he sees me. "You, you're a demon. So that's what everyone was being so secretive about." A haughty look crosses his face."Release me, I'm your superior."

"You're a traitor," Mav spits in response, more venom in his tone than I've ever heard before. "You arranged for those insects to attack us."

"Did I? Or was I only practicing my portal skills? This is an uninhabited planet, so I can do what I want here." He sneers in response, his words distorted by the headgear.

The rain has stopped, and the night sky brightens unnaturally. A flicker in the sky draws my eye, bringing a panicked look across Hugh's face. "Let me up! That's the solar flare. We can't survive it out here," he pleads with us, and I look at Mav with worry, but he's calm.

"Really, Hugh? You know *we* survived one last time we were here."

"I'm not sure how you did; that the solar radiation should have fried you." His blatant admission is causing me more shock, but Mav just nods with acceptance. I guess now that he's caught, Hugh's decided the need for games is over. Frankly, his confidence is disgusting, and I would love nothing more than to smack it off his face.

"Yes, it should have, but you sent us here anyway knowing full well one was on the way."

"I was ordered to get rid of you," he whines, "but you still managed to survive. You're like cockroaches. So hard to kill." Just as he says this, Kai appears out of nowhere. But this is like my Kai on steroids. Everything about him is extra, and I stare with amazement. Fangs, horns, and tail larger than before. His purple skin bright with the incoming light, and his body bulked up like the fictional Hulk from Earth. His wings stretch out above him like a demon of death. Hugh takes one look at him and screams, making a delicious sense of satisfaction fill me as the sound.

"What do we have here?" he growls, his voice deep with amusement that booms out across the now silent ruins.

"A traitor. Do what you want with him." Mav waves his hands at him, and Kai picks him up, slinging him over his shoulder, and with a wink in my direction, they disappear.

"What was that?" I ask, pointing at where Kai had been standing.

Mav smirks in response before grabbing my hand, and we start walking back to the others. "That was Kai's Archdemon form. It's like their normal form but bigger and badder. I guess he wanted to make an impact. Did they not tell you about it yet?"

"Ah, no! Do you think that's why I get the scales, the tail like a laser, and the invisibility?"

"Maybe." He shrugs. "Another thing to talk about when we get underground again."

I roll my eyes at his flippancy. "You think?" *So many* words need to be had. He smirks, pulling me close to him. Running his hands up and down my scales, sending tingling sensations through my body. "I haven't had a chance to tell you how sexy you look." My mouth drops open in surprise at his demonstrative behavior. He's usually quiet and reserved; still waters run deep and all that. He snorts at my reaction, swooping in to give me a searing kiss. Before I can even react, the sky starts to get lighter quickly, and Mav pulls away, releases his wings, then picks me up in his arms bridal-style. "We need to get underground before the flare gets here. Are you ok with this, or do you want to fly?" he asks, about to put me down again.

"Ah, yeah, no," I tell him, wrapping my arms

around his neck, not wanting to share that I haven't done the flying thing yet. "Fly on, my taxi." He gives me the sweetest smile and then rubs his nose against mine, and I giggle like a schoolgirl — cue internal eye roll.

With that, he launches himself into the air, his big gray and silver wings glistening as they thrust powerfully to take us higher. We quickly make it back to where the others are waiting. A tired, muddy lot, we stumble back to the secret passage and make our way downstairs.

Chapter Twenty

Jessamina

It's déjà vu or like we've gone back in time. Again, we walk from the underground elevator to the palace. Mind you, this time, we're dirty and exhausted, but the demons in our path stop and clap throughout our journey, thanking us for protecting their home. Kids run after us asking questions as they drag their hands through the guys' wings. They've left them out for washing because they're filthy.

Not far from the palace doors, I feel something tug on my hand, and I look down. A small female child of about five is standing and looking up at me. She has tight blonde curls sticking out at all angles, and her grin shows she's missing a tooth. Pretty rosy cheeks, the left side creased with a dimple, have a childish roundness to them, and her lavender eyes are alight with curiosity.

"Where are your wings? Why don't you have them out like all the others?" she questions, gesturing around like a game show host. She has such a sweet, hopeful smile on her face, and I would hate to let her down, so I suck up my insecurities.

"The first one to laugh goes to the bottom of my feeding schedule," I threaten, and they frown, not knowing what I mean, but I see Jagger and Kai trying to hold back their smiles.

With a small smile to the little girl, I release my wings. The humongous poofy things spring out behind me like a drag queen at gay pride. Like my tail, the damn things have a mind of their own, stretching out to their widest on full display like a freaking peacock, and the crowd of surrounding demons cheer with enthusiasm. The little girl's eyes are wide with amazement as she reaches out her hand, but an older female jumps in front to stop her.

"No, Mollie, you mustn't touch the lady's wings," she scolds the little girl. Her cute little mouth turns down into a pout, and her forehead wrinkles with a frown as her eyes well with tears.

I jump in quickly, trying to comfort her. "No, it's ok! I don't mind." I bring them in close to my body, and she runs her hands through the fluff, cooing with delight at the softness of them. The feeling of her hands on my wings tickles, and they shudder. *Well, that's definitely weird. Can they feel other sensations?* Something to ask the others later.

She jumps back then laughs, the sound sweet and melodic. "They're the prettiest wings ever. I hope I have a pair as pretty as that one day."

Crap, how can I respond without promising something I can't guarantee? "I'm sure whatever your wings are like, they'll be beautiful," I reassure her.

The little girl's companion picks her up, smiling gratefully at me. "Let the pretty lady go, sweetie. She's on the way to the palace." We turn and leave, waving goodbye while I focus on not meeting the rest of the team's eyes yet.

"Do you think they're her boyfriends, Mommy?" the sweet voice asks. "I want that many boyfriends when I'm a big girl." A smile breaks out at her words. *Yes, she really does.*

"Was she a Barbie, Mommy? She looked like one!" *Fuck!* Her final words make me cringe, and the guys chuckle. We make it back to our assigned room and walk inside before they crack.

"Wow." Sander is staring at me, seeming to have lost his ability to speak. From the gleam in his eye, I'm pretty sure he's wondering how they're going to feel on his naked body.

"They're beautiful, Mina." Trick places a kiss on my cheek and moves away. He's so intuitive, knowing that right now I need some reassurance. Jagger and Kai have disappeared, leaving me alone with the rest of Team Alpha. I didn't see them go into the bathroom, so they must be using one of the ones in the bedroom.

I find Mav and Zeph staring at them in contemplation. "Can you fly?" Zeph asks, ever the Team Captain, and I shrug my shoulders.

"Not sure. I haven't had a chance to yet." He rubs at the stubble on his chin, and Mav's eyes are glued to the feathers. I'm not sure what's going through his mind, but before I can ask him, Zeph pipes up.

"Get clean; we'll eat and have our meeting, and then once the solar flare is over, we'll go to the top of the tunnel and have a flying lesson. Best place to have it since there's no one around to see a pink angel soaring through the air." He winks and walks away, and my heart trips at his sweet words.

"Or drop like a ton of bricks," Mav adds in with a grin before following Zeph.

"Asshole," I growl after him, but he only waves a hand in my direction, and my heart sinks. *Shit, what if he's right?* My thoughts head down a dark tunnel, but before I can wallow in self-pity too long, a hand on my shoulder distracts me.

"Mina, I'm going to go and wash up." Sander's voice is gentle, but there's a hint of lust behind it. "If you can pull yourself out of your head long enough, you're welcome to join us."

The smirk on his lips is taunting and precisely what I need to knock me out of my funk, sending my appetites roaring to life. But I don't want to let him know it worked. Keeping my face neutral, I just smile and nod, and his eyes dim in disappointment.

He turns and heads for the bathroom with Trick behind him.

After those comments, I'd planned on making Mav suffer, but I'm going to try out my new invisibility on Sander and Trick first. Looking around, I notice I'm the only one left in the living area, so I retract my wings, get rid of the scales, and tiptoe toward the bathroom. Cracking open the door, I can hear the showers running and the rumbling sound of their voices. *Perfect!*

Allowing the invisibility to flow over my body, I cross my fingers and hope it worked, easing myself past the door. They're still in the showers talking about something, and as I walk carefully toward them, neither look up, so I feel confident they can't see me. They're standing close together, and I can hear Trick reassuring Sander that I'm probably just tired and not upset at him.

Assessing the situation, I'm pleased to see they're close enough to each other for what I want to do. Both have raging hard ons, and as I reach them and get down on my knees, I'm pretty sure I can reach both of their cocks, but first, a little teasing.

Sticking out my tongue, I run it along the underside of Sander's thick length, holding back my hair so it doesn't drape against his leg. He has a ring at the end of his cock that wasn't there the last time I was this close, so I tug at it. He twitches, looking down with a frown, but he doesn't say anything.

Maybe he thought he imagined it with the water running over him or that Trick had brushed against him? Ok, then I guess we're going to need something a little more...extreme.

I wrap my mouth around the whole head of his cock and suck hard. The moan that escapes his mouth is low and long, but the following scream of shock almost makes me burst out laughing as he jumps backward when he realizes he can't see anything.

"What's wrong?" Trick asks, looking around. Sander sputters, and while he's trying to explain, I do the same thing to Trick. He reacts in the same way.

"What the fuck?" He grabs at his bits just as I pull my lips away.

Slapping a hand over my mouth to keep the giggles in, I move back a little as they search the area, talking about blow job-giving ghosts. Oh, fuck, I have to concentrate hard on not peeing myself or giving away my location.

They have their hands out, feeling around, but after five minutes, they give up and get back under the shower. This time I don't mess around, grabbing a cock in each hand and starting to pump my fists up and down, my grip firm. Their knees buckle in shock, and then they moan in unison.

"Is it cheating on Mina if we let a ghost give us a handjob?" Sander moans to Trick, his voice hitching in the middle of the sentence.

I take Trick's dick deep into the back of my throat, and he thrusts his hips slightly while moaning his answer to Sander. "Probably, but how are we supposed to stop it?"

I release his dick with a pop and give Sander the same treatment. He thrusts his hip into my throat, releasing a growl to match Trick's, and I can feel it pulse as I try and swallow around it, the ring rubbing against my throat. Sander grabs hold of Trick and clenches his hand hard on his arm, moaning loudly in a way that sounds more like he doesn't want to enjoy it but can't help himself. I see him clench his eyes shut against the onslaught of sensation and hold onto Trick even harder, who winces at the pressure.

"Maybe if we explain we've got a girlfriend, it'll go away." Sander's voice is strained as he makes this suggestion. Tears leak out of my eyes as I pull back. It's not from the huge cocks in my mouth, but the laughter I'm trying to hold down. I watch Trick nod his agreement. The fact that he thinks about me as his girlfriend even though I'm mated to Kai and Jagger is so sweet. Caught up in the moment, I stop and wait.

"Is it still touching you?" Sander asks, and Trick shakes his head, both looking around with eyes filled with relief.

"Maybe she heard us say we have a girlfriend." Trick's breathing is evening out now that my lips aren't wrapped around him, but they're both weeping their desire from the ends of their cocks. They wait a little longer in silence, scanning the bathroom.

"I think it's gone," Sander says with a sigh of relief. "Fancy finishing the job it started?" he asks Trick with a cheeky smile, and I watch as the dominance arrives in Trick's eyes. Before he can say anything, I grab them both again, alternating between the two, licking and sucking and using my hands to stroke them to release.

"Oh my god," Sander shouts in surprise. "It's back, tell her to stop!" he pleads to Trick, panting.

Then a possibly evil thought crosses my mind. *If I can turn invisible with just a thought, do I have the ability of illusion?* Thinking about a wrinkly old ghost lady, I let myself become visible, and it must work because their twin looks of horror as I appear are too much. They both release high-pitched, girly screams and pull their cocks away from my hands, covering themselves.

"What the fuck?" Sander's disgust-filled voice is music to my ears and Trick's open-mouthed speechlessness a joy to my eyes.

Standing up, I stretch my back out and my knees, having gotten a little cramped down there on the hard tiles. Their eyes track me as I do this before I ask, "Don't you want me to finish the job?"

"God, no!" Trick says with revulsion, and Sander just shakes his head, the look of horror still on his face.

"Oh, so it was okay when you couldn't see me, but now that you can, it's not?" I tease them in a little old lady's voice.

More shaking heads, the motion almost violent. "You heard us say we had a girlfriend and to stop," Sander accuses, getting upset. "In fact, you sexually assaulted us!" he claims as he crosses his arms, but that exposes his now limp penis, which is still a decent size, so he puts his hands in front again. I can't control the laughter anymore, and I let the illusion slip. Their eyes just about pop out of their heads as I step under the shower stream that they had abandoned.

"Mina? What the fuck?" I watch the distress leave their faces, replaced by amusement and a little bit of anger.

"Hello, boys, I have a couple of new skills I've discovered. I'm pretty sure you thought the first one wasn't half bad." Cocking my eyebrow, I watch them look at each other. I can see the excuses rolling through their brains, so I let them off the hook.

"Relax, I love that you at least thought about telling the ghost you had a girlfriend." I wink at them; the g-word is making me feel all warm and fuzzy again. A look of retribution crosses Trick's face as the dominance returns to his eyes, and I know I'm in

trouble now.

PATRICK

"Sander, I think Mina needs to be punished for her practical joke, don't you?" My voice is low and growly, and I can see Mina's body shiver in response, my cock getting hard at her reaction to my words. I think it's time we got to finish what we started earlier, and her practical joke has just stirred the fires of lust even higher. Sander nods his head in enthusiasm as he walks toward her.

"Mina, you've been a very naughty girl, and it's time to pay the price," I tell her as Sander grabs her by the wrists, and she shivers even more with antici-pation. I can see the want in her eyes before she bows her head in submission. "That's a good girl," I purr, stroking my cock. "Put her on the bench, Sander," I order.

Sander leads her to a seating bench that isn't far from the showers as I shut the water off. It's wide enough for her to kneel, and he makes me climb on my hands and knees. It's the perfect spot for her to have Sander's cock in her mouth.

Going over to them, I run my hands along her back, marveling at the mate mark between her shoulder blades. "You left poor Sander hanging," I lean over, whispering in her ear, and goosebumps rise across her skin despite the warmth of the bathroom.

"Sander, I think Mina needs to finish the job she started, don't you?" I say to him conversationally over her head. He nods enthusiastically, not that she can see with her head still lowered in submission.

We're teaming up now to dole out her punishment, and I can't wait. Sander walks around to the front of the bench where her head is, his cock hard and ready for her. Meanwhile, I grab both her horns and pull her head back, and the groan that escapes her mouth has my cock twitching with anticipation.

"Lick it, Mina," I demand, and she sticks her tongue out and runs it over the head, paying particular attention to the ring in it.

"Hmm, I think Mina may like the ring in your cock," I rumble while I caress her horns, running my hands up and down the ridges until her body shudders again. I purr my appreciation as she licks his dick like it's her favorite lollipop.

"If you're a good girl and take care of him, then maybe I'll take care of you too." Removing my hands from her horns, one of them comes down hard across one ass cheek, the crack echoing through the bathroom, and Mina jolts in surprise. But as I rub away the sting, a quiet groan leaves her lips. Looking down at the pretty red handprint my cock leaks with excitement. Smoothing my hand over her ass and down between her legs, I can feel how wet her pussy is. Mina's tail is twitching back and forth and wraps around my wrist as I pull my hand away from her dripping core as if to hold it there. I chuckle at the impatient thing. Unwrapping it, I bring my finger up and put it near Sander's mouth.

"Lick it off, tell me how she tastes." His eyes just

about roll back into his head with the command, and he eagerly does as I've demanded.

"Sweet as pie," he moans as he finishes licking off her juices.

"Swallow his cock now, Mina, show him how much you want it," I tell her while rubbing my hand all over her body. Teasing light touches that are broken up by the occasional nipple tweak or ass slap.

Grabbing hold of her tail, I run my hand along the length, and Mina's moaned response shows me it's as sensitive as I thought it was. She's a heaving, panting mess by the time I put my hands on her soft hips, and when I impale her on my thick dick, she screams with the instant orgasm. Her hot channel pulses around my hard length as I grit my teeth to hold off my own climax. Fully seated in her tight cunt, I hold still while she rides the wave of pleasure, but before long, I feel the pressure ease, and I issue a command, seeing she's stopped with Sander.

"Don't let her stop on your cock, Sander," I bark, and he grips her horns and thrusts deep into her open mouth, both of them moaning their enjoyment. At the same time as he pulls out, I thrust in.

"That's it, suck his dick, take it deep into your throat." My dirty words have Sander thrusting with enthusiasm, and she gags a little. Ssaliva drips from her mouth as she breathes through her nose. Her tight sheath pulses at the naughty treatment, and a chuckle escapes my lips. Our girl likes it a little rough and dirty. *God, she's perfect for us.* That thought breaks apart when I feel a probing I wasn't expecting, and Mina's tail breaches my tight ring, a shout of surprise leaving my mouth. Sander looks up in surprise, and a laugh escapes his mouth when he sees my predicament. The tail slides in and out, and it feels so good, my balls start to tighten. I know it's not going to be long,so I pick up my movements, thrusting more forcefully.

"Your tail has decided to get in on the action and is ass-fucking Trick," Sander explains as I start to pound my cock into her relentlessly. The warmth of her tight channel combines with the pressure, and my movements get more forceful. Sander matches my rhythm thrust for thrust. It's not long before we're all tipping over the precipice of pleasure and shout out in tandem as our releases coat Mina's throat and womb with our cum. She too explodes, her moans muffled by Sander's cock deep in her throat.

Before long, the pleasure dissipates, and Mina's tail pulls out of my ass as I collapse over her back, snuggling into her neck and whispering praise in her ear. "Such a good girl for taking care of both of us." Once Sander pulls out, she purrs in response and turns her head languidly for a kiss. Soft and gentle kisses are exchanged before we both sit upright. She has a satisfied look on her face, and she groans and stretches.

"Thank you, I feel full for the first time today." Feeling pretty pleased with myself, I'm sure I'm wearing the same smug look as Sander. Kneeling in front of her, I brush some wet tendrils of hair off her face.

"See what happens when you poke the beast? They poke back," I tell her, and she smirks in a devilish way that makes her even more alluring than I thought possible.

"Best payback ever. If that's my punishment, I plan to poke the bear a lot. Also, I think that you have to learn not to pull the tail of a tiger if you don't want to be in trouble." She winks at me, and Sander and I chuckle with agreement as he helps us both to our feet. My emotions are so overflowing with joy that I pull them both in for a group hug, truly happy at the situation despite the small seed of doubt that niggles in the back of my mind. Neither Sander nor I got mate marks, and I was under the impression that they came from sexual contact. My heart is heavy with this thought, and when I look Sander in the eyes, I can see his devastation, but we both hide it from Mina. The fact that this may be temporary is a hard pill to swallow, but neither of us wants to make this any more difficult than it's going to be. With that thought, I pull them both closer and hug them tighter, making the most of now.

Chapter Twenty-One

Jesssamina

We finish washing up and find some clean clothes left out for us in one of the bedrooms. Our uniforms are taken away by someone for washing, and we meet the others in the living area for something to eat; even if my demon hunger were fed, a girl's still gotta eat. Everyone is back and clean, making a dent in the lavish spread that's been laid out. I throw myself down on a couch between Jagger and Kai, happy to be back between my mates, their familiar scents calming and relaxing me further.

The conversation flow is disjointed and random. The insect swarm, Hugh being responsible for them, the demons cheering for us when we returned. How cute the little kid was who wanted to feel my wings. My heart starts to pound at the word *kid*, and something suddenly occurs to me. Jagger and Kai must feel it through our connection because they both turn to me at once.

"What's wrong?" Jagger whispers, not wanting to draw anyone else's attention to my panic.

"We didn't use protection, and I didn't use it just then with Trick, either," I hiss at him. "How do demons and angels get pregnant?"

A frown crosses Kai's face. "The same way anyone else does? We don't catch diseases, and the female demon usually does something to prevent pregnancy before her transformation. That way, she doesn't have to worry in case the process takes longer than a day. Most get the contraceptive shot. There's a special one developed for demons and angels."

"Well, I'm on the damn pill, and I haven't taken it since before the mission to Minzeon. By rights, I should have my period, but I don't. There's also a damn good chance I may be freaking pregnant already," I whisper back, panic riding my voice hard.

But Jagger is already shaking his head and whispers to me, "I had a word with Raphael before your transformation and asked him to check your medical records so that they could add it to the blood you were transfused with if you needed it." My eyes widen in surprise at his words. "I didn't want you to have another thing to stress about. I'm sorry I forgot to tell you," he apologizes, but I just throw my arms around him and hug him tight. *Jesus, how fucking thoughtful is this guy?* My feelings for him just increase because I wasn't even his mate then, but he was trying to take care of me.

He returns the hug, and I pull back. "Not that I'm against having your babies, or anyone's babies, in the future, but now is not the time." Kai and Jagger smile in response, and with a massive sigh of relief, I start back on my food.

"I checked when we finished in the bathroom, and Trick and Sander didn't get mate marks," I tell them both, the disappointment in my voice not hard to miss. I take a bite of a piece of flatbread before using the remainder to sop up the sauce in my bowl. They both stop eating again and look at me.

"Did you bite them?" Jagger asks, and when I look at him, his eyes are full of tenderness, not jealousy. I shake my head in response.

"That may be the reason, or it just might not be meant to be," Kai says sympathetically.

"But I wasn't biting both of you at the same time," I argue, and Kai shakes his head.

"No, you weren't, but we were all biting each other, so it was a continuous loop feeding your blood through us all, and ours through you." I nod my head thoughtfully.

"I guess I was biting Drusilla when her marks appeared. You could be right." With that, relief starts to damper some of my worry that Trick and Sander might not be mine.

"Just bite them individually to be sure, though.

You can't create a loop because they don't bite," Jagger warns me, and I make a mental note to bite them the next time we have sex, which fingers crossed won't be too long away. *God, I'm such a thirsty bitch.* I snigger at my thoughts but shake my head when they both look at me with questions on their faces.

The three of us stop our private conversation and listen in to the others again when a knock at the door draws our attention, and a demon enters. He's slightly older and has yellow skin with orange horns. No wings or tail to be seen, so he could be hiding them, but then again most of the demons we've seen haven't hidden any of their features; they obviously feel comfortable showing them, so maybe he doesn't have them.

"Lucifer has requested your presence in the questioning chamber downstairs, please." He bows and exits as Kai snorts, and I look at him with a raised eyebrow.

"That's a polite term I haven't heard before," he tells me, looking amused, and I frown in confusion. "Questioning chamber instead of the torture room." He must see my shocked look because he hurriedly reassures, "Not that we torture anyone. We have a truth serum that's pretty damn effective." Getting up, I take a few of the plates off the table and put them on the cart that had bought them. The others are putting on shoes, and I quickly run my hand through my hair to smooth it out a little.

Straightening my clothes, I look around the room, and we're all ready to leave, so Zeph gestures for the demon to lead the way. We weave our way through the palace until we're headed further underneath the city. All of us are curious about what Hugh may divulge and quiet in anticipation of what Lucifer has to tell us.

When we arrive in the interrogation room, we find Lucifer, Raphael, and a blue demon who has a strong familial resemblance to Jagger all waiting for us. I'm right in my assumptions when Jagger goes to the demon, and they hug each other tightly. "Hi, Dad," he mumbles, almost too quiet for me to hear.

"Son, I've missed you." The big demon sighs as he holds Jagger tightly to his chest. Before they pull away, he turns to look at Kai and me while he holds Jagger at arm's length.

"And I hear congratulations are in order." He smiles at us, and, leaving Jagger, he comes and drags us both into an embrace. My face is smushed against Kai's chest as Jagger's dad welcomes us both to the family. Smiling against Kai's chest, a giddy feeling of joy ecompasses me. Wow, more family, and happy about it too.

Despite the warm tone, he has a disgruntled look on his face as he pulls away. "Having to listen to Siffa gloat was tiresome, though." Laughter fills the room at his words, and Raphael introduces us all to Asmodeus before we take a seat at the rounded table.

"As you can see, the demon population has been slowly rebuilding itself since the war, and this is not the only underground city on the planet. What we really need is for the planet to recover," Mom tells us before Asmodeus takes over.

"Once upon a time, this planet was lush and fertile, with an abundance of wildlife. We managed to do a Noah's ark kind of thing, and we have small colonies of all the species, but living underground is not ideal," he explains. "They need sunlight, fresh air, and the outdoors to really thrive and flourish, and we can't offer that to them underground. It's always been a temporary solution."

"How can you fix something so broken, though?" Trick asks, a valid question, and Mom nods her head.

"We can't, but a god or goddess could. We're hoping that if Hammus is incapacitated, we can appeal to one of the others to help us."

"Incapacitated or gone?" Zeph asks curiously. Raphael, Mom, and Asmodeus exchange glances that have the rest of us side eyeing each other.

"Preferably gone," Raphael says quietly. "We need to find a way to take out Hammus. His tyranny has gone on too long, especially now that he's turning his eye to other worlds."

"This is what we know now, " Mom starts, Raphael allowing her to take the lead as he sits quietly.

"Your fathers were able to rescue Matoz from a

fortified stronghold on Minzeon. The Minzeon technology was quite good, but it was no match for their strength and magic, and they were able to get him free. He was unharmed," she tells us.

"How was the tech god taken in the first place?" Zeph interrupts.

"See, this is where not being able to harm their creations worked against him. Something his own people had created to incapacitate Hammus was used on him instead. Apparently, he was overpowered and injected with something before he could react. They were instructed to secure him in a remote place and leave him there." Raphael's voice is full of disgust when he says this.

"But what would be powerful enough to incapacitate a god?" Jagger asks, horror clear in his voice. Anything that can incapacitate the gods is not something we want in the hands of AoA and their supporters.

"We don't know. No one was around when we got there, so we couldn't interrogate anyone. Matoz was able to confirm overhearing them talking about AoA; he learned that Hammus is the person at the top of their chain, and the AoA is just a front for his actions. A way to stir up unrest on other worlds so that he could swoop down and be their savior or something. Honestly, nobody is sure of his motives at this point. Does he want to rule them all or destroy them? I think his mind is so muddled that not even he knows," Mom continues. Silence fills the room as the long-suspected truth is finally confirmed.

"Well, that's that then, isn't it?" Asmodeus says, rubbing his hands together. "We need to find a way to take out Hammus. This has gone on too long, and we don't need him destroying any other worlds."

Something about what he just said jumps out at me, but before I can catch the thought, it's gone again. Shaking my head to clear it, I interject a question. "What's all this about? Why is he doing this? Why did he do it to the demons in the first place?

"Jealousy and hate are very dark emotions, and I guess even gods are not immune. He succumbed to them, throwing balance out all over the world," Raphael says quietly, the room silent at the thought of having to destroy a god.

"Alright, are you ready to question Hugh?" Mom asks, a smile on her face, and the people around the table rumble their agreement. We watch as she flicks a switch, and what we thought was a blank wall becomes clear, revealing Hugh strapped into a chair. His eyes dart around nervously, and even through the two-way mirror, I can spot the telltale beads of sweat that give away the fear overtaking him. But I have no sympathy for him. He's a traitor to the Collectors Division and our general way of life. The AoA want to see everyone bow down to the superior beings that they believe angels are. A small minority group is ruining worlds for everyone. Everything he's done is in the oppression of others. So, no, I feel nothing but disgust.

"Wait!" Sander interrupts as Mom is about to go into the room. "We all suspect Sabboath is also involved with AoA. What if *he* was the one to go in and question Hugh? Promise to help him escape, tell some bullshit to get him to spill his guts? Hugh doesn't know where he is. All he saw was Mav and Kai; for all he knows, he's back at CD." Everyone but Trick looks at Sander like he's lost his mind, but I think I know where he's going with this.

"Dude, how are we going to get Sabboath to question Hugh and give it all away while we're watching?" Mav's voice is a bit annoyed at Sander's interruption, just as mystified as most of the others seem.

"Not to mention, I don't want him anywhere near this city," Mom snarls, but Sander bears his signature smirk with the confidence to back it up despite her anger.

"Mina here has discovered a new skill," he says, leaning back in his chair with his arms folded. "She has the ability of illusion and can appear looking like someone else."

Everyone turns to look at me in amazement. "Not to mention the invisibility," he adds in, and the amazed looks get wider. I squirm in my seat at all the attention, not comfortable being in the spotlight since I've transitioned and had my confidence shaken a bit.

"I'm sure there are other demons with these skills too," I protest, trying to wave off the attention, but Mom is already shaking her head.

"No, Mina, there aren't." The look on her face is so proud, and I feel a tear welling in my eye.

"Huh. I wonder where I got them from." Another thought tickles my brain, too, but I can't pinpoint why or hold on to it long enough to figure out what it is.

"How did you discover these skills, Sander?" Mav asks, his voice full of suspicion as he looks at me with a raised eyebrow. Shit, I know what he's thinking, and his eyes promise retribution. Sander wiggles uncomfortably with the question, and I snort with laughter.

Did you have some fun with your new skills, demon baby? Kai's voice is amused in my head, and I can feel Jagger's amusement too.

Is this something we'll have to watch out for? he asks. *Going to keep us on our toes, aren't you.* I don't reply, but I can't stop the smirk crossing my face while plans for all of them fill my mind.

"Doesn't matter," he replies stubbornly. I can tell that none of them are going to let it go, so I wave them off.

"That's a story for another time. I guess I can try; I did see what he looked like during that meeting."

Standing up, I let the image of Sabboath appear in my mind, and a wave of power flows over my body accompanied by a stabbing, needle-like sensation. *Huh, that's different from last time.* Looking around at their faces, I can tell it worked. There's a mixture of reactions; disgust from Sander and Kai, through to awe from the parents in the room. Raphael jumps out of his chair and walks over to me, a look of wonder in his eye. He circles me, inspecting the illusion from every angle.

"Is it right?" I ask, my voice nasally and whiny, and he does a double-take.

"Even your voice is right," he tells me, taken aback. He pokes me in the chest. "Holy shit, it feels real too. That feels like a male's chest."

My mom crosses her arms. "Did you just try and feel my daughter's tits?' she asks, looking unimpressed, and Raphael flinches away before he quickly apologizes.

"Ah, no, sorry, that's not what I meant to do." The room is full of unamused men, except Asmodeus; he has a gleeful smile on his face.

I roll my eyes, and apparently, so does the illusion because Asmodeus's grin gets wider. "Relax," I tell everyone, "I'm not offended. It also felt like he was touching a solid chest." It had felt like my boobs had disappeared. Actually, now that I think about it, *everything* feels different. My whole body seems to have changed shape. My lips are thiner, my nose is bigger, and my eyebrows, god, they're bushy as fuck.

Panic starts to grip my emotions and Jagger and Kai look at me sharply as they feel the anxiety through the bond.

Something occurs to me, and I start to open my pants to check out whether I have a dick or not, but Mom jumps up to stop me, and everyone laughs, so I shove my hand down my pants instead. Sure enough, I have a penis, a pretty small one by the feel of things, but then something else occurs to me, and I pull my hand out in horror. "Fuck, I just touched his dick." This time the whole room dissolves into laughter. While they try to compose themselves, I keep talking.

"No, what I mean is I could feel it. I don't think it's an illusion. I think I actually shifted shapes!" I tell them in shock. "When I did it earlier, I still sounded the same and looked the same as myself. This time I sound and look like him. Please tell me this is a skill you all have too." By now, they have their shit together, and Mom is shaking her head again.

"Well, where did all these new skills come from?" I ask, a little bit afraid.

She exchanges looks with Asmodeus and Raphael, who both nod their heads. "I think I might know," she tells me gently, "but it's another one of those, 'I can't tell you yet' things." She goes to put her hand on me to comfort me but recoils when she looks at me, and I flinch, that little part of my mind that still remembers she gave me away and feels rejected rearing its ugly head. But then it occurs to me what I actually look like. Right, it would be weird to be comforting Sabboath. "Just give me another few days, and we'll explain everything," she promises. Sighing, I agree to her request.

"Fine, but this is getting a little bit annoying, and to be honest, I need to know these things for my safety."

"I agree, and I will push for permission to tell you, but it's not just up to me."

"Ok," I say, looking around the room. "What do we need to know? What do you want me to ask him?"

"We need confirmation of Sabboath's involvement, so you need to get him to say that he ordered Hugh to do what he did. It also wouldn't hurt to hear confirmation about Hammus from someone else's mouth, " Mom tells me, and I nod.

"We also would like to know if AoA has any plans in the works at the moment. We need to get ahead of them," Asmodeus adds in.

"And we need to know if he has any idea of the Five's whereabouts," Raphael's voice rumbles. "We need to get them back into the menagerie."

Whoa ok, they're not asking much. My face, or should I say Sabboath's face, must look worried because Zeph stands up and comes to me, grabbing hold of my arms. "You can do this, Mina. We have faith in you," he reassures me, and when I look around the table, everyone is nodding except

Sander. He just seems disturbed, with his face all frowny.

"Dude, can you step away from her, please? You being that close to Sabboath is freaking me out." That comment breaks the tension, and with a grateful smile to both of them, I head toward the door.

"That's two-way glass, yes, but can you hear too?" Mom nods, so I continue forward. *Let's do this.*

Chapter Twenty-Two

Jessamina

Taking a deep breath, I step into the room, watching as Hugh's terrified face eases just slightly at the sight of me, or Sabboath really. "You can't keep me here; I've done nothing," he sneers. Trying to adopt the air of self-importance that I saw in my brief moments around Sabboath, I scoff, waving a hand at him.

"Save the act, I turned the cameras off, and nobody else is around. They're letting you sweat before they come in and question you."

I watch as Hugh relaxes at my words. "Thank fuck! You have to get me out of here before they get back," he pleads. "Some big ass demon grabbed me when I was on Habbalea. He wasn't one I recognized; I'm assuming he works for the Archangels because Mavromichali seemed to know him." His voice is whiny, and, knowing that Sabboath likely wouldn't forgive demands given in that tone, I backhand him across the face.

"Whoa, babe." Kai's voice in my head is amused

305

with a touch of impressed. Hugh, on the other hand, definitely doesn't share those feelings. His head snaps back, and he looks at me with shock and terror.

"You've disappointed us. What did you think you were doing?" I growl at him before turning around and pacing the room. Trying to think about how Sabboath may handle this interaction. I probably should have asked for some more advice before I started this. I run my fingers through my hair in frustration, pulling at the greasy ends.

He whimpers before replying, "I was just doing what you ordered. Taking care of Team Alpha." Bingo! Sabboath's guilt confirmed. *One question down, a million more to go.*

"I knew I shouldn't have trusted you with such an important job; you've fucked it up once before," I growl at him, whirling around to face him.

This gets a reaction from Hugh, who snaps in return, "Yes, but so have you and that pathetic excuse for a daughter. She almost blew the whole thing, lucky for her that Jessamina Michaels can't remember anything."

This shocks me into silence, and I stop my pacing. My memories must hold some vital information. Hmm, maybe I could get some more information about Connie here.

"You know very well how much my daughter has given to this organization," I probe carefully, but Hugh's too worked up to notice.

"Please, she jumped at the chance to be the guinea pig for his experiments." He scoffs, "She wanted more power, something to get people to sit and take notice. She begged for all of it. But she screwed up on Minzeon. The Michaels girl should never have seen her let alone been attacked. Completely blew her faked death and now it's just a matter of time before she remembers and everyone knows." He's ranting furiously and hasn't noticed me stopping in my surprise, thank goodness. Maybe it's time for Raphael to dig around.

"You're just lucky that Hammus still believes the two of you are useful with that formula you inject the new recruits with," Hugh continues.

Wow, the information is just flowing out of his mouth. Staying silent, I wait for him to cave under pressure. I turn to raise my eyebrow at him. "Maybe I'll just leave you to rot."

All bravado gone, he starts to beg. "You have to get me out of here. Bravo has been discovered; there's too much on the line now. Let me help with the Five's next mission. The tech they're planning to steal from Minzeon is too valuable to our cause to be left in their unpredictable hands. God, I don't know why you trust them to get it right. That's like using a chainsaw for brain surgery. " Hugh's contempt for the plan is obvious, but this time he's tempering the attitude enough that another backhand might be too over the top. I pretend to think about it, knowing this isn't my call to make.

"Kai, what should I say?" I ask, knowing they'll all be discussing it.

"Raphael says to tell him you'll give him one last chance, but if he fucks this one up, he's dead. He also said he's going to come into the room, and you're going to have to hit him again like you've been questioning him, and knock him unconscious. This will allow us to inject a tracker into his skin." His voice is calm as he gives me instructions. Thank goodness because my heartbeat is racing a mile an hour, and I can feel his calm penetrate my mind and absorb some of those feelings. Taking a deep breath, I just let it flow, easing my tension and then I focus on what I need to do.

Hugh is prattling on in the background, so I shout, "Silence while I think!" The ensuing quiet of the room is suffocating, and I find myself pulling at my limp hair in frustration.

"This is what will happen. I'm going to rough you up, so when they arrive, you're unconscious and can't be questioned. Once they dump you in a cell to recover, I will ensure you can escape."

Hugh's face fills with gratitude at my words, the slimy fucking weasel. "But if you fuck this up, I will kill you myself," I threaten him, and he nods, eyes wide. "Get the thing from Minzeon." I pause."Do you even know what it is we're after?" I probe, and he nods furiously, eager to please now that he knows his escape is on the horizon.

"You want the new DNA scrambling tech they've created. Something to do with creating new viruses. Making humans more susceptible to things that animals carry," he sputters out.

God, I'm good at this, I think smugly before answering him.

"Good, don't fuck this up." I hit him again, and grabbing his hand, break a finger.

Over Hugh's scream, I hear the door open, and Raphael walks in. "Sabboath!" His voice is filled with anger that's so believable it's a little scary. The fury practically radiates off him, and we both shudder with the intensity. "What are you doing to our suspect?" Hugh's eyes widen, and through his tears, I see him begging me. Without answering, I make a fist and clock him in the temple, knocking him out instantly.

Slumping with exhaustion against the table, I shift back into my own body the moment his eyes close. Raphael wraps his arms around me in a hug, stroking my hair. "You did so good, Jessamina. We're very proud of you. You got all the information we needed to move forward," he says softly.

He helps me back to the conference room while Asmodeus uses a big needle to inject what I guess is the tracking chip into Hugh's neck. Collapsing in the chair, my team all give me praise for the job I just did, but I only feel disgust. *I hurt that man while he was tied down and defenseless*—my stomach rolls with the thought. *How far am I willing to go to save the people I love?*

"What did he mean about Bravo being discovered?" Jagger asks, bringing my attention away from my self-pity. Lucifer and Raphael exchange another one of those glances that I'm beginning to hate before they answer.

"I'm sorry, Jagger, but the remaining members of Bravo were supposed to be doing some under-cover reconnaissance for us, but they must've been discovered or betrayed."

A look of sadness crosses his face, and he slumps into his chair, Kai reaching a hand out to comfort him. "Well, shit." He runs his hand through his hair; his voice tinged with sorrow. "It was only Brock that was an asshole; the others were okay guys. They tried to get him to lay off, but he was the team leader and wouldn't be swayed."

"Actually, Brock is missing," Raphael tells him, and Jagger sits up straight in his chair, fury crossing his face. Eyes alight with the need for revenge, his voice is filled with disgust as he asks, "Are you saying he's a traitor as well?"

"Yes, that's what we think; otherwise, how would he get away unharmed?" The fury is Jagger's eyes is blazing, and I'm worried he's going to do something stupid, so I get out of my seat and plonk myself down on his lap, wrapping my arms around his and snuggling into his chest.

"Good job, baby." Kai's voice is sweet in my head, like fingers tips softly brushing across my skin, his approval at my actions thrumming through the bond.

"He looked like he was going to do something stupid." With Jagger effectively distracted by me, we listen to Lucifer, Raphael, and Asmodeus's plan.

"I'm heading back to update the others on what has happened and to promote Clementine to head of CD. We've never had any reason to doubt her in the past, but let's ask her to allow us to check her mind for traitorous thoughts. That will assure us all that we're not making another mistake. Asmodeus, why don't you dump that jackass somewhere on Reath and plant some false memories to replace these? Maybe he got away from Habbalea, and he needs to track down the Five to carry out his mission."

Asmodeus agrees to the suggestion. "Then I will keep an eye on him, and when I find out the location of the Five, I'll let you know so that we can apprehend them."

"Sounds good," Mom agrees. "I need to get back and open Eternal Damnation, so nobody gets suspicious that it's been closed for a while." Asmodeus and Raphael nod their agreement while she turns to our team. "What are your plans?" she asks Zeph.

"Technically, we still can't go anywhere due to the solar flare. We're not supposed to be able to portal through it, so I guess we'll spend the night here. I'd like to give Mina a flying lesson too, once the flare has gone. We need to know if those wings are just for show like a peacock or if she can actually fly." He grins at me, and I roll my eyes, snuggling further into Jagger's lap. I'm exhausted all of a sudden; shape-shifting really took it out of me.

"Alright," Raphael agrees, "I'll let Dru know, so she's not worried about you." He gets up and gives Trick a quick hug, whispering in his ear before he nods to us all and leaves. I keep forgetting that Raphael is Trick's dad; he's always so business-focused. It can't be easy for either of them. I can see so many similarities between them. I'm wondering if this is why Trick likes to take charge in the bedroom. So much of our lives are out of our control that that's the one thing he *is* able to control.

It makes me wonder about the elusive Michael, head of the Archangel council and Mylea's right-hand man. *Will I ever meet him?* Maybe now that Matoz has been found, he'll start attending meetings again.

My eyes start to drift closed as I feel a hand on my cheek. "Jessa, baby," my mom's says quietly next to me. A hand touches my forehead as if to check for a temperature, I smile at the very mom action. Cracking my eyes open, I look at her.

"You need to eat again; the shape-shifting must take a lot of energy," she tells me. I nod okay and close my eyes again. As I drift off, I hear her ask the others, "Is she getting what she needs?" The softness with which she'd addressed me is gone;

Lucifer's voice is now a fierce growl that speaks to her desire to protect me.

———•••———

Lysander

"Kai gave her blood before the fight, and Sander and Trick took care of the other needs after," Zeph tells her, annoyed, like he doesn't appreciate his ability to look after his team being questioned.

"Ah, see, that's the problem. For the first few months, she's going to need both at the same time. Actually, now that I think about it, with her unique abilities, she may always need both at the same time," she explains gently, calming now that she knows the team at least tried to take care of her daughter. "And depending on what she's doing during missions, she may need it more than twice a day."

I look over to where she has fallen asleep in Jagger's lap. She's pale and has dark circles under her eyes, and a wave of guilt hits me at the thought of us not giving her what she needed earlier.

Lucifer must see how I feel because she shakes her head. "No, you weren't to know, and you guys will only each be able to feed her blood once a day. Unlike Jagger and Kai, you don't have the ability to regenerate that quickly. Their bodies have evolved to allow for it, as blood is a demon's food source. But as she's fated to have more mates, they may not be enough either until she finds the others. Just remember that you should only feed her once a day to stay healthy."

"I think it will be best to set up a schedule," Zeph suggests. "That way, it's not something that's overlooked. Are you okay with that?" he asks Jagger and Kai, and they both nod their heads in agreement.

"Ideally, we would like to be able to take care of our mate, and it's a kick in the guts to know she needs more than we can give her, but Lucifer's right. She has more mates out there, and until we find them all she needs alternate food sources. We can swallow our jealousy for her," Jagger says while Kai frowns but agrees.

Jagger stands up with her in his arms. "Let's head back to our rooms, and you guys can take care of her again since she didn't take your blood," he says to me, and my cock is instantly hard at the thought of taking care of Mina again. I can see in Trick's eyes he feels the same way. He knows that she'll never replace him in my life; she's an added bonus to our relationship on the days she needs us.

Zeph and Mav start to complain, but Kai puts his hands up. "If you guys plan to take her flying, you don't want to be losing any blood before that." Both their faces lose the annoyance at that, and they nod their agreement.

few hours later, Mina is tucked into bed on one side with me in the middle and Trick behind me, his arm wrapped around my waist, his breath tickling my neck as he breathes deeply in his sleep. A feeling of utter contentment surrounds me at being sandwiched between two people I love. Yes, I *love* Mina, have for years, and the thought that she has mates and that Trick and I may not be a part of that rips my heart to shreds. He didn't have to say it earlier, but I knew Trick felt the same way when neither of us got mate marks after being with her. If this is the only chance I'm ever going to get to be what she needs, I'm going to make the most of it. If we're going to lose her to her future mates, I'm going to give her memories she's never going to forget because god knows I never will.

I'm watching Mina's chest go up and down when Trick finally moves behind me. He snuggles in and rubs his stubbled chin against the back of my neck, bringing goosebumps to my skin. His hard cock pushes against my brief-clad backside and places gentle kisses on my neck.

"Is she still sleeping?" he rumbles in my ear, one of his hands coming up to tweak at my nipple ring, giving it a little tug that causes my dick to pulse. As much as I like his dominant side, I really like the sweet and snuggly Trick too. We've been together for long enough that he can always read what I need and when. It makes me feel loved and secure in our relationship with this new addition to it.

"Mhmm," I answer his question, trying not to wake her. She needs all the sleep she can get. She's still trying to recover from her transition and whatever it was that sent her into that coma.

His hand leaves my nipple and moves downward, pushing aside the waistband of my briefs and palming my cock in his hand. With a firm grip, he rubs up and down a few times while thrusting against me from behind until I'm squirming on the bed.

"Do you think we can give her a little incentive to wake?" he asks, leaving my cock and turning my head to give me a long, languid kiss over my shoulder. I nod in agreement, and he places kisses down my spine as he removes my briefs and throws them on the floor behind him before his join them.

The snap of a bottle opening fills the quiet, and I guess he's grabbed lube from somewhere because as he snuggles back into me, I feel his fingers against the ring of my tight hole. He slowly eases them in as the other hand grabs hold of my cock again. With lazy strokes, he stretches my ass in preparation, then he lifts my top leg up and back over his hip, so he can slowly slide his cock deep.

The groan that leaves my mouth is louder than I expected and has Mina stirring in her sleep. As she wakes, Trick slowly thrusts in and out, his hand on my hard length moving in time. Mina's eyes flutter open, and as she looks around, another moan leaves my mouth at the thought of her watching or, even better, joining. She finally wakes enough to realize where the sound's coming from and rolls over to face me, her eyes glowing red with hunger, her blonde hair with the red streak falling over her shoulder.

"Well, what a lovely sight to wake up to," she says sleepily. "Have you got room for one more?" she asks, the huskiness in her voice turning me on even more as she moves closer and pulls one of my nipples into her mouth, her arms wrapping around me to caress Trick.

"God yes," I moan, my words a prayer of delight as I grab her and pull her closer, my head coming down to nuzzle at her neck, placing kisses as I move closer to her breasts. Giving her nipples the same treatment she just gave mine, I nip and suck at the perfectly hard, rosy peaks, her groans of delight ramping up my desire as Trick continues to thrust teasingly slowly. She pulls away from me, so she can kiss him over my shoulder, their tongues twining around each other in a play for dominance.

He pulls away. "What do you want, Mina?" he asks softly, the dominant man nowhere to be seen. Right now, we need to take care of the beautiful woman in front of us. *Dominance games can always come after that.*

She thinks about it, a slight blush coming to her

cheek before she replies, "How about instead of using your hand, Sander uses my pussy?"

Fuck! My cock twitches and I just about blow my load there and then, but Trick clamps down hard on it, and the need recedes slightly.

"I would say that Sander thinks that's a pretty good idea." His voice is deep with want as he takes his hand off my cock and pulls out of my ass, allowing me to push Mina onto her back and pepper kisses all over her body.

"Oh, baby, I would love to use that pussy, " I tell her before running my tongue along her already wet slit then moving up her body and kissing her on the mouth. Without messing around, I thrust my cock deep before pausing so that Trick can slide his cock back into my ass. Her pussy is warm and tight as it wraps around my thick length. Once Trick is balls deep, he takes over the rhythm, thrusting deep and using me to push deep into Mina. The three of us groan together. His cock is thick and hard in my ass, and her pussy has a hot, vise-like grip around my dick. The combination making my eyes roll back into my head.

She opens her eyes that had drifted closed. "Can I bite you?" she asks, her pretty eyes filled with want but worry too. *Fuck, I'm not going to last long at this rate.*

"Yes, please?" I beg her.

From behind, Trick adds, "Me too." Without hesitation, he wraps an arm around my chest so that she can bite into his wrist. The offer has her breath hitching and her fangs extending as she bites deep into his vein. When she pulls back a moment later, I can see the two puncture holes as she starts to suck. His eyes roll back in his head at the sensations.

"How does it feel?" My voice is part curious, part envious.

"Fucking mind blowing." His mind stutters on the thoughts as the sensations rush through his body like a shot of pure adrenaline and leak into me through the bond. This sets off a chain of events as her pussy tightens around me, her orgasm exploding through her body, and Trick thrusts even faster before shouting his pleasure to the roof.

So many sensations, and when she removes her mouth from him and plunges her fangs into me, slurping away, I come harder than I ever have before, following the others into this blissful moment. The sensation of her drinking my blood is like a shot of ecstasy to my cock. It pulses repeatedly inside her pussy, still gripping me tightly as her orgasm also flows onward.

Just as she finally removes her mouth and runs her tongue over the holes, then does the same to Trick's arm, I feel a pain shoot through my body like I've been stabbed in the chest. My shout of agony joins Trick's as he collapses on top of me, unable to hold his balance through the searing sensation.

Mina, too, is groaning with pain, but she

manages to bring up both her hands and runs one through each of our hair. She's cooing and praising us, her words not really making sense yet soothing nonetheless.

"There, there, it only hurts for a while, my lovely mates." The word *mates* has me lifting my head to look at her in shock, and she has a huge smile on her face. Trick pulls out and rolls over, letting me pull out of Mina. We both lay on the bed with groans, but she's recovered and is sitting up, practically bouncing with delight.

"Look," she exclaims, pointing to a spot just above my heart on my pec. Sure enough, a pattern has appeared, and I eagerly look at Trick. He has a mark too, but it's different to mine.

"Why is his different?" I ask with worry. "Is there something wrong with them?" My worry overshadows the joy that both Trick and I are destined for this woman.

She shows me her back. "See the marks? They're all different for each mate, and they seem to be growing into one cohesive tattoo." I examine the marks already on her back, knowing I'd seen them before but hadn't paid attention. There seem to be five different designs on there.

"I know Jagger and Kai are your mates, but who's the other one?" My tone is a little harsh, but I don't remember anyone else with her, and a little hurt spikes through me that she would keep a secret from us.

"It's Drusilla, isn't it?" Trick adds in, a smile in his voice, and shock at that revelation has me frowning. I can't believe Drusilla didn't brag about it in her usual way. She must be busting a gut to scream it from the roof of the CD building if she feels anything like I do. Poor thing.

"Yup," she tells us, and she must see my frown. Biting her lip with worry, she adds, "Don't be mad! We didn't want anyone worrying about whether they were going to get marked as well. I'm going to ask you guys to keep this news to yourselves for now too." I start to argue with her, but Trick nods, always the patient one.

"I understand we don't want to distract Zeph or Mav when we've got so much going on. Though I have a gut feeling that they'll be your mates too." I guess what he says makes sense. But damn it, I want to be the one to shout it from the roof, and I want to beat Drusilla. Evilly, I plot to tell Mom and Dad before she can, but I keep that to myself.

A wide smile crosses her face. "I sure hope so."

"What about Sam?" I ask quietly, and she shakes her head.

"I can't worry about Sam anymore. He's a big boy, and he has his own choices and decisions to make." Her forehead gets a little frown. "Are you guys okay with this?"

Looking at each other, we both pounce on her and share a three-way kiss. Switching back and forth from one to the other, it's a tangle of tongues and lips, but so much fun, and we all dissolve into laughter. The sense of relief, joy, wonder, and huge amounts of love flowing through our newly established bond wipe away the sadness that I'd felt earlier when I'd lost hope that Mina might be ours.

"I couldn't be happier. I was worried before when nothing happened," Trick admits, the delight in his voice evident even as he admits he'd had concerns, and I nod enthusiastically in agreement.

Smacking Trick on the ass, I get up. "Let's go clean up and get some dinner before coming back to bed." I wink at her. "These mates have some practicing to do."

Chapter Twenty-Three

Jessamina

After spending a lovely evening with my two new mates, I sleep like the dead and wake up feeling refreshed the next morning. Leaving Sander and Trick snuggled up together, I go in search of my other two mates and find them snuggled up together also.

Both in demon form, their colors vibrant against the white background of the sheets, I watch them for a moment. Soaking in the joy at having five people bound to me for my whole life, to love and be loved by. Never when I started this journey did I think that anything like this would happen.

"Are you going to stand there staring like a creeper, or are you going to come over here and help me suck Jagger's dick?" Kai's question is all husky with sleep, but it does things to my body that have me panting with anticipation. Letting my human form drop, I feel a prickling sensation as my demon form flows over me, but it's not uncomfortable. In fact, it's more like a sense of relief.

Stretching my arms, I feel my tail stretch out straight too. It must get sick of being hidden all the time. Taking a running start, I fling myself onto the bed where twin grunts greet me when I land on top of them. Pulling the blankets back off their faces, I give them both big smacking kisses on their mouths.

"Morning, my mates, I've missed you."

"What's got you so happy this morning?" Kai grumbles. Jagger has a smile of amusement on his face but seems to be happy to indulge us. "Apart from the double dicking you received last night." A snort of laughter escapes my mouth.

"Oh, Kai, don't be jealous. I'm pretty sure you didn't miss out on a dicking last night either." Jagger's amusement turns to smugness as Kai grunts an inaudible response.

"Also, I'm pleased to tell you, you were right. Sander and Trick are also my mates." I turn around to show them my back and the way the mark has grown. Two hands run over the marks, a shiver following down my spine at the tickling feeling.

"Demon baby, I'm happy for you." Kai's statement is surprisingly light and full of joy, and I turn to him in surprise.

"Look, I knew I was going to have to share you, and if I have to share you with anyone other than Jagger, at least I know these assholes are good people." His voice turns all grumbly at the end, and I throw myself at him, wrapping my arms around him and covering his face with kisses. Again, Jagger smiles in amusement, the easy-going bastard.

I whisper in Kai's ear, "Bet I can suck him off quicker than you." Without waiting for a response, I dive under the blanket and wiggle my way down toward Jagger's dick, where I find Kai's hand already wrapped around it. *At least Jagger's expression makes sense now.*

"That's not fair! You started before me," I complain before pushing his hand away and wrapping my lips around Jagger's delicious cock. Laying my whole body on top of him, my pussy almost straddling his face, I hope he gets the hint to make my morning memorable. Warm breath on my pussy tells me that Jagger has gotten the right idea, and as his tongue strokes through my folds, Kai grumbles disgruntledly.

"Hey, what about me?" Chuckling internally, I remove my mouth from Jagger's dick and bring it down over Kai's, and the sulky boy quickly groans with pleasure. Feeling a nudge at my cheek, I open my eyes to see Jagger's tail. Removing my mouth from Kai's dick, the tail forces itself in, and I understand what it wants, so I lube it up with my spit. A moment later, Jagger's tail probes at Kai's tight ring before slipping past it, and he moans in delight as my core clenches with arousal.

I spend the next little while swapping between Jagger's and Kai's cocks, licking and sucking, their lusty moans echoing through the room around us.

The musty smell of sex fills the air under the blankets, and sweat drips between my cleavage. Jagger's tongue is pulsating inside my cunt, and I grind my pussy into his face with groans of pleasure. Before long, my mouth and Jagger's tail must be too much for Kai because he shouts a warning, then his cum is splashing down my throat, and I swallow with ease.

Licking him clean, I turn my attention back to Jagger. With my mouth on his dick and my finger pushing into his tight ring, he's coming in no time. I slurp his cum down my throat like a drunk on a bender, the shot of energy leaving me shivering with delight. Once finished, I turn my head, and, using my fangs, I drink from first Jagger's and then Kai's femoral arteries. They moan with every draw of blood, their cocks rigid and throbbing still.

The rich, delicious blood combines with Jagger's talented tongue and mouth, bringing me to my own orgasm. I ride his face, grinding my mound against it and shouting my passion through muffled blankets.

Just as I start to come down from the first orgasm, I feel a sharp pinch on either thigh, and the boys latch on. Their sucking sets off another round as they both drink their morning fill, and one of them uses their fingers hard and fast in my already quivering pussy.

Once they're finished and close the holes in my inner thighs, I drag myself back up to the top of the bed, panting and pushing back the sweaty tendrils of hair from my face. They wrap their arms around me, and their love and smug satisfaction pulse through our bond.

"Damn, what a way to start the morning." My voice is scratchy from screaming through my orgasms. Turning, my head, my lips meet Jagger's in long a lazy kiss before breaking away and giving Kai the same treatment. Then I throw the blankets back, ready to climb out of bed.

"Oh, I see how it is, hit it and quit it?' Kai's voice teases from behind, slapping me on the ass as I try to climb over Jagger.

"Nope, I think she's in a hurry to get to her flying lesson." Jagger's voice is full of laughter as I stop dead at the reminder. Panic quickly replaces the feeling of well-fucked satisfaction, and I quickly change direction, flinging myself back between the two, hauling the blankets back up, and pulling them over my head.

"Ah. No. I'm done. Not sure I got enough sleep last night. Probably need to spend the day in bed," I ramble, my voice muffled by the blankets. The guys chuckle with laughter at my reaction, but before anyone can say anything, the bedroom door flies open with a bang.

"Get your mouth off their cocks, princess; we've got work to do," Mav orders, his voice dry and demanding.

I ignore the request and stay hidden, but both

Jagger and Kai climb out of bed, leaving me all alone. "Traitors!" I accuse as the noise of them getting dressed for the day is heard.

"Come on, didn't peg you for being a chicken," Kai taunts me, but still, I stay hidden.

The noises recede, and I assume I've been left alone, but before I can roll over and get comfortable, the blankets are ripped off me, and I'm left naked and exposed to Mav's eyes. His gaze is heated as it runs the length of my body, and his tongue comes out to wet his lips. My whore pussy clenches in anticipation, and my tail decides to wave at him like it's saying come on in. *Damn it; you just got fed.*

But the gaze turns cold again. "Get up now. You're a liability to us if you can't fly. You've got ten minutes to get ready before I grab you and teleport to the highest peak and push you off. Let's see how quickly you pick this skill up." He walks away, leaving me feeling hurt and ashamed at being afraid. *Asshole.*

Rolling out of bed, I find my uniform on a chest of drawers; it's been cleaned and folded, ready for me to wear again. I have a quick shower to wash all the sex fluids and blood off me before dragging it on and zipping it up. After a minute of silent debate, I change back into human form; this is going to hard enough as it is without having to worry about a tail and horns and how they affect my flying. Just as I'm doing my hair and looking for my magic wand, Zeph pokes his head in the door.

"You ready?" He has an expectant look on his face and seems pleased that I'm ready to go instead of still hiding under the blankets.

Nodding my head, I follow him out to the living area. Trick, Sander, Jagger, Kai, and Mav are all sitting around eating breakfast. They all seem to be chatting about my upcoming flying lesson.

"Mina, your wings are unlike any I've ever seen," Zeph says, passing me a cup of coffee, which I accept gratefully. Blowing over the top, I take a sip, and the warmth soothes me a little bit. "The feathers are more like an ostrich or a peacock, and ostriches can't fly and peacock for only short distances. So, we're going to just give this a shot and see if you can. Mind you, they're the largest I've ever seen apart from one other, and he can fly, so maybe that will make up for the lack of streamline." By the end of his words, my head is down and shoulders hunched in embarrassment, but a firm grip on my chin has me looking up.

"Baby, they're beautiful wings, and I'm sure they'll do what they need to." Kai's sweet words, such a contrast to his typical cheeky ways, have me smiling again.

"Mina, you've had so much thrown at you just recently and come out shining; you'll be fine," Zeph assures me.

"And if you're not, he'll catch you before you hit the ground." Mav's flat tone has everyone frowning, but I think I'm onto him. I have a feeling he's playing bad cop to Zeph's good in the hope that one way or another, I'll leap off the cliff. So instead of getting upset, I stick my tongue out at him in a childish way, and a twitch in his eye has me knowing I've gotten to him. I've learned Mav's all about control, and this is something that's out of his hands. Of course, it's going to send him into a tailspin.

Draining the last of my coffee from my cup, I put it on the sink and follow Mav and Zeph out of the room and through the palace. The city is still relatively quiet at this time of the morning, with only early birds out and about. A few people are sitting down and having coffee or breakfast in cafes while the occasional jogger runs by, but the sounds of yesterday are missing as of yet. We make our way to the elevator shaft and patiently wait as it rumbles upward toward the prick of light I had noticed the other day.

The shaft having been built into the rock is quite ingenious, and as we get closer to the top, I notice that the light isn't coming through a window of any kind. In fact, the elevator just deposits us at the top where we can step straight out onto the clifftop.

Confusion must show on my face as I look around because Zeph explains, "Lucifer told us that the shaft is covered by a force field-type barrier that keeps the weather out and camouflages the hole from anyone looking for it." As he says this, the platform rumbles and starts its descent downward. Once it disappears, a hologram appears over the hole, hiding it from view.

"What happens if someone walks over the illusion?" My curiosity can't stop me from asking.

"They fall a very long way down," Mav's voice rumbles from behind me.

Stepping away from the shaft, I look around at our location. Today the sky is clear even if the atmosphere is still hazy. Any sign of yesterday's storm and solar flare has vanished, and from this height, I can see the land stretched out far below us. The ruined city is vast, but there are small patches scattered around where things have been rebuilt. The landscape beyond is rocky, dry, and dusty, the solar flare from yesterday having removed all evidence of the storm and dried out the ground again.

"How did the demons survive the solar flares in the past?" I can't understand how this was a lush and fertile planet with all the radiation that they put out.

"Habbalea was originally surrounded by a force field that Hammus maintained. When he discovered the demon resistance, he got rid of it as punishment," Zeph explains.

"But if that's the case, how are they ever going to get the planet to recover?" I feel so sad for the demons underground. I've only known about my demonic heritage for a short while, but I do know what it's like to be on the outside of something. Feeling like I'd been unwanted by my parents then being taken in by Peter and Maggie made me realize the true importance of having a home. The underground looks nice, and the demons have definitely made a paradise out of a really shitty situation, but my heart aches for them not being able to turn this world into what it should be, what it once was. Living a life in secret just doesn't seem like a life at all...no matter how nicely they've made it work.

"I guess that's what they're hoping one of the other gods will help them with. Once everything with Hammus and AoA is settled, then Lucifer and the resistance would stand a better chance at trying to give the demons here a real life aboveground. Minzeon has forcefield technology, so maybe Matoz would be willing to help the demons. Their tech is where the shaft illusion came from, but whether that's big enough to cover an entire planet, we don't know."

"That's enough procrastination; let's see those wings." Mav's patience has run its course, and his voice is demanding as he steps in front of me, arms crossed.

As he says this, he releases his. In the sunlight, his wings are so shiny and bright, and the light reflects off them, bouncing around the landscape as he moves. Zeph steps up next to him, and his wings are glistening too, the mottled blues and browns set off by the silver and gold threaded through them. They look at me impatiently, and I guess good cop/bad cop is over for the morning. Huffing out a breath, I release my wings. They burst impatiently out of my skin and ruffle wildly before they settle into place. Zeph does a lap around my body, examining them, while Mav stands there, face full of nothing. Seriously, I know he's struggling, but a bit of some kind of emotion would be nice.

"Okay, I guess the only thing we can do is try. I'm going to be in the air in case you need help, and Mav will wait until you take off to join us," Zeph outlines, totally too calm and relaxed.

"Flying is completely instinctive. Your wings will know what to do, just the same as your arms and legs do what you want without really thinking about it. You really just have to steer. Now be aware, if you do this in demon form, your tail may throw you off balance slightly, so don't forget to take that into account. Jagger or Kai will be able to give you some kind of instruction regarding that." I nod my head, soaking in the knowledge, but my nerves must show because he shakes his head.

"Where's that brave girl that took on recruits that were twice as big as her so many years ago? Come on, let's do this."

He jumps into the air, the rush of wind from his wings blowing back a red tendril of my hair that has escaped. "Probably best if you get close to the edge and just jump off. The wings will catch the air currents. Once we know you will stay aloft and propel forward, we can work on those kinds of take-offs."

He flies away from the cliff, so he's hovering over nothing, and I step forward until I reach the edge. Taking a deep breath, I'm just about to step off when a large hand in the middle of my back gives me a big shove forward. Arms pinwheeling, I tumble over the edge, a scream of terror escaping from my mouth. "You fucking asshole!"

I can hear his chuckles not far away, so he must have followed me over. The wind rushing by brings tears to my eyes. Waiting for something to happen, I'm still dropping like a sack of potatoes, and the ground is getting close fast. Terror flows through my body; these stupid things don't fucking work. Looking around, I can see panic on Mav's face as Zeph arrows toward me like a bullet, wings flat against his back as he streamlines himself to get to me as fast as he can.

Saying a prayer that my new demon status will protect me, I'm about to let my scale armor cover my body when the wings snap out to the side, slowing my descent and catching the wind currents, allowing me to glide along parallel to the ground. "Woohoo!" Zeph's shout of glee brings a huge smile to my face as I instinctively start flapping them to gain altitude.

"I knew you could do it." Close to my ear, Mav's voice has me turning my head and shooting him a death stare, but he just shrugs his shoulders. "Everyone always needs a shove. Uriel was the one who was tasked with shoving all of us when we first learned to fly." I picture a scene of six terrified young children having the same thing done to them, and I don't feel so bad.

Zeph flies in front of me, a look of excitement lighting his face. "Come on, follow me, we'll put you through your paces." For the next hour, Zeph, Mav, and I play 'follow the leader,' looping and weaving through the air, riding the currents and racing each other. The relief at being able to use them gives way to the feeling of freedom. Although the atmosphere here on Habbalea isn't very clean, it still feels fantastic to be gliding across the barren landscape, letting my worries flow away even if just for a little while. While riding the flow of the wind, my mind soars, and I think about everything I've been through just recently.

During the fight with the lizard it felt good to be back to fulfilling my original dreams, but I realize that was the old me, and now I'm someone differ-ent. Someone who has a family, albeit a new and fragile bond, but I have hope for it to grow and build and become unbreakable. I have a team who have welcomed me with open arms, and mates. Mates that are destined to love me and care for me no matter what. It's comforting to know that they will always be there for me, that I'll always have someone to lean on through good times and bad.

I'm excited for what the future holds and am ready to embrace it with open arms.

When we finally land, I'm exhausted but happy, and I throw my arms around them both, pulling them close. "Thank you, thank you!" They both squeeze me tight and place kisses on my cheek, Mav thankfully seeming a little bit more relaxed now that this problem has been solved.

"Shall we head back to Reath?" Zeph suggests. "I think we've been away for long enough now. Raphael should have updated Clementine on her new position and filled her in on what's happened to Hugh. They'll have done a mind sweep to make sure she's trustworthy."

"So will she be clued in on your Archangel status then?" I ask curiously because I know Hugh hadn't been.

Mav grunts, back to his minimal communication. "I think it's time everyone knew. It's not like they can do anything to us now, and the hiding is getting tiring." The crease around his eyes makes him look tired, and his body is tight with tension. Something is bothering him, and I see that Zeph has noticed now too. When I get a chance to talk with Zeph on his own, I'll ask him about it.

"Mina, can you mind link with Kai or Jagger? I can't seem to get through to any of the others." There's an undercurrent of worry to Zeph's annoyance, and frankly, when he's worried, that's saying something. I guess all the chaos happening around us is putting all of us on the edge, and we just can't seem to keep our footing for too long.

"I've been thinking about that," I tell him as it jogs my memory. "Kai said something as we arrived about not being able to speak to Dru once we were underground. I think there might be some kind of block, and that's why I had trouble reaching Kai in the past. He must have come topside to speak to Jagger, but when I tried, he was below ground."

A thoughtful look crosses Zephs face, and at least the slight worry lines flatten out. "You may be right; it might be part of their defense systems." Just as he says this the rumbling of the platform can be heard.

"Looks like they didn't want to wait anymore either," Mav observes tensely, his body looking like it's ready for any situation in case it's not the team. Going to him, I wrap an arm around one shoulder and give him a squeeze, until his body relaxes slightly. *I wonder if Mav ever truly relaxes.* Standing there, leaning into him, we wait for the platform to bring the rest of the team topside so we can return home.

Chapter Twenty-Four

Jessamina

Arriving back at CD through the portal, the building is in a buzz, and the gossip that Clementine has replaced Hugh is the primary subject of the day. Apparently, he's missing, and his secretary Emmeline was seen being taken away for questioning. It's like a game of telephone, and by the time we report in and make it back upstairs to our apartment, we have heard so many different versions, including him being responsible for Bravo's death. Which I guess he was, albeit indirectly. The main buzzword being thrown around is 'traitors,' and the theme of who can be trusted is prevalent.

Walking inside, I don't even have a chance to close the door behind me before Drusilla is in my arms, her soft lips against mine. She pulls away before I can turn the kiss into the gesture I want, her voice filled with relief when she starts to scold us. "I was so worried about you, and Sander, being the ass-hat he is, would only give me an occasional update." Hmm, he must have gone topside a couple of times. I wonder when he did that, and then I feel slightly bad that I hadn't noticed. *Definitely have to work on being a good mate.*

I pull her over to the plush sofas and collapse into one, wrapping my arms around her. "Gee, thanks, Dru, glad to see you're worried about the rest of the team," Zeph teases her, and Sander, of course, has to add his two cents.

"Or your brother."

"Oh, hush, I'm used to you all going off and doing your thing. It's a novelty with Mina, and if you remember rightly, I was like this with all of you too when you first started." She jumps to defend herself, but I can see the guys are just messing around, so I rub my arms up and down her back and coo sweet words in her ear to placate her.

"Don't listen to them," I tell her telepathically. *"I think it's sweet, and I've never had anyone but Maggie worry about me before. It's lovely. Feel free to worry as much as you want.*

While we sit there talking about everything that happened, we watch the boys shuck clothing in a whirlwind of motion. Boots get untied and shoved at the front door, jackets unzipped and hung on hooks. Sander and Trick go to the kitchen, Sander grabbing some beers and giving each of the guys one. Trick makes me and Drusilla a cup of tea and brings them over to us before they all disappear, taking their beers. I guess they've gone off to have showers. Kai came back with us this time after deciding he doesn't want to let us out of his sight anymore. He asked Raphael if he could be temporarily assigned as a team member even though he hasn't been through the academy.

I've just finished telling Drusilla all about the demon underground, when she asks me about Kai. "What do you think he will do?"

"What do you mean?" I ask, confused.

"Well, didn't you say that Raphael okayed his temporary status but as only backup? He can't go on official missions until he's gone through the academy. Do you think he'll do that?"

"Honestly, I'm not sure. I know he wants to be here to help protect me, and I think that's his mate instinct riding him hard at the moment, but I don't really need him for that when I have all the others. I'd like to see him go back to helping his people instead of the academy when everything settles down. He's so passionate about it. He's promised to come home most nights, or we can go to him. Lucifer is having a large suite built in the palace especially for me when I want to visit with my mates. You'll have to come with us next time," I tell her, wanting to show her what Mom and the others have created. She looks excited at the prospect.

Eventually, we move from the couch to the kitchen, where we put together a quick meal of spaghetti for the team. Spending this alone time with Drusilla is wonderful, and I grow to love her more and more with her delightful quirks and habits. She's been telling me all about the gossip in the tech room and how me being a part of Alpha and taking up all their time and attention hasn't won me any friends.

"There are some very pissed off females who had been hoping to eventually catch the eye of one or more of the guys. I'm pretty sure that's why a lot of them are friendly with me, hoping they would have a way in." She shrugs when I look at her in surprise. "I'm also a good choice since I'm no threat to any of them because I'm into girls."

I wrap my arms around her waist and pull her close. "Mmm, yes, and I'm thankful you are." Her arms come up around my neck, and I bend down to press my lips against hers, her tongue slipping out to slide between and stroke mine. Taking a hand from her waist, I've dragged out her shirt and moved it upward toward her breasts when the door between the living and bedroom areas bangs open. She tries to pull away, but I hold her firm. Turning to look at the interruptor, Sander stares back, his eyes widening in shock. To be fair, I guess my red eyes and the growl that escapes from my mouth are slightly more jarring than walking in on me and his sister.

"Whoa, babe, didn't realize you were hungry again," he apologizes, holding up his hands and moving around into the kitchen to stir the sauce. "Why don't you go and take care of that, and I'll dish up dinner for everyone." My growl settles at his suggestion, and I drag Dru by the hand to her bedroom, passing the others in the hallway as they make their way out for dinner. They all keep their mouths shut, thankfully, and when we get to her room, I slam the door behind us and throw Drusilla onto the bed. As she bounces on the mattress, a moment of clarity breaks through my obsessive hunger, and I'm horrified at myself. I collapse to the floor on my knees, a wave of shame hitting me at once.

"Oh my god, Drusilla, I'm so sorry," I apologize, tears in my eyes at the realization that I just manhandled one of my mates.

She peeks over the side of her high bed. "Why? That was hot as fuck. Now get up here and finish ravishing me." Her demand has me blinking in surprise, but her face is flushed, and her eyes are sparkling; she doesn't look scared at all. So, I get up off the ground and start to strip off my clothes, but Dru just gestures with her hand, and they disappear. Looking down, I blink in shock, and her peal of laughter has me smiling.

"I forget we can do those kinds of things," I tell her sheepishly, and before I can climb up on the bed, she's gotten rid of hers as well, leaving her luscious body on display as a feast for my eyes.

She holds her hand up to stop me from going any further. "Mina, I can't strip off the rest; you have to do it."

My forehead wrinkles in confusion. "Demon form, please," she requests, "oh, and don't forget the tail and those sexy showgirl wings too." Surprised but willing to give my mate whatever she desires, I let the magic flow over my body, and the wings erupt with flair. *God, they are so dramatic.*

Using her legs, I flip her over to her stomach and shower gentle kisses over her body starting at her feet. My wings wrap around and drag across her skin with little strokes. The responding pressure sends little waves of feeling down each feather. They're like receptors telling me if the surface is smooth or rough, and Dru's skin is all porcelain smooth. I move up her calves, over her thighs, and to her tight little backside, digging my teeth in to bite when I get to it. A groan escapes her mouth at the feel of my teeth in her mounds of flesh, and I barely manage to keep my fangs in, unsure she's ready for *that* much of a bite.

Placing soothing kisses on the bites, I travel up her spine until I get to my mate mark on her shoulder, where I pay special attention, nipping and sucking, feeling possessive of that mark. Laying my body down on her, I rub my pussy against her bottom, grinding my hips. My arms wrap around her until I can get my hands on her breasts and tweak at her nipples.

Her breath is coming faster as my tail gets in on the action and gently pushes its way into her pussy. I can feel the tight, wet, heat as it thrusts in and out, and she grinds her mound against the blankets. My core is on fire, and I rub my pussy against her bottom, my clit rubbing and pulsing with pleasure at the movements. Her breathing gets faster and higher as I bite and lick her neck and whisper dirty words in her ear.

"Such a good girl, you like my tail in your wet cunt, don't you? It's so greedy, gripping tight around it."

Her breathing hitches, and just as I feel the final fluttering of her core before orgasm, I bite down into her neck. She muffles her scream against the pillow while my orgasm flows gently over me, and her blood trickles down my throat, a rich river of deliciousness. My body absorbs the feral emotions of her desire as she rides out her orgasm, my tail slowing as she comes down from it. Finally, I drink enough and pull away, sealing the holes with my tongue. Caressing her breast gently before removing my hands, I roll to the side, bringing her with me to snuggle in. Eventually, her eyes open, and she has a very satisfied look on her face.

"I'm not sure why I never considered a demon lover before, but I definitely should have with those tails." I snort at her rambling but don't get jealous. I know I'm the only demon lover she's ever going to have. At the thought of my own lack of jealousy, a question occurs to me.

"Drusilla, do you feel ripped off that I have other mates, while you'll only have me? Are you upset that you'll be sharing me?" She places kisses on my lips as she shakes her head in denial.

"Absolutely not. I'll be honest; there's no way I could handle your sexual appetite if it was just me. I mean, I'd try, but I would probably end up dead," she jokes, trying to lighten the mood.

"But what about the others?"

A shrug accompanies her next response. "I don't know, sweetheart. It's something you should talk to them about, but I doubt it. Jagger and Kai both seemed thrilled to be your mates." She rubs her hands gently up and down my back. "Also, you forget that as a team, we'd already decided we wanted to attempt a relationship with you. So for me I always knew I'd be sharing you with others, and two more extras really aren't a big deal. I think you have a big enough need for all of us, and as long as you share it around equally, I can't see anyone being upset."

That's right; I haven't told her about the others. "And Sander and Trick," I chime in, and she sits up, an ecstatic look on her face.

"Really? That's awesome. I was so worried we would lose them to other bitches. They must have been pleased." I nod my head but tell her we haven't mentioned it to the others yet just in case.

"I'm not worried at all; I'm sure this is meant to be. I'm trusting in a higher power to look after us." Her throwaway comment pricks my brain again, but for the life of me I can't think why.

"Come on, let's go and have dinner with the family. I want to hear Mav and Zeph's version of your flying lesson, and I want to hear about the invisibility and the shape-shifting and everything. Wow, so much has happened in the last twenty-four hours," she rambles, her voice filled with amazement, and I stop where I am, completely in shock. Crap, she's right. It's only been a short period since all of those things happened. *How can life change so much in so short a time?*

Smiling deviously to myself, I say to her, "Make sure you ask Sander and Trick how they discovered the illusion and invisibility abilities. The others haven't heard that story either."

—■ ·◆· ■—

Drusilla

Later that evening, after we've had dinner, done the dishes, and cleaned up, we're sitting around having drinks, and after a little prompting from me, they're all laughing at Trick's retelling of the prank Mina had played on them in the shower. Sander's disgruntled face has everyone nearly hysterical. Looking around the room, I feel content with my life, happy to be surrounded by my family and that I've been given to Mina as a mate. But it's with concern that I watch her rub at a spot on her chest, a frown on her face, even as she laughs along with everyone else.

An echo of pain radiates between our bond, and I notice her other mates also rub at their chest subconsciously feeling Mina's ache, barely managing to stop myself from doing the same. *What could be causing the ache?* As I look at Zeph and Mav, they're rubbing at their chests too, and then something occurs to me. Sitting up straight, I gape in shock. *They must be her mates as well, and if they are, what are the odds that Samuel is too? What if the fact that he's not here is causing her to hurt?*

A silence descends on the group, and I decide to address the issue in a roundabout way. "What are we going to do about Sam?" I ask everyone. I might as well get it out in the open. Grabbing Mina's hand, I give it a little squeeze as the radiating ache turns to sadness.

"Well, now we know for sure that Connie and Sabboath are on the wrong side of all of this," Zeph muses. "Maybe they, or shall I say, Connie, is doing something to affect him."

"It makes sense," Mav agrees. "He was such a freaking douchebag when she was around last time." Mina's eyebrows raise in surprise as she looks at him.

"Don't you remember sparring with him when we were at the academy? You always got hurt somehow, and it was worse whenever she was lurking on the sidelines." Mav's voice growls with those words, his forehead creased in anger, body radiating tension. Mina goes silent, thinking about it, and a range of emotions come through our bond. Surprise, hurt, sadness, and anger all war internally within her, and looking around the room, I can see we're all feeling it.

Frustration and vulnerability join the others in a riot of emotions, so I wrap my arms around her and pull her back against me in a show of support, and a wave of gratefulness seems to override the rest of her feelings. "Huh! Looking back now, I guess you're right. Samuel was the only sparring partner who ever hurt me, but I'd just chalked it up to my inexperience." Her voice becomes quiet at the end, and she adds, "I guess I never wanted to think that he'd ever hurt me on purpose."

"And the way he shoved his relationship with Connie in your face so much that you stopped coming to dinner if we were going to be there," Trick adds, mirroring her soft tone.

Sander's face is a thundercloud of emotions, and he doesn't bother tempering those feelings before he chimes in. "You weren't the only one he was a dick to; we also got a fair amount of it too," he tells me, and I remember the way they told me Connie almost tore their bond apart.

"But it all changed once Connie was gone," I add in, as it all seems to make sense now. "Once she was gone and he had moved on from his heartbreak, it was like he became another person. He was kind and happy and generous to a fault again, just like he was pre-Constance joining the team." We sit together, contemplating what it all means. Watching my team's faces, I see a range of emotions, dismay and guilt being the predominant ones, and I know exactly how they feel. *Is this partly our fault for not realizing how different his behavior had come, for assuming he'd just become an asshole? For not figuring out he needed our help. I guess we've all got something to make up for now.*

"So I guess an intervention is called for," Zeph says with a large sigh. "He'll need to pick a side."

"What if he picks the wrong one?" Jagger asks gently. He and Kai had sat quietly while we discussed it, having had nothing to add.

"Well then, we may have to ask for my dad to look him over for dark influences," Trick says firmly.

"And if there's none?" Kai plays the devil's advocate, which brings frowns to the faces of the others.

"Then I guess he becomes the enemy!" Zeph's voice is final, and an air of despair surrounds us all, making the thought of the future into a dark presence. The possibility of hunting down a team member sits heavy with us all, and it's with that heaviness we head off to bed.

— •◆• —

I 'm not sure how long it's been since we went to bed, but I'm woken with a sense of déjà vu when an alarm shrieks through the apartment. Jolting with fright, I untangle myself from Mina's arms and groggily get to my feet.

She, too, is climbing out of bed and rubbing at bleary eyes. I grab my wrist guard, checking it for messages, not liking what I find. "Emergency meeting. They've got a hit on Hugh and the Five; they're going after the tech now," I tell her.

She's wide awake by the time I finish relaying the message, and she's rushing to get dressed. With a gesture of my hand, I have us both in uniform, and she looks at me gratefully before I clasp my wrist guard on.

Running to her room, she returns with her own wrist guard, shoving her magic wand into her ponytail, and we both head toward the living area where most of the guys already are. Leaving the apartment, my sense of dread increases. I don't know if it's because this is the same thing that happened when it went wrong last time or something else, but I do know that she's better equipped to handle anything they throw at her now. Well, I *think* she is, and from the look on her face and the feelings through the bond she thinks so too.

It's with that thought I follow after the others to the conference room to be briefed on the plan.

Chapter Twenty-Five

Jessamina

Clementine waits for us in the briefing room accompanied by a gorgeous brunette angel I haven't seen before. "Who's that?" I whisper to Drusilla as we all find seats.

"That's her assistant and partner, Riarliel," Dru whispers back.

"Really? I thought I saw her making eyes at Headmaster Norris on selection day," I reply, and Drusilla gives me one of those 'seriously' looks.

"Honey, you have how many partners?" she says sarcastically, and I feel a little stupid.

"She was mostly a behind the scenes assistant. When Hugh was around, she couldn't get a word in. I guess now that Clementine has been promoted, she'll be more involved. Especially with Emmeline being taken away for questioning." As we settle, I look around to see if anyone else has joined us, but when Riarliel closes the door, we're the only team present.

"Okay, listen up." Clementine is all business, a

351

nice change from her predecessor. "Asmodeus has Hugh and the Five in his sight. They're on Minzeon at a scientific compound just outside of the capital city, so we assume the DNA sequencing device they're after is located there. We need the Five contained and returned to the menagerie, and we need to stop Hugh from retrieving the device." Her voice is commanding as she issues the orders, her confidence a powerful force that inspires you to follow her directions and try to please her.

"Don't use your angel-runed weapons as that would return them directly to their home realms, and we don't want that. Make sure you all take guns set to high stun. I want them unconscious for transport," she finishes as Riarliel starts to hand us each a holster and one of the light guns that Zeph had trained me to use. "Malakai, you've been approved to be on this mission." His eyebrows raise in surprise, but he nods his assent.

Taking the gun, I drop the magazine to check that it's full and then slam it back in, chambering one of the little light rounds. I also grab a spare magazine off the counter just in case.

"Okay, some of the Archangel council will be joining you as well, but no one else is in on this. The rumors of traitors in the ranks have swept the CD, and there are no other teams I trust right now. Raphael has assured me that this team is one hundred percent trustworthy, that none of you will defect." Guilt fills my soul at her words since

Samuel's status is still up in the air. She must realize that he's missing at the same time I think this.

"Where's Sam?" Her voice is sharp, but the concern is evident. I guess they've been a part of the CD for a while now and the number one team, so it would make sense that Clementine is worried.

"He's on another assignment at the moment," Zeph reassures her, and she seems to be happy with this explanation because she doesn't press any further.

"Okay then, get on with it. The others are waiting downstairs for you." She and Riarliel leave the briefing room, and Drusilla gives me a quick kiss before waving to the guys and heading off to Communications.

"Right, let's get this done. We need to get out in front; I'm sick of playing catch up." Zeph leads toward the elevators, and we make our way to the portal room. Downstairs the dads are waiting for us, suited up, colorful wings on display. The CD employees are looking on with awe as the open portal shimmers, waiting for us to go through it.

"Good, you're here. We're just waiting on one more, and this mission will be a go," Azrael comments as we arrive. Chamuel looks around with concern. "Where's' Samuel?"

"Ah, he's still assigned to Constance, so I guess he's with her," Zeph tells him, and I watch as he nods, and the dads exchange a look I can't decipher. Zeph looks confused too, but before he can question it, another angel arrives in a blaze of light, and we all cover our eyes to avoid being blinded.

A moment passes before the light dims, then Uriel laughs out loud with joy, and Team Alpha all turn to look at him with astonishment. *What's he so happy about?*

"Yes! *Now* we're ready to bring the pain." His face is covered with glee as we turn back to look at the new arrival.

The Archangel is tall and built with long flowing blonde hair that reaches far down his back and the largest gold wings I've ever seen stretched out behind him. In his hand is a blazing sword, and he's dressed like the others in combat fatigues. I thought Uriel was scary, but the power radiating off this man is awe-inspiring.

Team Alpha all bow their heads in reverence, recognizing him immediately. "Archangel Michael, good to see you again," Zeph says with confidence, his voice full of respect.

Okay then, no wonder this man has power, he's the head of them all. He nods to us, but his mind seems to already be on the task as he slaps hands and exchanges hugs with the other dads. A small smile crosses my lips at the overt macho exchange. No matter what species, I guess boys will be boys.

"Let's go," Michael commands, and everyone falls in behind him, no hesitation to follow his powerful voice and presence.

We step through the portal and with a thankfully smooth transition, arrive in an area full of trees. The wooded area surrounds the compound, making access difficult and creating a slight cover of darkness over the whole area.

"Asmodeus says that the Five and Hugh are on the other side of this compound. The Five are going to provide a distraction, and Hugh is going to steal the device." Michael's voice is melodic, and a feeling of invincibility fills me as I listen. The Archangel has this overpowering charisma that leaks from his words, and even in my short time around him, I can understand how he's the head of the council.

He looks at Team Alpha, a sharpness in his gaze as he seems to gaze into the very heart of each of us, giving a sense of justice and rightness. "We need to lock this down. Incapacitate the Five, and your fathers will transport them to the menagerie. Keep an eye out for Hugh; we *cannot* let him escape with that device. Who knows what Hammus wants with it."

"Mina, now might be a great time to use your invisibility," Raphael suggests to me, and this has Michael's head turning to look at me.

"You can turn invisible? How?" There's a bit of suspicion underneath his questions, but the predominant emotion seems to be the surprise that's now reflected in his eyes. He also seems a tiny bit uncomfortable, and I'm thinking it's because the Archangel isn't usually the one lacking knowledge about a person or situation.. Adrenaline floods my body at being the focus of this being of intense power. A little shiver of fear courses through my body, followed by one of reassurance. Huh, that's strange, but as I look around the room no one else seems to be afraid, so maybe that came from my mates through the bond.

Shrugging my shoulders, I respond, "I'm not sure, sir. We haven't quite figured that out yet." His gaze is calculating, and his attention turns to Raphael with a degree of anger, but the other Archangel avoids meeting Michael's eyes.

"Hmm, we'll discuss this when we return from the mission. But go ahead and use the invisibility; it may give you an edge. Team Alpha, you set your guns to a lower stun level and take care of any Minzeons. Knock them out and get them out of the way of danger even if you have to shove them into a closet." As he issues that instruction, an explosion on the other side of the compound lights up the night sky.

"All right, let's go," he commands. Taking off in a run, he dodges the trees and launches into the air over the compound wall. The dads follow behind, leaving us to run and scale the wall, in case any of the enemies are looking.

We watch as Jagger and Kai sail swiftly over, their wings helping them glide silently to the ground. Their bodies are in their much larger, hulked out Archdemon forms now. Debating whether or not I should also take my demon form, I dismiss it for now, needing easy access to my gun. "This shit is getting old," Mav grumbles as he hauls himself to the top of the wall and turns around to give me a hand. "We could have flown in too. I'm sick of hiding what we are."

"Agreed," Trick and Sander chime in, and Zeph nods his head.

"It's time we talked about outing ourselves. There's nothing anyone can do to us, and we need to be using our skills to the fullest. We'll talk to them about it in the debriefing."

Now over the compound walls, I allow the invisibility to flow over me. "Mina, stay on our six. You being invisible is all well and good, but we won't know if something happens to you," Zeph grumbles.

"Actually, we will. Jagger and I can feel her emotions," Kai reassures him, and a look of relief covers Zeph's face. With nothing more to add, we approach an unguarded door. They must have all been dragged away with the explosion on the other side. One of Jagger's huge booted feet comes up, and he kicks it, the door slamming open and lodging into the wall behind it.

"Guns on lower stun?" Zeph asks, and we all pull them out and check, keeping them in our hands, ready.

"Okay, stay alert, and if you meet one of the Five, don't forget to adjust the intensity. Trick and

Sander, you go right, and Mav and I'll go left. Kai, Jagger, and Mina, you go straight ahead."

Dru's voice is suddenly in our ears. She'd been quiet while Michael issued instructions but is now ready to run this mission. "Alright, the compound is like a labyrinth, corridors weaving back and forth. It's an ingenious design, easy to get lost and trapped. I've got a lock on your locations, and I'm ready to guide you if you run into trouble."

"Roger that," Zeph replies to Drusilla and waves us all forward. Trick and Sander then Mav and Zeph split off, leaving us to go straight ahead.

Jagger takes point, with Kai on his right and me on his left. We move quickly and quietly down the corridor, any noise of our steps covered by the loud shouts that echo through the compound as the workers are taken by surprise. We get to our first group of huddled scientists, all wearing white lab coats. Another feeling of déjà vu flows through me, and a flash of memory assaults my brain, bringing a stabbing pain with it. A groan escapes my mouth.

"Mina, what's wrong?" Jagger softly asks without missing a beat, as he and Kai stay focused and knock out the scientists then move them under a table in the room.

"I think I'm starting to remember what happened on the mission when I got injured." I pant through the pain, and as quickly as it arrived, it subsides.

"Let us know if you need to stop," he orders.

Unwilling to slow us down, I reply, "No, I'm fine, let's keep going." We run through a few more corridors, twisting and turning, following Dru's instructions, before we meet the next group of workers, and we make quick work of them too.

"If you guys keep on the current course, you'll make it to the main chamber very shortly," Drusilla warns us, and Jagger motions for us to slow down and keep an eye out. Smoke fills the air the closer we get, and whispers from the rest of Team Alpha come through the earpieces. They, too, are meeting occasional pockets of Minzeons, all scientists or other workers, no guards. Zeph suggests that they're all protecting the device so for us to be careful as we approach.

As we get closer, more stunned bodies litter the ground, and we enter the main chamber to find Michael and the fathers battling the Five. It is complete and utter chaos with stun blasts flying erratically through the room. Illusions are playing havoc with the Archangels, and the cackling joy of the Five is an eerie sound.

Not wanting to go further into the room for our own safety, we watch as Uriel aims at Loki, the blast he fires going straight through the illusion and hitting Zadkiel, who freezes, twitching before he falls over rigid.

"Fuck!" Uriel's bellow has us all wincing as he runs over and drags Zeph's dad out the way. Catching sight of Kai and Jagger, he grumbles,

"He's never going to let me live that down." We chuckle as he launches back into the fight, but our attention is quickly directed elsewhere. Movement overhead has us looking upward, and time slows for me as a giant spider with the head of man scuttles down the wall close to us. *Anansi*.

Flashes of memories bombard my mind as everything I went through comes back in a rush of color and frantic sound. All noise from the Archangels and the Five disappears as they replay, and I come to the horrifying realization that the thing that attacked me was *Connie*. But what the hell has been done to her?

A gun blast close to my ear has me paying attention again, and the spider's body drops to the ground with a thud. Kai hit it with the strongest setting, and he's out cold. Jagger conjures a net and wraps it around the unconscious chaos god, securing him tightly.

"Mina, are you okay? You sort of blanked on us for a moment, and all we could feel was terror and sadness." Jagger's brow furrows in concern as he looks to where he thinks I should be, surprisingly close to my actual location.

"Yeah, I'm okay. I just got my memories back in a rush," I reassure him, brushing aside the nerves that came with them. "I'll tell you everything when this is over."

Uriel has finally managed to hit the real Loki, and he and the two females are unconscious and secure, so it's only the Monkey King left standing. He's zooming around the room on a white cloud, waving his staff in the air and shouting in Chinese. But what he doesn't see is Michael rising into the air with his giant blazing sword that cuts right through the Monkey King's cloud. He plummets to the ground, shrieking with fury when no less than three shots hit him. Not another sound escapes his mouth.

As we watch, Raphael gestures at the bodies, and they are instantly tied together. The smoke starts to dissipate, and the screaming alarms are finally shut off, the room falling into blissful silence as the other two teams arrive from different directions, their faces are covered in disgust at missing the fight.

"Well, that was kind of anticlimactic," Sander complains, looking at the unconscious chaos gods. Team Alpha relaxes and holsters their guns, and I watch as Uriel tries to rouse the still-unconscious Zadkiel. After a couple of hard slaps, he regains consciousness and stumbles to his feet, bitching at the black-winged angel the whole time.

Huddling in the corner are a couple of conscious scientists, and I vaguely listen as the Archangels question them, but something out of the corner of my eye catches my attention. Not wanting to interrupt and still invisible, I quietly move toward a fire exit nearly hidden behind some machinery. I watch as Hugh quietly opens the door, propping it open so it doesn't slam behind him. In his hand is a metal briefcase, and he disappears through the door with it, my team and the Archangels none the wiser.

Not wanting to alert Hugh, I keep my mouth shut and follow him down the long corridor. Hopefully Kai or Jagger notice I'm missing before too long. He must have an earpiece giving him instructions because now and then he stops and holds his hand to his ear before going in the direction he's given.

Finally, we make it to the outside of the compound, and he pushes through the door and out into a debris-strewn courtyard. There's a great big gaping hole in the wall, and he heads straight to it.

Remembering I can communicate telepathically, I reach out to Jagger. *"Jagger, Hugh has escaped, and he has the device. I'm following him."*

"Fuck, Mina, you should have said something earlier," Jagger chastises, the sound more vicious than any he's directed at me yet.

"I'm sorry," I apologize. *"I forget we can communicate this way. Don't forget this is all new to me."* I try to purposely direct my emotions through our connection, so he can sense the sincerity behind my words and the slight embarrassment I feel at having such a dangerous lapse of memory.

"Sorry, baby," he replies, his voice laced with frustration. *"We're on our way. Michael and the dads are taking the Five but will return as soon as they're secured.*

Raphael is with us." Even in his mental voice there's a breathless quality, like he and the others must be running to follow behind Hugh and me.

Suddenly, I hear shouts through the earpiece, and they all talk about the compound being flooded with animals that are attacking them all. Pulling out my earpiece, I shove it in my pocket and keep following after Hugh. As worried as I am about my teammates, I know they can handle whatever is thrown at them. I don't need the added distraction, and one of my mates can always talk in my head.

Chapter Twenty-Six

Jessamina

I follow as Hugh clambers over what remains of the wall and hurries into the woods, where Sabboath meets him. Moving toward a tree at a safe distance from the gruesome twosome, I huddle behind it as I listen to the conversation.

"Good work." Sabboath's smarmy voice echoes clearly through the trees, and I momentarily marvel at just how well I'd duplicated his voice with my newfound shapeshifting before I remind myself that there are bigger issues at hand. "Now hand it over so that I can take it back to our laboratories."

"No," Hugh says, defiance lacing that single word in a way that is likely far too bold. "I need you to take me with you and guarantee my safety. The CD knows of my involvement, and I'm not safe any more. My wrist guard has been locked out of the system, and my world chip will have been inactivated. I'm a sitting duck." At the end of his demands, the defiance is slipping, giving way to desperation with an edge of easily noticed panic.

Watching on from where I'm standing, I see Sabboath study him carefully, a glint in his eyes that clearly says Hugh is prey. Hugh fidgets where he waits, but he has a tight grip on the briefcase and a determined set to his shoulders. Finally, Sabboath nods his head and puts his hand out. Just as Hugh raises it to give it to him, Asmodeus swoops down out of the trees and knocks Hugh down. The case goes flying into the air and lands further away at the base of the trees.

It must all be too much or Asmodeus has knocked him out because Hugh lies motionless where he fell, and Archangel and Archdemon face off against one another.

"Asmodeus, I should have known. Always sticking your nose where it isn't wanted." Sabboath's face warps into a sneer that matches the derision he aims at Asmodeus as he looks around for the case.

I slowly make my way to where it landed. *What is taking my team so long?* I reach out with my thoughts and feel like I hit a brick wall. *Ouch, that hurt.* Something is blocking me from talking to my mates. Panic creeps through my mind as I realize I haven't heard from them since that last moment through the ear pieces. Maybe I should've gone back when they had been attacked. Guilt follows on that wave of panic as I pray nothing has happened to them. It's too late now, and all I can do is to try and get that case. Shaking my head, I keep creeping forward.

"Sabboath, always trying to play with the big boys and never quite making the cut," Jagger's dad taunts as they circle each other, both of them with big swords in their hands. In a flurry of motion, Sabboath takes to the air. I'm not sure if he's trying to escape or get an advantage over Asmodeus, but he follows him up, and they come together in a clash of steel. In awe, I watch the epic battle taking place in the sky. Swords clang and sparks fly as they strike and parry, neither getting the advantage over the other.

"Get the case, Mina." Asmodeus's voice is a whisper in my mind, but it gets my focus back on the job. How he knew I was here, I have no clue, but I waste no more time and run for the case.

Picking it up, I turn to run back to the compound when I discover I'm not alone. Constance is standing with her hand on a giant white tiger surrounded by all manner of creatures. I see wolves and bears and other great cats, but as my gaze hungrily scans the area for the one face I desperately want to find, I see no sign of Sam.

"You might as well show yourself. Picking up the briefcase gave your location away, and I've got you surrounded. There's nowhere for you to go." I consider using my wings and flying to escape, but there's a good chance that Sabboath would block my exit, and I'm not ready to defend myself against an Archangel.

"Come on, don't be shy," Constance taunts, so I let the invisibility flow away, and her smug face turns ugly.

"You! I should have known. How is it you can turn invisible?" she spits out, her grip on the tiger tightening as it rumbles a warning.

I ignore her question and fire back one of my own. "Where's Sam? What have you done with him?" I can't hide the worry in my voice, and a cliché peal of evil laughter escapes her lips, the hair-raising sound only made worse by the way her sickly face twists into a smirk.

"Oh, dear, Sam had to make a choice, and he chose the winning side. You don't have to worry; I'm taking excellent care of him." The smugness in her voice makes me feel sick, as do the thoughts of her taking care of him.

"I don't believe you; Sam would never turn traitor! I have faith in him," I shout at her, and she just laughs a little more, rocking the unhinged look now.

"What happened to you?" I ask her. "I know you were the spider. There's no hiding it anymore." Trying to distract her, I slowly inch my way backward. If I can get a clear run through the trees, I'll turn invisible again and try to escape.

"Wrong? Nothing is wrong. I am simply better and more improved. *We* are the wave of the future," she declares, gestures to the surrounding animals. "We'll be at the top of the food chain." She blabs on, but I tune that crap out and watch my surroundings, looking for any opening. Unfortunately, the tiger isn't so easy to fool, and while she monologues, it breaks away from her and comes running straight for me. Before I can turn and get further than a few feet, his giant paws hit my back, and I'm falling to the ground, the briefcase flying from my hands as I try to break my fall.

"Argghhhhh!" Connie's scream is deranged. "I told you there was no escaping us!" The tiger rolls me onto my back and pins me in place. It's staring me down, a rumbling warning coming from its chest, its huge fangs inches from my neck.

A scream in the air has me looking up, and a dragon flies into view, circling the area. Breathing fire at Asmodeus, the Archdemon is unable to stop both it and Sabboath, and he's hit in the side, stunning him; he careens away into the foliage. His opponent distracted, Sabboath flies toward us, landing not far away. "Grab the case," he shouts at Connie, but before she can, the shouts from the rest of Team Alpha become clear.

"Damn it, leave it," he demands and opens a portal right next to me and the tiger. All the animals start streaming through. "Bring the girl; she may come in handy," he tosses over his shoulder as he marches through, leaving me to Connie, who appears behind the tiger. Looking the tiger directly in his somewhat familiar eyes, which is weird, I think I see a flash of sympathy before Connie's boot crashes into my head, and it's lights out.

———•◦•———

Patrick

We're sitting around watching as Michael interrogates the scientist regarding the device and have just established it's missing when Jagger's voice echoes across the room. "Fuck!" All of us turn to watch him yanking at his hair as he has a telepathic conversation. Dread fills my body, knowing the one question I don't want to ask.

"Where's Mina?" I can't believe we haven't missed her yet.

"She fucking followed Hugh, who has the device," he shouts as the room bursts into action. Michael and the other dads grab the Five and disappear, returning them to the menagerie while leaving Raphael behind with us.

"Let's go," he commands, heading toward the fire escape that has been discovered behind some equipment. "How was this missed?" he barks out, and Dru responds in our ears.

"It's not on the schematics of the building."

"Mina, talk to us," Raphael demands. "What's

happening?" She doesn't respond, and before we get much further, an abundance of animals pour from every corridor. Raphael lifts his gun and aims at the wolf that bounds in his direction. With the gun still set to stun, it falls to the ground, shifting shape and turning into Brock, Team Bravo's former leader. We are all stunned stupid for a minute, frozen.

"Holy shit," whispers Sander.

"Don't kill them, just stun," Raphael orders, the usually unflappable Archangel showing some of the same confusion mirrored on my teammates' faces. "Who knows how many of these are here voluntarily or not." We set about taking down the animals one by one, each shifting back into human bodies. They just keep coming, domesticated pets, wild animals, and even insects, all swarming the corridors, our path to the outside slowing dramatically.

I reach out to Mina, desperate to hear that she's okay. We haven't tried communicating telepathically yet, though I know it should be possible, but I hit a wall. Something has blocked communication, and I have a feeling it may have some divine interference. Damn Hammus just can't help himself.

Ducking as a hawk dive bombs my head, I follow its trajectory, shooting it from behind, and it slams against a wall before sliding down it and changing shape.

The unconscious bodies are piling up, but our way seems to be getting clearer.

Finally, it's just one or two stragglers, and we quickly stun them before we move forward out into the courtyard. We arrive just in time to watch in dismay as a dragon's fire strikes Asmodeus.

"Dad!" Jagger's cry is filled with anguish as we watch his father fall into the trees, out of control. Before we can get any further, we're stopped by another wave of animals. Raphael tries to shoot them, but the shot hits a barrier and bounces back, narrowly missing Mav as he jumps quickly out the way. Some sort of forcefield is stopping us from getting through.

We watch on helplessly as Sabboath lands and opens a portal, and they all start to escape through it. As the area clears, I can see a body lying on the ground, pinned down by a great white tiger.

"Mina!" I shout as I bang my hands against the barriers. The others see what I'm trying to do and join me, but it's no use; the barrier is restricting tele-portation too, so I go nowhere. Connie's boot connects with the side of Mina's head, and my heart sinks. We've failed her again. *What kind of mates are we that this keeps happening?*

Connie says something, and the tiger backs off Mina's unconscious body and shifts fluidly into a different shape.

"Fuck me!" Sander's words say it all. With horror, we stand by as Samuel bends down and throws Mina over his shoulder. With a wink in our direction and a smug smile, he follows Constance through the portal, and it closes.

"Nooooo!" Mav's tortured scream is an echo of how I feel, and my own feelings are beginning to be overwhelmed by the despair leaking in from Mina's other mates. The place in my chest where my connection to Mina sits is empty. Turning to look at my team, I watch as three others rub the spot where it was, exactly where my hand now is. As soon as the portal closes, the barrier disappears, and Mav stumbles forward, his hand bloody from repetitively banging on the forcefield. Dru's yells stream through the earpieces, demanding to know what happened, but we're all too shocked to respond.

Jagger rushes into the trees to look for his father. Sander and Kai look broken and in no way capable of helping, so I start to trudge after him to see if he needs assistance. Before I can get far, a hand on my shoulder stops me. Looking up into my father's sympathetic gaze, his big arms wrap around my shoulders, and he pulls me close as I shudder with sorrow.

"I'm sorry, son. I promise we'll get her back somehow." His voice is gentle, but I'm feeling too numb to find solace in his words. "I'll go help Jagger; you stay here with your team," he tells me, pulling away. Before he can get very far, a flash lights up the area, and Michael and the other dads appear.

The leader of the Archangels scans the scene, taking in all that is in front of him or not, as the case may be. A furious look crosses his face, and the words booming out of his mouth have us dropping to our knees from the sheer power of his rage.

"Where the fuck is my daughter?"

The end for now....

Glossary

Five Worlds

Reath Home-world to the Collectors Division. A mish-mash world of steampunk, magic, and some advanced technology. This world is surrounded by nine realms. Mylea, goddess of Magic, is their god.

Earth No Magic, no advanced technology but incredibly creative minds and talents. Earth's creativity clashed with Reath's magic and created the beings that inhabit the nine realms. Eagi, god of Freewill, is their god

Minzeon An advanced civilization of high IQs and innovative minds. Matoz, god of Technology, is their god.

Amilles Angel home-world. Azeyr is their god

Habbalea Destroyed Demon realm. Hammus is their god

Glossary

Nine Realms

Zeli Gods of the European continent
Lyneon Gods of Africa, India, and the
Middle East
Kolekin Gods of Asia
Resnea Gods of South and Mesoamerica
Neadna Gods of Australia and the Pacific Islands
Elkly Mythical figures realm, e.g. Santa,
Tooth Fairy, Easter Bunny
Ferijen Halloween and mythical monster realm
Glieh Fairy-tale realm
Dikan Fictional character realm

Glossary

Characters

Jessamina Michaels Daughter of Lucifer and Michael

Zephaniah Aldridge Son of Archangels Jophial and Zadkiel

Lysander Caldwell Son of Archangels Uriel and Haniel

Drusilla Caldwell Daughter of Archangels Uriel and Haniel

Samuel Mason Son of Archangels Chamuel and Sofiel

Mavromichali Atwater Son of Archangels Azrael and Gadriel

Patrick Longhurst Son of Archangels Raphael and Ariel

Jagger Archdemon Son of Asmodeus

Malakai Archdemon Son of Belphegor

Thank you for reading!
I hope you enjoyed the book. It would be super awesome if you could leave a review wherever you bought it, because I love to hear what you thought of the story

Need more of Mina and Team Alpha? Get Book Three now
ttps://books2read.com/CollectorsDivision3

Want to keep up to date with new books coming soon? Sign up to my newsletter here
https://landing.mailerlite.com/webforms/landing/s7a8a6

Another way to do that is to join me Facebook group. I drop teasers and giveaways in there all the time. Here's the link
https://www.facebook.com/groups/1068846123323085

ACKNOWLEDGMENTS

Gosh so many people to thank. Thank you to my Beta team, Laura, Ashley, Natasha and Leslie. You guys were great with your flexibility and working within my time restraints, and were solid sounding boards for when I struggled with the words. I couldn't have done this story without you.

Thank you to Ashley at Infinity Book covers for the fabulous cover.

Thank you to Michelle from Inked Imaginations for the editing. You were so awesome to work with, I hope you will still want to edit my stuff in the future.

Thank you to the #stayhomeandwrite word sprint crew. My ultra competitiveness kicked in and although none of you ever knew, you guys kept me writing under pressure

Thank you to Coles sweet party mix. You are life and kept me fuelled for all the words

Thank you to Lori Campbell and Melinda Ludanyi who let me use their angel names as characters, I hope you get a kick out of seeing them

Lastly thank you Emma Cole. You keep me company at all hours of the day and put up with annoying procrastination and listen to all my random shit. You rock.

If you want a taste of what I'm working on, turn the page to read the first chapter of my new contemporary adult bully reverse harem that will be out soon.

Lexie

Neighpalm Industries Collective

Chapter One

"Harlow! Are you up here?" My best friend Maxine's husky voice carries up the stairs to my apartment above the barn. She claims it's from all the dust and hay from working with the horses everyday, but she's had it for as long as I've known her, and that's from before both of us could talk.

"Yeah, come on up," I call back, my eyes glued to the TV in front of me, the noise of her feet on the stairs getting louder the closer she gets. She bursts into the room, and I can see and smell that she's showered. Unlike the smell of horses and hay, which my apartment and I both usually smell like, she smells spicy and sweet. Probably some expensive designer fragrance that costs a gazillion dollars a bottle.

Looking her up and down, I can tell she's here

to harass me to join her for a night on the town. She's wearing a black bodycon dress that hugs her curves in all the right ways. Her dark blue eyes are accentuated by her smoky eyeshadow, and her burgundy lipstick and perfectly tousled pixie cut make her look like Tinkerbell gone wild. Her short frame is boosted by the five inch heels she's wearing. You would never know this girl wears boots and jeans most days and handles horses that could easily kill her if things go wrong.

"What are you doing? You want to hit a club?" she asks, going to my fridge and grabbing a bottle of beer for herself. Flipping the bottle top onto the counter, she takes a long pull before heading back over to the couch.

Taking a sip of my own beer, I watch, smiling, as her nose wrinkles when she looks for a clean place to sit. Not that my apartment is *dirty*, but I'm not great at picking up after myself, and there are books and magazines lying all over every surface.

She glances at the TV. "You're not watching those damn abandoned videos again, are you?" she asks in disgust.

"Check this out," I say to her, pointing at the television. "They're visiting this abandoned zoo in Detroit!"

"Huh?" She looks at me, confused, while finally moving some of my vet journals out of the way and taking a seat.

I take another sip of my beer. "I don't get it.

Why do they leave all these buildings abandoned? Why don't they repurpose them? The zoo would make a great animal sanctuary for the animals that idiots buy but can't manage. Like big cats and huge ass snakes and things." Shaking my head, I take another sip of my beer. "All these places in the world, houses and hospitals and shit, that people have just picked up and left abandoned for various reasons. It's fascinating. And these guys go around checking them out and filming them, discovering all the history. How cool is that?"

The incredulous look on Max's face almost makes me snort my beer through my nose. "Fucking hell, Harlow, you need to get laid. Your obsession with abandoned things is disturbing. Isn't your little menagerie downstairs enough?" Her tone is disgusted. "We're going out, and I won't take no for an answer. How long do you need to get ready?'

Looking down at my dirty jeans and fuzzy wool socks that I haven't bothered getting changed out of, I shrug my shoulders. "Nah, it's been a long day. You go and have fun; I'm going to stick to my abandoned, lonely buildings."

The look she gives me is borderline homicidal. "Is that supposed to be some kind of metaphor for your life, because, bitch, I've got no sympathy." She chugs her beer down in one go. "You're no more abandoned and unloved than I am. My parents think you walk on water, and I would pick you over my own siblings every time."

I roll my eyes at her dramatics. "You have no siblings, you spoiled, rich princess. So there *is* no competition."

"Who cares? It's the thought, right?" She waves her hand. "I'm giving you half an hour and then calling the car around. If you're not ready, I'll tell Mom that you're up here crying."

I shudder and quickly stand up, flicking off the television. "Damn, you don't play fair," I snap at her and stomp off to the bathroom to have a quick shower. "You better be buying the drinks. You know I hate spending money in those pretentious fucking clubs you drag me to with all those damn stuck up people you call friends."

Maxine is what you would call uber-wealthy. She comes from old, established money and probably has every right to be as stuck up as the rest of the patrons, but her parents raised her to be down to earth and to work hard. There isn't a snobby bone in her body. Well, not too many, anyway.

"Bah, if you didn't keep giving money to that crack whore who gave birth to you, you wouldn't have a problem. You know she's just going to snort it or shoot it up."

Closing the door to my bathroom, a bone weariness crosses my body at the thought of my mother. Never has she been responsible or even partly concerned about my welfare, but I still make sure she has a roof over her head, her bills are paid, and she has money for food. Though

Maxine is right, most of the food money goes on drugs.

I peel off my dirty work clothes, leaving them where they fall, and turn on the shower. Hot steam fills the small bathroom, and I step under the sharp spray, groaning when the heat hits my body. Standing there, I give myself five minutes to wallow in sadness.

My mother used to be a personal assistant for Maxine's parents, and they were beyond thrilled when she announced her pregnancy at the same time as Melinda, Maxine's mom. I was an instant playmate for their daughter, and we lived on the estate, so we've been inseparable since birth.

Unfortunately, while pregnant with me, Mom fell in with the wrong crowd. Maxine's parents kept her on for as long as they could after I was born, but by the time I turned two, she was doing hard drugs and not turning up for work. On the occasion she did, she stole from them to feed her habit. They let her go but allowed her to continue to drop me off to be looked after by the same nanny who looked after Maxine while she tried to keep one crummy job after the other. By the time I was five she was permanently unemployed.

Moving from couch to couch of one sleazy boyfriend to the next or begging her druggie friends to give us a room for the night had child protective services stepping in when Melinda demanded enough was enough. I was promptly removed from my mother's care and moved directly into Maxine's bedroom, a perfectly pretty princess bed to call my own, and welcomed like I was one of them.

Melinda and Charles were everything a girl could want in foster parents, but the children at the schools they sent me to never let me forget where and what I came from. Maxine was my staunchest supporter and still is, but deep down, a simmering resentment brewed toward the one who should love me above all else. It wasn't until my late teens when I did some lashing out of my own and Melinda and Chuck sent me to a therapist, that I came to realize that none of it was my fault. My mother had her own deep seeded issues and was way too selfish to be putting the wellbeing of a child before her own. That's on her, not me.

The one thing I will always hold against her though is the fact that she would never tell me about my father. She would use it as a way to manipulate me, promising to tell me things, and one day I realized that every story was different every time, so nothing ever added up. That was when I decided she probably didn't know who he was and let go of the thought of ever being rescued. It wasn't long after that that I went to stay with Maxine permanently and tucked that dream down into the recesses of my soul. Mom's always been a stain on my life; on visitation rights, she would drag me down to whichever bar or strip club she was working in at the time, and I would sit in the corner coloring while she tried to find her next fix. Later on, I discovered she was also finding her nightly meal ticket.

I never told Melinda or Chuck where we went; Diane took care of that by threatening Maxine with harm if I ever told anyone. It wasn't until I was about fifteen and the men she was trying to score with started to hit on me that she finally declared our fortnightly visits done with. I didn't see her for three years after that until I had finally graduated high school and was awarded a scholarship to the local university. By then I was working for Melinda and Chuck on their horse farm and had been for years, being paid decent money. That's when the guilt trip came raining down, and I started paying her money to keep her away from Maxine and her family.

"Hey, what are you doing in there? You didn't fall asleep, did you?" A thump on the doors made me jump. Maxine's patience had never lasted long.

Grabbing the soap, I shout back, "Sorry, I was daydreaming! I'll be fast." Making quick work of cleaning myself and my hair, I'm out and drying off when I hear her shout through the door again.

"I've put a dress on the bed. Wear it," she demands, and I groan to myself but she must hear it. "No, don't complain! I know if I leave you to it, you'll throw on a pair of ripped jeans and a fitted shirt or something. We're clubbing, not heading down to the local pub." Sniggering to myself, I wipe the condensation away from the mirror and study my reflection. My skin is sunkissed from all the time I spend outside, but, as yet, there are no fine lines developing. I'm careful to religiously apply sunscreen if I'm going to be outside for any length of time. Using my towel, I rub at my natural sun streaked blonde hair to stop it from dripping before wrapping it around my body. I grab out the blow drier and blast the long length until it's almost dry before running a brush through it. It has the windswept tousled look, and I figure that's good enough. I put a hair tie around my wrist in case it gets too hot in the club and I need to tie the whole lot up.

Unlike Maxine, I apply minimal makeup. Just some shadow, liner to my eyes to make the hazel stand out, and mascara to darken the blonde lashes. A bit of lipstick to my full lips and I'm good to go. Blowing myself a kiss in the mirror and rolling my eyes when Maxine shouts at me again to hurry up, I leave the bathroom in search of what horror she's placed out for me to wear.

Her text notification sounds while I'm stuffing myself into the tight blue number, and it's lucky my work is physical and I'm in great shape because there isn't an inch of my silhouette that this dress doesn't show off. But once it's on, the stretchy fabric allows easy movement, and I don't feel uncomfortable at all.

"That's the car," she tells me, looking up from

her screen and giving me a wolf whistle. "Girl, you clean up hot."

Rolling my eyes again, I grab my phone and hold it and my wallet up. "Where exactly am I supposed to put these?" I ask her sarcastically. "The dress doesn't exactly have pockets. Why don't they make dresses with pockets? Designers really are letting the female species down."

This time she rolls her eyes. "Put the wallet down, you won't need it, and the phone just shove into the top of your dress. Lord knows those things are big enough to keep it safe." She points at my breasts which are looking fabulous in the dress, though she's exaggerating about the size. Really, they're just a little more than a handful for a man with average-sized hands.

Doing what she says, we head down the stairs to the waiting car. "Good evening, ladies," William's elderly voice greets us as we climb in. He's been the Bostons' driver for as long as I can remember and is in his late sixties.

I shoot Maxine a dirty look before replying to him, "William, what are you doing driving us this late? We could have called a cab."

Maxine scoffs at me before he can answer. "Bitch, don't get your nonexistent panties in a twist." My heart in my throat, I look down at my dress to make sure nothing is showing, and she laughs, winking at me before continuing. " I tried to but he insisted on driving us. When we get there, he's going to return and go to bed, and we'll get a cab or an uber home." She growls, looking at him in the rearview mirror.

He just nods and smiles. "Of course, Miss Maxine."

He points the car in the direction of Hartford, and we get moving. Maxine has her phone in hand, and her fingers are moving furiously across the screen. "The gang's all there already," she tells me without looking up. "They can't wait to see us." I scoff and sit quietly as I watch the rural area roll by and slowly build up until we're traveling through the city. 'The Gang' are all kids we went to school with. Snobby rich kids who always treated me no better than the dirt at the bottom of their shoe, but Maxine protected me from the worst of their petty bullying.

William pulls the car up in front of a building glittering with spotlights and a line that stretches back around the block. A neon sign of a horse head and palm trees with martini glass in the middle is lit up with the words Club Neighpalm splashed across the front. I groan at the sight of that line and look down at the heels that Max made me wear. Unlike her five-inch, mine are slightly lower at about three inches, but I'm naturally taller than Max. I'm also not used to wearing them like she is. She spends an equal amount of time in boots or heels, whereas I try to go barefoot whenever I don't have on my boots. Either that or flip flops.

We climb out of the car, thanking William, and he smiles and waves goodbye before driving back into traffic. I start to head toward the back of the line, but Max grabs me. "Where are you going?" she asks, looking confused.

"To the back of the line." I tell her, gesturing down the block.

She just shakes her head and mumbles, "It's like you don't even know me." Then she pulls me toward the door, giving our names to the big beefy bouncer who eyes us appreciatively before stepping aside to let us in.

"Ok," I concede, "I should have known better. How did you get us on the list?"

"You know my grandparents' besties Grace and Howard?" she says as we walk through the quiet foyer.

"Nanna and Poppy Summers?" I reply in confusion, thinking about the kind elderly couple that visit Nana and Grandpa Boston a couple a times a year.

Nana and Grandpa Boston, Chuck's parents, are an older, refined couple who I've always felt didn't agree with Melinda and Chuck taking on a stray junkie's daughter. They were never outwardly hostile, but they never went out of their way to make me feel like I was wanted.

Nanna and Poppy Summers were the complete opposite. They filled a much needed void when they visited the house. My mother's parents died before I was born, so I had no grandparent figures in my life, but every time they visited they treated me as one of their own. Nanna would bake with me or take me on excursions to museums and the zoo and things. Poppy would slip me candy and chocolate, and when I fell off my pony for the first time, he was the one who picked me up, brushed me off, dried my tears, and made me get back on. "You're not a successful horseman until you've fallen off at least a hundred times," he reassured me. They would always invite me to come and stay with them at their place in California, but that was the one thing I was never allowed to do. When Mom gave me up to Melinda and Chuck, she made them promise I was never allowed to leave the state. Just another way to control and manipulate me throughout the year

"Yeah, this is one of their clubs. You know Neighplam Industries is a huge family corporation, and they have an airline, hotels, record and movie studios, even an energy drink. This is the latest club to open, and they put us on the list when I asked them too. We also get to drink for free tonight. VIPs all night long." She does a little happy dance as we walk, and I shake my head at her, but a smile crosses my lips, amused at her antics.

We approach the large wooden doors that also have the horse head and palm trees on them. The thud of the music can only just be heard through them, the soundproofing doing what it's supposed to. We stop, and Maxine turns to me, eyebrow raised, putting her hand up on the door. "You ready for this?" I just add my hands to hers, and together we push open the heavy club doors and step into a pounding, hedonistic delight.

Want more? Get Abandoned Girl here https:// books2read.com/AbandonedGirl

www.ingramcontent.com/pod-product-compliance
Lightning Source LLC
Chambersburg PA
CBHW020542120726
47903CB00001B/87